Gladys Hazel aged 40

THE COURAGE GAME

Jeni Whittaker

Matador
9 Priory Business Park,
Wistow Road, Kibworth Beauchamp,
Leicestershire. LE8 0RX
Tel: 0116 279 2299
Email: books@troubador.co.uk
Web: www.troubador.co.uk/matador
Twitter: @matadorbooks

ISBN 978 1 8004 6451 3

British Library Cataloguing in Publication Data.
A catalogue record for this book is available from the British Library.

Printed and bound by CPI Group (UK) Ltd, Croydon, CR0 4YY
Typeset in 12pt Adobe Jensen Pro by Troubador Publishing Ltd, Leicester, UK

Matador is an imprint of Troubador Publishing Ltd

This novel is dedicated to the memories of both my great-aunt, Gladys Mary Hazel, who is the central character of the novel, and to my father, Peter Waterfield, whom she brought up from the age of two, when he lost the mother who was her sister.

A few weeks ago the last member of the Hazel family – the last at least to still bear that surname – sadly died of Covid-19. She was Janet Hazel, who was the daughter of Jim, Gladys's elder brother. Fondest memories of her also.

1

Blewbury, Berkshire 1950

Halfway through breakfast I pick up a dropped spoon and notice Truda has her slippers on. Meticulous Truda, who never leaves her room without being fully dressed, hair done up in her trademark knot. Alarm bells ring as I realise that for some reason she is rattled, so I watch carefully as she wipes her lips, rolls her napkin square into a neat sausage and feeds it through its silver ring. Behind her the window is filled with the high white sky of autumn, sparrows and tits jostling around the food I've hung for them in one of the apple trees. She clears her throat, looks quickly up at me, a bird-like glance, bright and shy, before dipping her head down. I ponder the top of her head, thin white hair barely covering pink scalp. I am now thoroughly alarmed.

Gazing earnestly at the polished surface of the dining table as if for inspiration, 'I enjoyed the person you were when I first met you,' she says with a kind of apologetic wistfulness. 'Fiery. The way you spoke at those meetings, standing straight as a candle with your hair blazing as hot as your anger …' She blinks up at me, perhaps to gauge my reaction, then presents her scalp again. 'Though I understand things are different now – *you* are different now. But I want you to know that what *was* – the past – wasn't all bad. She takes a breath and finishes in a rush. 'I think it's time to stop punishing yourself.'

I hate the inference that I am somehow less than in the past, but all the same I do not want to resurrect that me. When Truda first met me I was a travelling speaker for the suffragettes, my speeches inflammatory. I'd been filled with the self-righteousness of certainty: certain I was right, certain that anyone who didn't share my beliefs was wrong. Truda is correct: I consigned that person to oblivion, buried her. In fact, I was ashamed of who I had been, the mistakes I'd made and the price others as well as myself had paid through my fault.

I make a show of finishing my porridge, though I've suddenly lost my appetite and it sticks in my throat. Then, mastering my unease, I scrape my chair back on the parquet floor and take both our dark blue bowls – bought from an artist friend here in Blewbury who also once supported the Cause – into the kitchen to wash. The walls and ceiling need a fresh coat of paint. It's dark in there today, North facing, with little light spilling from the living room across the corridor. I focus on these things to blot out the past, that past which we'd agreed, both agreed I'd thought, to leave alone.

Of course there have been times when memories surfaced, especially at the start of our arrangement – she working busily as a doctor, while I cooked and cleaned for her, barely adequately. A poor exchange as I wasn't a natural housekeeper but Truda was kind, or absent-minded or both, and appeared to like my burnt offerings and not to notice the dusty surfaces, except in her clinic. There everything had to be just so; there she was queen of her own domain, fierce and protective.

It was she who encouraged me to grow fruit and vegetables

which became a passion, soon replacing all past passions. I had that, and I had my boy, Peter, whose childhood filled many happy years. Almost without my noticing the past receded. I had thought it quite gone.

Now I linger at the veined white sink, where I can look out of the window down the path, past the line of cherry trees – a few leaves still attached – past the blackberries, the raspberry canes and the sleeping rhubarb beds, to the narrow gate and the steps down to the lane. Faces emerge from the soapsuds: Millie, Emily, Dorothy – all people with whom I'd shared so much. Out of the suds another shadow forms. Michael. Quickly I stir the water and pull out the plug. Memory can take only so much at a time.

I hear Truda wondering aloud what I'm up to. She sounds herself again, so I make her a cup of coffee, strong and black as she likes it. The small demands of this task settle me once more and I return to the dining-room, convinced she's let the subject go.

But no. She's like a dog with a favourite bone. Her eyes sharpen as she sees me and she carries on as if I'd never left. 'Time you wrote it all down,' she said. 'It's important. People should know. Your family should know, what remains of them. And, with the benefit of hindsight, you can make sense of it and lay it to rest.' I recognise the tone. It's the firm no-nonsense voice she used to adopt with a recalcitrant patient, one who resisted when medical advice was offered.

I protest of course. For a start, I thought I *had* laid it to rest. The poet in me has reached out to another form of poetry that claims all my time, the simple alchemy of seeds, sunshine, water and earth. My garden keeps me rooted. It feels more real than words which slip and slide. Hands buried in the rich soil, sifting out weeds, crumbling it in preparation for seeds, the mind stays on the simplicity of the tasks.

My head appears to be manifesting its own denial, shaking to and fro like an automaton as I tell her that the vegetable beds must be cleared and prepared for the winter, or there'd be too much to do in spring. Then I babble on, listing the tasks until I run out of steam. Truda, needless to say, keeps silent. Knowing me as well as she does she knows that the suggestion she's made will ferment inside me until I act on it, one way or another. She used the same method when I was in denial about the boy, all those years ago. But I'm angry with her: she's stirred up the sludge and the memories are rising up however hard I try to stop them.

Instead of going out into the garden, I head straight to my bedroom, make the bed with hospital corners, which Mama taught me but I never normally did – the kind of petty rebellion that became habit – when my eye is caught by something on top of the wardrobe. It's my old Underwood typewriter, almost buried under dust. It's years since I last took it down, to write a play for the boy and his friends to perform I think, maybe even longer ago than that: those poems I was honing to send to the publisher. There's no harm in just looking at it, checking it over. There's no commitment in that and certainly I'm not reacting to Truda's suggestion. I just happened to catch sight of it, out of the corner of my eye.

Denial is still uppermost when I stand on a flimsy chair and lift it. Then I feel its weight, its solidity, heavy in my arms, like a spiky child, like my embryo self and find myself cradling it with great tenderness. It speaks to me out of its dust of ages, its neglect, its memory of forgotten things. And I'm afraid, but already it's working its magic. When did mere fear in the old days prevent me from anything?

Tentatively I remove the cover. The dust makes me sneeze but as soon as I catch the faint but familiar smell of the ink ribbon my mouth waters as it always did. My dear old Underwood. I can't help it, just the smell sends a bolt of excitement through me. Will it still work? Won't the ink have dried up? I place it on the little desk in front of my bedroom window, notice the vegetable garden outside, tired and dishevelled and in need of care, but now my mind is elsewhere: stirring, weighty with memories, seventy years of them.

My finger hovers over the x key and presses down. As I suspected – blank. The ink has dried. I stab the key again and again, and there, like a figure appearing gradually out of the mist, becoming clearer as I keep on stabbing, a series of xxx's. Kisses or warnings – who knows?

A quick rap on the door and Truda pokes her head around, her watery eyes barely visible behind her spectacles, thin white hair straying out of its topknot. 'You've started then,' she says, pleased.

Some childish instinct makes me want to wipe the expression from her face. 'No. I was just seeing if the old thing still works. It doesn't.' And I stand in front of the page with its line of xxxs, blocking her view. 'So that's that.'

'Pity,' she says, unfazed. 'But there's always pen and ink. And the village shop will sell typewriter ribbons I'm sure.' She gives me a brief smile and leaves. I can't help finding that last comment smug. What is she up to? Trying to hole me into a corner? I listen to her soft footfalls going down the carpeted corridor to her own room, then turn and replace the cover on the typewriter. I'll put it back, damn her. Later, when I can face the wobbling chair again. So I leave it on the desk for now, where it sits, very black, rather rusty, definitely dusty, and now undeniably threatening, and head for the garden.

After a desultory few minutes with a fork attacking the yellowing trails of dying vegetation I sit back on my heels. A new memory has surfaced, from an earlier time, too early to be weighted with guilt. I see again the thick uneven walls of the ramshackle cottage in Ireland where we all lived for the first ten years of my childhood. Whispering to myself, I speak aloud the names of my brothers and sisters, all six of them in order of age, over and over again like a mantra: Jim, Gladys – that's me – then Rita, Edgar, Duncan, Kay and finally Lina.

That's it, I think. I'll write about those days, my family, nothing else, and my feet carry me back to where the typewriter beckons.

2

Killybeggs, Donegal, Ireland 1887-1890

For a while I sit, staring at a blank page of paper. The mantra of names, the barrier I have made of them against anything threatening, intrudes. I go to the bottom of the same narrow wardrobe, on top of which the typewriter had rested out of sight and mind, and pull out a little brown suitcase. Usually my good shoes and Sunday boots live on top of the case. It's a long time since I've opened it.

The case is scuffed and stained with dry mud. When I open it two photographs lie on top, pasted on cardboard. One shows the family in front of the ivy-covered wall of the side of our house in Ireland. There is Papa in his good brown tweed double-breasted suit and his deerstalker hat with the flaps over his ears. His beard is short and neat and even through the sepia tints of the photograph I can see how light his eyes are, such a shining blue, the colour of speedwells. He looks like the Prince Regent of the time, Bertie, who became Edward VII. Papa has his arm around my waist and I am smiling broadly, the only one in the photo who is, amongst a number of scowling or bored faces. Probably I am smiling because he usually favoured Rita over me. Rita, his Aimée Marguerite to give her her proper name, was always the spoiled favourite. Is that why her pointed lace collar is so much bigger than mine? She is standing on the other side of Papa and looking sulky – an expression that doesn't suit her. Kay, obviously on the brink of tears, is between Rita and Mama in her best black bombazine.

Mama looks studiedly calm and rather plump. I count the number of children there – six, including me. So Lina is not yet born. Perhaps she is the reason for Mama's stoutness. Sitting on the ground are the three boys, all in their best sailor suits. Jim and Duncan still have their sailor hats on but Edgar's has fallen off. His hand is placed on Duncan's thigh and from Duncan's pained expression it is clear that Edgar has just given him a pinch. Jim, the eldest of us all, appears patient and rather absent while Edgar just looks naughty. His face is pulled into a grin like a gargoyle.

I am lost in the photograph, trying and failing to remember that day. Because the picture is not in colour you cannot tell, looking at it, that Mama and I had carrot-red hair, while the others were largely chestnut-brown. Papa's looks as light as Mama's but he was probably already turning grey. He was a good many years older.

Underneath this photograph is another of all us children crammed into the little donkey cart, with Mama standing beside it, the ruffles of her bustle making her backside look vast. She is still dressed in her Sunday best. It was not taken in front of our house, like the first picture, but somewhere in Killybeggs perhaps. You cannot see the sea in the picture, but I know it is there, opposite the houses, slapping against the harbour wall. In this picture Mama holds a baby. Lina has joined us. There is a stain on this photograph, almost obliterating Lina, but I can conjure up her face, with its slight twist as if to react to the twist in her spine, its fine eyes. And suddenly I can hear us all, the clamour of our voices piping and high as we seek to be heard. And memories fly out, like photographs escaping from the closed covers of an album...

There is Mama, a determined look on her face, teeth bared, as she clamps my wriggling body between her legs. The scissors in her hands clack.

'Keep still.'

... Clack clack, and released strands of hair fell into my eyes. I heard a gasp from one of the boys behind me and a giggle from Rita.

'Your turns next,' threatened Mama. 'You'll know to keep still now, won't you?' She gave me a push and I ran out of the room, up the stairs and into the bedroom where Mama, Papa and the two little girls, Kay and Lina, slept. There stood the only mirror in the house, a fly-spattered piece of glass hemmed between dark oak curlicues standing on top of the chest-of-drawers. It was as I feared, my fringe slanted at an alarming and comical angle from above my left eyebrow up into the right-hand hairline. I'd be a laughing stock.

Jim, the eldest of us seven children, is walking with me along the sandy lane to Killybeggs. To the left, peaty tussocks littered with granite boulders, as if a giant toddler has thrown his toys out of the playpen, ascend to a rugged skyline. To the right, high dunes spiked with tall grasses allow occasional glimpses of the sea. The sky is heavy and threatens rain. Seagulls wail like souls thrown out of Heaven. Jim and I are heading to the schoolroom, where a small number of local boys learn the rudiments of

*Latin, History and Mathematics from Father Cullen, the
Roman Catholic priest. There are no other girls ...*

... All but one of those boys was younger than Jim, which he
was ashamed about, and all but one were from the Anglo-Irish
families who owned the larger houses and businesses around
the town. Soon they would be sent to schools in England for,
unlike us, they could afford the journey and the boarding
school fees. All but one, and he was a local lad, as Irish as
the lads who were laughing at me as we walked through the
town, me with my wild orange hair and crazy fringe which
disappeared into the hairline and left a white naked expanse
of forehead on one side of my face. They hooted and threw
stones and ducked over the edge of the wall and down the
stone steps to the greasy sand of the harbour at low tide,
skidding on weed and doubled over with cruel laughter that
hurt like knives, and mocking words in harsh Gaelic, which I
could not understand.

As we approached the school room, which was the priest's
study in his cottage beside the church, we caught up with the
Irish boy, Michael, who heard the taunts following me like a
cloud of flies after horse droppings and suddenly turned and
ran behind, shouting.

My tormentors scattered, faced with Michael's stream of
Gaelic and his blue eyes like darts under the thatch of his light
brown hair. When it was quiet, he returned to slot in beside Jim
and me, and kept turning his face towards first Jim and then
me. I looked away from him, afraid that he would laugh too,
but then we were entering the priest's house, and the younger
Anglo-Irish boys gathered there began to point and snigger
but were silenced by the priest's words and Michael's glare, so
that soon we all settled on our two wooden benches, slates
on our knees, and the delights of learning lapped me around

and made me forget how ugly I was. The only difference from usual was that Michael sat next to me on one side with Jim on the other while all the younger English boys crushed together on the bench in front, their backs to us.

Michael again. Once he's swum past the barriers in my memory a shoal of other incidents surface. Now he is older – the Michael I remember from later years – looking out at me with his eyes narrowed as if he's looking into the sun or, as he once joked, the fiery sunset of my hair, which shines in light like the brightest of copper wires – his words. He turns his head and looks away, pretends to be dazzled, but I know the real reason. He cannot bear to look at me lest his feelings overwhelm him.

I blink away sudden tears and the snapshot in my mind reforms. Now just a lad, he squints into the sun as if looking into or from a great distance. I remember now the first time I met him …

… We had gone to buy bread and other necessities from the town. A boy of about eight, one of Mrs O'Connor's brood with a smattering of English, offered to hold Fern, our donkey, while Mama shopped. Gratefully we spilt out of confinement and, leaving Kay and Lina to accompany Mama, with Rita to hold Lina, the boys and I ran down the slipway and onto the beach. Unlike the white sand beach near our house, this one was darkened by the black grease used to preserve the nets, and sequinned with fish scales. Snakes of rope, anchors and buoys littered the whole area. One or two smaller boats listed sideways, looking strangely clumsy out of water. Edgar and Duncan climbed into one to be pirates. Soon the air was full of thick-accented expressions gleaned from *Treasure Island*, newly sent over by Papa's sister, our Aunt Sarah in England.

That day, being fine, most of the fishing fleet were out, or the dark sand would have been crowded with larger boats and with fishermen smoking their clay pipes and repairing their nets and crab pots.

Against the harbour wall, green with slimy weed, sat a group of boys, legs out straight and stiff in front of them as they threw stones at a bottle. Every now and again a missile connected to the target with a clang and a cheer rose from the players.

Duncan, tired now of pirates, spotted a lad he'd met on previous occasions and ran to join the group. Edgar hovered, less sure of a welcome. The boy who rose to his feet to meet Duncan had to be some years older than him. He was at least ten, dark, with a low brow and a sullen expression. He pushed Duncan in the chest and my brother laughed good-naturedly and pushed him back.

Edgar explained, 'That's the boy who always hits Duncan. He can't speak English. I think he's called Patrick though, Patrick Allen.'

Now the boy was sitting on top of Duncan and pummelling his chest and Duncan was still laughing, but wildly, in a more desperate way. I glanced at Jim and then both of us went to the rescue, but before we reached him the mean boy, apparently satisfied, got off our brother and slouched back to the wall where the rest of his gang had stopped their game to watch. We began to brush Duncan down from the wet sand that had stuck to his clothes and his hair. I could see Jim wondering whether he should go and challenge Duncan's aggressor and not much relishing the thought.

Duncan's face meanwhile was stuck in a smile like a grimace. 'He always does that,' he explained cheerfully. 'It's because I'm English. I don't really mind. Sometimes we skim stones in the sea and he's better than me. Then he doesn't hit me at all.'

A tall boy, perhaps twelve or thirteen, had already risen to his feet and now came over. He greeted us in fair English, though strongly accented. His voice was deepening, already almost a man's.

Jim responded cautiously, but with relief.

I could see that the newcomer was taller and older than my brother by a year or two. He had hair the colour of hay that has been left out in the rain, not quite blonde but not quite brown either. His fringe flopped into eyes of a very sharp blue and his face was unusually pale under a cap pushed well back on his head. The other boys in the group looked weathered in comparison.

Jim introduced the boy to the rest of us. 'This is Michael Allen. He has lessons with me sometimes, with Father Cullen.' From his attitude I could see that Jim was embarrassed. I resolved to ask him later what was wrong with the boy. To me he appeared pleasant and, better still to children who had no friends but their own brothers and sisters, he behaved as if he wanted to know us. Best of all, he spoke passable English.

To make up for Jim's shortcomings, I smiled at the Irish boy and he smiled back. First he apologised for his brother Patrick who was, he said, 'a bit of a ruffian.' He explained that he studied with Father Cullen to improve his English and further his Classics, because he wanted to go to England one day to find better work than he could find in Ireland. To me his language seemed already quite good but some of the words were strangely pronounced and their order was rather muddled. I found myself offering to help him too.

Even then, there was something about him, something that attracted me.

Jim pulled me away and, as we made our way back up to the road to meet Mama, Duncan and Edgar running ahead with their cries echoing the gulls above them, I craned back to look at the boy, standing there so still and apart. He raised one hand a fraction in farewell.

As we stood by the trap, relieving the lad who was still holding Fern, Jim looked fiercely at me. 'I don't like that boy. He may seem friendly but he's like all the rest. His whole family want us to leave Ireland. Walking to school in the mornings, I've come across the Allen boys many times. They throw stones and clods of mud at me and shout abuse. They may speak Irish, but they have learned one phrase which they never tire of yelling: *Go home English*.'

I saw his bent head and realised the torment of his lonely treks to school. He had never complained. But I was puzzled. The eldest boy had appeared so pleasant.

'That Michael Allen – he's one of the boys that throws stones?'

Jim shook his head. 'No. But only because he hasn't far to go from his own house to Father Cullen's. He's usually sitting in the school-room with the Father when I arrive. I think he has a lesson on his own before everyone else is there.'

'Is it only you that's treated so badly? I thought there were lots of English boys at school.'

'There are. But they're rich boys. They're driven to school by their families' servants.' Nothing in Jim's voice suggested envy but I began to see why Mama warned us against straying far from home. The beach by our house, a mile away from the town, was our terrain. Suddenly the town and its environs felt uncertain, as if my rose-tinted curtain had been drawn back exposing a darker place, full of threat and shadows.

I looked around, seeing the familiar sandy street, the sky a watery blue above. 'Aren't there other Irish boys there too?' Suddenly the schooling I longed for appeared less attractive.

Jim explained there was only the Allen boy who wanted an English-style education.

The others were schooled locally, if at all.

'Why do they hate us?' I felt aggrieved. 'We've done nothing to them.'

'Because it's their country, they say, and we are taking it for ourselves. It was Michael Allen who explained that to me. That was when I arrived one day covered in mud, before the Father saw me and took me into the kitchen to wash. So that's how I know that boy is not to be trusted any more than the others.' He looked around blindly and checked we were alone – Edgar and Duncan had joined Mama in Mrs O'Connor's. I saw his eyes were full of tears which he blinked back fiercely before whispering. 'I hate this place. I wish we could go back to England, to where we belong.'

The idea felt impossible to me. Leave Ireland? I had known nowhere else, though I knew I had been born in England. And despite Jim, I couldn't get the Irish boy out of my mind – his smile, the way his eyes crinkled at the corners. 'I don't think he *is* like the others. I think he was just explaining things to you. It doesn't mean that he shares his brother's feelings, does it? He says he wants to work in England one day. Is he clever?'

Jim shrugged and from that I surmised that Michael was at least as clever as Jim and that Jim didn't like that. He was jealous of him, an Irish boy from a poor background studying hard and trying to further himself. This understanding made me resolve to get to know Michael better and I'd have a chance soon, since there had been some talk about me studying with Father Cullen myself, though I would be the only girl there. Mama and Papa had said that I'd already outgrown the kind of teaching they could give me: a smattering of history, masses of literature from Mama's books, and the rudiments of French and German from Mama's travels with her parents, who'd often travelled to the continent. Mama was particularly fond of French, as she'd been born in Avignon, France – by accident, she said, because she'd arrived early.

I thought of Michael Allen, his smile, his eyes, and resolved to help my parents make up their minds. 'I'll be walking with you soon,' I said with a certainty I didn't feel. 'Then you'll be safe. Those boys won't hurt a girl.'

Mama, Rita and I are walking towards Killybeggs, Rita holding Mama's hand and me dragging behind. Mama is carrying a cloth bag with wooden handles full of cast-off baby clothes from the youngest, Lina. This snapshot memory has a fuzziness to it, as if it were unreliable or came from an earlier time. But how could that be? Mama would not give up useful baby clothes unless she were sure she'd have no more. Unless Lina was an accident, as perhaps she was because her birth ensured Mama would have no more children, ever, and the protracted horror of it ensured, too, that Lina would always be different, with her twisted spine and face …

… I hated it when Mama made us come on what she called charity visits. Her eyes took on a far-away look and her chin went up as she remembered her childhood, when her family owned a grand house on the edge of a Hampshire village where they had lived for centuries and where the villagers pulled their forelocks, their memories long with servitude. There, Mama had been taken by her mother to hand out toys or clothes for the children, possets and tonics for the adults. Each new baby born to the villagers was graced with a visit and fussed over. Most importantly, nobody laughed at her or her mother. They expected such visits. It was how things were.

Here, where on Papa's naval half-pay we had little more money than the locals, it was a different matter. Whatever

Mama's dreams of grandeur, to our neighbours we were just another bunch of pretentious English, looking down on the Irish and not even bothering to learn their language. They hated us. Even at that very young age I knew it.

Rita appeared indifferent to the sullen glances of the locals. She was the beauty of the family and, with hindsight, I could see how canny my mother was to take her with us. Rita's pretty ways opened doors that might otherwise be barred. Even the children, despite the language barrier, were drawn to her and included her in their games when we bought our bread and eggs at Mrs O'Connor's, where Mama stayed sometimes for a chat.

Looking back, I can see now that Mama must have been lonely for adult company. Our cottage was a way out of the town, set on a spit of land that meant we were surrounded on three sides by the sea. When there were Atlantic storms, the spray from the huge waves rattled our windows and streaked them with salt. There were no neighbours. Most of the shopkeepers in Killybeggs spoke English as well as Gaelic, but they were cool and business-like in their dealings with customers. Mrs O'Connor was different: a red-faced woman with dark hair raked back into a savage bun, she was always friendly and eager to try out her English. With her, Mama occasionally relaxed enough to share a joke, notice Mrs O'Connor's many children, even once or twice sit in the cramped front room and take a cup of tea.

It was a different matter when the husband was there. He was a fisherman, often away for days on end, but when the weather was stormy he'd fill up the space in front of the fire with his bulk and glare around at our English voices, a pottery tankard in one large fist. Mrs O'Connor was a different person then, her head held low, her voice thin. Usually she spoke Gaelic when he was around, so that Mama, understanding, pointed to what she wanted and lifted her fingers to indicate how many. The gaggle of small children who usually shrieked and tumbled around their home and in and out of the door to play in the lane were noticeably absent when their father was there, as if, like mice, they'd disappeared into the gaps in the walls.

On the days that Mama stayed and chatted, those same children grabbed hold of Rita and pulled her off to play with them. Never me, though once a wee tot showed me a tiny shell she held in a sticky hand and then, encouraged by my polite interest, beckoned me to follow upstairs.

I glanced back at Mama, rosily sipping tea and exchanging tips about cooking for large families. I was bored and restless, so I followed the tot, who jabbered incomprehensibly the whole time, up to a cramped room entirely taken up by one large bed, its coverings horribly stained and a pile of coats and a single coarse blanket heaped on top. The room stank dreadfully and a black mould crept down the walls from the tiny window, emitting its own damp aroma. My captor showed me a ragged doll with one eye sewn into its cloth face, the other having unravelled to lend the toy a rakish look. This treasure was thrust into my reluctant arms while the child reached under the bed to pull out a reeking bucket, almost full to the top with urine. As I backed away towards the top of the stairs, looking for escape, the child lifted her skirt, revealing no underclothes, and squatted with a sigh over the receptacle. It was enough. I dropped the battered doll and fled back downstairs from where, finding Mama still talking, I bolted out to find Rita, surrounded by an admiring crowd to whom she was teaching the basics of hopscotch. I took deep breaths as I watched the game, but my lungs felt clogged and nostrils held that stench till long after we left for home. It was like coming up for air after nearly drowning.

How clearly this memory has taken shape. I fear it does not show me in a good light – often the case in those days. It was Rita who charmed people of all ages. I would notice how eyes would follow her and a soppy smile would appear on the faces of even the most hardened of adults. And my parents indulged her of course, or that is what I felt. Was that true? I grew up thinking so, feeling like the odd one out. But maybe my vision was skewed. My parents were so busy then, with so little time for any of us in particular, that mostly we were left to entertain ourselves.

And how did I feel about Rita? Was I jealous of her? Yes, often, but she was also my best friend, the closest to me in age. We shared a bed, whispered together with our arms around each other, far into the night, held pillow-fights which sometimes began out of anger but always ended with laughter until our stomachs hurt.

How I miss her, even now in my old age. I shall never not miss her: Rita, whose real name was Marguerite and whose forgotten first name, Aimée, means Beloved.

I spent a little time today, reading back what I'd typed yesterday. Truda wanted to see what I'd written, of course, but I told her to wait. I am no longer cross with her for I am filled with a kind of relief as the dam opens and the memories trickle out. I've even admitted that I'm enjoying myself, can hardly wait to get back to the typewriter.

'Will you go on to write about the suffragette years?' she asks casually, as if she doesn't care if I do or if I don't. But I know she sees the necessity, that this is the healing she wants for me so I admit that I may well end up there and, seeing her disappointment at the slowness of it all, I explain that already the paths my life took are becoming clearer.

One path is the awareness of poverty. It began with the O'Connor's house, though they were by no means the poorest.

Mr O'Connor worked, after all. They did not starve. There was fish and other spoils of the sea, and the flat bread Mrs O'Connor baked, and eggs from the hens.

No, to me, poverty was wrapped up in smell. There was the reek of that bucket and the insidious rank creep of mildew and damp in every little cottage, including our own, though Mama scrubbed at it with a noxious mix of ammonia and ash that blistered her hands. There was the stale earthy smell that came from bedding in which too many people tossed and slept – that one bed in the O'Connor's cottage, I later found out, held all their many children at night. I never knew how many there were. Like puppies they wriggled and squirmed and were never still enough to count and, again like puppies, I imagined them heaped together in the bed, snuffling and snorting in a tangle of bodies, warm but unbelievably smelly.

Don't misunderstand me, there are good smells too. The smell of earth as I dig the soil, the sharp clean smell of the coastal air around our Irish home, the wind carrying the scent of summer flowers on the high downs where I live now and where the racehorses run.

I suppose it was human smells which disgusted me the most in those days. I was too young for pity. All I saw was the way in which people – as I imagined – *chose* to live. I made comparisons between our cottage, full of two adults and seven children with only three bedrooms, and the houses of others which we entered on those charity visits. How could they allow their clothes and their bedding to become so dirty? How could they not clean the dust and the spores of mould away? We managed, didn't we?

But now I see: three bedrooms, compared to one and little more than a bulge in a corridor, which is where the O'Connor parents slept, is no small difference. And Papa's earnings, even on only half-pay, must have been considerably more than a fisherman's, subject to vagaries in the weather, or the small pittance gathered in by his wife's efforts. Nina, my Birmingham friend, tried her best to make me see that, despite the romantic illusion I'd built up of our childhood deprivations, and it was Nina who showed me the underside of Birmingham and shocked me into the realisation of what it truly means to be poor.

Another charity visit, this time to Michael's house, the Allen's, where a new baby to join the other five has been born. Rita is holding the baby and jiggling it up and down, a big smile on her face. I see then her sly look as she offers the infant for me to hold. She knows I dislike babies, even though I have been around so many of our own ...

... Of course, I explained to Michael later, holding my own baby brothers and sisters was different. They smelled different. There was a family smell perhaps, that we all shared. Michael just laughed and teased me. Did I never play with dolls? Wouldn't I want a baby of my own one day? A resounding No was the answer to both. He asked whether I had played at being a little mother to my new-born siblings, whether I'd enjoyed washing and changing them. My answer was a shudder. I'd passed all those chores to Rita who didn't mind them a bit.

Michael and I were sitting in the dust outside his house, our backs against the wall. For once Patrick and the others were nowhere to be seen. I can't remember whether they were in the house. Perhaps they were, in the shadows of the dark room, watching the English usurpers handing out unwanted gifts.

Michael drew patterns in the dust with the end of a stick. 'You'll be a woman one day,' he said and gave me a sidelong look, 'a beautiful woman, surely, is what I'm thinking. Can't

I see you now with a smile on your face and your hair like a sunset, cradling an infant to your bosom … ?'

I sprang to my feet. 'Not me,' I spat. 'Rita perhaps. I shall be a writer, a famous poet…' Then I thought of what he said. No one had ever used the word beautiful about me – it was a word reserved for Rita. And mostly people focused on my hair in a negative way, as in Mama's laments over its springy curls which resisted the hairbrush, or Rita's attempts to tame it, tip of her tongue protruding, before leaving for Father Cullen's. Mama's hair was also red, like mine, but softer and straighter. Mine, she said, was simply a torment. Yet Michael had called it a sunset. I liked that and looked down at him more kindly, even though he'd used the word bosom, which was a word to be giggled over by Rita and I under the sheets.

I would have sat down beside him again, but at that moment Patrick and the rest of his brothers emerged glowering and Michael got up protectively and steered me away. We peeped in the door where Mama and Rita still crooned over the baby.

'Why are your brothers so angry?'

'They think your Mama is patronising our mother.'

'What does that mean?'

'Don't worry yourself. I don't think so, that's all that matters.' He nudged me with his elbow. 'Will you look at her? The first girl in a passel of boys.'

'She'll be spoiled rotten,' I commented, already jealous of anyone who took Michael's attention away from me.

Michael and I had been friendly since the fringe episode, nearly two years before. Though he was much older than me – by now he was fourteen and I ten – we had been thrown together, with Jim, by our shared lessons with the Father. I started with the younger boys but quickly outstripped them and within a year found myself sharing lessons with Michael and Jim instead. Their sharp minds, Jim's no less than Michael's, challenged me and the to and fro of our arguments caused my brain to seethe with excitement. Two years of this followed, by which time a reluctant Rita, followed by Edgar, joined the younger, ever-changing group of Anglo-Irish. I was no longer the only girl.

It was good to have more of us to walk to class but the dynamics had changed. Rita quickly became the centre of attention, admired by all the other boys. I didn't mind this so much, but I did mind the gentle teasing she received from Michael. Was no one blind to Rita's charms? The result was that I drew away from Michael and was obstinate and snappy with him.

Then in that same year everything changed. We heard we were to return to England.

We are all sitting round the large scrubbed kitchen table with Mama and Papa at either end. Apart from a small walk-in larder, this is the only room downstairs. We have a large black range which warms the whole house and on which Mama cooks. There are two easy chairs near the range, in which Mama can sit and read of an evening while Papa does his paperwork or reads the news. Hanging on the wall is the tub in which we all take baths. Above the range are Mama's prized collection of copper pans, polished like mirrors. It is hard for my parents to hang their pictures or place ornaments because the walls are so lumpy and uneven. That is why pictures are crowded in little clusters, where the wall is smooth, and why there are large areas with no ornament at all. The wall is whitewashed, but it always looks more grey than white. Mama has tried to impose some gentility on her living space. I can see now, in hindsight, how hard it must have been for her, the daughter of a wealthy family, brought up in comfort.

At Mama's end of the table the two little girls sit one each side of her. Lina has her thumb in her mouth; her constant sucking has created a large raised blister, which concerns Mama and when she can she forces the thumb out, to no avail. Back it goes within seconds.

Rita and Jim sit closest to Papa at the other end. These things appear set in stone. Duncan and Edgar don't mind not sitting next to one of our parents; they have each other. But I mind terribly. I want to be next to Papa. I feel I should be, by right of age. But I know Rita has always been his favourite child. Now I watch as he reaches out and pats her head. His palm fits round the crown and she pushes up into it, like a cat.

Papa has just given us the news of our return to England and I notice he looks younger and happier than he has for ages.

Mama takes up the story. We are to go back to Papa's family home, Rowstock, in Berkshire. There we are to have our own separate bedrooms, and there are fields and orchards to play in because there are three farms there, all belonging to the Hazel family.

'Is it near the sea?' asks Duncan.

No, it's not, and we all look at each other anxiously …

… Later that evening, sitting on the bed Rita and I shared, we elder children, all five of us, pummelled Jim with questions.

'You must remember what it was like. You were born there. You must have been at least two when they left.'

'Don't be silly. What do you remember about being two?'

'Mama said we'll all be going to school,' said Edgar glumly.

'You already go to school,' Jim said.

'Father Cullen's doesn't really count, does it? Papa said we'd board at Warwick School. Jim and I from next September.' His voice wobbled. 'Then Duncan the September after that.'

'A whole year,' wailed Duncan. 'On my own.'

'Why do we have to board?' persisted Edgar.

'You heard what Papa said,' Jim explained. 'There are naval scholarships for the sons of officers. That means it won't cost much to send us there.'

'I'll hate it, hate it, hate it,' yelled Edgar and ran out of the room. We could hear his bawling at the end of the corridor. Duncan looked at us, his lower lip trembling. Then he too, ran out of the room bawling.

'We really do need to stop being such crybabies,' said Jim crossly.

'*We're* not crying,' Rita pointed out.

'No,' said Jim. 'But you will when the time gets nearer. Everyone's going to be blubbing away like anything when we leave this house.'

'And the sea,' I put in softly.

'Well, I for one will be glad to go. There'll be a proper school to go to, with proper teachers and chaps of my own age.' He swung his legs over onto the floor, straightened his back and marched out like a soldier with his head held high.

Over the next few days Papa told us more about the house where we were to live, which was free because one of his two brothers had died suddenly, and we began to get used to the idea. Promises of animals and a pony to replace Fern and friends to make at the village school in Harwell, which is where Rita and Duncan would go for a while, had appeased everyone but me. Was I the only one who loved this place? And what was to happen to me when we arrived in England?

Papa wasn't certain. 'I think my sisters, your Aunts Mary and Sarah – they live in one of the other farmhouses at Rowstock – are looking into possibilities.'

'And *my* sister, Louise, who lives in Oxford will have ideas too,' comforted Mama. 'Don't worry. There are so many good schools for girls nowadays, we'll find you one that'll suit.'

That mattered. I loved learning. It seemed I was the only one of us who did.

'The best news is that Papa won't have to work any more,' Mama continued. 'Won't it be lovely to have him with us at home?'

Jim looked at him, puzzled.

'The Navy are discharging me,' Papa explained. 'I'm at retiring age, or nearly, so I'll have a bit of a pension and be able to enjoy life more.'

'Didn't you like your work here?' asked Jim, surprised.

Papa took his empty pipe out of his pocket and clamped his teeth down on the stem, a sure sign he didn't want to answer.

Mama said, 'Sometimes the Irish Customs Officers aren't very patient with him. He doesn't know this particular coastline like they do and …'

'That's enough, Katherine,' said Papa. 'No need to say more. We'll only be here for three more months. Then we'll be home.' His whole face lightened as he said it.

I was confused. Wasn't this home?

'Papa was born at Rowstock,' explained Mama. 'He spent his childhood there.'

So, if home was the place in which you spent your childhood, this cottage in Donegal was my home and always would be. I knew I would never forget it. But I felt sorry for Kay and Lina, who were four and three respectively. Was that like being two? Would they, like Jim, not even remember?

It is during that last summer. We are all playing on the beach near our home. The tide is out, revealing huge flat expanses of white sand, streaked with runnels of water that gleam in the sun.

Lina and Kay are sitting quite far down the beach in a hole which the boys dug earlier. When they duck down into it they are quite invisible.

Edgar and Duncan are rock-climbing at the base of the cliff which flanks part of the beach, while Jim sits on a ledge some way above them, telling them where to put their feet if they want to join him. Rita and I are decorating the castle we have just made with bits of weed and shells.

Suddenly everyone freezes as we hear Kay scream …

… There were two horses galloping up the beach. The leading rider, on a big bay, had his head turned away and was shouting back at the rider following. I couldn't hear what he said, but I could see that the rider behind was a young woman. Her hair was caught up in a net, but stray strands flew behind her and she was laughing, her face in a hectic flush of excitement. The horses too were caught up in the competitiveness of the race, long legs stretched out, sand flying behind them, manes and tails streaming.

Kay had poked her head out of the hole and seen the nearest horse frighteningly close. She'd clambered out and staggered away just in time. But Lina was still in there.

From our higher vantage point I could see the fluffy top of her head beginning to stir. It looked a matter of seconds before the front horse, sharp hooves slicing into the soft sand, would be on top of her.

We were too far away to do anything, though all of us began to shout and to run towards our baby sister. Everything so far had happened in a split second – the man with his head turned, the woman following, the horse's hooves tearing into the sand, Kay staggering away with her mouth open in horror and her screams carried up in the air to join the screams of the gulls.

It was clear that neither the horses or their riders had spotted the hole in the sand. And then, woken from her baby slumber by the noise, Lina's little brown head popped up and looked up at us, her thumb still in her mouth. Suddenly she turned her head and saw the horse. I saw her hand reach up as if to touch it and the horse reared. For a second or two it fought with its own body and flailing legs, but with a grunt and an alarmed whinny, it threw the front of its body sideways and came to a trembling halt. Its front hooves were no more than an inch away from the side of the hole, so close that we could see the sand wall collapsing inwards under its weight.

By this time, Rita and I had reached Lina and lifted her to safety as the side of the hole finally gave and the horse lurched and whickered, its flanks heaving and foam dripping from around the bit in its mouth.

Its rider threw himself off, pale with shock. He stammered apologies to us all – by now the boys had reached us – but it is the woman's response that I remember to this day.

'What stupid children,' she said through clenched teeth. 'One of them could have been killed. Why are they even here without anyone to mind them?' Her voice was upper-class English, not so different from our own had she bothered to speak to us directly. 'It's typical of these people,' she concluded, her eyes roaming coldly over us.

Jim started to explain that we lived in the house close by but she ignored him and raked us all up and down with her eyes, not even bothering to get off her horse, a pretty dappled grey beast with dainty legs.

As if she couldn't understand Jim's speech, 'Common little brats,' was all she said to her partner. 'Why are you bothering with them?'

I filled up with a spurt of anger that shook me from head to toe and rendered me speechless.

'Let's go,' she said to the man, as she pulled her horse's head around and began to canter back the way they had come.

But he didn't follow her, not yet. Instead he asked Lina if she'd like to pat his horse and the little girl, not at all aware of what had so nearly happened, reached out an eager hand to the foam-flecked neck and soon she was sitting on the saddle, held firm by the man, and Duncan was clamouring to have a go too. Then, with another apology, he said he'd have to catch up with his friend and he mounted up and was off, straight away into a canter which sprayed us with wet sand. He did not look back.

'Let's hope there're no other children playing on the beach today,' commented Jim grimly as we watched them disappear.

'Lucky that horse was so clever. His rider wasn't even looking where he was going,' I said.

'Horses will never willingly trample a human,' said Jim. 'Or so I've heard. Mostly they're gentle creatures.'

I looked around at Rita and the others. For a moment I saw us through the English woman's eyes. We were a ragged lot. Kay, not surprisingly, was still shocked and crying; snot streamed from her nose and onto her upper lip. Edgar's legs beneath his cropped trousers were scratched and bleeding from his rock-climbing, all of our hair, even the boys, was long and tangled by the wind and all of us were brown from the sun and covered in sand. Somehow that made it worse. I could see why that woman had looked down on us and seen us as Irish brats but also I understood for the first time why our neighbours hated the English. If all were like her, and I guessed many were, then no wonder.

The seven of us are sitting in our secret place, above the beach, where the stiff grasses of the dunes surround a deep hollow. The house, around two bends in the lane, is out of sight, and the shore too, but we can hear the waves

churning against the rocks and rushing up the sand.
Above us, seagulls loop lazily, adding their ghost-cries to
the sounds of the sea …

… Something had changed in Jim since the episode of the
horses. Far from blaming the careless riders, he had begun to
blame Ireland itself for everything that was wrong and to wish
ceaselessly that time would hurry by till we were in England.
He'd started to protest against going to Father Cullen's, but
Papa had prevailed, telling him that he needed the Father's
knowledge of Classics in particular if he were to pass muster
at Warwick School.

Jim muttered under his breath but obeyed, though his
black looks in the little schoolroom caused the Father to
remonstrate with him.

'We know that you are leaving soon,' he said sympathetically,
'but you need to learn to control your feelings. To be sure, you
will miss this place after so long…'

'I won't!' Jim shouted. 'I hate it here.'

Michael reached over to touch him, out of sympathy I
suppose, but Jim flailed out with his fist and hit him in the
eye. Michael's eye teared up but he made no sound. Jim was
standing, fists clenched by his side, his chest heaving, all eyes
from the younger boys in the rows in front turned on him
in excited glee. Rita and Edgar drew slightly apart, their eyes
wide with alarm.

Father Cullen kept his voice steady but he took Jim outside,
loosening the belt around his priest's garb as he did so and
we could hear the sound of the strap falling once, twice, three
times on Jim's bare flesh. Afterwards, he followed a stony-
faced Jim into the room and demanded that he apologise to
Michael.

I don't know who was more embarrassed of the two boys.

Both heads were ducked as Jim forced an apology out of lips that scarcely moved, after which Father Cullen left us with our slates and a mathematical problem to work on while he took Michael into his housekeeper to have his eye seen to.

As soon as they'd left I questioned Jim. Rita left the ranks of the younger boys in front and joined in. But some of her admirers were of the opinion that Jim had struck a blow for England and congratulated him. I could see that Jim was not displeased by this and I fell quiet.

I did understand, more than I wanted to admit. Though our beach and the dunes above it would always remain in my heart, I was becoming more and more aware that we were intruders in this country. I began to notice how people fell silent when we entered into a shop, how our progress down the street was marked by hard-eyed stares. Particularly, I noticed the hostile looks levelled at the smart carriages which came to pick the English boys up from Father Cullen's. I'd seen grown men levelling a sneaky stone at the back of a carriage.

But why did he have to hit Michael who was not just any Irish boy, but my friend? I understood with a rush of feeling that of all things Irish, it was Michael I'd miss the most.

Jim was sullen for a few days after Father Cullen's chastisement. It was the beginning of our last summer. Then, sitting in our secret place in the dunes, driven out from under her feet by a wild-eyed Mama trying to sort what would go with us to England, he suddenly announced that he'd invented a new game. He called it the Courage Game. We received the news with equanimity. Jim was always inventing games. Mostly they were of the indoor kind, with wooden boards he'd made himself and painted, and tiny ships or figures he'd fashioned in loving detail. There were always rules, lots of them. Jim liked rules.

This game, he explained, as Lina sucked her thumb and followed a struggling insect with her eyes and Duncan heaped the dry sand over Edgar's feet till they were invisible, would help to Form Our Characters and Make Us Brave. It was a Challenge that we all needed.

'Why?' asked Rita carelessly, throwing her head back into my lap and blinking up at the bright sky.

'Because we need to stop being babies.'

Rita sighed. 'Some of us *are* babies,' she pointed out, against Kay's protests.

Jim rolled his eyes and chivvied us down onto the beach, where we were lined up and told to stand straight. Then we were marched up and down until both the little ones complained. So then we were made to stand still and straight without moving for the longest time, until Edgar pushed Duncan over and both boys rolled about in the sand.

'You need discipline and focus,' yelled a frustrated Jim.

'But it's boring,' said Duncan, and Edgar, taking advantage of the lapse in his brother's concentration, sat triumphantly on top of him.

'Look,' said Jim, calming his voice with an effort, 'our lives are going to change. We'll have to face up to schools where people will already have made their friends. We'll be bullied and we need to be prepared.'

Now he had all our attention. Kay sat on Rita's lap and Lina on mine. The two boys settled next to us. Jim sat and faced us as he explained that most children would already have become used to school where we were going but that punishments such as strapping and the cane were common practice. 'And we're all a terrible bunch of crybabies.'

'You're not,' I said, thinking of the punishment meted out by Father Cullen.

Jim smiled gratefully at me. 'And I don't want Edgar, who'll be joining the preparatory department where I can't protect him, to cry, nor Duncan next year. They'll be terribly scoffed at by the rest of their class. We need to toughen up.'

'They won't hit girls,' said Rita confidently.

'Won't they? Remember Mama telling us once how she couldn't remember a times table and was caned on the palm of her hand. She said it hurt for days. And she was only seven.' He looked solemnly around at us. 'You don't want to be thought of as weaklings, do you? All of us, no exceptions, need to face up to what's going to happen. Papa told me that the most important thing about school and his training for the Navy was to keep a stiff upper lip. That means being brave whatever the pain, never showing that it hurts you, never shedding a tear or uttering a sound.'

Everyone looked at Jim. None of us spoke as he proposed what the 'game' would entail for the rest of the summer. Some of it sounded fun: drills and races and competitions. He had it all planned. We would help the little ones through and make allowances for their ages. But other suggestions sounded frightful, sticking pins into the palms of our hands without uttering a sound, cutting our thumbs with a knife till the blood flowed... 'Like blood brothers,' chorused Edgar and Duncan, who wanted to try that immediately... being locked up in the dark alone, being tied up with rope and rolled over the big stones at the top of the beach, walking barefoot through nettles... there seemed no end to Jim's imagination.

Some of these ideas might be hard to manage behind the backs of a watchful Mama, I pointed out, but Jim had thought of everything.

'Mama and Papa have a lot to think of. They're used to us playing together on our own anyway and Mama is packing and sorting all our belongings to go back to England. How will she know that Gladys, for instance, is locked up in the garden shed on her own for a whole afternoon? No one ever goes there.'

I shivered. The garden shed was a grand name for a kind of cave dug into the side of the steep hill behind our house with earthen walls from which white roots protruded. It was a playground for insects and spiders of all kinds, shapes and sizes. The door was roughly made out of planks and 'locking' it meant that a large roundish boulder was pushed against it from the outside. Once in there'd be no escape.

Jim looked at me knowingly. He knew my particular fears and that this would be a trial indeed. I looked back at him, determined not to show my feelings and he gave a little approving nod. Then he rooted around in the pocket of his short trousers. 'Look.'

We all shuffled closer in. In his hand he held a small cardboard badge, coloured red. 'I've made lots of these already.' He explained that one of these would be awarded to every winner – it may be for conquering a fear, or for not showing any emotion, or simply for winning a race. 'I'll write the initials of the winner on the back of every badge. But you won't be able to show them off, because Mama and Papa must not know what we're doing. It'll be our secret.'

Badges! Now that everyone knew there was a reward for every effort, we were all eager to begin.

How badges and rewards matter I think, as I visualise our young selves in those last days in Ireland. We children pushed ourselves to extremes to receive one little cardboard circle. Our parents would have been horrified if they'd known. But we learned to conceal: feet swollen with nettle stings, scratches from that tangled maze of brambles the day we were told to battle through them up the hill behind the house, bumps and bruises from being rolled over the stones and nightmares from being left alone for hours in the dark. Even Kay and Lina were part of it, though Jim carried them through the worst of the nettles and the brambles and they only received the tiniest prick on the day we all had a needle pushed into the palm of our hands.

The suffragette leaders knew the value of badges too and I remember the pride and pleasure with which I wore mine. Despite the pain. Despite the torture some of us suffered. Till I had time to think, during all those War years where suffrage was forgotten for our heroes at the Front, when I began at last to doubt everything I had done for the Cause.

And here it is, the Cause for Suffrage, emerging from the tangle of memories like an exotic flower – the kind that lures mortals to death and destruction for its sake.

Long-ago Ireland fades as memories of England surface, England with all it had to offer of education and opportunity. It was the beginning of something entirely new, when everything would change.

We left Ireland on a windy day, which made Mama and I too sick on the crossing to gaze at the receding shore. Our furniture had preceded us and the last few days had been like a continuous picnic, eating outside on a rug if it was fine, cross-legged on the uneven stone floor of the kitchen, appearing huge without the table in it, when the squally rain blew in from the Atlantic.

We'd said our farewells, which were few – the old fisherman who used sometimes to take us out rowing, who always grinned with his black teeth when we managed a straight course; Mrs O'Connor, who seemed genuinely affected, until her husband loomed in the doorway and she quickly mopped her tears; Father Cullen, who wished us well; and Michael, who bravely came to our house where he met my parents, too busy to notice him. They and a couple of local men were loading our belongings onto two carts which would take us to the station, from where we would travel to the ferry.

Michael shook Jim's hand, then Rita's, Edgar's – and Duncan's, not to be outdone, though he had never started at Father Cullen's – all the time looking past them at me. Last of all he grasped my hand and held it. He bent close and whispered, 'I'll be seeing you again for sure, Gladys. One day. When I'll be coming to England.'

After he had gone and while the others were settling noisily into the carts, Rita and I crept back into the house where we had spent the whole of our childhood so far – ten years for me, eight for Rita. It looked sunk in on itself, too small to have housed us all. Holding hands, we climbed the uneven stairs to our old bedroom and gazed round the empty space.

'Look,' said Rita suddenly and, letting go of my hand she dived towards a crack under the skirting and brought out a little notebook. It was mine, full of jottings and attempts at poetry. I riffled the pages but when Rita left the room I replaced it where she'd found it. It was of the past, it was gone, and now the future beckoned.

3

Berkshire, England 1890

I can remember the arrival at Rowstock as if it were yesterday. Just closing my eyes – there it is, with its generous sash windows, the virginia creeper covering the main square house on the side which faced the road, the sweet-smelling pink and white rose that covered the lower section of the house, which was the original older dwelling. And there we were, standing in an awed cluster, close together for comfort, until encouraged by our parents to choose our own rooms. The excitement of that, short-lived for the boys who were more eager to explore the farmland and visit the animals, kept us happy for the rest of the day.

It was the Ambroses, father and son, who had met us from the station. They worked on Middle Farm, where Papa's one remaining brother, William, a confirmed bachelor and, as we soon discovered, averse to children, lived in grim solitude. The Ambrose family inhabited the farm cottage, near enough at hand for Mrs Ambrose to clean such parts of the main house as Uncle William would allow and to bring him his meals, while Ambrose, as we all learned to call him, managed the farm with his eldest son, Joe, a lad of fifteen or so but already well-muscled and weathered from years of heavy work.

Our furniture had already arrived in advance of us, so the exploration of the upper floor of the house was punctuated by cries of delight as we came upon familiar objects. In addition, new beds had been ordered so that we each had our own and in the first few weeks after we arrived, Mama, often with Rita, who immersed herself in house management and cookery from the first, travelled into Oxford to find suitable pieces to grace our drawing-room, dining-room and Papa's study.

Duncan and Edgar hoped for cousins to play with, now we were surrounded by Papa's family, but it emerged that neither of Papa's sisters had obliged. They had never married and both were now in their forties.

Aunt Mary, the elder of the two, was tall and hatchet-jawed, bolted into her clothes as if they were armour, a single eyeglass hanging from a silver chain across her chest. Her eyes, bright blue like Papa's, were sharp and her hair in the front was so tightly curled that it completed the picture of a woman made entirely of some strange newly forged metal. Even her clothes, black and stiff in mourning for brother Robert – whose demise had given us Rowstock House – scarcely moved when she walked.

Aunt Sarah was smaller, younger and softer in every way. Though in mourning also, she wore clothes of a soft lilac-grey muslin, which flowed around her so that she seemed always in movement, in contrast to Aunt Mary's rigidity. We were already predisposed to like Aunt Sarah, because she had sent us *Treasure Island* the previous year. That book had became the source of many games, especially on rainy days when we turned the boys' bedroom – so small that the two beds in it were crammed together with little floorspace around – into an imaginary ship, our pinafores as sails, which bloomed with piratical phrases gleaned from Long John Silver and his crew.

Both aunts lived in the third farm house, called Lower Farm, a square ugly building on the Abingdon road. The farmland, however, from all three houses was managed as one unit by the Ambroses with the help of labourers from neighbouring Harwell.

On her first visit, Aunt Mary looked around at what Mama had done with the house, quizzing the offending item of furniture with her monocle when she found it offensive or frivolous. Mama followed in her steely wake, face strained and hands twisting the fabric of her skirt. But Aunt Sarah asked to see the new pony which, as promised to the younger boys, was there when we arrived: sturdy, dapple-grey and immediately named Bracken, so that their old donkey friend, Fern, wasn't completely out of mind. Relieved to be out of Aunt Mary's reach, we all followed, deserting poor Mama.

Aunt Sarah melted completely once she was out, petted the pony and gave it an apple from the orchard and was even inveigled into playing games with us all. Red Rover was our current favourite, played on the main lawn where in later years we would play croquet. Edgar and Duncan loved this game, which usually ended with them rolling on the grass in helpless laughter, since they always targeted each other over anyone else. The game required trying to hop from one end of the lawn to the other without being caught by whoever was allotted the middle ground, who had to catch those trying to dodge past. Our youngest aunt was a good sport, hitching up her skirts so as to free her legs for hopping, and removing her hat to rest it on the hedge bordering Bracken's field.

Afterwards, at supper, we giggled because we had seen the lacy bottoms of her bloomers, and because Bracken had munched through the straw of Aunt Sarah's hat, but there was not one of us who hadn't liked her or admired the way she had joined in, like a child herself, hooting and laughing with the rest of us and not minding a bit that her hat was ruined.

Once settled in our home we quickly established new habits. Edgar and Duncan gravitated towards the farm, where kindly Ambrose allowed them to 'help'. I suspect they were more of a hindrance, especially as their loving rivalry never ceased. Thus Edgar would boast of being allowed to help hold the plough, while Duncan would boast that he was allowed to lead the shire horses to their field at the end of the day and even to groom them, though he could surely only have reached as high as the top of those vast legs.

Jim spent more and more time away from us all. Perhaps he was preparing himself for the huge changes ahead, of school and naval training. For hours on end he would shut himself away in his room, only calling us in when he had a new game he had designed and wanted us to try out.

The little girls played outside when they could, on the large lawn where they would set up complicated obstacle courses for their pet rabbits or play with the dolls' house that Aunt Sarah had brought down for them, which, she explained, had been hers and her sister's when they were small. The idea of fearsome Aunt Mary ever being a child made us all grin, but Papa reproved us. 'You wait,' he said, 'when you know her better you'll discover how nice she is underneath all that ...' His hands made helpless gestures for even he could not find words to describe what the elder of his sisters had become.

Not all the changes from Ireland to Rowstock were good in my opinion. The worst was that I felt I'd lost my family. Even Rita, who'd always been my closest companion, was spending a great deal of time with Nora, our cook. Rita loved to bake. Even in Ireland, she'd tried to help Mama and proudly came up with a birthday cake for me when I was nine, so covered with buttery icing that we all wore creamy moustaches for the rest of the afternoon. Whether it was wet or dry, much of that late summer before our schooling would start she spent slavishly following Nora's instructions in the kitchen.

At a loose end, I spent much of my time reading in my favourite spots: under the lime tree at the bottom end of the garden, where it swooped round the side of the house and inclined downwards to the fence bordering the orchard, or in the orchard itself, full of ripening apples and pears – the gnarled tree branches weighed to the ground with fruit as July progressed. In this manner I devoured many of Mama's novels, housed in Papa's study. Walter Scott fed my imagination with dreams of adventure, romance and chivalry while Victor Hugo disturbed me into realisations of the underlife that lapped at the foundations of the safe world we knew.

Night times were the worst. I missed the comfort of Rita's body next to mine and our whispered confidences. Sometimes the missing became so acute I would leave my bed and make my way along the corridor to hers. There she would stir in her sleep and mumble, but soon turn towards me and our bodies would fit around each other's as they always had.

When not reading I was worrying, mainly about the future. I still did not know where I was to go to school. It was this that loomed largest at night. Why was everyone certain of their immediate future but myself? Was it because I was the least loved? I brooded on my name. My three sisters all had names which meant Beloved: Aimée for Rita, the 'leen' parts of Kathleen and Eileen, which were Kay and Lina's proper names. That 'leen', I knew, meant the same as Aimée but in Irish. It wasn't fair. All my name meant was a gladiator's sword, something sharp and hard and entirely unlovable. Is that how my parents saw me?

That summer Mama and I clashed even more than usual. I was often being sent to my room, or scolded for being difficult and rebellious. Is that why no school would have me?

Seeking comfort, I knocked one morning on Jim's door, to find him at the little desk in front of his window. He was staring at one of Papa's old school books, head in hands. He was afraid, he said, of being behind at school, of being laughed at because he didn't know the right things. I could see he was struggling with tears, that very weakness he had tried to train all of us to avoid.

'Father Cullen ...' I began, meaning to reassure him.

'What did Father Cullen know of what is taught in English schools?' His voice was harsh. 'It might have been good enough for the likes of that Irish boy ...'

'Michael,' I whispered, instantly seeing his face in front of me.

'... or a bunch of seven-year-olds heading for preparatory schools in England but for someone of my age ...'

He hid his head and I put a hand on his shoulder, but he shook it off, so that I tiptoed out even more disturbed than when I had entered.

Running downstairs, I sought out Mama. She was with Papa outside the front of the house where, flushed with happiness, he was planning a rose garden. Papa was gesticulating with one hand; the other was clasped in Mama's.

Seeing me, both turned, and gave me a look that I knew well: patient, but masking impatience. Though I knew it was the wrong time such was my need that I blurted out my fears about the immediate future.

'Aunt Mary is up to something,' said Mama. 'And when I was last in Oxford, I asked my own sister, Louise, what she thought. She was rather busy, packing up ready to visit my other sister, Jane, in Edinburgh, but she said there were plenty of places and she'd ask around.'

'We haven't forgotten you,' said Papa, already turning away.

They had no idea what this meant to me. Already both were absorbed in their gardening dreams. Those linked hands swung to and fro with a new kind of freedom, one I'd never seen in Ireland.

With no answers forthcoming, I decided to take my mind off things with something new. I would go up to Middle Farm, where Edgar and Duncan spent every day, and find what they were up to. Perhaps there was something in which I could immerse myself. But the cows were in a far field and neither the two boys, nor Ambrose and Joe were anywhere to be seen. I knew I wouldn't be welcome at the big house as Uncle William had made it clear from the start that children were foreign territory to him and one that he had no desire to explore.

I knocked at the cottage door to ask after my brothers. It was answered by Mrs Ambrose who had a frantic look about her that immediately made me think of the people we knew in Ireland. She was arranging tomatoes and lettuce on a plate of cold chicken while small children tugged at her skirt, or tumbled with each other and a yapping terrier outside in the muddy yard.

Mrs Ambrose was polite but knew nothing about the boys except that they were with her husband.

'Happen they'll be back directly,' she said. Then, eyeing me doubtfully, she asked if I wanted to come into the big house where she was about to take Uncle William's lunch.

I shook my head, knowing I would not be welcome and she looked relieved.

'You can wait here with Edie and Flo if you want,' she

continued. 'They mind the younger ones while I'm with the Master.'

That idea would have been fine if they were my own brothers and sisters, but Edie's eyes narrowed when I looked at her while Flo's mouth was wet and open and her eyes were somehow empty. Neither appealed.

Mrs Ambrose, pleased with her solution, disappeared into the big house and I spent half an hour or so being shown around the little cottage by the younger Ambrose children, three or four small boys, herded with flapping movements like skittish goats by their sisters, before I could make an excuse and escape.

All of it had reminded me uncomfortably of our occasional charity visits in Killybeggs: the crowded cottage, the shared beds, the harried mother, the dirt and smells which, to be fair may not have been the product of neglect but the normal result of human beings and animals living in close proximity. All the way back home I brooded on this. Like a revelation, I saw that what I had found disgusting both in Ireland and here was more a matter of too little space and too many children than laziness or lack of concern from the parents.

Once home, I burst into Jim's room to share my thoughts. The Ambroses had many children and William none, nor even a wife, so why did he have a large house and the Ambroses such a small one? To me there was an obvious answer: William must be made to see the injustice. It should be he who lived in the cottage and the Ambroses in the farmhouse.

Jim's first response was to laugh. That made me mad; I pummelled him about the chest until he caught my wrists. Soberly, holding my wrists firmly, Jim explained that that was how it was in the world. Rich and poor were divided and always would be, and the rich lived in grand houses, sometimes with many rooms unused, while the poor had to squeeze into smaller dwellings.

'But why?' I said. 'It doesn't make sense and it's not fair.'

Of course I'd known that most of the English landowners in Ireland had big houses, but I'd never seen them. Everyone we'd been acquainted with were squeezed into tiny cottages or delapidated farms. Our house had been perhaps a little larger than some, but we were still tumbled on top of each other like our neighbours, so differences were not so apparent. This was the first time I'd woken up to the contrast in close proximity.

As I calmed down Jim began to laugh again. 'Imagine telling Uncle William that he ought to swop with his tenants. I can just see his face.'

I could see it too and I knew the change would never happen but that still didn't make things better or fairer. Everything was topsy-turvy and I wasn't about to let go of my revelation. 'If someone – Papa perhaps – explained to him …' I began.

Jim stopped laughing and turned away from me. 'You'll understand the way the world works better when you go to school,' he said loftily – like a grown-up and not like my Jim at all.

'We'll see about that,' I flared, slamming the door to his room and heading out to the lime tree. And, *if I ever do go to school*, I thought, convinced as we moved into the end of July that no one wanted me, that Mama had told everyone how difficult I was, that my whole family would become knowledgeable and educated around me, even Lina who I'd once heard Mama saying might never be able to leave home or have a normal life. I would be left behind to pick up crumbs of learning from books they left open or from crusts of knowledge they let drop over mealtime conversation. I would turn into a wild ravening beast, a kind of imbecile, unloved and denied the light of education, like something out of one of those Victor Hugo novels.

Leaning my back against the lime tree, I began to enjoy this vision of my future and wallow in it. No one would talk to me in the end, I thought, for no one would want to know me. My eye fell on the barn at the side of the orchard. That would be my home. Only Lina, I fantasised, who was always kind to animals, would take food to me and give me an occasional stroke.

Eventually I stopped pitying myself and put my mind to the differences I'd seen both here and in Ireland. Why were things so unbalanced? Was it just a matter of birth, of luck? It certainly appeared so for what had we done to deserve such a change of circumstances, from our little place in Ireland to our large house in England? We were not especially good or deserving of favour. Poverty or riches must, then, be simply a matter of chance, like the fall of the dice in one of Jim's games. Why couldn't Jim see that too?

Michael used to talk about the English looking down on those who worked as tenant farmers on their land, about the unfairness of the rents they set and how sometimes, in times of hardship, whole families could be turned out of their homes for being unable to pay their rent. Chance again – the failure of a harvest from something as out of human control as the weather.

Not all the English in Ireland were harsh, however, but that didn't seem to make them more popular. Sometimes Michael had used the word 'patronising' for the way kinder English ladies would sometimes set out to help their tenants. He'd sounded angrier even than when he'd talked about people losing their homes… as if ill treatment was expected and kindness was suspect, an insult even.

I wondered now if he'd seen us in that way after all, when

we trailed after Mama on her charity rounds. The thought made me squirm and distorted the memory I had of him, till I began to doubt all I remembered. Did he really mean it when he said he'd see me again? An English girl who had been an intruder in his country? I felt sadly certain that, as he grew up, he'd side with his brother Patrick – whose hatred had been obvious and who'd made little Duncan a kind of whipping-boy for his feelings – and remember my whole family, myself included, as *patronising*.

Aunt Mary did not visit often, so when she sailed in, her stiff skirts crackling over the floor tiles, and her booted feet tap-tapping imperiously, her mouth in a wide line that might have been her version of a smile, I knew at once that something important was happening. Was this it? Had Aunt Mary found a school for me? Indeed she had, but instead of allowing me to come and hear all about it, which would only be right and proper in my opinion, I was dismissed along with the others. I pleaded but met the Aunt's steeliest look and subsided. Casting a wild-eyed look behind at us which said as clearly as if spoken, Stay Away and Make no Trouble, Mama followed Aunt Mary into the drawing-room.

Once outside I grabbed Rita fiercely by the arm. 'Please, take the little ones off. I want to hear what they have to say.'

'You can't!' said Rita, equally fierce. 'What if they see you?'

I explained I'd go on hands and knees under the drawing-room window and then sit quietly with my back against the wall. 'I'll be mostly hidden by the virginia creeper anyway.'

Rita rolled her eyes. 'You'll be in such trouble. Again.' This was a reference to my rebellion over tidying my room the day before. I didn't think piles of books and scraps of paper on which I was writing poems counted as mess. Apparently I was wrong.

The ground under the creeper was deep with dead leaves from years of moulting. They harboured age-old damp, a dank mould which stained my white stockings and streaked my patent shoes, though the best Sunday dress – forced on, amidst protests from all us girls, to make a good impression – proved dark enough to absorb stains well.

The window was open. I heard something about schools and pricked up my ears. There was mention of the village school, which was expecting Rita and Duncan, and then there were reminiscences about Papa's time at Warwick School where Jim and Edgar would be.

This was all old news. Was I to be left out again? If only I could go to Warwick with Jim. I drifted off briefly, imagining what special naval things might be taught. What would it be like if girls could go to Warwick too and learn about knots, and to reef sails and climb rigging as in *Treasure Island*?

At last I heard my name and pushed myself up a little, to just under the window ledge. 'I have contacted your sister in Oxford.' Aunt Mary said.

'Oh?' said Mama, sounding anxious.

'I told her that Gladys is precocious.'

'Yes, she is. She loves literature, reads anything she can get her hands on.'

'So Calleva House, the girls' school in Wallingford, a short train ride from Oxford, will take her and she will board with your sister. It is all arranged.' The chair creaked and I could hear the tinkle of a spoon against china. I raised my head a little further to hear better.

Mama was saying that Louise was a busy woman, that she might not...

But Aunt Mary was having no protests. 'As I said, it is all done. And Sarah and I will meet the small rent your sister requires for the child's keep.'

Amid stammered thanks from Mama I heard the rustle of skirts and the opening of the drawing-room door. 'Calleva House,' I whispered to myself. At last I had somewhere to go.

I began to extricate myself from the creeper when I was taken by surprise by Mama suddenly appearing at the window. She looked down at me and swiped ineffectually at my head. 'Why can't you behave?' she whispered grimly, and closed the window firmly. I was left to brush myself down as well as I could and, chastened, seek out my sisters.

Later that day, over supper, Mama caught my eye and asked to see me in my room when the little ones were in bed. Despite the excitement I had felt ever since I overheard the news, a pit opened in my stomach; I had hoped she'd forgotten.

When she came in, Mama's face was more sad than angry. She sat down beside me on the bed. 'Why are you always so wilful?' she began. 'You are the one, as the eldest girl, on whom I most rely and yet you disappoint me.'

I felt a wrenching in my chest, as if something hard but alive had lodged there. There was no satisfactory excuse I could give so instead I asked whether Aunt Mary had known I was there.

'Of course,' came the reply. 'Didn't you remember that you were wearing a hat? I was so very ashamed of you.'

Stupidly, I protested. 'But she didn't say anything. She may not have noticed...'

Mama stopped me with a glare. 'I'm concerned for your future. Especially when you go to school and stay with my sister Louise.' She began to pace around the room, appearing to forget I was there. 'I didn't expect that Mary would have already made arrangements. It's quite taken the wind out of my sails. Louise won't like to have been dragooned.'

The thought of school had kept me buoyant all day. Even though I hated upsetting her, there was nothing she could say that could damp that feeling. So I waited and at last she looked back at me.

'My sister is difficult,' she said. 'She's much older than me, of course, and her life has not been easy. She lost her husband young, and she was not lucky enough to have any children.'

'So she's lonely.' I felt full of sympathy for this sad woman, whose life would be reignited by my arrival.

'Not exactly,' answered Mama. 'She's very involved in charitable works and committees.'

I felt further warmth for my aunt, who was obviously a person with her heart in the right place, just like Mama.

Mama gave me an anxious look. 'I just want to warn you to be on your best behaviour. Sometimes you're your own worst enemy, Gladys. You ask too much and you expect too much.'

I opened my mouth to argue. How can it be possible to ask too much? Wasn't life about seeking answers to even the knottiest of questions? But Mama's face didn't invite argument. Instead I asked, 'What should I take with me? Will there be plenty of books at Aunt Louise's?'

'I believe so.' Mama's relief at talking practicalities was palpable. 'She was married to a don, after all. He taught Classics.'

Wonderful! The Greek myths were a great favourite of mine. I began to look forward to my stay in Oxford. Perhaps I could learn Greek and Latin. And my mind reached out with excitement to the new school in Wallingford. I saw a long dark corridor, in which, as I peered down its length, doors opened one by one, emitting slices of beckoning light.

Mama had risen from the bed and was preparing to leave. Her face as she looked down was in shadow, but the wisps of red hair straying around her head caught light from the passage outside, like a halo.

'Oh, Mama,' I leapt up and threw my arms around her. 'I really will try. I'll be a credit to you, you'll see.' I thought but did not say, 'Then you'll love me as much as you do my sisters.' It was a problem I chewed on whenever I felt low, the fact I was always in trouble with Mama, that I was not, as she so often said, a credit to her.

But I could not stay low for long. I was going to school. I was not left out. Like the others, for even Rita and Duncan were to go to the village school for a year, the rest of summer just became a time of waiting for our education to begin. We faced it mostly with equilibrium, fortified by Jim's constant reminders of the lessons learned from the courage game.

It was the two younger boys that appeared most affected. They became quieter and quieter and disappeared during the daytime for longer than ever. Often Jim would be sent up to the farm to shepherd them back. Duncan would plead with him to ask Papa if he could go with Edgar, and Jim had to explain that since he was still only six, he was a year too young – but they would be reunited eventually.

One rainy day, Rita and I were up in Jim's room while the rest of the family were visiting the Aunts at Lower Farm. We had been watching raindrops running down the window and guessing which would reach the bottom first.

'What will Duncan do without Edgar?' I asked, bored with the game.

'What will I do,' put in Rita, 'without you, Gladys?'

We watched the raindrops for a little longer, how they hesitated, streamed down for a little, and paused again. Mine was neck and neck with Rita's but Jim's was ahead, nosing its careful way to the bottom.

'At least Edgar will be at school with you, Jim,' said Rita eventually. 'But Duncan will only have the two little girls here to play with.'

'And you, Rita,' I said, though I was aware that Rita saw herself as too old, even though she was only two and a half years older than Duncan, a similar gap as lay between the pair of us. 'And there's Bracken. And Aunt Sarah.'

'He'll quickly find chaps to play with at the village school,' said Jim. 'Remember how he always tried to make friends with the local boys in Killybeggs? Even that awful Patrick Allen! He'll be all right.'

'There was another pause, then *Hoorah* from Jim, half-heartedly celebrating his winning. Neither Rita nor I were concerned.

'It's just the waiting for it to happen that's hard,' I said, thinking how difficult waiting for any known change always seems to be. First you go through excitement and then disbelief. You can't envisage yourself in the place or the circumstance that is coming, so you stop believing in it. And that is quite comforting: it will never happen because you can't see yourself there. I could not imagine being without the big comfortable knot of my siblings so mostly I chose not to, against reason, against the inexorable march of the summer towards autumn. I saw seeds float off and separate from their flowers. On the other side of the garden fence, where broom flourished, I heard the sharp gunshots of the pods burst as they fired their small dark seeds into the air. Uncaring nature managed it, why should I worry that we were untangling into disparate strands that would lead who knows where?

Not even going into Oxford to buy uniforms for Jim, Edgar and myself gave reality to the situation. But all at once it was a week away. In Jim's room again, his new clothes hung over the back of a chair, he and I listened to the rain against the window, the tap of the creeper in the wind, Nora's voice raised downstairs as she talked to Papa, and looked at each other.

'I never thought I would, but I miss Ireland,' Jim said.

'Even the rain is different here,' I agreed.

'I'm still afraid I'll be behind at school,' confessed Jim. He scowled to stop the tears coming, but I saw the shine of them.

'It's the same for me,' I said hurriedly to distract him. 'I'm afraid too, of being ignorant and not able to keep up.'

'Oh, you'll keep up, Gladys,' he said with great emphasis. 'You're the cleverest of us all, don't you know that?'

'I'm not,' I said automatically, but his words bolstered me anyway. I remembered the excitement I'd felt at the thought of going to school, when our return to England was first mentioned, and my spirits flickered and rose a little. 'Wish I'd met Aunt Louise,' I said, but it had been impossible. She had been up in Scotland for the whole of August. The thought of that meeting and the start of school loomed like twin mountain peaks, equally daunting.

I patter down the corridor in my stockinged feet, and run a glass of water from the kitchen tap. Its coolness in my throat revives me.

Truda pops her head around the corner. 'I thought I heard you. Taking a break?'

'I think I'll go into the garden for a little. It'll help order my thoughts.' I slip my feet into my wellingtons, convenient by the kitchen door.

'I'm off to visit Marjorie for a cup of coffee and a chat. Do you want to come too?'

Marjorie is a woman of great energy, a little older than us and a former member of another suffrage group, The Artists' Suffrage League, which often worked together with the Women's Social and Political Union – the suffragettes. Marjorie had designed posters for us, and cards to sell in our shops to raise money for the Cause. She was one of the reasons we moved here to Blewbury, she and other artists like her. There was quite a little enclave of us, all passionate about women's rights, in the early 1930s when we moved from Leicester. Oh the tea-parties we had, the reminiscences, and the grumbles too, for nothing that we had worked for happened quite as we'd envisaged.

Truda, as a secret suffragette, was as much a part of this group as I. Her calling and delicate position as one of a very small number of female doctors had meant she could not show her colours openly when the fight was on; she would have lost her practice. But she had furnished money and a safe house for suffragettes on the run from the police, as important and potentially dangerous an input as any.

These get-togethers had, in the end, had a detrimental effect on me. The more we talked, the more I questioned. The more I was praised for my daring deeds the more uncomfortable I felt. Had it been courage or something more insidious and self-serving that had motivated me? A nasty sort of pride perhaps. Finally, using the excuse of Peter's upbringing, I dropped out from their society and began the task of burying the past. Denying it really.

So 'Not now,' I say to Truda and watch her face fall. Clearly she sees reigniting my friendship with those suffragettes that remain in the village as part of my therapy. I relent a fraction. 'Maybe when I've got to that part of my memoir she'll help to refresh me on some of the details.' I watch her expression clear as she turns to leave. 'Give her my love,' I call after her. 'Will I see you at lunch?' Her carolling *yes* leaves me looking after her with fondness as her thin legs in their thick stockings negotiate the slippery path. That's something else I must do before someone has a fall – scrape away the moss that has accrued.

First I apply myself to the trailing brambles that have been taunting me from their position in front of the kitchen window. Within minutes I have a large thorn caught in the fleshy part of my thumb. The bright bead of blood reminds me of the day we all stuck pins into our palms as part of Jim's courage game. Edgar and Duncan did it to each other, looking into each other's faces: just a blink, a pucker of the mouth, would have meant a failure. Jim pretended with Kay and Lina, just breaking the skin enough for them to feel a part of it. But we three eldest children did it to ourselves, in turn, watching each other lest anyone move a muscle. Despite, or maybe because of, Edgar's fierce look, six-year-old Duncan was the only one who welled up with tears, but he fought them so valiantly that Jim awarded the Badge of Courage to him that day, though none of us had uttered a sound.

It was Duncan who fought those tears again as he waited for us to leave for school that first time. He covered by petting the neck of Ambrose's mare before we set off. 'Time to leave,' announced Ambrose, heaving the last of our luggage into the well of the cart. Duncan stepped back and his face creased as he looked up at us.

'Look after Bracken for me,' said Edgar.

Duncan nodded. His mouth trembled, but he was saved by Ambrose's timely 'Giddy-up,' and the crunch of our wheels on the gravel of the drive.

You're very easy to spot,' said Aunt Louise, 'you look just like your mother. Your hair is a trial, just as hers always was.'

Her tone implied criticism and made me nervous. I looked at her face, oval like Mama's but with small sharp eyes that snagged on mine and looked instantly away, as if what she saw was not to her taste. Brown hair was pulled severely back and tucked tidily under a wide flat hat, which sported two red feathers and a wide red ribbon that tied under her chin. Her figure looked narrow in its light-brown dress with red trimmings, and she sported a gorgeous umbrella, which I instantly coveted. It was trimmed in the same red as her hat and had a long narrow point with which my aunt poked at the uneven platform in front of her, as if searching for hidden treasure.

Holding this accessory aloft, my fashionable aunt waved imperiously to a porter, who helped carry my bag out onto the street and into a waiting hackney. I admired the bay horse standing in the shafts, its head low, and patted its thin neck.

'No time for that,' called Aunt Louise and I scrambled into the cab after her.

The route took us past wonderful buildings, which I craned my neck to admire. 'The colleges,' my aunt explained. 'You'll soon get used to them.' Her tone was bored and she looked straight ahead of her, oblivious to the sights on both sides. I knew I'd never be bored. The buildings were steeped in learning. I could feel it. Experimentally I breathed in deeply and opened my mouth. Yes, I could smell and taste it too.

'Don't be ridiculous,' snapped my aunt. 'What are you thinking of, your mouth open and tongue hanging out. Are you some kind of idiot child?'

I closed my mouth so suddenly that I bit my tongue and had to turn away to conceal the sudden tears.

We were out of the college area now and my aunt leant forward and instructed the driver to turn first left. We stopped in front of a pleasant house of a similar yellow stone to that used for the colleges. The windows were small and mullioned. There was no garden to speak of in front of the house, just short iron railings to separate it from the street. Some glossy dark green shrubs were the excuse for a garden and I very much hoped there would be a proper one at the back, or what would I do for trees and grass?

The cab-driver came round to take my bag but, 'I can manage it,' I said, determined to show that I wasn't a nuisance. The bag wasn't heavy, since I was going home at weekends. I swung it to and fro to prove the point, with a big smile fixed to my face, hoping to shift the little frown on Aunt Louise's high brow.

'Hurry up,' she called over her shoulder as she entered the house, pulled off her gloves and slotted her umbrella into an ornate stand beside the grand-father clock. The hall was quite narrow with a black-and-white tiled floor leading down a long passageway. I put my bag down and made to follow my aunt as she clipped down the corridor and opened the door at the far end.

'Stay there,' she called behind her. 'Eva will show you to your room and help you unpack. I have some ladies coming here shortly for an important meeting, so I'll thank you to keep to your room and entertain yourself.'

The room was small and dark, placed above the front door so that I looked out onto the street. I sat on the highly-polished window-seat and peered out. The building across the road looked quiet and similar to Aunt Louise's. As I watched, a door in the wall opened and an elderly man, pushing a bicycle, emerged. The basket on the handle-bars top-heavy with books, gown flapping, he pedalled determinedly towards the main road and turned right. I could see he was heading towards those colleges. Dreamily I imagined myself riding through those streets on my way to study. Did University students go to classes like school-children? Could they choose what they learned? There was so much I wanted to know. I had no idea about Oxford other than that it was a famous place of learning, that much of it had been founded centuries before. What would I study? Could one just do poetry? I hoped Aunt Louise would help me, could hardly bear to wait till supper when I could ask her all the things I ached to know.

For a long time I sat on the window-seat and dreamed, gazing outside for clues to this new place in which I found myself. There was a rap on the door and the maid, Eva, came in. A tall thin woman with iron-grey hair pulled back under a white cap and a frilly white apron that looked incongruous on her bony frame, she had a wooden tray with a china egg-cup, two boiled eggs and bread cut neatly into soldiers. A glass of milk, dangerously full, slopped over as she pushed the door open with her foot. I ran to help her. 'You're to leave your tray outside when you've finished, Miss,' said Eva. 'I'll wake you in the morning in time for breakfast. Your aunt will take you to the station for the school train.'

It seemed my questions would not be answered now after all. Aunt Louise was no doubt being kind and imagined that I was tired and needed sleep before my first school day. Tomorrow I would ask questions and my aunt would show me all the exciting spots around Oxford. This illusion stayed with me for a surprisingly long time.

Ambrose came to fetch me from the station, with Bracken and the trap, at the end of that first week. I was delighted to see that Rita was craning round his solid form to catch a first sight of me. Her cheerful wave did much to lift my spirits.

She could hardly wait till we were home before questioning me about school and about Oxford. Not surprising, for she was to join me at Aunt Louise's in a year's time. After tea, we ran outside and sat by the lime tree. I described the school, which was organised and timetabled to the nth degree, but which I thought would suit me in the end. The English teacher was particularly kind, and had already encouraged me. I had written about Ireland, pouring all my love of it into the words, and she read it out to the class.

'That must have been embarrassing,' said Rita. 'Did all the other girls hate you for it?'

Such a thing hadn't even crossed my mind. Had they? I saw the row of polite faces sitting behind their desks. One girl had even smiled at me. 'I don't think so.'

'You have to be careful, Gladys. No one likes a know-it-all. Mama calls you precocious and it's true that you do often use very long and difficult words. I'd be careful not to be too showy-offy if I were you.'

Normally I'd have defended myself but the rest of the term loomed ahead and I couldn't find the energy. Instead, I threw myself back into the sweet long grass where my face was partly concealed. The sun was shining. I wanted just to stay in this moment. But Rita's voice carried on relentlessly.

'I bet you're spoiled by Aunt Louise. Is she like Mama?'

I described my room in meticulous detail, to avoid answering. Rita was having none of it, so I gave my first impressions of our Aunt, her smartness, the gorgeous umbrella. Rita's eyes narrowed.

'You're not telling me something. Is she horrible?'

So I told her how Aunt Louise had taken me to the station and showed me the right platform on the first day, but how for the rest of the week I'd been accompanied by a taciturn man, Douglas – apparently Eva's son and as gaunt as she – who did odd-jobs for my aunt. We'd walked there and back and I enjoyed this the most of anything else in that first week. I could admire the colleges, the bridges over the river, and the many signs of greenness, which were lacking from life at my aunt's. Douglas wouldn't let me linger, or poke my head through those inviting doorways to peep at the secret life within, but I hoped when Rita joined me the following year, we would be allowed to walk on our own. Then we could explore.

Rita asked about the garden and I had to admit that there was just a poor excuse for one, full of large bushes with dark-green leaves which Eva said were camellias but which I couldn't see any point to at all. 'They don't have fruit, so they're no use to anyone and most of the year there aren't even flowers, though Eva says the flowers, when they do come, are beautiful and a cheerful sight at the end of winter.'

'You talk about Eva a lot, but hardly at all about Aunt Louise. Is she as pretty as Mama?'

I shook my head. Mama was much rounder and infinitely more comfortable, even when she was being sparky. I didn't see much of our aunt, I explained. She was always too occupied, and often out. It was Eva who woke me, gave me breakfast and supper in my room, but Eva was always too busy to talk.

Faced with Rita's shocked disapproval, I staunchly defended Aunt Louise from neglect by boasting of how much she did. She was on committees for the poor and needy, where she assessed who would receive financial help and who would not. She was on a board which raised funds for the hospital and another which collected money to send to Africa. She visited sick people ... My voice trailed away.

'She must be a very good person,' said Rita respectfully. And then she gave me a huge hug. 'And you must have been so lonely. Poor Gladys.' She pondered a little. 'But at least we know she's got her heart in the right place. She's trying to make things better in the world.'

'Y-yes,' I answered doubtfully, trying not to think of Aunt Louise's sharp blue eyes and her mouth, which lacked all the softness of her younger sister, our mother.

'And are there cousins?'

'Well, yes. But Aunt Louise never had children. There's Mama's other sister, Aunt Jane, but she lives up in Scotland. She has two children, I believe, but they're older than us.'

'Oh,' said Rita. 'The others will be disappointed. Especially Duncan. He's convinced that weekends will soon be heaving with cousins, all ready to rough and tumble and – well – to replace Edgar.' She thought a little. 'It's strange that Mama has never talked about her sisters.'

'Perhaps they didn't get on. Mama is a lot younger. It's like if there were only Lina, me and Jim. A big gap.'

'Hmm. Even so, it's odd, isn't it? I shall ask Mama when I get a chance.'

I sensed that this might not be a good idea, but if anyone could extract an answer it would be Rita. So I kept quiet and threw myself back in the grass again, closing my eyes against the low, late afternoon sun.

Rita lay back too, chewing on a grass-stem, and for a blissful moment all I could hear were the sounds of Ambrose far off, calling the cows in, and other farm workers, nearer at hand, talking sparsely as they harvested apples. Here Duncan found us and dragged me off to the farm to see the puppies that had been born to Ambrose's aging collie. It was supper time before we got back, my school clothes smelling comfortably of dog and my good shoes dented by puppy teeth. Already I dreaded the return to Oxford.

I flex my fingers remembering the disappointments throughout that first year of school. Aunt Louise never did take me to see the colleges. Nor did I spend much time with her at all. It was as if she did not really want to face up to the fact of a child in the house, a child who might be lonely and unhappy. Once or twice I was invited to join her for the evening meal, where I watched my behaviour to such a degree that my head ached and I longed for the tranquillity of my bedroom.

On one occasion – it was quite early on in my stay – I plucked up courage and went downstairs to ask if I could borrow a book. Although I heard voices in the drawing-room, I knocked before realising that was probably a mistake. There must be a committee meeting going on. My heart pounded but I could not take it back. It turned out that it was lucky I did. My aunt was gracious to me in front of the other ladies, even boasting of my cleverness and aptitude at school, though how she knew that I could not fathom. She said of course I could borrow books from her husband's study, and that was my saving. I devoured every book that the school gave us to read so fast and had so much time after school to myself that the discovery of so many completely at my disposal was a godsend. These became my companions, for none of the girls I met at school lived close enough for friendship, and I lived from then on in a dream peopled with ancient Greek heroes and gods. There was poetry too, though much of it I found too difficult and not to my taste. Instead, in those lonely evenings, inspired by heroic deeds, I began to write stories for myself and to play with the idea of rhythm and metre from such poems as I studied at school. My English teacher was kind enough to encourage me in these efforts.

Surprisingly, Aunt Louise asked me to join her for the next committee meeting. There were to be a couple of cases under discussion which she thought might interest me, and I had made a good impression with her colleagues. Whether this was to show herself in a better light I cannot say, but if so it failed. First was the case of a young woman whose husband was absent and who had lost her job because she was pregnant. I listened to the ladies of the committee discussing whether she should be housed in a charitable foundation that they helped fund, since her current rent was in arrears. One of the ladies said she had researched the case and had found there was no husband nor ever had been. Instantly the others, including my aunt, said that she should be given no help since she had brought her downfall on herself by – with a glance at me – her 'imprudence.'

Did they think I could not understand, myself as one of seven and brought up in the country? I knew where babies came from, though admittedly the mechanics of the whole procedure were a mystery. So I opened my mouth and asked how the young woman could live without a job and with no husband to bring in money to feed herself and a child. She should have thought of that, they answered. I opened my mouth again, incensed by their attitude, but before a word could emerge, Aunt Louise sent me out of the room.

That was the last time I was a party to their committee work, but the case of the young woman and what might happen to her haunted me that night in bed. The next morning I dared to confront Aunt Louise in the breakfast room overlooking her neat but flowerless garden and was roundly chastised for my presumption and lack of manners. Apparently I should not have spoken but simply have listened, no doubt in awe, to the way they saw the world and how they ordered it – they with the power and the money to make or break whole lives. That whole day in school, I brooded and raged inwardly, until, as is the way of children, my attention was caught by something new which pushed it all away.

Strange to remember that now, but bringing Aunt Louise before me and wondering why she was so harsh with me then, I have started to see her in a new light. Her lack of knowledge of children is one excuse; the fact that she was 'dragooned' into taking me by Aunt Mary another. I know how Aunt Mary could be; she would suffer no argument once she had made her mind up to something. And then my own nature has to be blamed. As Rita once said, I am not good at understanding people. I have my own idea of right and wrong and a vision of the world that to me appears quite clear. I often fail to see how others can hold a different view from mine. As I grow older I have come to see how different people are, and to value that diversity, even when it means that our opinions differ. But I still fail sometimes to 'look deeper,' as my friend Nina often used to say.

So between reading, school and home visits at weekends, I limped through that first year. Everything became easier once Rita joined me, not least because she could handle our difficult aunt where I couldn't. And though Rita merely skated through school, skimming the surface of every subject and putting in the minimum of effort, she excelled at games and hurled herself around the hockey pitch, pulling me in her wake. To my surprise I enjoyed it. Sports, my English teacher and Rita's company saw me through until we left both school and Aunt Louise's, both at the same time, since Rita confessed – to my surprise – that she would not be able to cope with Aunt Louise without me and nor did she have any hankering after further education.

I look at the time. Another morning has passed and if I don't bestir myself Truda won't have any lunch. Luckily there are left-over vegetables from last night's supper which I can make into a soup.

Seated at the table, steaming bowls of soup in front of us, I notice to my surprise it is a pleasant day, high blue sky, wisps of striated cloud. I hadn't even noticed.

'Was it raining earlier?' I ask, my head revisiting those last wet weeks before we began our schooling.

'A drop or two. Just enough to cleanse the air.' She looks at me over the top of her glasses. 'Is it going well?' she asks cautiously. 'I heard you clacking all morning on the typewriter.'

'Well enough. Dwelling on my school days at the moment.'

'Oh,' she says, clearly disappointed. She blows on a spoonful of soup, sips and swallows. 'Not yet got to grips with it then. Marjorie did ask.'

I take a deep breath. 'Truda, it's always there.' I tap my head.' And it's nothing to do with Marjorie. I'd thank you not to involve her. Let me just try to find the threads that led me there in my own way. It's important to me to understand *why*. Can you not see that?'

'Seems to me that dwelling on your education is a delaying tactic.' She says this softly, as a mutter that I can ignore if I like.

I scrape my chair back, trying not to snap, and clear the plates away. There is fruit from the garden next: stewed apple and blackberries. We have the biggest juiciest blackberries I've ever seen. I tend them lovingly, comparing them to the hard little fruits we picked on that wind-swept hill behind the Irish house.

Calmer now I serve Truda, who picks up her spoon and says, 'You're thinking of Oxford. You were there twice, weren't you?'

'Yes, as a child at Calleva House, and then after my degree when I trained to be a teacher.'

'Did you stay with that Aunt of yours both times?'

'I did, but it was very different the second time.' I can't help smiling to myself as the memories come flooding back. 'That was a happy period of my life. I had many friends in Oxford by then.' …

… I thought of Bill Waterfield who was courting Rita at that time, but who, until he had met my lovely sister, I had hoped might be interested in me. Bill and his group of friends accepted me into their circle, all of them lively, musical, arguing far into the evenings about everything and anything under the sun. I envied Rita then for Bill was the shining star of that group, grandson of the famous astronomer John Herschel, whose daughter Matilda Rose had married his father; great-grandson of William Herschel, who had discovered the planet Uranus and whose telescopes were still the best ever invented. All of us at Rowstock had fallen under Bill's spell, listening to his stories at family suppers, or watching his clever fingers move over the pretty little piano Mama had found in an auction. None of us played, so it had sat there through all our adolescent years, horribly out of tune until Bill spent a day tinkering with it and brought it back to life.

That group of friends had allowed me access to those hallowed colleges which, during my first miserable stay with Aunt Louise, were always just tantalisingly out of reach. Shy at first, I listened more than spoke but, encouraged by Bill, I began to share my thoughts, especially about the social structure as I saw it.

'Quite the little socialist,' they would tease but Bill didn't laugh. He drew me out, gave me some of his poetry to read – it wasn't marvellous, but I was flattered nonetheless. When I made suggestions, he listened carefully and congratulated me on the clarity of my thought. 'You'll make a wonderful teacher,' he said.

'Unless she gets diverted into saving the world,' teased his best friend, Victor, a rather bohemian young man, wild black hair and an ugly-charming face.

'I shall be happy to make sure that a few young women in my classes are led to see the world in a different way. That seems the surest way of bringing about change.'

'Yes,' agreed Bill. 'Sure and…'

'Perhaps rather slow?' put in another.

'But safe,' said Fred, the cynic of our group.

'What do you mean?' I challenged, hurt.

'I mean that you'll be changing things at second-hand,' he answered, 'without actually engaging yourself with what needs doing. And change done that way will be nothing but hit-and-miss. The class-room is a little cell cut off from the real world.'

I can see still see Fred's eyes behind their spectacles, blinking at me earnestly. At the time I was offended, but how right he was …

Lost in this memory I become aware of Truda. 'Where had you gone?' she asks.

I tell her how suddenly that conversation, sitting on the grass by the river under a blue April sky full of blossoming trees, popped into my head. 'I'm on the right path,' I reassure her. 'I'm not dwelling too long on things, just finding the links. Because everything's connected. This is not just about becoming a suffragette and the damage that choice did to me and those I love. It's as much about who I was, how I was changed by what seemed at the time to be random events but which I now am beginning to see were all pushing me in one single direction.'

I remind her of the first miserable years with Aunt Louise and suddenly a memory of leaving her house at the end of school surfaces. I had forgotten it, so busy had I been demonising this aunt for that first year and for what, years later, she had done to drive me and my family apart. As this new memory surfaces I can hear Rita tunelessly humming upstairs as she packs her things to go home…

… Already packed, I'd waited in the corridor downstairs when Aunt Louise clipped up towards me. She was wearing that day an ensemble of ivory with brown accessories. In the gloom of the corridor she gleamed like bone. She put a manicured hand on my shoulder and I jumped, expecting a criticism of some kind. But instead she turned me towards her and bent at the knees a little so that her face with its thin slash of a mouth was very close to mine. Now both her hands rested on my shoulders.

'I know, Gladys, that it has always looked as though I've favoured your sister,' she said.

I shrugged. 'I'm used to it. Everyone does.' Rita, I had long recognised was a born manipulator. Where I blundered in and upset people, she appeared to know exactly what to say to get her own way. Thus, when she arrived in Oxford my strict aunt showed her off to her committee friends and even, under Rita's wheedling, took us on occasion to the park, or to sit by the river. Of course none of this was new. Aunt Louise was only the latest victim in a long string of Rita's admirers.

My strange Aunt continued: 'You're a clever girl, Gladys, I want you to know that. You'll do well. I know it's been difficult for you here but I want you to know that I admire your commitment. Once you've decided to do something you work hard at it and you don't let yourself get diverted, unlike your flibbertigibbet of a sister, who'll never amount to much except to attract and charm. I don't like children, I freely admit, but if I'd had a child, I'd have liked one with your qualities of grit and determination. John, my husband, would have appreciated you. Now off you go and make your mother and I proud of you.'

Now I remember it is because of that surprising speech that I elected to stay with Aunt Louise again, during my teacher's training. And though she was often crabby and always about to rush off somewhere important [as if I were nothing of importance as a mere guest who just happened also to be her niece] we came to a kind of understanding, built more on mutual respect than affection, but a support nonetheless. I can even remember being sorry to leave her and giving her a hug...

… I relay this to Truda, unable to keep the astonishment out of my voice. 'I'd forgotten all that. Funny what tricks memory plays… what it buries.' And yes, I tell her defensively, everything is relevant. Calleva House was a stepping-stone and led to the Royal Holloway College, where I did my degree in English Literature, followed by my second bout in Oxford, to study to be a teacher. Without this pathway I would not have ended up at my teaching post in Birmingham. 'Which,' I conclude, though she's heard all this before. 'is where it all began. That is where I broke out of my sheltered cell' – I shake my head ruefully at my own echo of Fred's words – 'and that is where I began to engage directly with the damaged world about me.'

Truda nods. 'You're right. But don't forget to list some of your achievements too. You're always too unassuming about yourself.'

'No one's going to see this journey I'm writing, are they? I don't have to put every detail in. And it's not a good thing to boast.'

'Being honest with yourself is not boasting. Part of the picture of who you are, part of the acceptance you must make about yourself, is the fact that you are more than ordinarily clever. Your family saw that and allowed you to go to University. That was still unusual at that time.'

I bow my head in acknowledgement. 'Luckily it didn't cost them so very much as I won a scholarship place.' How nice she is to think I am being unassuming. Over the years I have battled with my own arrogance. If only she knew how horribly full of myself I was as a child. But of course she knows. Wasn't I still like that when we first met?

'And received the English Prize when you left Royal Holloway.' Truda is still listing my trophies.

'Yes, yes.' I brush it aside, embarrassed. 'It's nothing to your achievements. One of the first women doctors, and you and Bessie as the first in Leicester to bring contraception to women. All of which you did without your father's support.'

'My brothers helped me.' She looks away. I shouldn't have brought up her father, who she never talks about. I have always imagined him as some kind of a monster, in consequence.

'Dear Bessie,' Truda clears her throat and continues. 'She's living in Devon now. I had a letter from her last week. But I'm afraid she's not well.'

Truda falls silent, no doubt thinking of her long years of friendship with Bessie Symington, both of them pioneers in their own right, Truda for birth control and Bessie for venereal diseases, the first woman to set up a clinic for female sufferers. After the Great War, where many soldiers contracted the disease, there was a dreadful spread of it amongst women.

'You should be the one writing a memoir,' I tease.

She looks sharp-eyed at me. 'There is no need. I am at peace with myself, whereas you are not. And I am not a writer. You are.'

I open my mouth but bite back my words. If my facing up to the suffrage years and the destruction it caused in my personal life is some kind of therapy, then shouldn't she face up to whatever her father did to her as a child?

That is what ran through my mind, but I'm glad now I didn't utter the words.

4

Aston, Birmingham 1905

There it was, Number 18, Walsall Terrace, one of a row of identical Birmingham houses, neat and tidy and within walking distance from the school where I was to teach. I was already a barrel of nerves about the staff meeting on the morrow as I climbed the steps to the front door. Below the pavement level I could see the dark windows of the basement and hoped that my room would not be down there in the gloom.

'You must be Miss Hazel.' A broomstick of a woman greeted my tentative knock on the door. Her hair was pulled upwards so severely, and fastened with so many pins, she must have suffered from a continual headache. 'I'm sorry you had to wait.' She had one of those voices that always sounds resentful, as if the world had rolled the dice against her. 'I have one maid who does everything so, as you see, I must answer the door myself.' Her eyes raked me up and down and her lips curled, as she opened the door just enough for me to squeeze inside. 'I am Mrs Cartwright. Wait here one moment and I will have Annie show you to your room.'

I stood in the dark hallway, my new carpet bag at my feet and my leather satchel, crammed with as many books as I could fit in, hung on the bottom post of the banisters. Soon a flustered young woman came through the door at the end of the corridor, hooking stray tendrils of thin hair behind her ears.

'Follow me, Miss,' she said, lifting my carpetbag. I hefted my satchel and did as she requested, up the narrow stairs and down a dark corridor, off which there were a number of closed doors. Annie reeled off a list which I presumed described the contents of the rooms behind those doors.

'Mr Lawrence, Mr Peters, bathroom, broom cupboard, laundry cupboard, Miss Norris.' She stopped dead and turned big red-rimmed eyes onto me.

'Is that it?' I asked. 'Where am I to be?'

'With Miss Norris, of course. The ladies share. Men are more difficult. Mrs Cartwright finds it easier to keep them in rooms on their own.'

She spoke in a flat, stilted way, as if all the zest had been squeezed out of her. Fishing in her apron pocket for a while, she came up with a note printed in black ink on stiff card and handed it to me. With a perfunctory bob she disappeared at a trot down the corridor, leaving me to my own devices.

From the card I learned that I was expected to pay four pounds, twelve shillings and sixpence commencing today and hereafter on the same date every month. I considered this to be fair. It would leave me sufficient out of my annual salary of £95.00 for clothes, presents for my family and the occasional luxury. Reading on I learned that breakfast was in the dining-room at seven a.m. and supper at the same time p.m. I was reminded that no visitors without prior arrangement were allowed, and no male visitors at all. Clean sheets would be provided and laundry attended to.

I turned to face the door of my new room. What would Miss Norris be like? I guessed she'd be a teacher like myself, since the school had organised the lodgings for me. Gently, I turned the round brass handle and held my breath. Whatever I'd find, at least it wasn't in the basement.

The room was a pleasant surprise. Small, of course, I'd expected that, but the two narrow beds were covered in a floral fabric, and the wall-paper, similarly floral, carried pictures of idyllic cottages, their gardens bright with flowers. One had children playing in a sandy coloured lane with a terrier, another hens pecking in an orchard full of blossom. Though idealised and sentimental, or perhaps just because of that, they brought a lump to my throat for my Berkshire home.

I looked out of the window: a scrubbed back-yard, a small outhouse in one corner with a green-painted door, a washing-line, and against the wall – under a tin roof – a mangle. Over the wall, I could see another similar yard and the back of a two-storey house, almost identical. Beyond that were more houses, stretching as far as I could see. This was my first time in a big industrial city, my first proper view of Birmingham.

The door opened and a stocky young woman with a wide smiling mouth entered. 'Sorry, sorry, sorry,' she said. 'Meant to be here when you arrived but got delayed. Welcome. I'm Miss Norris. Nina since we're to share a room.' She extended a friendly hand.

I took it gratefully. 'Gladys. I was just wondering which bed was mine.'

'Nearest the window,' she said. 'Do you mind? I like to be nearest the door so I can creep in without disturbing you if I'm late. That's the arrangement I had with Freddie, the previous girl who lived here.'

'Freddie?'

'Frederica.'

I could see from Nina's face that Freddie was missed, and hoped I wouldn't be too dull and earnest a substitute.

'Frederica's gone to be married. She was a teacher too, and at the same school as you and me.'

'King Edward VI Grammar School?'

'Yes. It's close by and the only women the Cartwright will take are teachers.' Her eyes danced. 'She thinks they're respectable. We'd better not disillusion her, had we?'

I was dying to ask her why she sometimes needed to creep in late. Did she have a man-friend? The question was on the tip of my tongue but I bit it back. I'd know soon enough. We were living in close proximity after all.

Nina pulled back a skimpy, too short curtain opposite our beds with a music-hall style 'Tah-dah!' Behind it were some wooden hangers and a dress, two blouses and a skirt. A pair of lace-up shoes and smarter button boots were stowed neatly underneath.

'Behold our wardrobe,' announced Nina and asked if I needed any help unpacking.

'Is there anywhere for books?' I poured the pile of favourites I'd brought from home onto my bed.

'I keep my work-books for preparation and stuff in the little cupboard between the beds, so that's taken. Hope you don't mind. Freddie put her books on the window-sill. I mainly teach the younger girls by the way, in the preparatory department.' She paused for breath and laughed. 'No time for reading.'

She came over and turned over one or two of my books curiously. 'They're mostly poetry, aren't they?' She sounded disappointed.

I nodded. 'Poetry's my passion. But there are one or two novels that I couldn't be parted from.' I lifted up *Middlemarch* and *Great Expectations*.

'I've no problem guessing what you're going to teach anyway. Good luck trying to fire up a class of girls with poetry or Shakespeare. You'll get the chorus of groans treatment. But persist. They're nice girls on the whole. By the way, have you a bicycle?'

I shook my head.

'You'll need one if you're going to do any more than walk to and from school. There are some wonderful parks near here, but they're a fair distance – oh, except for Aston Park, just behind the school – but where we are the countryside isn't too far away. Don't worry, I'll help you find a bike. I wonder what happened to Freddie's.' She looked thoughtful. 'Wait there a moment. I'm going to ask the Cartwright.'

She dashed out of the door and I could hear her thundering down the stairs. Just her mention of countryside brought an ache to my heart. It would be good to escape from the city when I could. I arranged my books while I waited and listened for the return of her confident steps. For one so short – not that I was tall but she was even shorter than me – she had a heavy footfall and a loud voice. Good for the classroom, I guessed, but rather hard on the ears at close quarters. It was difficult to imagine Nina creeping anywhere and once more I found myself wondering about her evening activities.

'Got you one! The Cartwright wants five shillings for it, which isn't really fair since Freddie left it and it was hers. I tried to argue, but there it is. Five shillings or no bike.'

Her bright gaze rested on me and I nodded and thanked her, mentally counting out what money I had left with me. It wouldn't leave much, but there it was. A bicycle would make life more fun. Despite my financial misgivings I felt my spirits rise.

Nina took me down to the basement and Annie allowed us to go through the kitchen to the pantry passage, where the

Raleigh bicycle was leaning against the wall. It was a dark green and I'd like to say it shone like a new penny, but it didn't. Its handlebars and spokes had a thick coating of rust but the tyres were good and firm, the chainguard sound and there was a pump attached and a shabby basket fastened to the handlebars.

'You'll be able to put your exercise books in there,' said Nina, 'and it'll be much faster getting to and from school. I'll go with you the first time, to show you the way. Tomorrow's staff meeting's at nine.' She made a grimace but then laughed. 'It's pretty dull, but you'll meet everyone and there are one or two younger members of staff closer to our age.'

She chattered on as I paid Mrs Cartwright for my room and the bicycle. Our landlady's scowl didn't appear to upset Nina, or even make her pause, as she described some of the staff I'd meet, and then helped me out with my new purchase through the kitchen passage and into the back yard. From here a narrow alleyway, blocked by a flaking wooden gate, led to the street. The shed at the back of the yard had room for both our bicycles, amongst slop pails, some smelly cloths, a stiff broom and numerous glass jars and bottles in a wooden crate.

'You can't arrive at school on a bike looking like that,' said Nina, eyeing the rust, which out in the open air looked much worse. There were clumpy cobwebs in the basket too. She handed me some cloths and a wire pad that she kept in her saddlebag and we spent a happy hour cleaning it up till it sparkled in the afternoon sun, while Nina kept up a constant stream of chatter, describing who to court and who to avoid among the staff I'd meet in the morning.

I pedalled hard and concentrated on the journey, trying to memorise the route. The streets appeared all the same, a maze of terraced houses. Nina wove her way confidently through them, taking short cuts through little alleyways, wobbling around a cat sleeping in a sunny spot, avoiding a group of children playing with a ball against the wall. I craned back to look at them, ordinary children, paler than my brothers and sisters used to be, who were always out in all weathers. A small boy stared back, his nose running, no socks but good boots on his feet.

Nina was waiting for me at the end of the alley. 'Those children – they're so pale,' I said.

'Oh, for God's sake, you think that's bad?' she replied and pedalled off so fast I could barely keep pace. Her tone was crabby, but I was getting used to her mercurial changes of mood. When she was sunny, there was no one more fun. But shadows moved in fast and were not always easy to spot coming. Already I had learned that she wasn't the easiest of room-mates.

At last we entered a wide tree-lined avenue where houses stood back from the road, masked by trees. Many had coach-houses and stables standing nearby. These were affluent people, city-dwellers who could afford to bring slices of country life into their own backyards.

Soon after this, Nina swooped to the left and we arrived.

There in front of me was a large bright-red brick building, aflame in the autumn sunshine. I came to a halt and balanced on my bicycle, gazing. This place would be my crucible. I would be immersed and rise from it as tested metal. My throat felt full. All I wanted was to try myself and not be found wanting.

'Hey, dreamer,' interrupted Nina, already cycleless. 'Leave your bike at the side of the building. Remember, when you come on your own, you must always enter from this side, Frederick Road, as must the girls. The other side, from Albert Road, is the entrance to the boys' half of the school. And heaven forfend that the twain should ever meet!' She rolled her eyes upwards and clasped her gloved hands together as she intoned in mock Shakespearian, then dropped her voice dramatically. 'Notice the high wall across the playground? Boys that side,' she pointed over the wall, 'invisible to all, their times outside staggered so that no girl or female member of staff should have even an inkling of their existence. On this side, our girls, properly hatted and gloved whenever they leave the building – you will have to take your turn at the door, to check gloves are on for the street – because never, even if he is a brother, must a girl meet a boy, speak to him or even acknowledge his existence. When you are on duty, you will have to peer round the corner to prevent a girl waiting for someone of the opposite – er – dare I use the word? – *sex* – to talk or walk with her.

'Same goes for you too, of course. Decorum, decorum. Shouldn't be hard for you, Miss Goody-good,' she grinned to take the edge from her words. 'Now, must hurry, I've got to make a quick visit to my classroom. I'll see you in the meeting. Go straight through that door there. There'll be plenty of people about to show you where to go after that. Look for the girl with wavy dark hair, about our age. That's Miss Strachan – Amy. She's all right.'

'Thank you, Nina.' But still I stood, drinking it in and suddenly unable to move, through shyness and a plummet in confidence that left me wanting to leap back on my bicycle and head off anywhere else but there.

The large main doors were painted forget-me-not blue. One side of them was open and beyond was darkness, my unknown future. I gave myself a good shake, steered my bicycle to a rank where others, some as battered as my own, were already parked. Fishing out a notebook and pencil I took a deep breath before resolutely heading through that door.

I found myself in a gracious hallway, with a curving stone stairway leading upstairs; craning my neck, I could see where the banister rail continued into a long gallery above the hall. A table with a potted palm stood below the gallery. The impression was of space, even of stately living and I felt reassured. The air of this hallway felt laden with knowledge and a sense of purpose.

I looked around. Passageways headed off in three directions. The smell of ammonia and beeswax tickled my nostrils and made me want to sneeze. I loosened the hankie tucked up my sleeve in case. Then, footsteps. A tall woman of uncertain age, her mouth in a pinch that lent her face an unwelcoming expression, clip-clopped by me in stout button shoes. She turned to glare. 'If you're a new member of the teaching staff, you'd best come in before the meeting starts.' She had the trace of a foreign accent, French? German? She looked French. Narrow black eyes raked me up and down. 'Are you?'

I nodded and, after a brusque order to follow her, obeyed.

Head down, she trotted down one wood-panelled passage and then another until we found ourselves in a large sunny room that overlooked patchy grass and one careworn tree. Many faces turned to stare as I followed my guide into the room. I cleared my throat, which had suddenly tightened, and gave my name. Immediately, a young woman about my own age – dark hair, very pretty, maybe the person Nina had mentioned – shifted up on the long window seat that lined one end of the table and invited me to sit.

There was a hum of chatter around the table as all waited for the entrance of the headmistress, Miss Nimmo. My friendly neighbour leaned in, 'Amy Strachan. I take one of the younger classes. I think you're maybe the replacement for Miss Pullen, English?'

'That's me. Did she retire or get married?'

Amy laughed, a high snort that she quickly suppressed. 'Sorry. The thought of Miss Pullen marrying!'

I hadn't seen Nina come in, but she pushed through to sit on Amy's other side and plumped down, leaning over to ask if I was all right.

'Just telling her about her predecessor,' explained Amy. 'She asked what had happened to her.' She turned back to me and dropped her voice. 'I don't think she would ever have retired. She was very old, wasn't she, Nina? And one day last term, she just dropped down dead. In front of the class – my class as it happens. She'd turned round to write something on the blackboard and all at once she gave a little sigh and just fell to the floor.'

'How awful! The poor girls having to see that.'

'Yes. That's why I know the details. A lot of them wanted comfort afterwards.'

Something about this story made me more fearful than ever. How could I ever fill the shoes of someone so dedicated that she died delivering knowledge to her no doubt rapt pupils? But this bubble was burst by Nina, who remarked in a hoarse whisper that if the old bag hadn't died when she did, then she'd no doubt that some of her pupils would have expired out of sheer boredom.

All chatter ceased as Miss Nimmo entered and smiled graciously around at us.

Then she caught my eye.

'Oh, good,' she said. 'Miss Hazel is here, safe and sound, and ready to take up Miss Pullen's mantle.' She smiled warmly at me and looked around the table. 'Good. And most of you here will know that our Miss Brown...'

'That's Freddy,' Nina whispered.

'... left us for a new career as a married woman. So we welcome Miss Forbes in her place. Miss Forbes comes to us with a great deal of previous experience and we're lucky to have her.'

'She looks a bit dry,' commented Nina, still in her over-loud whisper, and earned a sharp look from the headmistress.

'Now,' continued Miss Nimmo, 'to help our newcomers, I ask that everyone around this table introduce themselves.'

———

How well I remember that inspirational headmistress; her thin upright figure, her plain face with its steady gaze. She had an admirable ability to be able to keep her feelings and opinions concealed, which made me feel flustered. I have never been able to hide anything – Mama always said she could read me like a book – and Truda says I'm not much better now, despite Jim's efforts to school both our bodies and our minds. Come to think of it, Truda and Miss Nimmo are cut from similar cloth; they even look quite similar, both very straight, both with thin hair forced into a bun, though Truda's is untidier. The first time I met her, at my interview, I'd been nervous and certain that I wouldn't please.

When she'd asked me why I wanted to teach I'd answered truthfully that I wanted to be of use but also to share my own enthusiasm for literature. Miss Nimmo's face had warmed into the smallest smile. She said she liked my attitude, that it made a change from the self-absorption of some of the young women she met straight from training.

If it hadn't been for Miss Nimmo, the respect I had for her and for her attitude to education, I doubt whether I'd have stayed as long as I did, once the Cause had pulled me in.

My eyes drift to the window again, but I do not see my garden, not this time. Instead I remember the corridor of the school and the closed door of my classroom before the very first time I entered it…

…I breathed deeply, afraid to go in. A cold sweat ran down from my armpits and I flapped my arms a little to disperse it. One, two, three, four… I counted to myself as the hum of the voices from the other side of the door began to rise and separate into different shrill threads. Only the tapping of shoes coming my way down the corridor propelled me through the door. I was immediately dazzled by the light, which made me see the children first as a blur, from which colours separated out slowly, like looking through a kaleidoscope. The scrape of their chairs as they stood up was delayed. Perhaps, from my aspect and abrupt explosion through the door, anxious not to be caught dallying by those encroaching footsteps, they didn't see me at first as a teacher. I knew I looked young, soft, and that my hair was as unruly as ever. I cleared my throat.

'Good morning, girls. I am your Year 5 class teacher, Miss Hazel. I will also be teaching you English.'

The ritual of greeting, the obediently droned reply and the settling back into seats calmed me. I took the register and made a kind of game of matching names with faces.

'Let's see,' I said, having run through the names from the back to the front of the class a couple of times. 'It's a little too easy, as you're sitting in alphabetical order. I wonder, will I get you correctly if you change places? Quick – I'll turn away – swap places with someone else in the class.'

There were nervous giggles and chairs scraping. I waited till all was quiet and turned back to face them. 'Now, let's see …' and had the pleasure of hearing the girls laugh a little as I stumbled through the names again. Two blue-eyed girls with long straight blonde hair were now sitting together. 'Oh dear,' I said and the class grinned. 'Is it Letitia and Jane?'

'Yes!' they chorused, 'but which is which?'

I'd noticed Jane earlier as a shy rather nervous girl. One of the pair wouldn't meet my eyes and I guessed that to be her, but for enjoyment's sake deliberately got it wrong and was put right with such evident delight that I knew I'd done the right thing, proved myself fallible and human.

We were all now more comfortable with each other and I moved on to discover what kind of things they had encountered in English lessons. Having heard what they had read to date I said I'd like to find out how they wrote. 'You can write just a paragraph or two – more if you want – about your favourite place in the world.'

'I haven't been anywhere else than Aston,' said one disgruntled child.

'No, I don't expect many of you have. You can write about a place in your house or garden. Or you may have been taken for a picnic in the park, or the countryside. Anything will do – it's your choice.' …

By the end of the first day I was exhausted. Who had learned more – my new pupils or me? Probably me. Most helpful had been to realise that each new class was as nervous as I and like me hadn't known what to expect. For me, they might have been a pack of wolves, poised to tear me to pieces, while for them I could have been any kind of schoolmarm, formidable, boring, uninspired. If these were classes that had been taken by my predecessor, I resolved to lift their spirits with my teaching and surprise them into enjoyment.

5

Nina, Amy and I often took the steam tram into the centre of Birmingham on Saturdays. Amy liked nothing better than to wander round the shops admiring items that were far out of Nina's and my financial reach. Nina could never see the point of this.

'Why are you even looking?' she grumbled, after a particularly long session of window-shopping. 'Let's go to the Art Gallery. Glad will like that.' She looked at me sidelong. When she first called me Glad I wasn't sure and said so, so now she often used it. Nina liked to needle.

'Boring,' said Amy. 'I've been there so many times.'

'Glad hasn't,' said Nina.

'Oh, all right then,' Amy gave in. 'You should see it, Gladys. It's a museum too. And the weather's improving. Afterwards we can sit by the fountain.'

There was an exhibition on from Newlyn in Cornwall. I admired the groupings of fisherfolk and their children, the details so real I felt the people were about to break into action and speech. Stanley Alexander Forbes, I read. In another grouping were paintings of children so characterful and lively it was clear that the artist had known them and painted them out of her own experience. Yes, a woman! The painter was, I presumed, Forbes' wife or sister, for the label below the grouping called her Elizabeth Forbes.

Nina gave me a nudge and spoke in a hoarse whisper, in exaggerated deference to the quiet of the building. 'See you outside,' she said. 'We're going to sit by the fountain. You'll find us easily.'

'Sorry. I'll come now.'

'No, take your time. Do something *you* want to do for a change, and stop trying to please everyone else.'

Nina's criticisms of me were frequent. Was I such a goody-good as she liked to call me? Did I always try to please people? If so that was something new, for I'd been very different as a child. I'd always felt the naughty one, the rebel. Aunt Louise had tamed me a little, by rendering me invisible and inaudible – perhaps that is when I changed. More likely, that is when I learned a modicum of concealment.

I suppose I always have felt that I'm a charlatan, that I'll be found out somehow. There is a basic insecurity in me, a feeling that I don't belong. But at that time the trying to fit in, to be a good teacher was real – or I'd built a convincing shell around myself, one that convinced even me.

I had buried Fred's comments about the prison cell of the classroom and the newness of it all was still, in that first term, exciting. The future appeared straight and shining, a path leading into a satisfactory career in education. I wanted to do this to the best of my ability and, having met Miss Nimmo, I wanted to please her in particular.

I opened my mouth to defend myself but Nina had gone already. She was like that, always taking me by surprise with a comment that made me question everything about myself. I hoped I wasn't the goody-good she often called me. What could be more irritating than that?

As time passed, some of the gloss of my first resolve to be an inspirational teacher became tarnished, as it collided with reality. I learned to accept that, however I tried, some youngsters would never see a poem as I did, would never be fired by the way words could be flung into astonishing forms. It didn't stop me trying and, in every class, there was at least one pupil who rose to the shining bait with pleasure and gratitude.

It was enough to satisfy. The classes began to separate in my mind. I learned strategies to cope with the more difficult pupils, spent hours of preparation to think of ways of teaching the nuts and bolts of grammar in an exciting manner, and listened with a generous ear to their stumbling recitations of the poems I had given them to learn.

At morning break, I escorted my class down to the hall where hot milk was available to all and buns or doughnuts for those who had a penny to spare. Porson, the porter, dignified and formal, served each girl with their milk and took their pennies if they wanted one of the vast currant buns.

There were frustrations of course, particularly that I did not teach the girls at the top of the school, in Class 1, which I ached to do. Miss Hadley had this privilege by right of seniority and until I had earned the right myself I would have to be content. But how much I wanted the to and fro of debate, the tussle with meaning at a higher level, which had been so enjoyable in the senior class at Calleva House and, even more so, at the Royal Holloway College and with Bill and his friends in Oxford.

One day, cycling into school through a misty November morning, I realised that I was happy. I had found my calling and could see myself pottering on in a teaching capacity for years, maybe for the rest of my life. I saw myself white-haired and perhaps stout, as Mama was becoming. I fancied myself, like some of the staff here, as being by then a little eccentric, and the thought made me smile. With a jolt, I remembered that this comfortable vision would mean I could not marry. Married women could not be teachers. I still harboured hopes of finding love. Might I at some point have to make a choice?

Suddenly, the image of Michael Allen surfaced. Michael with his bold blue eyes and slow smile. I hadn't heard from him since the day we last saw each other fifteen years ago. We had just been children. Why should I think of him now?

Jane Evans, the quiet, shy girl in my own class was of concern to me, so much so that I mentioned it to Miss Hadley. We sat in the staff-room, after lunch in the small school dining-room, which always sent me to the comparative quiet of the staffroom with my ears ringing and in search of relief. Most days lunch could be taken separately with the other staff, but we took turns, in pairs, to monitor the children at their meal. Today, it had been the turn of both Miss Hadley and myself. Fetching a cup of tea for her from Porson at the trolley, I wondered how best to approach the subject of Jane.

I'd ignored her first attempt at writing for me, the exercise about a favourite place, for which she'd written just one word: 'Nowhere.' That was on my first day, and how was I to know whether this wasn't merely an attempt to be rebellious? So I'd decided to let it pass. Further written work proved no better, however, and often she was absent from class. Even if she were present in the morning, she'd go home for lunch, as quite a proportion of the girls did, and not return afterwards. I'd mentioned this before, but no one appeared concerned. Apparently absences were common amongst a few of the girls.

'She's one of the poorer ones,' said Miss Hadley. 'A difficult family. Frankly I'm surprised she still comes to school at all. There are a number of younger children. I expect there's pressure on her to help her mother.'

Miss Hadley's tone was bored, as if she'd heard all this before, and more. 'You'd think school would be an escape for her,' I said, irritated, and more to myself than to her.

'Yet you tell me she doesn't put much effort into her studies.' She sighed. 'An order mark might encourage her to pull her socks up. That's my advice.'

It was a struggle to keep my temper. Not once had the woman shown any intimation that she cared. What sort of a Head of English was that?

Something of my anger must have penetrated, for at last Miss Hadley raised her head, her brow furrowed. 'Don't get too involved, Miss Hazel,' was her last instruction before she turned back to correcting exercise books.

Why not? I thought rebelliously. What kind of teacher confined her activities just to the classroom? Surely my remit should include concern for the children's welfare too.

Nina was also unsatisfactory over the problem of Jane. We sat on our beds one evening, pillows propped up against the wall behind, legs stretched out. Both of us were correcting exercise books. Jane's was as usual full of blots from a leaky pen and the individual letters ill-formed. I passed it over to Nina.

'I have one of her sisters,' she said curtly. 'Their father's lost his job.'

My attention was caught by this problem. 'Do you know why?'

'Why would I?'

I recognised the tone. Nina was having one of her moods. Normally I kept quiet when she was like this, but this time I wanted answers. The problem of Jane was niggling at me and coming between me and my rest.

'Nina!' I protested. 'You've just said you teach Jane's sister. Is she a poor attender too?'

I waited, but just got a grunt for a reply.

I wasn't going to let it go. Miss Hadley hadn't cared, Nina appeared indifferent, but I wanted to know the best way of dealing with the problem. 'If a pupil's attendance is poor and her work not up to scratch, then surely we need to find out why and help if we can.'

Nina sighed. 'Then find her address. Visit the family. You won't get any thanks for it. There are many things so much worse all around us, Gladys. Forgive me if I can't get worked up about bloody Jane Evans. All her mother has to do is apply for a remit of the fees if the family's struggling. Half the children at the school receive remittance, for one reason or the other.' She paused and her mouth creased with bitterness. 'Yet I've noticed that most of those children still have a penny in their pocket for a currant bun.'

'I didn't know that,' I said. 'About the remittance. Are many of the children on it?'

'Almost as many as aren't.'

'You think that might be Jane's problem? Her parents can't afford to pay?'

'Perhaps. More likely she's been asked to help her mother. Or even to earn some money for the family, since Mr Evans is off work. There are far worse cases than hers. Now for God's sake let me get on with my correcting.'

I felt a little overwhelmed by so much new information. Children taken from school to help at home? Remittance given if money was short? What else about the workings of the school did I not understand? I looked sideways at Nina, waited till she'd put a finished book aside and admitted my ignorance.

'I'm not surprised,' she said. 'You have an amazing lack of curiosity about so much. Surely you've noticed that some of the children's dresses are worn and patched, and only a few have those pretty lace collars?'

'I hadn't really. I look at their faces.'

'Look deeper, Gladys.'

At least she was facing me now. Her expression was strange, troubled. 'Jane Evans and her like are still among the lucky ones,' Nina carried on at a calmer pace. 'They've been accepted at a Grammar School. They are privileged compared with so many poor children. Do you know how hard it is to pull yourself out of poverty without education? And most people get nothing but a few years at elementary school, if they attend, where they are lost in noise and make little progress, despite the best intentions of their teachers. I'll take you to one of those schools one day. There's one I visit every now and again.'

'I wish you would.' I wasn't going to be put down by Nina. Ignorance wasn't a crime. I didn't deserve her scorn.

'You'll find it too much, I suspect. But at least it'll show you how lucky you are with your post at the Grammar School.'

'You too,' I fought back. 'You're not so different from me.'

'No. But I don't think I'll be there much longer. Whereas you have all the signs of settling in for ever.'

'What do you mean – you're not going to be there much longer? Where are you going?'

Perhaps it was to do with the mystery person she met on Wednesdays. Could she be getting married, like Freddie? Though Nina was difficult, she was still my room-mate, the nearest thing I had to a friend. My stomach knotted at the thought of her leaving.

Nina ducked her head further into her pile of books. There was a longish silence while I watched her. She wasn't reading what was in front of her. She was very still.

Then, 'My mother's sick,' she said in a small, lost voice. 'If she's worse at Christmas, I will have to stay and nurse her.'

This worry must have been what she was hiding. No

wonder she was moody. I thought of Mama. What would I do if she were ill? Would I give up my teaching for her? But she had Rita, Kay and Lina still at home. It probably wouldn't be necessary.

I swung my legs off the bed and perched beside her.

'Don't touch me,' she said through tense lips.

'I only meant...'

'I know what you meant. I just can't stand fuss. Even well-meaning fuss.' She gave me a watery smile. 'It's bad enough keeping controlled, holding the stopper in, but if you talk nicely to me, out it'll pop and I'll be a bawling baby.'

'Oh, Nina.'

'See? Stop it.' Tears ran freely and silently down her cheeks. I gave her my hankie. 'Oh, Glad, what will I do without this job?...' She sniffed. 'With no one but my mother to talk to, nothing to keep me busy but housework and cooking and nursing her.' Another sniff and a protracted blow of her nose. 'I can't bear to think of it.' The tears were flowing again and I could think of nothing to say. 'What if it's years and years? What if I never teach again?'

'Oh surely, it won't be as bad as that.' I handed her another hankie. I'd never seen Nina like this. Actually, I'd never seen anyone like this. Our family were buttoned up about tears. If we cried, we did it in private. Jim's stiff upper lip had rubbed off on some of us, though I was still more prone to venting emotions than he would approve.

As if sensing my unease, she gave her nose one last blow and blinked back her tears. 'Sorry, sorry. I'm being very embarrassing.'

'Not at all. I don't blame you. Can't imagine what I'd do in your shoes. When did you hear about your mother?'

'A few days ago. A neighbour wrote to me at the school.'

'And you didn't think to tell me?'

She shrugged. 'I guess I was just mulling it over. It didn't really sink in. But just then – marking those silly books, I just thought – what if this is the last time?'

'Nina! There's a few weeks of term left yet. You are getting a bit het up, and it may be unnecessary. Perhaps Miss Nimmo will hold your place for you. Have you asked her?'

'You're right, silly me.' She blew once more and laughed – shakily – but still a laugh. 'Thanks. Sorry, Glad. I feel better now.' She gave me a playful tap with her fist, 'You're still very irritating a lot of the time, but on the whole I like you.'

'That's very generous of you,' I said sarcastically, pleased to see the old buoyant Nina resurface. 'What irritates you so much?'

'You can't help it probably. You're just a little innocent. You see nothing but good in everyone and everything, plus you're so flaming bubbly and enthusiastic that it's a little wearing at times, that's all.' Her tone hardened as she spoke and I felt it deeply. Was that really how she saw me? I'd thought she liked me – she'd just said she did, but with reservations. Liking, I felt strongly, shouldn't have reservations. You either liked someone or you didn't. I began to feel that she didn't. Not really.

I opened my mouth to argue the point but she looked at me, her face closed as she put her books aside. 'I'm tired. All that emotion. If you don't mind, I'll go to sleep now.'

I turned down the gas lamp a little and tried to finish my work. Nina's back was humped in my direction. I could tell from her breathing that she was awake. What if she didn't come back after Christmas? This thought and the problem with Jane – what Nina said about her being lucky, so much luckier than many children – jostled around in my head with Nina's cryptic summation of my character.

The girls' work lost the battle for my attention and I gave it up and turned down the light. In the darkness, I thought instead about what she'd said. Did I not look deep enough into people? Did I just accept the outer show as the whole person? If I did, the same could be said of others, most people probably. I turned my mind away from the subject; it made me feel resentful, just as I used to when Mama or Aunt Louise criticised me.

Instead I thought about Nina's troubles. I tried to put myself in her place and failed. We were such different people. I felt sure she was exaggerating the problem, that something could be done.

Between that and resentment at her criticism, I tossed and turned most of the night, sometimes aware that Nina was too still and quiet for sleep herself. Normally she made little breathy grunts, which I'd found comfortable for it reminded me of sharing a bed with Rita. I thought of speaking to her, but her humped back looked somehow forbidding. In any case, what else could I say? I had to respect her silence. Finally I slept, thinking of dear Mama and Papa and wishing for the comparative peace of home.

Over the next few days, I tiptoed around Nina and tried to curb the usual chatter about my pupils, since that appeared to annoy her. I didn't find it pleasant watching what I said and I was still harbouring resentment, even though I tried to make excuses for her.

We went separate ways at the weekend, myself to a field near the canal, some way out of Aston. There I watched the slow descent of autumn leaves to the water and imagined their journey all the long way to the sea. The inactivity and fresh air calmed my spirits and I began to feel more generous towards my room-mate. It helped that the quiet allowed me time to make some contingency plans. If Nina did leave after Christmas, I decided I'd find a room elsewhere, on my own.

I didn't want to share with another stranger. The thought excited me and made me look at everything in a better light.

I saw Miss Nimmo about Jane Evans and she said she would ask a board officer to visit the family. They would remit the school fees if it were necessary, and find out if anything else was keeping Jane from her lessons. She thought it would be inappropriate for me to make a home visit as it might be read as interference of the wrong kind. I had to bow to her opinion. At least, if money was the problem, something was being done.

However Nina had spent her weekend appeared to have mellowed her too. She even apologised.

'I did say some hurtful things, didn't I? Sorry, sorry. I didn't mean them.'

I thought she probably did mean them, but I didn't say so. 'It's your mother, I know. It's understandable. You must be so worried for her.'

She gave me a strange look. 'You don't know her.'

This was so obviously true that I didn't feel it needed a response, but I got one anyway. With her back turned to me Nina painted a verbal portrait of her mother that had not an ounce of love or kindness in it. 'She's a witch,' she finished, turning to face me. 'I had to slave for her all my childhood, while she lay moaning in a darkened room, too ill, or so she said, to do a thing.'

'Perhaps she *was* ill,' I said, shocked to hear such a catalogue of dislike.

'Never too ill to greet a caller; and there was a man once that I knew she was meeting behind my back. At least then she was often out of the house and I had some peace from her constant nagging.' Nina's mouth turned down; her whole face registered contempt. 'She was furious when I left to train as a teacher. And now she's driven away half the village who, when

I left home, rallied round to help her – everyone believed that she really was ill, you see. But I know that she was just lazy. She didn't feel that it was her lot to keep house; she was meant for better things, or so she continually told me.'

'Oh, Nina. What about your father?'

'Dead.'

I moved towards her, with the idea of putting an arm around her, but she shook me off. 'Don't waste your sympathy. It was a long time ago. I don't remember him. He was a Captain in the Army. There's a photograph I had to look at on a regular basis, but it meant nothing to me. He was just a strange man with an extraordinary waxed moustache. Mother told me he was killed in South Africa, at Majuba Hill, in the first Boer War.'

'What did you do for money after that?'

'There was an army pension. And my uncle gave her a bit of an allowance too. It was tight. We managed. And there were only the two of us. Father had died too soon for there to be any more children.' She gave a bitter laugh. 'Sometimes I used to imagine that he left because he discovered what he'd married.'

I plumped myself down on her bed, careful not to touch her. Now I understood a little more. I'd never asked her about her family, not once, but I'd babbled many times about my own. I'd been angry with her for her criticism of me, but what kind of friend had I been? Shame made me feel sick.

Nina ducked her head. 'It'll be like going back to a prison. She'll never let me go again.' Her voice was a frail thread. 'Don't tell anyone, Gladys, will you? Not even Amy.'

I wondered why not, but guessed she had her reasons. Amy did like to gossip. 'I won't. Not a soul.'

She blew her nose fiercely, got up and ran her fingers through her tangled hair, plaiting it expertly and wrapping it round her head. 'Thank you.' Her laugh was tattered but she had mastered herself. 'Now,' she said brightly. 'Time to pierce that innocent shell of yours. We're both free on Wednesday afternoon. I'd like to take you somewhere.'

'To the elementary school you mentioned?'

She nodded. 'Then, if there's time we may go on somewhere else.'

She wouldn't be pressed into any further information. I would have to wait. I wondered if I'd finally get to meet the person she met up with on Wednesday evenings. Whatever her secret life contained, sharing it with me was a privilege. Something only a real friend would want to do. Apart from my own sister I'd never really had a girl friend.

There were things I still wanted to say but I knew that it would be wrong to pierce that brittle shell Nina had wrapped back around herself. Perhaps later on we could plan a strategy so that she didn't have to leave her teaching post. Friends worked together to conquer problems and that's what we would do.

6

We left the school premises together, me with a pile of exercise books in my basket. Nina was unusually silent. We cycled in tandem for the first part of the journey, then veered left into the cut-through alley, where I dropped behind. Here Nina jammed her foot down and came to an abrupt halt.

'Watch out!' I shouted, having nearly gone into the back of her. 'What do you think you're doing?'

'Sorry, Glad.'

I heard the abbreviation with relief. It meant that her spirits were back to normal.

Nina perched awkwardly on the saddle, rocking from toetip to toetip, a feat that was necessary with her short strong legs if she were to keep balance. I drew level with her and watched her mouth move as if she were having a conversation with herself. Finally, with a kind of grimace, she spoke.

'Glad, I was wondering if I ought to prepare you for this.' Her eyes were anxious and I waited.

'You may have noticed that sometimes I come home particularly late...'

'Late and hungry,' I added gently, to ease her awkwardness.

I was often awoken by her eating of the sandwiches left out by Mrs Cartwright, in quick snatches as if scared of losing out to someone else, someone hungrier.

She grinned and then drew her face back into a frown. 'The thing is, what I do is… I go and help out at this club in a very poor area.' The last was blurted in a rush.

Instantly I was intrigued. 'A far remove from a man friend then.'

She laughed. 'Golly, yes. Is that what you thought?'

'What sort of club?'

'It's run by women and it's for women. And their children, of course. It's pretty dire, actually. These women live desperately hard lives. I thought that, after visiting the elementary school, you might like to come there with me.' She looked at me to see my reaction. 'Might you be shocked?'

'How can I answer that? I don't know,' I answered. 'But yes, I'd like to go with you and help if I can.' I tried to picture in my head what such a place would be like, what would be its function. It was impossible. I had no experience on which to build my imagination.

Nina grinned with delight. 'If your concern for Jane Evans hadn't been so evident, I'd never have thought of inviting a prissy goody-good like you. Only teasing. We'll have to drop off first and warn the Cartwright that there'll be two of us for cold cuts. I meant to tell her earlier but this morning was a bit of a rush and I forgot.' She nodded towards the basket of books. 'You'll have to leave your bike and exercise books. Do you mind? Not doing your correcting?'

I did mind. I was driven by a desire to keep up a certain quality of efficiency that I'd begun. The girls needed immediate feedback, expected it. And they were right to do so. Guilt, always my shadow, lurked under my skin waiting to surface. But this opportunity – for that is what it seemed to me – to see more of life tweaked my curiosity. I'd manage the marking somehow, perhaps later, when we returned.

We walked at first in silence and then, as the area narrowed into meaner streets, Nina began to prepare me for what I was to encounter.

'The school we are visiting does its best, but you mustn't expect too much. Miss Derris, who will welcome our visit, has no degree and came up through the pupil tutelage system, like most of these elementary school teachers.'

'I met one or two, who'd managed to get grants to attend at the Royal Holloway College. They'd learned from their teacher, stayed at their school until they were thirteen or fourteen, so that they had a good grounding in the three Rs and then been asked to take over the younger children. It seemed to be a sensible system. The couple I met were really fired up about being teachers. I had great respect for them.'

Nina agreed. 'It is a good system, so far as it goes. But not many go on to do degrees. Most will just stay a year or two in the school that taught them, get married and leave. Luckily there're always a few more coming through, but though they may have learned the basics themselves, not all of them are good at passing it on. Well, you'll see for yourself.' She pointed at a church spire rising above the rooftops ahead of us. 'That's where we're heading. The school's close to the church.'

'It's a long way,' I complained. My boots pinched the toes as my feet swelled and I was beginning to hobble. 'Why couldn't we cycle?'

'Bringing our bikes into an area like this would be the last time we saw them.' Nina laughed at my puzzlement and shook her head. 'You really haven't seen poverty, have you?'

'We were poor in Ireland,' I blurted, before I could stop myself. I saw ourselves running around barefoot, the boys' hair as long as the girls', Mama's dire attacks on our fringes. I loved to dwell on those days; they made me smile.

Nina didn't bother to comment but just looked at me. I'd talked about my childhood to her before and I knew what she felt about it. 'There's a difference between having just enough and true poverty,' she'd said then. 'You were decently clothed, you chose to be barefoot but you had boots to wear when needed and you had food on the table. Maybe you were a little short of money, but you weren't grindingly, miserably, depressingly poor. Though I'll bet some of your neighbours were. Knowing you, you probably didn't even notice.'

I'd protested, even mentioned Mama's charity visits, making out by not elaborating that I was more involved than I was. Nina however was scathing and gave me a look that silenced me, a piercing contemptuous look, just like she was giving now.

Since that conversation, which had appeared to get Nina so rattled, I'd kept off the subject of my childhood and now I wished I hadn't mentioned it again. Luckily Nina didn't pursue my inadequacies this time but turned away and marched ahead, her stocky body tense with determination. She turned off the main thoroughfare with its mix of terraced houses, pubs and shops and into a narrow street. Immediately we were in a different world, still Aston, but an Aston I'd never imagined.

The streets we walked down were the most confusing I had ever seen. Between the blackened brick houses were sudden openings onto cobbled courtyards, flanked by four or five dwellings on each side. It seemed to me like a rabbit warren. Everywhere we passed, women, holding babies wrapped in a shawl and with other small children clinging to their legs, emerged from doorways and eyed us with suspicious curiosity. Their chatter stilled as we walked by but started again as soon as we were a few paces away. The skin at the back of my neck prickled, aware of many unfriendly eyes.

It being a fine day, though cold and still, women were hanging washing on lines crisscrossing the courtyards. The narrow streets that linked these 'courts', as Nina called them, were also strung with wet clothes, from one upper window to another opposite. Blueish-grey sheets dripped on the cobbles. They hung so low we had to duck our heads. Overlapping the stained bedding were shapeless garments, in a spectrum of colours that ran from rusty black, through browns and greys, to a white smudged with spreading drifts and continents of ochre and nicotine brown. All materials strained and fought to become grey, and not just the clothing and bedding intended for warmth and comfort. The sky, the buildings and the people who skulked in the narrow doorways, they too appeared drowned in the same hideous all-consuming colour.

Ahead of us was brightness, the end of the street. My spirits lifted a little and for the first time since we'd entered the area I spoke to Nina and received the news that the elementary school was just around the corner. We broke out into the space of a small square, dominated by the church with its impressive spire, its yews the one spot of green even on this October day.

Close by was a brick building with a small cobbled yard in front of it. 'Here we are,' Nina announced. Ahead was a single large door flanked by two tall arched windows, while on each side of the yard were a couple of shabby buildings, whose slate roofs appeared more hole than roof.

'The privies,' Nina whispered hoarsely, though no one could hear us. 'Girls that side, boys the other. And the same in the school. They're lucky to have separate rooms.'

From the building ahead a dull buzz emerged, as if from caged and angry hornets. The sound rose and fell, up to a roar punctuated with screeches and staccato whoops and then back down to that background murmur of insects looking for escape.

'Let's go in,' suggested Nina, with an ironic smile as I stood frozen to the spot.

I braced myself and swiped futilely with a handkerchief at my black skirt, stained by a spatter of damp spots from the washing we'd passed under.

Nina elbowed me. 'Stop fussing. No one will notice.'

We approached the door, the buzz from within increasing as we did so. I glanced through the window on my side, to see a room crammed with furniture and children of all sizes. How many were there?

I took a deep breath. 'Are they expecting us?'

'I warned them last time I visited I might bring someone else. She – Miss Derris – won't mind. Helping hands are always welcome.'

She rang the bell hung outside the door. The sound of it cut through the noise within like spreading ripples from a pebble thrown in water. Looking through the window, I could see the front of the class fall quiet first, until silence and accompanying stillness gradually reached the far corners of the room. Every member of the class was now looking at me through the window.

I took a step back and we waited quietly, until a girl of small stature but somewhat older than most in the room opened the door for us. She smiled shyly through an over-long fringe.

Once I'd been introduced, the children remained quiet, seated in rows of four, along wooden benches with their sloping desks in front of them. I supposed the spectacle of a new face was enough to keep their interest for a while.

Proudly, Miss Derris explained that this particular school was lucky. The boys were taught by a schoolmaster in a separate classroom and the infants were taught underneath, in a basement room. Most schools, she told us had a single room with a partition down the middle to separate boys from girls and a gallery above for the infants. Sometimes the partition was no more than a curtain and the noise was tremendous. From the outside I had thought the noise here was deafening. How much worse could it be?

She asked the same girl who had let us in to introduce herself and tell us a little more.

'I'm Ada Taylor,' the girl began, 'and one day I'm gooing ter be a teacher meself. Already I help the littl'uns read and write...'

A few jeers greeted this remark but were suppressed as Miss Derris cracked her cane down on the nearest desktop.

'You will be polite to our guests,' she said, 'and show them nicely what we're doing here. Go on, Ada.'

'My job is to tek some of the littl'uns over theea ...' she pointed to the sides of the room, where some desks faced the walls. There was hardly an inch of bare wall visible; all were covered with pictures and improving texts. 'Be grateful for what you have,' I read, and next to it 'Consider the lilies of the field.'

I ran my eyes over the fidgeting class. Some lilies! Most wore clogs, though there were some in boots, and clothes were patched and stained. Faces were superficially clean but hair looked untamed and greasy. One or two girls had hair cropped close to their heads and I knew enough to understand that this was probably to rid them of nits.

Nina nudged me. I had stopped listening to Ada, whose accent I still found hard to follow, though some of the girls in my own class had accents almost as strong. 'We're being invited to see some of the work of Ada's 'little'uns.'

I smiled approval and went over to a side of the room where four of the youngest in the class now sat two to a desk facing the wall. Miss Derris meanwhile, began to rehearse the main class in their times tables, which was done by rote. To a noisy background of 'two times two is four…' and so on, Ada struggled to help her charges with their reading. There was a narrow ledge which ran round the whole room, where slates and primer books were lodged and two of these were taken down for the children to share.

'Aggie,' said Ada. 'You begin. Goo on now.'

Little Aggie, about six years old I guessed, looked up at me big-eyed, and then at Nina, and set her mouth.

'I'll do it,' said her neighbour eagerly.

'Awright,' agreed Ada.

'The boy steals the pears and is whipped…' began the girl hesitantly. 'Ada, what is pears?'

'They's like apples that groo on trees,' explained Ada. She looked up at me for confirmation.

'Ain't never 'ad pears,' said the girl, 'but if them's like apples, them's nice.'

'Goo on readin' and less of yer lip,' said Ada firmly.

'The dog p-p-p…' She ground to a halt.

'Pur… sues,' I said slowly. 'What a difficult word.' I looked up at Nina, and she grimaced in agreement.

'Pursues,' the girl said hesitantly and looked up at me again.

'It means 'chases',' I said.

'Then why dain't it say so?' spluttered the indignant child.

'Goo on,' Ada interrupted. 'What do the dog chase?'

'The deer,' finished the child triumphantly.

'Have you seen a deer?' I said, pointing at the picture in the primer. Four little faces peered at the picture and shook their heads.

'No, I never,' said one.

'Cats and dogs is wot we sees round ower yard. But they dain't look like that,' said another, pointing at the greyhound in the picture.

'I seed a pig once,' said Aggie, "angin' in the butcher's.'

'Ower Mum went to the country when she was a young-un and picked 'ops. She said theea was mower cows 'n' pigs than people.'

The look of disbelief on the other children's faces was both wonderful and sad.

In the rest of our time there, Ada saw four more little readers, who struggled through sentences about country living which bore no resemblance to their real lives. Two other pupil teachers were doing similar work around the sides of the room and both Nina and I took on some more. This meant that all the youngest children were taken from the main group and the thirty or so remaining could be taken through their geography lesson on the countries of the world. So far as I could hear, against the background of my own work with the youngsters, the lesson consisted of writing the name of a country on the blackboard, then choosing a pupil to find it on the globe – a process that took a long time, and was accompanied by yells of encouragement or ridicule from the rest of the class – after which they all wrote the name of the country on their slates, three times.

More and more restlessness was evident and as the noise level rose, it was punctuated by savage cuts from the cane on the desks of the principal offenders. It made me jump out of my skin every time, but at least the teacher didn't actually hit a child. It was a relief when the end of the afternoon arrived, the bell was rung in the corridor between the two classrooms and the children lined up ready to leave. The noise level had started a dull headache above my eyes.

One of the youngest children had fallen over, racing to get into the queue. Her skirt flew upwards and I was shocked to see she had nothing on to cover her bare bottom. The child was crying, but Miss Derris strode over and tapped her backside with the cane, not hard, before using its tip to pull the skirt back down.

'Make sure your mother provides you with some bloomers before you next come to school,' said Miss Derris sternly.

Through her tears, the child told her that they couldn't afford bloomers.

'It's not decent,' said Miss Derris, still stern. 'She must find some covering or other.' Ada joined our group, while Nina monitored the waiting line of children.

'Now, stop yer blartin' and blow yer nose,' said Ada as she hauled the child to her feet. 'Me Mum 'ad to sew together sum rags to make me daicent. Yower Mum must do the same.' She gave the child a little push and finished with 'The cold Winter's roond the corner and yower bloomer's'll keep yer warm, see.' Then she grinned up at both of us and accompanied the child, still sniffling, to the queue.

Once Miss Derris had seen her pupils out of the door, the boys emerged in the corridor from their classroom. A tall broomstick of a schoolmaster accompanied them. His long stringy neck and the wild tufts of hair scattered over a balding scalp made him look like a heron. He saw out sixty or so, one at a time, speaking each of their names out loud as they passed, in a doom-filled voice that seemed to suggest each one of them was a hardened criminal and there was no cure. The quietness and discipline of the boys were remarkable until released by their name, after which they exploded down the steps into the courtyard and out into the street as if shot from a gun.

'I try to avoid a rabble flocking the streets,' explained the schoolmaster, Mr Keane, after we'd been introduced. 'They will wait for each other further down the road, of course, but they know better than to shout and misbehave in my hearing.'

Nina gave me a warning look as I opened my mouth to

speak. 'How do you manage to keep them so well-behaved?' I asked, ignoring her.

He stooped closer to me. 'By fear,' he said. 'Nothing else works. Fear keeps them attending and fear drums the rudiments of learning into them. If they can read, write and manage simple arithmetic when they leave here, I count myself rewarded.'

I couldn't understand how fear might make them attend. Wouldn't it be more tempting to truant?

Something of my doubts must have shown on my face, for he correctly read them and turned his mouth down as if used to criticism from random and uninformed visitors like myself. 'We are lucky to have a school board that is hot for education. The board officer for our district was brought up in the area himself. There are not many hidey-holes he does not know about and he will track truants down and bring them by the ear to me.' He glanced at Miss Derris. 'So my boys rarely truant. Whereas the girls' numbers, I note, are down again.'

Miss Derris opened her mouth to speak but, without waiting to listen, and grinning like a crocodile, Mr Keane nodded curtly to us, bestowed one last glower on Miss Derris, and turned into the black hole of his classroom door. Behind this I imagined the torture of small boys, hung like onions on strings around the room, would continue to amuse him until well into the night.

Miss Derris waited until he was safely out of earshot before she invited us back into her classroom. A small thin-faced child was busily wiping slates and slotting them in batches of five along the ledge on the wall. Here they were prevented from slipping by a rope that ran, like the ledge, right around the room.

'My slate monitor for this week,' smiled Miss Derrick, patting the girl on the head and sending her home.

Once the door was closed, Miss Derrick confessed that Mr Keane disapproved of her and thought her too soft on her charges. Hence the cane. Apparently the sound of this, thwacking the wooden desks, reassured the school-master that children were being made to toe the line. 'But I rarely hit anyone,' she said. 'And I believe they make better progress because of that.'

'How about truancy then?' I asked.

'It goes on, of course it does. Whatever Mr Keane says, many boys know how to duck the board officer and simply never turn up. They'll spend the whole day on some peck or other, entertaining themselves with others of their kind.' She saw my puzzled expression and explained. 'Pecks are the local word for areas of waste ground. If you stay in Birmingham, you'll get to know how rich the language of the working classes is.'

'I do hope to stay,' I said, aware of Nina's caustic look. 'But tell me about truancy among the girls. Mr Keane mentioned it and I couldn't help but notice there were far fewer in your classroom than there were boys.'

'Mr Keane has an axe to grind but mostly it's not the child's fault if they can't attend school. Sickness is rife and that eats into school-time. On top of that, girls in particular are expected to help their mothers. The families are so large, even though many of the babies and smaller children die, of consumption, measles and whooping cough mainly. Despite the death rate, families still grow. It is common for there to be seven to twelve in one family. And of course the mothers are worn out by the constant child-bearing and often die young themselves.' She was dry-eyed but there was strong emotion in her voice.

As I continued to ask questions, Nina watched with a small grim smile on her face as bit by bit my illusions and innocence were stripped away. I learned that in this school most were so undernourished that the school provided breakfast. A mug of cocoa and two big slabs of bread and jam were given to each child considered poor enough to warrant it. 'But they have to be there on time to claim it,' explained Miss Derris. 'It's a way of getting them to school and teaching them punctuality. If they are not in the breakfast queue by the time the bell stops ringing in the morning, they won't receive the food. Of course, that still doesn't stop truancy, though it might mean at least that they receive some education in the mornings. In the afternoons, because they all go home for lunch, many won't return.'

'That happens in our school too. At least half the pupils go home for their lunches.' I said to comfort her. 'And we have some poor children too, even one or two that come from this area.'

'But they've been accepted in a Grammar School,' said Miss Derris quietly. 'Whatever else, they'll have a chance to get out of here, out from the slums through earning better wages. They're very lucky.'

'I told you so,' said Nina. 'Your Jane Evans cannot be put in the same category as the children we've seen today.'

'Will Ada go on to the Grammar? She's certainly bright enough.'

'There's some resistance from the family, who think she'd be more use going out to earn a living, but I'm working on it. I hope she'll go and be able to win herself a better life.'

I had warmed to Miss Derris more and more during this conversation, so when she suggested I visit again if I could spare the time, I accepted with enthusiasm.

'The children liked you, I could tell, and another voice encouraging Ada to apply for a scholarship would be welcome.'

We shook hands and left, both of us promising to return on any Wednesday afternoon we could manage.

Once we were back in the square, Nina asked if I felt capable of going with her to the Club she'd mentioned. 'Aren't you too tired?'

'I do have a bit of a headache,' I confessed. 'The noise of so many children in one room.'

'There are other opportunities,' said Nina, turning back the way we'd come. 'Encounters with the underclasses are very wearing.'

'Why do you say that in such a sarcastic tone? As if you think of me as a weakling who has to be wrapped in cotton-wool? I'm stronger than you imagine, Nina. So let's go to your bloody Club.'

'Oooh!' was Nina's sarcastic response, but she had a beaming smile on her face as she steered me past the church and into another narrow street.

Above the door was a wooden board, with ASTON WOMEN'S CLUB written in beautiful calligraphy. I followed Nina into a large room, full of small tables and wooden chairs. Noise and odours that fought for attention embraced me. Someone had tried to cheer the room by covering the tables with checked cloths, but the first impression for a stranger like myself was of unrelieved gloom.

This was not so much the fault of the room itself, though the flaking paint was dark green and the ceiling so stained that its colour could only be guessed at, but of the demeanour of its human contents. At some tables a single person sat. I saw two girls, young enough to be my own pupils, seemingly asleep with their heads resting on their table, cushioned by their folded arms. They slept on despite the racket from crying babies and the sharp chatter of their mothers.

A brisk efficient-looking woman came to meet me and Nina made the introductions. 'Call me Violet,' she said. 'We're all first names here.' She looked at my face with sympathy. 'It's a shock the first time,' she said. 'You'll get used to it.'

Would I? I thought of Ada and the stalwart efforts of teachers like Miss Derris in board schools all over the City. I saw again the jumble of streets and courtyards, the black fungus growing on the brickwork, the dripping laundry, the pinched faces of the children, the pungent smells that assaulted one at every turn. The thought of getting used to this already made a knot in my heart. It reminded me too much of Mama's charity visits. Those smells! Everything in me rebelled against further immersion into the lives of these people.

I saw Nina looking at me, her face knowing, and steeled myself. This time I'd stay, but only this time, to prove to her I could do it. Then, nothing would bring me back here. Even the thought of it brought back the nausea I hadn't experienced since my childhood.

That first visit passed in a blur. I made tea and ladled soup from a huge copper. Another helper had brought apples from her own garden. The children fell on these and retired to eat them, their eyes darting, fearful they'd lose their treats.

'They get nothing fresh, you see,' explained Nina. 'And it makes them ill, weakens their bones. Often they suffer from scurvy, like sailors on long voyages used to in the old days.'

I worked on in a daze made up of bewilderment at so many new impressions, exhaustion as the hours passed into evening – when a new set of women appeared and some left – and a kind of dull horror and disgust.

As on Mama's charity visits in Ireland, it was the smell that got to me the most. Filthy clothes and bodies caked in grime. Worse, a sweetly sickening odour, like decay or perhaps urine, that rolled off them in waves at every movement they made. This compound of scents encased me, clung to me like a miasma, so that it pursued me as we made our way home in the darkening evening – on the steam tram this time to save my sore feet – and, like sticky invisible cobwebs, covered my own clothes and skin with an imaginary layer, even in the refuge of our shared room.

I lay wide-eyed in my bed, listening to the rustle of bedclothes that meant Nina too was awake. All thoughts of those exercise books had fled. They no longer seemed important. My mind was full of the school children, of Ada, but even more those other children, the ones at the Club, the lack of light in their eyes, the acceptance of despair in their mothers' faces. Later in the evening had come a second wave of women, ranging from mere children of twelve or so to hard-faced creatures whose ages were impossible to guess.

'Nina?' I whispered into the cushioning autumn night air that drifted sweetly through our open window. It may not be the scented air of Rowstock, my family home, untouched by anything worse than the natural rhythms of life, but it was welcome to me. Through the casement it carried echoes of the green hills and valleys beyond the city. There birth and death happened, of course it did, but all flowed along in the brown stream of nature, wrapped around with earth and sky, so that poverty and hardship there appeared kinder than what I had witnessed that day, ancient and time-honoured compared with the man-made horrors of those mean streets and dwellings.

'It's hard to take at first,' Nina whispered back. 'Don't let it get you down. You did so much better than I'd expected, Glad, I was proud of you. A few more visits and you'll get used to it.'

Something about that last statement, the second time it had been said to me in a single day, bored into my brain like a worm. Get used to it? Never.

7

When the next Wednesday came, I went to the elementary school but pleaded too much school-work to go on to the Club and returned home after saying farewell to Miss Derris. Nina gave me that look again, as if she could see my thoughts and wasn't impressed. I hardened myself against it. I counted her as a friend. But friends didn't have to do everything together, did they?

I am ashamed to think that a part of me didn't care what Nina thought. Such was my desire to separate myself from what made me uncomfortable I was prepared to make any excuse. A worm in my brain whispered she probably wouldn't be around for long anyway. We had explored and discarded any number of useless strategies concerning her mother, and had settled on the only one that might work: that Nina go home in the short term, but that she should try to find someone to care for her mother, who would have to be paid. That uncle might help out. Or Nina could use a part of her salary when she returned to teaching.

Meanwhile, I was a teacher, a good teacher, or so I believed. I was doing something useful. I didn't need to prove myself further, to Nina or anyone. I would continue to go to the elementary school, sometimes, but not every week, for my own pupils deserved my full attention. Nina would just have to get used to the fact that she and I had different values.

⸺∞⸺

The following Wednesday Amy asked me to accompany her to the theatre, where she was meeting a couple of friends of hers. Amy was a local girl and had many friends in the area. I was excited and decided to stay away from the elementary school too, to ready myself for the evening.

The Prince of Wales Theatre was on Broad Street, a long ride on the steam tram. I fretted a little lest I be late, as I'd not been to that area before and worried whether I'd find the right building. I needn't have. The tram stopped right outside and the friendly conductor pointed the place out, a handsome building with Corinthian pillars on the outside and wide steps leading up from the street.

Amy waited at the top with a middle-aged couple. The woman was dressed smartly, in the latest style, with a light green hobbled skirt, flared slightly over the ankles. Her coat, muff and hat were all made of a rich brown fur, very opulent, but suitable for a crisp autumn evening.

I felt dowdy climbing up towards them in my Sunday best navy frock with a heavy cape. I didn't own a coat. Nor did I have a muff, though my gloves were good enough, and my navy felt hat kept the evening chill off my ears and the sides of my face. I lifted my chin. I had nothing to be ashamed about.

The couple were introduced as Bertie and Eveline Foster-Smythe, friends of Amy's family for generations, she said. He was tall and very dark, with eyebrows that jutted over eyes such a deep brown they appeared black. His face bristled with hair, neatly groomed, but still leaving little skin uncovered. In the midst of all this hair, two red lips moved and stretched, creating quite a dance between the whiskers of his curling moustache and those of his beard. I dragged my eyes away from the sight and tried to concentrate instead on Eveline. I must admit that, despite a kind of horror created by Bertie's saturnine looks, both he and his wife were very pleasant and quickly made me feel at ease with them.

As we settled into our seats in a theatre buzzing with excitement, Amy whispered in my ear, 'Bertie owns a manufacturing business in Hockley.' As the noise of people greeting each other from box to box increased, she raised her voice. 'The factory make all sorts of machine parts. I was shown round as a child. It was exciting to watch the skill with which the workers handled the hot metal. Oh, and the noise of all those vast machines, the clanging and the clacking, you could never imagine it. I felt quite deaf after my visit.' She turned and nudged Bertie, 'Just boasting about your factory, Bertie. I hope you're pleased. Perhaps you'll show it to Gladys too, one day.'

'I'd be delighted,' said Bertie, smiling so that his red lips curled like a small animal stretching in its nest.

I hoped this offer would never happen. I removed the bulky cape from my lap and tucked it under my seat. Seeing how hot I was, though it was the heat of embarrassment, Bertie's wife leant over and passed me her fan. And after that the lights began to dim and the dark red curtain with its gold trimmings to move and my neighbours were forgotten in the excitement of the beginning.

The play was *Caesar and Cleopatra* written by George Bernard Shaw. I had heard of this gentleman, whose opinions on all sorts of matters, from politics to vegetarianism, were often quoted in the paper. Papa didn't approve of him and called him a filthy Fenian, based on nothing that I could figure, except that Shaw was Irish and politically minded, so was assumed by Papa to favour Home Rule.

It took a little time for the play to take hold but I found the childish Cleopatra charming in her imperiousness. Her pert remarks to the elderly Caesar, vain as men can be about their age, made me smile. I began to relax into it. As the actors warmed up, so did the audience and the atmosphere infected me with such enthusiasm that I turned to the others in the interval and held forth about the play – that the actor playing Caesar was surely much too old, and Cleopatra too, supposed to be a mere child, was clearly played by a woman of about my age – in a way that clearly amused the gentleman and irritated the lady. Amy, however, smiled with pleasure and told me she was glad I was enjoying myself so much.

Evie, as her husband called her, rose languidly from her seat and made her way out to meet up with some friends of hers in the foyer. She left her outer clothing curled up on her seat like a large amiable dog; I almost saw its tail wagging. Amy also rose and, after checking I was all right, said she would visit the cloakroom and soon be back. I was left alone with Bertie.

'You're enjoying the play, I gather,' said he. His lips glistened in the yellow light. He put his gloved hand on my knee.

I pulled sharply away and he withdrew the hand, but not without a brief caress first, a lingering of the forefinger, which moved up and pressed unpleasantly into the flesh of my thigh. In panic I recoiled. What should I do? Was it best to ignore or reprimand? I decided that a reprimand would make too much of the event. Instead I rose to my feet with some idea of seeking out Amy.

'Don't go,' he said, both hands now firmly curled around his silver-headed walking stick and facing the stage, so that he talked to me without looking. 'It won't happen again. I saw you as a modern woman, Miss Hazel, beautiful and aware of your effect on our weaker sex. It won't happen again … unless you want it to.' He glanced quickly at me, his eyes amused and predatory. Those lips curled.

By now I was on my feet, angry and upset. His action had quite driven out my enjoyment of the play.

'You took advantage of my solitary state, undefended by a male escort, in the seclusion of your theatre box,' I hissed. 'I shall let it pass, but it is not forgotten.'

At that moment Amy came in. She looked from one to the other of us, a puzzled frown on her face. 'Everything all right?' she asked. 'Did you need the cloakroom, Gladys? Only the play will begin again soon, so if you can wait it would be better.'

'I'll be all right,' I muttered and pulled myself together. Avoiding Bertie's sardonic gaze, I sat back down.

Amy turned to Bertie. 'Tell Gladys about the work you do for Birmingham City Council.' She turned to me proudly. 'Bertie's recently been elected to the council and has been much praised for his charity work and his plan to rebuild some of the slum dwellings.'

I looked at him afresh. Of course, no person is just good or evil. Even this one, who I could not personally like, did some good. 'Tell me about the plan,' I asked politely.

'Have you visited any of the slums?'

'Yes,' I said with a shudder. 'If you are planning to rebuild any, that would only be for the good.'

'My factory needs to expand,' he said. 'So I shall clear away the dwellings in Hockley directly adjoining it, and rehouse the occupants in newly built places elsewhere. Many of them work for me in any case. It'll mean they have to travel a little further to work, so more likely I shall dismiss those particular ones and employ others living closer to hand.'

Something about the casual way he said this really upset me. 'Don't those people rely on the wages they earn to feed their families?'

'They'll find other work. Or not. It's not my problem. I employ a hundred or more men and nearly that many women, so I think you could say I do enough for the working classes already.'

I gritted my teeth. A dull anger was beginning to seethe inside me but I kept it under control. This was a public place and we were here for our recreation. I knew I shouldn't make a scene.

'What do the women do in your factory?'

'They check some of the smaller parts and put them together. Some of them file the edges of the metal down. None of the work is difficult.'

'And how are they paid?'

He looked at me with amusement. 'With money, of course!' He laughed and looked around at Amy, eyebrows raised, as if to say, *Isn't your friend a card? An ignorant one at that.*

'The men earn more than the women,' Amy explained. 'About twice as much. But then women's work doesn't require as much strength as that of the men's.'

'Their hours are just the same though, I imagine.' I tried to keep my tone friendly, but the comment came out sarcastic all the same.

'Ten hours,' Bertie answered, 'which is normal.'

Evie returned at this moment, which was as well. I had to bite back the desire to say that if I worked for ten hours on end, I'd be exhausted to the point of collapse. While she removed her furs from her seat and settled them around her for comfort, Bertie leaned in to me and said, 'You're concerned for those women I employ. You shouldn't be. Take it from me, I know the type well, have employed them for years. They're little more than animals, living in warrens, breeding like rabbits. If some are laid off, there are always others to fill their shoes.'

I leapt to my feet, all resolutions blown away. 'How dare you speak about human beings like that! Human beings!' I repeated, my voice shrill. I was shaking from head to foot.

Evie looked at me in consternation, finely drawn brows raised and her mouth in a moue of disdain. Bertie kept his eyes on me too, amused by my antics, as if I had been a wasp in a jam jar that he had been shaking to see what it would do.

Amy pulled me down. 'People are looking at you.' It was true; I could see white faces turned up towards our box from the seats below. 'You're being very embarrassing, Gladys.'

And I was. But I wasn't ashamed. Something in this conversation had triggered a feeling inside me, one which I did not recognise at first, except as anger. I remember nothing of the rest of the play, but sat still and rigid. The explosions of laughter or clapping around me sounded far away. Over and over in my head, I heard Bertie's smug tones, his dismissal of a whole section of humanity as a sub-species, beneath contempt. I recognised that he had enjoyed stirring me up, but I didn't think that he was exaggerating. He spoke his feelings and watched my response, just as he had tried out my response earlier when we were alone. I don't think I'd ever actually hated anyone before and I knew I should be ashamed, but I wasn't. Mama's voice sounded a reproach in my head and I shook it away. I wanted this anger.

After the play, a rather stiff Amy saw me into a hackney, which Bertie with a smile insisted on paying for. 'Trams are all very well, but you get all types. And I wouldn't want you to walk to your lodgings in the dark at the end of your journey.'

In the jostle of leaving the theatre I apologised to Amy, but nothing would make me apologise to Bertie. I even found it hard to say thank you for paying for my journey home. But I made myself, forced it out through a throat half-closed by tension. He instructed the driver and then took my elbow to see me in. It was all I could do not to jerk it away, but Amy and his wife were watching. The sensation of his hand burned me all the way home.

This incident drove me to a good deal of soul-searching. Why had I reacted so extremely to this man? Was it just a personal aversion, or was it because I recognised something about myself in his careless attitude to his workers? Had I not, since childhood, avoided contact with those I didn't want to acknowledge? Worse, whom I found in some way disgusting? Wasn't that why I was making excuses not to go back to the Club? I was no better than him.

I lay in my bed, Nina snoring lightly nearby, and found much to dislike in myself. Nina was right to view me contemptuously. She called me goody-good, but what she meant was that I was priggish and full of myself.

The result of this sleepless night was an understanding that I did not want, in any way, to be a part of a class that saw others as less than human. My anger had hardened into a resolve to face up to my own prejudices. Especially I didn't like the fact that I too had dismissed these people, not as animals, but certainly as something I didn't want to deal with or take any responsibility for.

So I forced myself back to the Club. I chose to go on a different day, when Nina was at school. It was a Monday, when I finished early, though not as early as on a Wednesday, so I was tired, but determined to take myself in hand. I found it easier without Nina, without the consciousness of our other life together: school and shared lodgings. Especially without her judgmental look, her expectancy of my failure.

Despite my resolve, I stood outside the building for a long time. My legs simply did not want to propel me through the door. I imagined the stench of the occupants seeping under the sill and wreathing round my feet. I felt sick. It was no good, I simply could not do it. I wasn't made of the right stuff for compassion of the kind required, compassion that Mama clearly had, and Rita perhaps, but especially my youngest sister Lina, whose heart, as she had grown up, embraced any suffering creature. Me – I found suffering, illness, babies and their emissions, all of that disgusting. It wasn't personal, nothing to do with class. I wasn't too keen on my own bodily functions either. Was that normal? I'd met a young nurse once, who described what she had to do and, though I admired her for her dedication, I knew I couldn't do what she did. It simply wasn't in me.

Having acknowledged this about myself, not without some shame, I decided to leave, but before I could make a move I heard the clack of clogs behind me and a woman with two children came up.

'You want ter goo in, do yer?' she asked, in the thick accent which I still struggled to decipher, despite having lived in the area now for close on three months. 'Noo need ter be afeard,' she continued. 'The babbies'll tek yer through the dower if it's yer first time.'

The 'babbies' duly took me by each hand and, grinning up at me under their peaked caps, pulled me to the door. Perhaps nothing else would have got me in. Escorted as I was, I could not flee and, faced with such friendliness from this unknown woman, how could I at least not have the grace to try?

'Been 'ere befower?' she asked, and I told her I had. 'This place is a godsend for the likes of us. Don't know what we did afower it were 'ere. Sat in ower mucky rooms with ower neighbours, talkin' in the damp and cold, that's what.' She chuckled. 'What's yower name, luv? Mine's Mary.'

Then we were through the door and Violet greeted us, with another couple of volunteer helpers, and I felt surprised to be so welcomed. Their fuss made me feel I was doing something really brave, out of the ordinary. It made me wonder if my previous thoughts had not been so abnormal after all. Perhaps others of my class – as most of the helpers were, mine or higher – had felt them too.

It was Mary's words, though, that really resonated with me. Without them, I'd probably have gone home and never returned. The Club was a godsend, as she said, and a refuge from the dreadful places in which they had to spend their lives. I had a long way to go yet, but if I stayed the course this time, I would have begun.

Following this resolve, I went again next week, on the same day. I had to force myself. My feet dragged, as I left the familiarity of King Edward's. I felt all sorts of pains in my stomach or my head. It was as if my whole body was siding with my secret fears and rebelling against my resolve. With gritted teeth, I overcame the rebellion and took the steam tram as close to the club as I could go.

Violet introduced me to a group of mothers, surrounded by children indistinguishable from each other, at least to my eyes. I felt my mouth in a fixed smile as Violet chatted easily with everyone. My eyes roamed over the children. Working with slightly older ones at the Elementary School had made those children individual. But these! It was even difficult to tell their ages. And they wouldn't keep still. Only the 'babbies' were easy to spot, clasped to their mothers, often asleep, or watching their siblings with listless eyes.

I kept at a safe distance. Memories of our charity rounds surfaced and I had to force myself to show interest as one mother or another pointed out the charms of her brood. Violet, who had learned some skills from the doctor who gave his services, free of charge, to the Club, wanted to examine the skin of one of the toddlers. But he wriggled and yelled and would not allow her to peel back his clothing. Before I knew it, the mother dumped her baby onto my lap and captured the toddler. My hands grasped the infant automatically. I held it firmly on my lap, while Violet and the mother examined its enraged brother.

The infant and I regarded each other. The change of ownership had woken it. Two reddened eyes regarded me. I could see no discernible expression. Its hands emerged from the rags that wrapped it and pleated together. Little nails, I saw, perfect in their way.

I held the baby nervously. My fingers dug into the back of its creased neck to support the head. It had a floss of black hair, spiky and untamed, like a young hedgehog. Between the spikes of hair was flaking, reddened skin and the top of the scalp pulsed with a secret life of its own. Its eyes, slightly milky at the edges and an indeterminate colour somewhere between brown and blue, continued to regard me. The creature was hideous but fascinating. The warm weight of it fitted exactly into my braced hands.

Suddenly the mouth pulled down into a grimace of pain and the tiny body twisted. Alarmed, I was about to pass it on to its mother, but she was absorbed with Violet and the toddler. The baby straightened from its contortions and its face settled into an inward look of great concentration. I became aware of a warm damp feeling permeating my skirt. I shifted my hands downwards to lift the child away from my clothes. It was soaked through. The shift of position had stirred up the stench of urine and worse. I wanted to throw the bundle of rags, with the child inside, away from me. This is what I had always hated: this smell, the mixture of dirt and bodily effluents. A whimper escaped me.

Violet turned and looked at me. 'Are you all right, Gladys?'

'Of course,' I said, through gritted teeth.

The mother gave me a hard look, but her attention was quickly reclaimed by the protesting toddler.

One of the group of children approached. 'Poo-ey, poo-ey.' she said, wafting her hand in front of her nose. 'Frankie's bin and done a poo-poo, Ma.'

'Give 'er some clean rags then,' said the distracted mother.

The child dug in her mother's burlap bag and extracted a pile of greyish strips of cloth. She heaped them on my lap. My skirt was stuck to my leg now and I wanted nothing more than to get rid of the offending infant and run home to wash the skirt. I felt I'd never lose the smell, which clung to my clothes and the skin beneath. The infant and I were frozen, eyeing each other in mutual distaste. Gradually, the new rags slid off my lap onto the floor.

'Get on wiv it then,' said Frankie's sister, all of three or four years old. She looked me up and down and heaved a sigh. Then she lifted her brother up, holding him under the arms and not minding the wobble of his head on its fragile stalk. I watched as the child began to strip her brother of his wet clothes, to use the wet but unsoiled ones to clean his bottom, lifting him like a chicken by the ankles, and to wrap him round very competently with dry rags. When she had done she gave me a contemptuous look worthy of a person six times her age and sat on the floor, jouncing the baby on her lap.

I felt as though a hundred Mamas had judged me and found me wanting. I remembered how I'd always left the intimacies of baby-craft up to Rita, even with Kay and Lina, who I'd never found hideous. It had not seemed a failing in me at the time. Rita so obviously enjoyed all of that and I did not. It had always appeared merely sensible to allow each of us to follow our inclination.

To cover my feelings of inadequacy, I moved beside Violet and listened as she lamented over the sores on the toddler's skin. 'See, here,' she said. 'These are bites from bed-bugs and fleas that have become infected.'

I looked in dismay at the swollen lumps covering the child's flesh. My own skin began to itch in sympathy.

Violet turned back to the mother. 'That ointment I gave you yesterday should help. Are you using it?'

'Yes, 'm,' nodded the mother. 'And Jack 'as distempered the walls again. Bugs dain't like that. But nuffing's any real good, 'cos all them fleas and wot 'ave yer live in them walls.' She turned to me to explain. 'The walls are made wiv plaster and 'orse-hair. Bugs luv 'em.'

Violet grimaced at me. 'The housing's to blame for everything,' she said sympathetically to the woman. 'You do your best, Katie, I know you do.'

In due course Violet finished her examination of the toddler and resumed her rounds of the club room with me in tow. My skirt dried on me. For a while, until I returned home to wash it in the scullery sink downstairs, I forgot the smell, overwhelmed by new faces and impressions. If I could not quite congratulate myself on my progress, I had at least made a start.

8

As time passed the fog of poverty, thick as porridge, began to hold fewer alarms. My skin forgot to flinch when I touched these poor souls. I learned to pick up children, sodden with their own urine and hold them on my newly-aproned lap. Though I breathed shallowly.

I was proud of myself but people, especially the 'babbies,' were still not my strong point. I was happiest when preparing soup, cleaning tables or anything else impersonal. Fired up with a desire to help in a practical way, by the beginning of December I'd managed to beg a few items of clothing from friends and teachers at the school. They were mostly clothes for adults, but I thought it was as necessary to clothe them as the children. All the women I saw were dressed almost identically, their black alpaca dresses rubbed almost green with washing. On top of these they wore black blouses with high collars, a black apron and now that cold weather was here, a black shawl. Hair was coiled and pinned up in rough buns and only the hats differed from woman to woman, as if that were the one way they could express a separate identity. One regular always wore a man's flat cap jammed onto her head at a jaunty angle, another a black bonnet, much frayed, with drooping faded flowers round its rim. Yet another had a natty straw boater with a piece of moth-eaten ribbon tied round it.

I looked forward to seeing their faces at some of the clothing I had managed to assemble. I'd filled my carpet bag with them and borrowed Nina's gladstone for the rest. By the time I reached the Club, my hands were red and sore from the weight of them, but I was filled with happy anticipation.

I spread the clothes out on two tables and, sure enough, inevitable children roiling and moiling around them, the women ambled over, prodded the garments and turned them over, very much as if such good stuff filled them with disdain. I guessed this was a matter of pride; they wanted to appear as if they chose to wear the clothes they did and that such unwonted finery was something they had in quantity back home, but had chosen not to wear today.

Eventually, one woman lifted up a white blouse with a pretty lace frill down the front. 'How much fer this?' she asked.

'It's free,' I said. 'Take whatever you like.'

The woman recoiled. 'I dain't tek charity. Theer's stuff as good as this at t'second-hand stall in ower street.'

I was baffled until Violet wrenched herself away from examining some of the babies with kindly Doctor Hayes, who gave his time when he could.

'A rumpus, I see,' she said with a smile. 'What's the matter?' She turned to face the group of angry women.

'It's one thing havin' a cuppa tea wiv yer,' said an older woman, Ellen. 'But we'll not be patronised.' She waved in the direction of the clothes.

I recoiled, horrified. Patronised! I was guilty of that very evil of which Michael had accused the English when they tried to be kind, including by implication Mama and myself. As I inwardly reeled, the fracas continued around me.

'Wot's this woman doin'? Tellin' us we ain't good enough dressed fer the likes of 'er?'

'Bloomin' cheek! Tell 'er to tek 'em back wiv 'er. We wunt wear 'em.'

Violet pointed out that I meant no harm, that I meant to be kind, not to patronise anyone.

'Well tell 'er to goo on out the dower and tek her bleedin' rags wiv 'er.'

This last was yelled by a hard-faced woman called Elsie, who I'd had a run-in with once before. She was a trouble-maker, liked nothing better than to have a good slanging match. Why she came at all I didn't know because most of the other women gave her a wide berth.

With Elsie alternating her black looks between Violet and myself, I stepped forward. 'I'm sorry if I've given offence,' I said. 'I didn't mean to but I'll know better next time. What if we said a penny per garment, and the money will go towards improving this Club?'

I looked at Violet for approval and she nodded.

'Well I ain't gotta penny to 'and over fer rags the likes of these,' Elsie bellowed and stalked off, but not far, I noticed.

Violet pulled me away and sent another helper to take the pennies. 'You'll only rile them further,' she said. 'Better let someone neutral oversee them now. There's a group of children over there. Why don't you help with them? Send Evelyn over here instead, and you make dolls with her group of little girls.'

'I'm sorry, Violet. A lesson learned.'

'There's no pride greater than that of the poor. The only thing they have left to them is their spirit of independence. We must respect that.'

On the far side of the room I helped the children make their dolls out of old black stockings filled with straw, twisted rag limbs sewn on and red woollen lips. Bits of straw were allowed to protrude for hair and one of the children had brought in some damaged buttons for eyes. Her mother worked in a button factory, so it was a neighbour who brought this child along, with a gaggle of her own.

For a time I was happily lost in the creation of dolls, which caused us all much laughter as the mis-matched buttons lent them such strange expressions. We gave them names and it was touching to see these little girls cuddling the dolls with such tenderness.

'I love this dollie,' said one little mite. 'Can I tek 'er wiv me?'

'You made it. So of course you can,' I said, pleased that at least the children weren't riven with the same stubborn pride as their mothers.

———

In the lull of mid-afternoon, when the mothers extracted their children and took them home, and we waited for the more lonely later visitors, Violet and I sat down with a cup of tea. I had noticed that all the clothes on the table had gone and Violet showed the little heap of pennies she'd got for them. 'Though I don't suppose you'd be surprised if I told you that I saw Elsie take a couple of items and stuff them down the front of her blouse.'

'Never!' I said, laughing. 'So taking charity is not done, but stealing is quite acceptable!'

'That's the way it is,' said Violet with a shrug.

———

On my first visit here there had been two girls sleeping at a table. I hadn't seen them since and had almost forgotten about them. Around four o'clock on this December Monday they came in like shadows and took up a table in the furthest corner of the room. I went over to welcome them, taking with me some soup and bread, which they fell on with gratitude.

After they'd mopped round the bowl with their bread and sighed with satisfaction I asked their names and ages. They could have been sisters, so alike were they in looks. Twins perhaps, I'd thought. But no, they turned out not to be related. At least not directly, though the tangle of families living in close proximity meant there was likely to be some shared ancestry. Their names were Millie and Sarah and they were twelve and thirteen respectively, though their pinched little faces looked older.

I compared them to the girls I taught. How healthy, strong and, above all, young my pupils seemed. They had no cares to wear them out. They shone like jewels, precious to their families and to themselves. Even Jane Evans looked a different breed from these two. It was hard to see any of that shine in the two girls facing me over the table top. Their skins were grey-white, the unnatural damp sheen of creatures living their lives buried beneath layers of soil, out of the sun. Even their hair lacked the lift that made that of my pupils appear to fizz with energy. And their eyes were full of a knowledge that no person so young should have.

I asked them both why they had come.

'Sumtimes we wait till the littl'uns goo. But we're 'ere lots o' afternoons. It's yow who ain't,' answered Sarah, the older of the two.

This was true of course and made me realise how I'd begun to live from Monday to Monday, as I became more immersed in the workings of the Club. The times in between had become a blur of lessons, faces, marking and preparation in the evenings, and trips out to the countryside north of Aston with Nina and Amy on fine weekends.

Wednesdays I had not forgotten Miss Derris and the elementary school and, when I didn't need to catch up on school work, I spent those afternoons, sometimes with Nina too, listening to the stumbled reading of the children there. Lately I'd taken with me one or two of the reading primers Nina had found in the preparatory department, not without trepidation that this borrowing might be found out and condemned as theft, though every time we returned them on the following day.

'Do you go to school?' I asked the girls.

'Sumtimes,' said Millie evasively.

'When her Mum don't need 'er to mind the kids,' put in her friend. 'Me, I've left school now and I'm lookin' fer work. It'll 'elp me Mum no end,' she finished proudly.

I ascertained that both their mothers worked when they could, but noticed that neither girl met my eyes when they told me this.

'Our muvvers are friends, see,' explained Sarah. 'We live back-to back in the same court, so we've been friends too, since we were babbies.'

'And your fathers?'

'Hers is dead,' Sarah replied. 'The pinchers took mine away but 'e'll be back afower too long. He only got two months. Then I 'spect 'e'll goo on back to the coal-yard where 'e works.'

'Things must be tight for you both then,' I said sympathetically.

'Oh, it's not soo bad,' said Sarah. 'Me Mam's got Poor Relief till 'e's home, but it ain't never enough. We tek stuff to Uncle too, every Monday, when they's clean. That gives us pennies for the gas. But sometimes we cain't get 'em back again. So that's no good. And wivout ower Dad, Billie dain't work either.'

'Who's Billie?' I asked.

This time Millie answered. 'He's her bruvver, only seven, but soo proud to do a man's work with his Dad. We'd watch them cum back from work and strip down at the tap, Billie and 'is Dad. First 'is Dad would wash the black dust orf 'is self, then Billie would, wiv the same expression on 'is face. But now Billie 'as to stay round ower yard and 'e en't 'appy.'

'Always up to mischief 'e is, out on the peck playin' pitch an' toss wiv the bigger lads.'

'Still,' said Millie,' sumtimes 'e wins and brings a few pence back wiv 'im.'

'Why can't your uncle, if he's got money, lend you some more? Till your father's back at least.'

The girls laughed.

'Uncle's the popshop,' Millie explained.

'Look at 'er,' said Sarah. 'She still don't understand.' She leaned forward, elbows on the table and spoke very slowly, separating each word. 'Everyone in our court, when the washing's done, presses the clean clothes and teks 'em down to Uncle's, the popshop...to pawn them. Then, at end of week, we buy 'em back again, if we can.'

'What if you can't?' I was appalled. I'd never imagined life could be like this.

Sarah shrugged. 'We goo wivout.'

'That's why she's lookin' fer work. And I do the odd job when I can. To help out, like.'

'What sort of work are you looking for, Sarah?' I asked.

She shrugged. 'Metal casting of sum kind, I 'spect. It's 'evvy work fer a lass, but the pay's better than moost jobs.'

Millie's eyes were drooping and I noticed her head flopping forward and recovering with an effort. I apologised for keeping them when they were so obviously tired and suggested they went home to bed.

'Noo, thank yer,' said Sarah with some dignity. 'We'll sleep 'ere fer a bit.'

'Theer's no sleep fer us at ower place.'

Violet was busy talking to Dr Hayes, a concerned look on her face so, rather bewildered, I left the girls and sought out one of the other helpers. The only one available was Mrs Hardy, an elderly woman who always wore an old-fashioned frilled black dress and a large white apron, so stiff with starch that it stood out from the dress like a board.

Mrs Hardy was very unforthcoming in the normal way. She was kind to the women and would sometimes sit with them, listening but largely silent. Usually, though, she busied herself round the edges, always cleaning and, when she was not, filling the copper to make more of the endless cups of tea the visitors consumed.

Since this lady was the only one available, it was to her I had to address my questions about the two youngsters.

'They're not the only young girls who come here, you know,' said Mrs Hardy, rather snappishly. 'And a good thing they and all these women have this as a refuge.'

I agreed and waited, hoping for more information. Meanwhile Mrs Hardy sighed, picked up a pile of dirty cloths and took them over to the sink in the corner of the room. She took some hot water from the copper, carried it over to the sink in a bowl and began to push and pummel the cloths around with a large bar of carbolic soap.

I looked around at the room. There was a group of older women sitting at a table. I'd sat with them before. They were friendly enough, but it was always clear they could hardly wait to get back to the good gossip they were enjoying. This was the time, when it was quiet, that I usually left and went home myself. I was tired and thought longingly of warm sheets and blankets. But I would have to wait. With the darkness rolling in earlier, it wouldn't be safe for me to leave on my own. I'd had this drummed into me by Nina, Violet and others. Especially to be avoided was the time just after six o'clock, when the men spilled out into the streets from their long day's work and flocked into the many beerhouses in the area.

Both girls were sleeping, heads on their arms. I was puzzled by this. Surely even a bed full of siblings would be more comfortable. We'd never had a problem getting to sleep in Ireland. In fact, when we first moved to England I found it hard to sleep without Rita snuggled close.

The doctor and Violet finished their conversation and briefly he took a detour past the gaggle of women still sitting at the table.

'Not at home cooking the meal for your husbands?' he asked jocularly.

'Now, Doctor, yer know them men aren't home afower nine,' laughed one.

'And reelin' drunk too, all of 'em,' said another.

'More likely to fall through the dower and flat on 'is face snorin' than wanna eat,' added the first.

Dr Hayes turned and exchanged a look with Violet before departing.

'It's the alcohol that's at the bottom of so many of their troubles,' said Violet to me. 'No, I'm wrong. It's too easy to blame the men, but who'd want to go home to those hovels? It's the houses that are to blame. They're what need to be torn down and replaced.'

Fresh from my conversation with the two girls, I wondered how anyone could condone the men throwing away any of their precious wages on drink. 'They are taking the food from their children's mouths and the clothes from their bodies.'

'A rather dramatic way to put it, Gladys. But no, I don't condone it. I merely understand it, having seen something of the conditions in which they live.'

'Why doesn't anyone do anything about those conditions then?' I asked automatically, shoving out of my memory the unwelcome thought of Bertie with his promise of new houses. Would he keep his word?

Violet didn't answer. I looked at her more closely, noticed that she looked grey-faced and more tired than usual. I tore my mind away from my conversation with the girls and saw again Dr Hayes' anxious face. I took Violet over to an empty table and sat her down.

'Thank you, Gladys. That's very kind.' She fell silent as she sipped a tea, brought from the shadows by Mrs Hardy, and I curbed my tongue to allow her space. Finally, 'I know you asked a question about the housing,' she continued, 'and the answer is no one cares except us women, it seems. The Council don't care and the Government certainly doesn't care. Anyway, they're all men. They don't have the compassion that we women do. There's a meeting in a couple of weeks' time by a group of women suffragists, in the Town Hall, and I think I'll go along to it. Why don't you come too?'

'What does a group of suffragists have to do with slum housing?'

Violet shot me a startled look. 'Sometimes, Gladys, I wonder which planet you live on. You're concerned enough about the plight of the poor to give your time here freely, but can't you see that nothing we do here does more than scratch the surface of the problem? It's like rubbing salve onto a festering sore. The salve alleviates the outer skin but does not reach the cause deep within the body, which will keep on surfacing and spreading out its spores.'

She blinked and put her head in her hands. 'Oh, Gladys, the doctor has told me of an epidemic of mumps running through the hovels. Two of those babies he looked at earlier had it and will likely die. It will kill many of the young and the weak. It has taken that good doctor years of telling the women in the area not to allow their children to drink from the canal running at the back of their streets. Cholera epidemics are less common now, thanks to him. But the canal still runs, foul smelling and evil, and its banks are a tempting playground for the young. It's only a matter of time before that disease returns. Because they have no gardens, no ground given over to them for play. And children must play.' She came to a halt, close to tears.

I passed over my hankie, but she waved it away. Calmer now, she said in a firm voice. 'So I will go and see what the suffragists have to say because women are so helpless to change anything. Nor are women listened to in the corridors of power, where their voices could count. Who knows, suffrage may be the answer to all this.'

'I'd like to know what the suffragists say,' I said. 'The meeting sounds interesting, but we're reaching the end of term and the school's in a frenzy of activity. I'm not even sure I'll be able to come here again until after Christmas – I was going to warn you. So I'll be busy until next term begins. Going to a meeting isn't a possibility, I'm afraid.'

'Pity,' said Violet and got up to resume her rounds of the room.

Pleased with how things are flowing out of me now that I have reached my time in Birmingham, I have given the first part of my memoir to Truda. I enjoy seeing her smile with pleasure as she reads about my childhood and hearing her laugh aloud when she realises how naive and clumsy I was in my first efforts at the Club.

'Are you being too hard on yourself?' she asks as she turns over the last page. 'There's a lot of soul-searching.'

'I thought that was what this was supposed to be about. And I made a lot of mistakes.' I flinch inwardly and whisper: 'Particularly about Nina.'

'Find the truth,' is all she says and 'Don't wallow.' Then she reaches a hand out to me and covers mine, aware that she has hurt me. She changes the subject. 'Is the Millie you've just mentioned the one who ...?

'Yes,' I smile. 'That's where I first met her,' and I feel my face relax in pleasure as I bring her face in front of me: her wiry dark hair, her determined little face. How strong and tall she became once she'd begun to work with me for the Cause.

'I wonder what would have happened if you'd gone to that meeting with Violet,' Truda mused. 'How much longer was it till you joined?'

I laughed. 'Years! Frustrating years too, where I tried to effect change through my own efforts. Another example of my naivete. And obstinacy.'

'Call it persistence. It's an admirable quality of yours,' says Truda. 'And I can't wait to read the next part.'

9

As it happened I had time for just one more visit to the
school, where I was welcomed by Miss Derris. Nina
wasn't with me. In fact it was some time since she'd been. The
closer to the end of term, the more she shut herself off and
stayed over and above her allotted times at King Edward's,
absorbing herself in school-life, offering extra duties. She
looked increasingly pale. Gone was the confident, boisterous
Nina that I'd first met. She'd withdrawn into herself.

When I showed sympathy, she shrugged it away. I asked
her if there was anyone else who could help at home – until
she found someone to take over. I still clung to the idea that
she would come back to the job she loved as soon as possible
but when I reminded her of it she gave me a scathing look.

'There is only me,' she said. 'A neighbour keeps me up
with events and has told me that Mother is now as good
as bed-ridden. I didn't believe it at first; I'm so used to her
pretences. But perhaps it is true and she really is sick. Only
this neighbour, who is elderly herself, lives close enough to
visit regularly and make sure she is eating. She needs proper
food and care and I am the only one available to give it. So I've
decided. No … don't say a word, Glad. I know you mean well.

But I have to do the right thing. I shall limp on until the end of this term, but I have already told Miss Nimmo that I shall not be able to return. She is looking for someone to fill my place. I love teaching, you know I do. I love being my own person. But I owe my mother a daughter's duty.' After this long speech, which came after days of miserable silence, Nina stomped off.

I explained Nina's absence and her circumstances to Miss Derris at the end of the day, after the children had filed away to their homes and the little slate monitor had also left. She was sympathetic. 'It's hard sometimes, being a woman,' she said. 'So much rests on us. We are supposed to keep the home and family yet we also want to work.' She laughed. 'At least, some of us do. Others see being married as work. And from some of the men I've met, perhaps they're right. Marriage might, after all, be the hardest job of all. Do you think you will marry, Miss Hazel?'

I thought of Bill Waterfield, what I'd felt for a while about him, who would soon marry Rita. He was in Canada at present, with a cousin, looking at the possibility of living out there. Then I thought of Michael and shook my head. I'd loved him as a child and had never forgotten him. Did he ever think of me?

'I don't know,' I answered. 'What about you?'

'I think not. But aren't we lucky to have that choice? There's nothing to beat the satisfaction of what I do with these children. If I left, they might get another like Mr Keane. I wouldn't wish that on any child, let alone these, who with all their faults I've grown to love.'

'I feel the same. My teaching job is nothing like as exhausting as yours. Though I do have the marking of exercise books – at least with slates you don't have that!'

We laughed and were thoroughly companionable as we cleaned and tidied the room ready for the next day. When it was time to go, we walked together till the end of the street before we turned our separate ways. I did not quite know what the time was, but it was at least a long time before the danger hour when the men left work so, although the light was beginning to seep from the sky, I decided to walk home.

The walk took me past some of the entrances to the mean streets of the poor. I avoided these, keeping only to the main routes, busy with small shops and little businesses. Suddenly, ahead, I could hear a rumpus. Raised voices, a flurry of action, which I couldn't quite make out in the gathering gloom.

All at once running footsteps headed my way and a crowd of youths hurtled down the road towards me. They were pursued by another gang of a similar age and stones were being hurled. One flew past and hit the wall of the building closest to me. I cringed against the wall, but still they came on, the first cluster turning now to face their opponents.

I had heard of these battles between rival slogging-gangs, who sought to claim a street or an area as their own territory. Now it seemed I was caught up in the middle of one. I did the only thing I could think of, picked up my skirts and ran round the nearest corner into one of the narrow streets. I didn't stop running until I was some way down, slipping and stumbling over the uneven cobbles. Then I looked back and saw the mouth of the alleyway where I'd entered was blocked. The fight had moved on and one gang was using it as a barrier to duck into and dart out from, armed with fresh stones. Howls and abuse accompanied the throwing of their chosen weapons, which were hurled with alarming accuracy.

I flattened myself against the wall as a couple of youths came further up the street towards me and began to dig with knives into the cobbles. Before long, one had lifted up a large stone and was charging out to wield it at the enemy. The other, muttering under his breath, still dug with his knife, loosening the cobble with his other hand.

I looked behind me and saw an opening a few paces away. It was an entry into one of the courts of back-to-backs, the most usual set-up for slum dwellings in this area. The opening was shadowed and very dark. Still peering around the corner to follow the course of the battle, I did not at once realise that I was not alone in my hiding place. I could hear grunting and heavy breathing, the rustle of material and a man's voice. There was a couple close by, just the other side of the entry, doing what?

I was about to go and see when a hand grabbed me from behind and pulled me away.

'Wot're you doin', Miss?' said a familiar voice.

The light from the street's single lamp fell on a white face floating in the darkness.

'Millie?'

'Yeah, Miss, it's me. Cum away now. Please. Cum away.'

'What for?'

'D'you really not know, Miss? That's Sarah, that is, wiv a man friend. Best we leave 'em to it.'

'But she's just a child,' I said, as understanding flooded in.

'Yes, Miss. But theea's no room for children in ower world. We just 'ave to get by. Do ower bit ter put food on the table.'

'You mean …?'

'Yes, Miss. It's normal. Most of us do it at sum time or other. And ower mothers as well, when they has ter. It's time y' knew. That's why we goo sumtimes to the Club ter get sum sleep. Ter stop the men botherin' us when we're home.'

'Bothering you? What men?' I could hardly breathe for shock.

'Cum away, please, Miss.' She plucked at my sleeve, and I moved further off with her, to where the sounds of the man's panting breath, as he did the unspeakable to a mere child, didn't swamp my ability to think.

I shook Millie's shoulders. 'What men?' I repeated. 'Who could do this to you and Sarah?' I had some vague idea that if I knew who it was I could do something about it. I wanted very much to pull that animal off little Sarah and perhaps Millie realised this and took me further off for that reason.

'Me Mum sumtimes does it in ower house, upstairs in ower bedroom. I was up theea meself, sleepin' cos me brothers 'n' sisters were at school, when my uncle came in. He were dead drunk.' She turned her face away, but I could still see it gleaming palely. 'He thought I were me Mum.'

'Her brother?' Horror piled on horror.

'No, me Dad's.'

I reached out to stroke her hair. 'No wonder you sleep at the Club when you can.'

Perhaps my sympathy unleashed something in her, because out tumbled stories of prostitution and unwanted pregnancies; abortions performed by neighbour women that resulted in death; children her age walking the streets to feed the babies, that themselves were the result of rape. The dreadful catalogue went on and on until I could take no more, but pulled away from Millie's restraining hand.

I saw the man leave the entry, where he had been with Sarah, and made a move to pursue him, with what intent I couldn't say. I was beyond thought. I wanted to hit him with every force I could muster. I wanted to beat him into a pulp.

Millie pulled me back. 'No, Miss. It's not yower place. Sarah wouldn't thank yer, she'll 've teken a few pence fer 'er trouble, and the man would laugh in yer face. Or hit yer. Yower not very big, Miss.'

My body was so rigid with tension that I shook, not in the helpless way that intense cold brings on, but because every muscle in my body was in a kind of spasm. Nor could I speak. The muscles in my throat wouldn't allow it. In any case, what could I say? Millie had told me everything in such a matter-of-fact manner, that I was left incapable of response.

As if she sensed this, she took me gently by the arm and pointed out that the fight had stopped, or moved away. The street ahead was clear.

Not long after this the Christmas break finally arrived, the end of my first term as a teacher. To cope with it at all, I had to bury all I'd learned from Millie deep in my memory, but it surfaced in nightmare visions when I slept. Luckily for my peace of mind the end of term had indeed, as I'd warned Violet, been full of too many extra duties – examinations and the marking of them, in particular.

The thought of home pulled me now like a promise of peace and normality, while at the same time guilt at leaving the women who helped in the Club pulled me the other way. Did Violet know about the young prostitutes that came to the Club? I suspected she did, but I began seriously to consider staying in Aston over Christmas and going to the Club to help in whatever capacity I could. I planned toys I could make for the children but knew better than to think of presents for the women themselves.

In the end it was Miss Nimmo, my headmistress, who decided what I should do.

She called me into her study at the end of the last day of term. 'How do you feel your first term here has been?' she began.

I felt wrong-footed. 'Have I not been satisfactory?' I asked in a voice that came out squeaky with tension. Had my work suffered from my increasing emotional commitment to the Club and the elementary school?

'Why do you ask that?' she answered kindly. 'Your pupils have responded well to you. Their grammar and spelling have improved noticeably and some are showing promise in their imaginative writing. You have nothing to be ashamed of. That is not why I called you in.'

I shifted in my seat, found it difficult to meet her eyes, for reasons I could not understand.

'Miss Hazel, my faith in you is paying off, just as I expected, but I'm concerned about the toll it appears to be making on your health. If you don't look after yourself better you won't be able to cope. Teaching is a vocation that drains the energy more than people realise. You need to find ways of replenishing yourself.'

I bowed my head. 'Thank you, Miss Nimmo. I will try. I do get too excited to remember to eat sometimes.'

That made her laugh. 'I know. It's that excitement in you that makes for a good teacher. But feed yourself both physically and spiritually. Both areas need replenishment. A good rest at home with your family will help. Build up your strength, Miss Hazel. Do not neglect yourself.'

When I left her office I reordered my plans. I would spend Christmas itself with my family, but just for a short period. I would go back soon after, replenished as Miss Nimmo suggested, and devote myself to a different course: not just to helping in the Club, but finding out more about the slums themselves. I would explore the area and make up a document of living conditions with which to arm myself. For what I didn't yet know. At least it would allow me more understanding of the inmates of those hovels. Two people, Nina and Violet, had accused me of what amounted to naivete, so that was the area of my character I would try to tackle.

For now, it was as if Miss Nimmo's words had given me permission to let go. She was right. What good would I be in any area of my life if my health broke down? Acceptance of this fact made me aware of a deep-down exhaustion. Every muscle in my body ached from the tension in which I habitually held myself. When was the last time I'd slept a full night through, without last minute marking by the glow of a feeble candle so as not to disturb Nina with the hissing gas-light, or tossing in my bed haunted by the faces of Millie and Sarah? Home, my family, re-entered my thoughts like a beacon.

10

The last morning with Nina was emotional. Before I headed off home for the school holidays, I pushed a few clothes into my carpet bag, making sure the gifts I'd bought and wrapped for the family were well protected. Nina sat on her bed and watched me. There was no sign of her packing or preparing herself to go home. She looked glum so, with one last check of my bags – I didn't want to leave anything behind for the Cartwright to nose through in our absence – I sat down opposite her. I told her how much I would miss her next term and that I felt sure she would be back before long.

'All you need is a week or two to make other arrangements for your mother. She will understand, I'm sure, how much your work means to you. Why, if it were me I couldn't stand it for a moment ...'

'I'm not you,' Nina muttered, in a strange stifled kind of voice. 'Even if I couldn't stand being shut up with my mother day after day with no one but her to talk to, even if that is what I have to do I have no other choice. It is what Fate has visited on me.'

I was struck by the melodramatic tone and the oddity of her language and moved to touch her but, shrugging me off,

Nina got to her feet and squeezed along the far side of my bed to open the window. Despite the coldness of the weather, she flung it open as far as it would go and hung out, gulping air as if it were life itself. When she closed it again and returned to sit back on her bed, her face was wiped of emotion but for a small stiff smile and the tone of her voice was bright.

We talked for a little about my own Christmas plans, the kind of Christmas we always had with such a large family, but how I intended to pull myself away and return before term began to help Violet at the Club.

'You're so lucky having a family. I always wished I had a sister. Brothers would maybe have been nice too, but I don't have much experience of boys. A sister, however, that must be like having a built-in friend.'

'It is very special,' I agreed, thinking of Rita. 'Though we have our moments. There's rivalry between sisters that are close in age, and jealousy at times. But on the whole, yes, it's wonderful...' I would have said more but I could tell that Nina wasn't listening.

'I shall miss this room,' she said, looking blindly around. 'And this area. I plan to spend a few days visiting some of my favourite spots. Before I go.'

I looked at her, puzzled. Her shoulders were slumped and she was looking vaguely past me and out of the window. Poor Nina, she was most unlike herself. I went over and stood beside her, though what she saw in the panorama of brick houses I failed to see.

'It's not a life sentence, you know, Nina, even if you do have to look after her for a while. You're a qualified teacher. Perhaps you won't have to be a nursemaid for very long and then you can go back to work. You might even be able to teach at King Edwards' again.' I meant to comfort her and for a brief moment her face lit up into the old grin that I knew.

'You mean my mother might die soon?'

'No, of course not. Oh, Nina, you know what I meant. I'm not trying to finish your poor mother off. I probably phrased what I said wrongly.'

'You don't always stop and think before you speak, Glad. It's one of the things about you that I find rather endearing. I'll miss you, you irritating, well-meaning goody-good.' She turned clumsily and gave me a hug, nearly knocking me back onto the bed. 'Sorry, sorry. Have I hurt you?'

'Not a bit. I'll miss you too. I don't want another stranger in this room, even for a short time while I try to find somewhere else. I suppose it's likely to be your replacement ...'

Nina turned away.

'Oh dear, that was clumsy again. I didn't mean to rub it in. I only meant that no one could possibly replace you. You've been such a good friend to me. Woken me up in the areas where I needed it. Pushed me into places I didn't want to go, but am beginning now to value.' I faltered to a stop, close to tears. 'I've got you a little Christmas present. Well, it's something I made with the children at the Club and I thought it would amuse you. Here.'

I pushed over my gift, wrapped in tissue paper. She opened it slowly, her fingers lingering over the wrappings. Finally, she pulled out one of the dolls we'd made. It's mismatched button eyes, both blue, but one significantly smaller, made it look as though it was winking and made her laugh.

'I'll treasure it,' she said, stroking its spiky hair. 'Really. It'll remind me of you and of the Club. Couldn't be more perfect.' She kissed it on its wide red mouth and laid it on her bed. 'Now I shan't miss you so much tonight after all.'

'It looks a bit like you,' I teased. 'Don't you think it has a kind of strong, determined look, with a bit of laughter always waiting to burst out?'

'Is that how you see me?' Nina's face was very pale. 'Oh, Gladys...' She appeared to be about to say more but turned instead and began to dig around in the little cupboard between our beds. When she straightened, her face was flushed. 'I didn't buy you anything for Christmas. Had a lot on my mind. But perhaps you'd like these.' She handed me some flowery handkerchiefs, neatly folded, and made of a kind of muslin instead of the usual cotton.

'They're beautiful.' A faint scent rose up from them and I buried my nose in the delicate material. 'It's much too nice a present. They're treasures. Whose were they?'

'My grandmother's. I never use them. Don't suppose I ever will. Please have them. I shall like to think of them in your possession. Oh, and... I nearly forgot.' Now she had pulled the curtain of our wardrobe aside. 'Please have these too. I'll have no need of them where I'm going.' She held out her heavy walking boots. I'd seen them on her every weekend that we'd cycled out to the countryside and walked by a canal or through the meadows.

'No, Nina. These are too good. You won't be stuck inside the house with your mother all day, you'll need them.'

'They may not fit you, I suppose.' Her face had fallen. 'Try them on.'

'I do have feet like spades,' I laughed.

'Me too,' she said. 'But they've been good feet, carried me well.'

I pushed a tentative foot into the right boot and laced it up. 'It does fit. Who'd have thought it? But you must have them back. You sounded as though you were saying goodbye to your feet then, and that's just silly.'

'Silly or not, they're too heavy for me to lug home. I've got so much stuff.'

'Nonsense!' I thrust the boots back at her. 'Wear them on the train. You'll thank me later. But the hankies are really special... if you're sure.'

'I'm sure, dear Gladys. Now go. Don't miss your train.'

She wouldn't hug me, said it would make her cry. Instead, she backed away towards the window. Beyond her I could see the houses stretching into the distance, spiked with the occasional steeple. The light from the window blurred the outline of her body, so that she looked insubstantial. It might have been the water that filled my eyes for I could not make out her face. It looked drowned, featureless, as if she had already travelled beyond and left just a fading memory of her behind.

'Write to me. Tell me how you're doing. You haven't even given me your address. You said you would.'

'I'll leave it with the Cartwright. Now, go.'

I hurried down the stairs, aware I'd taken too long. My face was wet with tears. I hadn't expected that. But at least Nina had sounded firm at the end, as if she'd come to terms with her future. I would write, after Christmas. It would be good to remain friends.

11

'You're too thin,' were the first words from Mama as I cycled up the drive.

'And wet,' laughed Rita. 'Don't you have a brolly?'

'You can't ride a bicycle with its basket full of presents and hold a brolly. I'm not the best of cyclists at any time.'

'I know,' said Rita, always more athletic than I. 'That's because you're never in the moment. You wobble along in a dream.'

I hugged her so hard, then Mama. How precious they were. All at once Birmingham and its dark underworld seemed like something seen through the wrong end of a telescope.

All three of the boys were round the dining-room table tussling with Jim's latest board game. Duncan's face looked chubbier, but the other two lifted identical long narrow faces to me.

The game was quickly abandoned.

'It was impossible anyway,' said Duncan, rolling his eyes.

'It does perhaps need more thought,' Jim said reluctantly.

'But the idea's promising,' said Edgar to cheer Jim up. 'How are you, big sis? How did you get here?'

'I cycled of course.'

'All the way from Birmingham?' asked Duncan, impressed.

'No, silly. I took the bicycle on the train to Didcot and cycled from there.'

All three pairs of eyes looked at me. I felt re-absorbed, as if my time away from them had sucked me dry and now, like a thirsty plant, I drank deep of their familiarity. I wondered if all people when they left home, encountered the wider world, felt the same: cast up, dessicated by the hot air of foreign emotions. I must ask Jim. He'd been a Marine for some years now. How had loosing the anchor ropes felt to him?

And then I was enfolded in a rocking group of bear-hugs where I was passed from one to the other like a parcel.

'Where're Kay and Lina?' I finally managed out of thoroughly squeezed lungs.

Edgar made a face. 'Out in the stable, I expect, with Lina's latest find.'

I waited for further explanation.

'Lina has become obsessed with saving every damaged creature she can. Today it's a rabbit she found in a snare. She'll be making a nest for it.'

'It's quite a menagerie out there,' put in Duncan.

'I'll go and find them while I'm still wet.'

They didn't hear me when I entered the sweet-smelling stable. The pony, Bracken, bent round to look, a wisp of hay drooping from her mouth, but the girls were bent over a wooden apple box. I squatted down next to them.

'Hello, you two.'

'Gladys, Gladys, how wonderful! When did you get here?' Kay jumped up but Lina remained by the box and only turned her head up to smile.

'Just arrived. It's so good to be home.'

'Look at the poor rabbit,' said Lina. 'How can anyone do such a thing?' She lifted the little creature, its sides heaving, frantic with terror and pain. One of its back legs was half sliced through from the cruel wire. I knew just from looking at it that the creature would die. I knew too that I hadn't the courage to say so to Lina.

Lina stroked the ears flat along the animal's back and replaced it in the box, full of straw and with handfuls of grass and weeds for its repast. Her eyes were huge with sorrow. 'I'll return soon to check on you,' she told the rabbit. Have a lovely rest now.' Then she struggled to her feet and took my hand.

There was something wonderful about Lina, something that none of us had. She had a quiet way with her, which drew creatures in. Even unknown dogs wagged their entire bodies with enthusiasm at sight of her, and flattened themselves for her caress. Cats, too, lifted their tales like masts at sight of her and wiped round her ankles. Now she was turning the torch of her compassion onto other creatures.

Walking back through the orchard I squeezed Lina's hand. With a jolt of recognition I realised that here was a kindred spirit, another person who had found a cause and was, like me, throwing as much of her energy into it as she could. Ashamed, I realised that I had marginalised Lina since her birth, seen her as less than she was because of her crooked spine which had never straightened as she grew, though all of us had hoped and prayed for that to be so. Just because she had an imperfect body I had made the mistake of seeing her as a lesser human being. And she was emphatically not. Perhaps she had more love in her than the rest of us put together.

'You're not listening,' protested Kay on my other side. 'I told you all about this boy who Mama doesn't approve of and you haven't heard a word!'

'What boy? And why doesn't Mama like him?'

'You see? I told you all this already. Honestly!' She ran ahead, picking up her skirts to avoid the soaking grass.

Lina turned to me. 'He's a boy from the village who she met at the Church Social Club. He's just an ordinary boy, but he's nice.' She looked thoughtful. 'Probably he's not quite right for Kay,' she admitted. 'But she likes him, which makes it all right, doesn't it? That's all that matters, that they like each other?'

'We-ell. I'd have to meet him to make a judgement of any kind, Lina. But she is only eighteen. I expect Mama has a point. What does Papa say?'

'He's not giving an opinion.' Lina unconsciously took on Papa's tone and I laughed, instantly saw him in my mind's eye clamping his teeth down onto his pipe stem, his eyebrows raised.

'I expect he's right. Perhaps he can see that it won't last. I mean, how do they meet? It's over a mile to the village.'

'She takes one of the boy's bicycles. Oh!' Lina clamped her mouth shut. 'I shouldn't have said that,' she added through gritted teeth. 'I promised.'

I sensed an impending drama. Christmas looked to be more lively than I'd envisaged.

That first evening meal was a delight. Everyone plied me with questions about my classes, the girls I taught and what I taught them. I felt lit up from within by their interest and wallowed in the telling. It rekindled all the love of the work I was doing and banished the shades of the darker Birmingham.

'Who's your favourite?' asked Kay cheekily. 'I bet you have one – secretly.'

'I don't, I really don't.' But it was true. In every class there were one or two faces in particular that formed a gallery in my head, whose interest in poetry or Shakespeare had fired me to greater efforts.

'All right then,' said Duncan. 'If not a favourite then someone you don't like.'

'It's not that I don't like any one of them,' I responded. 'But some are more difficult than others, it's true.' And I amused them with tales of Frances in one of the younger classes who had got up in the middle of a lesson, sneaked behind me and then run up and down the keys of the open piano against the wall. 'She's a very small girl for her age, perhaps a little undernourished and I just picked her up bodily and carried her over to her chair where I plonked her down. She wriggled so much that I had to hold her there by pushing down on the top of her head to keep her still. Her hair was wild and wiry, like a brush, and felt unpleasant.' I pulled a face and the others laughed. 'And then she protested so loudly at my treatment of her, set up such a caterwauling, that Miss Bragge came in and rescued me. Though she was divided in her blame afterwards in the staff room.'

'Isn't Miss Bragge the one you wrote about?' asked Rita. 'The one who doesn't like you?'

'I don't think she likes anyone who is younger than she is. It's not personal. She's the Second Mistress, a Deputy to the Head, and has a face like a walnut being pinched in a nutcracker. I don't think she enjoys anything very much and young people in particular have been put on earth to be disciplined within an inch of their lives. A good child is not just neat and obedient but also without opinions and would never, never interrupt.'

'How can a person like that be a teacher?' wondered Lina.

'To be fair,' I conceded, 'she's quite popular with the older girls and her lessons are said to be lively. It's just a personal thing with me, I expect. She didn't take to me from the start.'

'I expect she started out with all the best intentions, like our Gladys here, but something disappointed her and made her like she is now,' said Mama in her generous way.

Lina, who had inherited her kind spirit, agreed, but Jim and the two younger boys argued that some people went in to teaching because they enjoyed the power it gave them. Torturing the young with punishments for any show of high spirits was all that gave them pleasure. 'There's one in every school,' said Jim and all three of the boys regaled us with stories of their past school days.

Through my laughter, I spluttered that both the younger boys must have been every teacher's idea of hell.

'We were good in class,' protested Duncan. 'Mostly.'

'Only because you weren't in the same classes,' said Jim. 'In the dormitories and in our house it was another story. You were always being hauled in front of the house master.'

'I can imagine,' I laughed.

'Be careful you don't turn into a crab like Miss Bragge. It's a very real danger,' warned Edgar solemn-faced, miffed at our teasing, and I clouted him.

'Now boys, time to help your mother with the clearing up,' Papa, his own smile lop-sided around his pipe-stem, interrupted a whole table descending into giggles and companionable romping.

I caught his eye, then looked around happily. It was good to be home.

Later that evening, Rita came into my room and plumped herself down on the edge of my bed. She looked a little down in the dumps.

'What's up,' I asked. 'Missing Bill?'

'Every day,' she sighed. 'He's been gone such a long time and writes so seldom.'

Oh dear, I thought. Was Bill drifting away? Had Canada and those Columbian mountains claimed him, like Ulysses among the lotus-eaters?

'I know what you're thinking,' she continued. 'Don't worry, he still loves me. All his letters are about the land he and cousin Horace have bought, right amongst the mountains, and the house he is building for us to live in. Horace's house had to be built first – that's why it's taken so long – because his wife Elspeth is already with him and they've a baby on the way. It's just that it's so dull waiting for each letter and missing him so much. Sometimes I wish I'd never met him, settled like Kay for someone closer at hand.'

'Who is Kay seeing? Do Mama and Papa …?'

She put her finger to her lips, but her eyes danced. 'Tell you later. Anyway, I always knew Bill was addicted to adventure and travel, so I shouldn't be surprised. Don't you remember, he always talked of far-off places when he and Victor came to dinner? Edgar and Duncan as little boys hung on his every word. It's Bill that Mama blames for those boys' desire to join the East India Company.'

"But he will come back for you, won't he?"

'When the house is finished I suppose.' She brightened. 'Then we'll get married. Oh, Gladys, it's not before time. I feel I'm getting old. I'm twenty-four already and all the girls I know of that age are already hitched and mothers of two at least. Except you, of course.'

I didn't like the *of course* and must have showed it because she got abruptly up from the bed and wandered over to finger the clothes hanging in my wardrobe.

'Is this what you wear teaching?' She felt the coarse cloth of my black skirt.

I nodded. 'With a white blouse usually, though I have a darker one, a kind of sage colour, which is more practical.'

'I'm just trying to imagine it – to see you as a teacher. Remember the ones we had at Calleva House?'

'Of course.'

'Were we as dreadful as some of the girls you were talking about at dinner?'

'Probably. Sometimes. But we were mainly country children, or the daughters of Oxford dons. My pupils, some of them, come from very different backgrounds. A lot of them appear much older than their years.' I was a moment away from telling her about those other children, Sarah and Millie, who were not much older than Rita and I when we first went away to school, but who seemed a different breed when it came to worldliness and experience. I didn't want to think of them. Not now.

'You look sad,' said Rita. 'Has it been hard?'

'In some ways.' I didn't want to go further so I changed the subject. 'You know, you could have done something like me, something worthwhile. Wouldn't you have liked to have a degree? You were clever enough. The Royal Holloway College was the best fun I've ever had. Like minds. Like interests. I would love to have studied for ever.'

'It wouldn't have suited me. I'm not like you, Gladys. I don't enjoy reading and discovering new facts. And I couldn't have put up with Aunt Louise, not without you. At school all I loved was playing games. Afterwards I missed hockey especially but not for long. There was the village team at Harwell.'

She looked smug. Of course! That's how she'd met Bill. I'd taken Victor and Bill home to bump up the Harwell hockey team with their expertise. I'd introduced them myself, so only had myself to blame, but I was so stupidly sure that Bill and I were made for each other, with our literary leanings, our long conversations into the night with his Oxford friends, that I never saw the danger. Rita! Why hadn't I learned from the past? Always, always I was left in her shadow.

I pulled my self together, hankering for what could not be was a high road to misery and jealousy. I was used to losing out to Rita. I dragged my thoughts back to our aunt. 'I don't think I'd realised how unhappy you were at Aunt Louise's. Believe me, it was much worse there before you joined me.'

She looked at me sideways. 'That's because you don't understand people, Gladys. You never have. I buttered the old trout up so that we could at least eat our evening meal with her. I even showed an interest in her endless committees. So boring. Everyone on the committees hated her too, you could tell. They let her have her own way in everything. All but one, who would drop an idea of her own in, watch it being squashed, then repeat it in a very off-hand way and let it lie. By the end of the meeting, that idea would be put forward by Aunt Lou as if it were her own. Clever! That's how I learned to handle her too. I'd use my best wheedling voice...'

'Ugh! The one that makes my toes curl...'

'Yes, it wouldn't work with any of the family. They'd be suspicious right off. So: first, the voice... "Aunt Lou, if it's a nice evening, I'd love to see the river and go through the garden you're always talking about." She'd always say she was too busy for such frivolities. Then I'd wait but look wistfully, with my head on one side, at the sunshine on her horrible garden and sigh. It always worked.'

I was lost in admiration. She was right. Rita was born with a gift for handling people. It didn't matter whether she was with men or women, everybody fell for her. Ruefully I thought of Bill again. I knew that he'd be back one day and that I would have to watch him marry my sister, who I envied and loved and had missed so much in the loneliness of my first weeks in Birmingham. When she married Bill and they moved to Canada, both of them would be lost to me, for all time.

Thinking this I hugged her where she sat on the edge of the bed. I could never remain jealous or angry with Rita for long. She knew how to play me as well as anyone.

After church on Christmas Day, all of us buoyant with carols and good will, we were joined by Papa's sisters Aunts Mary and Sarah who would be our guests for the rest of the day. Aunt Mary had mellowed towards us somewhat over the years. She no longer regarded us as Irish ruffians, I suppose.

Bracken took our parents home in the trap while the rest of us walked the mile and a half from Harwell church. Edgar and Duncan, both now in their early twenties, and still bound together like twins, belied their ages by slicing off the dead heads of thistles and knapweed with sticks while the rest of us talked.

'What do you do in your free time?' asked Rita.

'Mark and prepare lessons mainly,' I answered, though a disturbing vision of Millie's pinched face entered my head and undermined my casual tone.

'Is Birmingham fun to live in?' asked Kay wistfully. 'I've never been to a big city. What's it like? Is it huge?'

'Well, it's much bigger than Oxford, of course. It has a fine centre. There's Chamberlain Square, which has all the best buildings, very grand. There's a wonderful Art Gallery there. And there are parks and green spaces quite near where I live. Sometimes I cycle to those for a breath of fresh air after a week in a fusty classroom.'

'But what do you *do*?' persisted Kay. 'Do you meet with friends?' She paused meaningfully. 'Anyone special?'

I ignored her inference. So far I'd hardly met any men at all – I didn't count Bertie, who was married anyway – and I didn't think my life as a teacher would lead me to the kind of places where meetings were likely. Kay was just at that ripening age where her mind was filled with little else. I spoke firmly, to discourage more of the same. 'I'm friends with my room-mate, who teaches at the same school as me. Nina. But she's having to leave.' Quite unexpectedly I found tears threatening.

'What's wrong?' asked Lina and put a hand on my arm.

'It's so unfair. Nina's had to leave to look after her mother and she doesn't want to at all. She loves teaching.' I saw her face clearly as I spoke. How pale she'd become. How sad.

'But if her mother's sick?' said Lina.

'That's it. There's no one else to look after her. She's doing what she must, I suppose.'

'She's doing what any of us would do, if Mama became ill,' said Kay.

'I suppose,' I said. But I wondered. Would I give up all that I loved for Mama? The thought prickled at me and, uncomfortable with it, I put it aside. Instead, I focused on all that Nina had done to open my eyes to the under side of Birmingham. Kay had asked, what's Birmingham really like? And I'd mentioned only the showcase centre, the civic heart of which Birmingham's upper classes were so proud. That, I knew, wasn't the real Birmingham. Nor was my school, populated mostly by the children of the rising middle-class, the factory managers, the owners of the successful stores which catered for the rich. The real city was a teeming mass of workers, kept in appalling conditions, in stinking warrens no wealthy person would consider fit for their own habitation.

As my anger rose I must have let out an inadvertent exclamation, because Rita immediately asked what was up. And I'd sworn to myself I'd not talk about it, that I'd keep Christmas and the family separate from all of that, but under the puzzled gaze of my siblings out it all came. The narrow alleyways linking the courts of back-to-backs, draped with grey washing, the faces of the women, old before their time, the cobbles running with stinking fluids, the vermin, the grey-white faces of the children and their rickety limbs, all spilled out. Just in time I stopped myself blurting out the story of Millie and Sarah. That would have been a step too far in front of Lina and Kay. But thinking of them made me cry.

Tears gushed and my speech became broken with

hiccoughs of distress. Through this I tried to explain my frustration that people lived in such conditions and I could do nothing about it.

Everyone looked at me in horror. Crying was permissible – just, but only if absolutely unavoidable – but to cry so openly! That was against the rules of the game. Kay, white-faced, regretted she'd pestered me, Lina took my hand and squeezed it in silent support, while Rita mopped my face with her handkerchief.

'Go and splash your eyes with cold water,' counselled Jim disapprovingly, as we lurked out on the lane running beside Rowstock House. 'You mustn't invite questions over the Christmas dinner.'

I took his advice, lingering in my room after I'd wet my face and neck from the washbasin, filled from the icy jug in my room. For good measure, I lifted my blouse from the belt around my skirt and cooled my clammy armpits. Then I sat on the edge of my bed and breathed deeply. Jim was right. The family meal should not be spoiled. And yet – how did Ada spend Christmas? Or Millie? Or Sarah? Were there presents for any of the children? I couldn't imagine that the festivities would lighten the burden of the poor; it would be like any other day for them.

In this frame of mind, outwardly calm but inwardly troubled, I joined the family at the dinner table.

'We missed you,' Mama smiled at me.

'Just had to put the finishing touches to my gifts,' I apologised and saw Jim scan my face and nod with approval as I placed my small offerings under the tree.

The room looked exotic, decked out in its annual splendour. Elbow to elbow we sat around the table, lengthened by the addition of two extra leaves. The candles on the tree made a curtain of liquid light, while those in branched candelabra down the length of the table, made a luminous path that threw our faces into relief. As an early dusk gathered, for our Christmas feast was always mid-afternoon to allow Rita and Mama time after church to cook, that candlelight gave back our images again in the darkening window-panes, in the silver brought out for the occasion, in the shining china and Lina's foil decorations. The different surfaces distorted faces and bodies into unrecognisable shapes: illustrations from the *Arabian Nights* perhaps, or from the fairy tales on which we were nurtured as children. We girls bustled back and forth from the kitchen, carrying in dish after dish heaped high with the produce of our garden, orchard and the family farms. We ate and ate. Our faces bloomed fuchsia-red with laughter and greed. We swore we'd never eat again, had room for no more, but managed it just the same. We wore our tinsel crowns like monarchs at a medieval banquet. We were Old King Cole and King John leading up to his surfeit of lampreys, his just desserts, as we celebrated Rita's pudding, topped with holly and flaming like our cheeks.

Of course it was all wonderful. Of course I enjoyed seeing the faces of those I loved best in the world relaxed and merry. But deep inside a worm of guilt continued to stir and would not rest, so that each mouthful of food swelled in my throat. Each time I saw the distorted view of my family, glittering chips of colour as if shaken up by a kaleidoscope, I saw a darker picture behind, moving slowly, at a different pace, as those move who lack the lustre of plentiful food to fuel them and give them energy.

After the meal were the games. This is where Aunt Mary came into her own. Her skill at word games and those that needed fast responses had become legendary.

Every Christmas since we'd been at Rowstock, we'd been in awe of this ability. Edgar and Duncan would spend days before Christmas practising ways in which they might catch her out. They never succeeded, but their efforts did not go unrewarded. Aunt Mary, with a glint in her eye, would crease her face into a rare smile while she quelled all attempts to depose her.

This year I ducked the games, pleading a headache, and busied myself instead with the washing-up. After a while, Jim came in.

'Why are you in here playing the martyr?'

'I wanted time to think.'

Jim eyed the teetering pile of dishes on the draining-board and picked up a tea-towel. I fiddled with cutlery, slotting the clean versions into gaps between the dripping plates while waiting for Jim to make space. We were silent for a few moments.

'What you were talking about on our way back from church …' He broke the silence. 'You have to accept that there's always going to be injustice in the world. There's nothing that can be done about it.'

I wheeled to face him, propelled by such a burst of fury boiling up from within that I shook. 'What do you mean, there's nothing that can be done? If everyone felt like that, it's true nothing would be. But there are those of us who are trying.' And I described the work of the women at the Club who were at least attempting to alleviate the lives of others less fortunate than themselves. 'It appears to be only women who are doing anything at all. And why is that? Because most men are like you. They don't see further than their own noses and they lack the compassion that women have in plenty. Perhaps because we're used to caring, to looking after children, elderly relatives, so we see how these poor women are suffering. And their children…' My voice broke. I turned back to the sink and eyed the scum of grease on the surface of the water without seeing it. 'Put another kettle on the stove, please,' I said wearily.

'You haven't mentioned the men in your equation,' Jim said. 'What's life in a slum like for them?' His voice was sharp. I knew he felt I'd left something important out, was looking at things skewed by – I couldn't help seeing this as his implication – my inferior feminine perspective.

'You think just because I'm a woman that I've got it all wrong.'

'Of course I don't. I just think you haven't seen enough yet to be sure of your facts. There is an argument that people find their own level.'

This incensed me. How dare he suggest that the poor were poor because they chose to be. It was the lazy argument of those whose lives were comfortable, who didn't want to be troubled by a social conscience. I knew that but for the last weeks I might have held the same views, out of the same ignorance. I held back, however, from saying things that might cause a rift between us, told myself that I had been privileged to find out something about the way the world worked but that he had been sheltered from it. It was his ignorance speaking, not his good heart, that kindness which I knew he possessed.

So I sat him down at the kitchen table and told him about Millie and Sarah, how they slept at the Club rather than go back to their homes, where their mothers had been driven to prostitute themselves to make ends meet. I told him how both these children had been raped themselves, how they too dabbled in prostitution. I didn't hold anything back. I wanted to shock Jim into realising how some people had to live, through no fault of their own.

In my telling, the men were as much to blame for the plight of their families as Society, or Birmingham Council. 'It's the drink that's half the problem, and then they go home, inebriated, and abuse their wives …'

'Stop right there,' said Jim. 'Some men might be as you say, some men might drink and abuse their families, but there must be others who try their hardest, who are loving and caring. Think of Ireland. For every O'Connor, who drank, and Donnell who deserted his family, there was a Carthy or a Heggerty who worked hard and supported his wife and children as well as he could. Think of that farmer who bought our donkey, Fern. He had nine children. Nine! And yes, they were barefoot most of the time but they were loving and independent. It is possible to be poor and happy.'

'It's all about the living space,' I answered. 'Our Irish neighbours may have been poor, but they had the green land and the shore to run on, and the wide sky stretching above them, to nurture their souls.'

'Souls!' scoffed Jim.

'Yes, souls. Because the slums are mean and narrow. They close their lives into damp boxes which trap every stench and germ. The sky is all but invisible, just narrow slices above the buildings, and they'll be lucky if they ever see anything green and growing in their whole lives.'

Jim was silent as he absorbed the passion with which I spoke. 'I'd have to see it for myself, I suppose,' he conceded finally.

'Yes, you would.' I smiled ruefully at him. 'But you probably never will. You're a Marine. You spend your life on ships.'

'Not just any old ship, Gladys.' He drew himself up and spoke with pride. 'We Royal Marines are the fighting units of the Navy. I could be sent anywhere in the world.'

'But probably not to the Birmingham slums.'

'No,' Jim grinned, 'It's not likely.'

While we hugged, our differences forgotten, or at least forgiven, Kay came in and looked at us curiously.

'Help me make tea and bring in the cake,' she said.

'More food!' I exclaimed in mock-horror.

'You'll manage,' said Kay with unusual sharpness. 'Christmas pudding and fruit cake are the things you're usually greediest about.' She busied herself getting things ready. 'Do you realise how long you've been hiding in here? Come and join the family. In case you've forgotten, it's Christmas.'

With a jagged bounce to her step that betrayed her irritation, she marched out carrying a tray of tinkling china. I followed bearing Rita's beautiful cake, its icing as smooth as the newly-shed snow it emulated. The decorations were Lina's: robins, deer, rabbits and mice, all made out of marzipan.

It wasn't my family's fault that the slums existed and there was nothing I could do for now. I rejoined them with a better heart, promising to myself that I would do whatever I could, whatever it took, even if it meant bombarding the Birmingham Council with letters and petitions, till I managed to bring about change.

The rest of the holiday passed peacefully, except for one drama where Kay could not be found as supper approached. It was dark with a moon flying sharp-etched, as if cut out of paper. Earlier in the day a sprinkle of snow had sugared the garden and paddock. Now, hardened by frost, the moon silvered this lacy whiteness and lit our way over the paddock to the barn, where we knew we'd find Lina putting her animals to bed.

Close questioning revealed that Kay had gone to meet her boyfriend, Harry, although Papa had expressly forbidden such unchaperoned meetings with an unsuitable local boy. Lina reluctantly admitted that she sometimes took one of the boys' bikes and sneaked off. Now it was dark however and we were fearful that something might have happened on the icy roads. We decided to find her without telling our parents.

It felt like a return to the old days, when we'd concealed the courage game from Mama and Papa. Now of course we were all a whole lot bigger and some of us were already heading for lives that would take us away. Jim and I had already gone. Rita – well, Rita was heading soon for marriage to Bill, while Edgar worked in the offices of the East India Company, in London, where Duncan hoped to join him soon. Both dreamed of going to India. The scattering of all the family pieces was close. Only Kay and Lina would be left on the gameboard, and for how long?

Here and now, though, all of us slotted into our usual places in the family pecking order. We deferred to Jim.

'You go and chat with Mama,' he said to Rita. 'Keep her talking and help prepare the meal. And you, Gladys, keep Papa in his study. Tell him more about Birmingham.' He gave me a sharp look. 'The comfortable bits only, mind.'

'I'd rather be with you,' I said, unwilling to lose this feeling of companionship, this echo from our childhood. 'And I'm not sure I could be trusted not to spill some uncomfortable bits into Papa's waiting lap.'

'Papa won't even have noticed Kay's missing,' Lina backed me up. 'He's always in his study before supper. He reads his newspaper from cover to cover.'

'All right,' said Jim. 'Let's not waste any more time.'

The night was very still and the air crackled with frost. Our cheeks stiffened with the cold and eyes streamed. We picked our way for the first few yards but quickly realised that we'd all be missed if we didn't speed up. As soon as we were out of earshot of the house we began to call Kay's name, but it wasn't till we neared Harwell that we found her and by that time our throats were hoarse and we had not called for some time. She was walking in our direction, a young man's arm around her shoulder. With the other hand, Harry, we presumed, steered the bicycle. They were so absorbed in each other that they didn't notice us till we were nearly upon them.

Jim grabbed her by the shoulder and pulled her away from her beau. 'What do you think you're doing?' he raged. 'Don't you know it's nearly supper?'

I echoed her comment to me on Christmas Day, because it still rankled. 'In case you've forgotten, it's still Christmas. It's family time.'

She shook Jim off and took a few steps back. 'This is Harry,' she said coldly, 'in case you've all forgotten your manners. We've been talking about getting married.'

January 1906

As I left home at the end of the Christmas holidays for the start of term – contrary to my original intention to go back early – Papa hurried out and thrust into my hand a page torn out from his newspaper.

'Something to read on the journey,' he said. 'It's about Birmingham. You may be interested.'

I watched the wet countryside out of the window and thought of Kay, who had been confined to her room after her escapade, and the liaison with Harry broken off by a Papa none of us had ever seen so angry.

After a while, I pulled the crumpled sheet of newspaper from my carpet-bag. A journalist was reporting on the sorry state of Birmingham slum housing. He listed many of the facts: the short cuts taken by builders, the thin walls that allowed no privacy, the watered down plaster thickened with horsehair. This only confirmed what I had already heard from the women at the Club.

He moved on to praise a particular landlord for doing something about it and building new houses with 'every modern comfort.' This paragon was named as Councillor Albert Foster-Smythe. I realised with a jolt that this had to be Bertie. 'Here is one landlord with a conscience,' I read, 'and a genuine concern for his tenants.' I heard again Bertie's voice dismissing his workers as animals. Genuine concern indeed!

After this, the journalist who, even if mistaken, had at least a good heart, finished his article with a description of some of the saddest tales he had encountered over the Christmas period in Birmingham. There was the family, unable to pay their rent, who spent one of the coldest nights of the year on a patch of waste ground in Hockley, wrapped in sacking for warmth. There was the young woman found floating in the canal that runs through Aston. There was the woman who died in child-birth on Christmas Eve, leaving three further children with no alternative but to go to the Workhouse. 'Look at your children's faces aglow with joy, full of Christmas cheer,' the writer exhorted, 'and remember these stories, of people for whom Christmas has only meant misery and hardship.'

His list stirred up all my buried guilt about deserting the Club. I thought of Nina, too, who had loved to walk by the canal that ran through Aston. How had her Christmas been, alone with her sick mother? I had walked by that very canal with her sometimes, at weekends. Often the slow-moving water carried dead animals: a dog, or a cat and once a sheep. What a shock it would have been to see a dead person in the water. I shivered. As soon as I had picked up Nina's address from Mrs Cartwright, I would write to her about it, along with the news of staff and pupils from school.

This thought turned my mind from home to the beginning of term with a renewed energy. If I was going to prepare my lessons and fulfil my latest vow to reveal the plight of the poor to those who could do something about it, then I had much to do.

12

The moment I arrived, Mrs Cartwright greeted me coldly on the step outside the door and told me that Miss Norris – Nina – had not paid her rent.

I was surprised. 'Surely she paid up to the end of the month? She gave in her notice from the New Year.'

'Did she indeed? Says you, but what do you know? She gave in no notice. Not by mouth or by written note. She has deceived me, that's clear, and left me short.' She glared at me. 'Deceived you too, it seems. Are you able to pay her share too? For that's what you'll have to do until the place is filled.' She gave me a look of grim satisfaction, as if threatening me in this way allowed her to vent her spleen at Nina's defection.

'I'm sure there's been some mistake,' I stammered, aghast at the thought of having to double my rent. 'She told me quite clearly that she was leaving to nurse her sick mother...that she'd given you notice.'

Mrs Cartwright emitted a sound like the spitting of a cat. 'Do you have an address for her?'

I was ashamed that I didn't. ' She told me she'd leave one with you, so that I could write. Oh dear.' Surprise had frozen my brain. I couldn't think straight. 'The school will have one. I'll find it out tomorrow, when term starts.'

'Mind you do. Meanwhile, I'd be pleased if you paid me for this month immediately.'

'Give me a chance to get in the door,' I forced a laugh and a clear and determined tone to my voice.' I do not have more than the agreed amount, Mrs Cartwright, but I'm sure the problem with Miss Norris will be quickly resolved. I'm surprised the school hasn't contacted you with news of her replacement.' Unless they'd found someone local of course, who didn't need a room. Several of the newest staff lived nearby and had been trained by the recently established University, here in Birmingham.

I handed over my half of the rent and she allowed me past, with a reluctant cracking open of the door, no more than was absolutely necessary to allow me to squeeze through.

When Nina had first told me she was leaving, the idea had popped into my head of finding somewhere else to live. I'd imagined a little haven, filled with books and comfortable furniture, where I could write poetry and expand my soul. Originally I'd intended to seek lodgings before the end of the Christmas term, but events had taken over and those last few weeks had been so busy that I simply hadn't had time. This interchange with my landlady reminded me how tired I was of her mean spirit. The idea of moving became top priority.

The next shock came when I entered our room. I pulled back the curtain in front of the wardrobe rail to discover that Nina's clothes still hung there with her boots placed neatly underneath, those same boots she had offered me before Christmas. The bedside cupboard was crammed with Nina's teaching books, her pens and pencils, even some exercise books which she had failed to return to her class. I flipped over the pages, full of comments in her round neat script. The last exercise had not been marked.

I sat down on her bed, feeling shaky. There was a lump under the counterpane. Diving my arm down under the sheet I came up with the doll I had given her. She had not even taken that! My Christmas present!

What had Nina been thinking of? Had she expected me to return the books to the school? I could, of course, and would. Did she have clothes more suited to nursing an invalid back at home? Was that the reason she'd left her good black skirts, her two white blouses with their high ruffled necks, her jacket?

I shook my head to clear it. No. That could not be the answer. Nina had very little money. It would be idiocy to leave good clothes, useful items like her stout boots, behind. There must be another reason.

I revisited our farewell conversation in my mind. Were there any clues there? She had been sad and abstracted. She'd talked of visiting old haunts, of saying goodbye to them. I'd thought her unnecessarily morbid, wallowing rather in self-pity. But she'd snapped out of it, hadn't she? I remembered her laughter, her hug, her pleasure in our exchange of gifts. I struggled to remember her last expression, as I'd left the room. She'd stood against the light; I couldn't properly see her face. But she'd been all right – hadn't she?

The room felt haunted by Nina. I kept expecting her to stomp in and throw herself on her bed, to tear into the sandwiches left out by Mrs Cartwright, as she used to do on her late Wednesdays. I kept hearing her voice in the passage, her footfall on the stair. I dipped in and out of pockets of sleep, to strain after imagined sounds. The night air was heavy, vibrated with after-shock – as if something had just finished and I had missed it by a mere second, or it had been whisked out of earshot. It could have been the sound of Nina's lips sucking on nothing in her sleep, or her little whistling snore. Twice I got up and tried to retrieve the sound, to seize it by the tail before it vanished. I looked out into the corridor, once catching sight of the peculiar man who lived in the next door room as he returned from the bathroom. The next time nothing at all but the beating of my own heart. It was a strange and restless night.

By morning I'd convinced myself that something must have happened to change Nina's mind. She just wouldn't leave all her stuff behind unless she was staying. It could be that her mother had died, and she was away at her funeral but she'd soon return. Everything I knew of Nina reminded me of how conscientious she was. Of course she would have returned her class's exercise books. So by the time I'd reached the school, cycling the well-known route and imagining Nina's stocky body cycling in front, I'd convinced myself that she would be back soon, familiar and awkward and fun in equal proportions.

All the same, I entered the staff room and searched the faces with my eyes, suddenly certain that Nina would be there. The light poured through the glass behind the window-seat where she, Amy and I always sat. And wasn't that her, there, smiling at me, her face indistinct against the light? I moved forward eagerly, questions crowding my lips. The figure patted the seat next to her. The hair was too dark for Nina. It was only Amy.

I sat down next to Amy, all the anxiety resurfacing so that I barely registered her greeting. Miss Nimmo would join us soon, I thought, and when she did, all would be clear. Nina would have contacted her and everything would be all right.

'Hello, grumpy.' Amy's voice broke through in a conspiratorial hiss. 'I've been looking round for likely candidates for Nina's replacement. See if you can see one.'

I just looked at her. The words meant nothing to me. The buzz of voices around the table, Amy's breathy voice in my ear, none of it made any sense.

I had put Nina's exercise books on the table in front of me.

I kept my hand on the pile, as if that would summon Nina there too.

'What's wrong?' Amy's voice was still quiet, not to attract the attention of the other members of staff. 'Did you have a good Christmas? Mine was just a whirl of parties. The time simply flew.' She nudged me. 'Hope the new member of staff is young, don't you? We're the only two under thirty left. If we're not careful, we'll be overwhelmed by old bats.'

I took a breath. 'I don't think Nina's left after all.'

'What do you mean? She gave in her notice last term. Of course she's left.'

I indicated the exercise books. 'And all her clothes and belongings are still at our lodgings.'

'That's very odd. Had she told you when she was leaving?'

'Just before Christmas. She mentioned the twenty-third.'

'That's very late. Shows she didn't really want to go.'

'I know. I'm wondering if something happened, her mother dying perhaps – I know that's awful to say, but it would explain a lot. Perhaps she received a telegram…' I pushed aside the thought that the Cartwright would likely have known if a telegram had arrived. But Nina could have met the delivery-boy on the doorstep – there were any number of possible explanations.

'Hmm, yes. It could be, I suppose. But then, why's she not here now?'

'If her mother has died, then there's probably a lot to sort out at home. Perhaps she's taken a few days' leave from the beginning of term. Miss Nimmo will know.' The more I put these thoughts into words, the more comforting I found them. The scenario I'd invented was by far the most likely, after all. So why did I still have a knot like a coiled snake in my stomach?

The door to the staff-room was opening. Porson was the first to enter, pushing a trolley of hot drinks and doughnuts to warm us up on a January day. Behind him came Miss Nimmo. Both Amy and I sat more upright.

After the usual round of greetings, the headmistress looked over towards us. 'Isn't there someone missing?' she said. 'I don't see Miss Norris. Miss Hazel, you share a room with her. Is she indisposed?'

Shock strangled my voice and tightened my chest. Amy laid her hand on mine.

'But Miss Nimmo,' she finally said, when it was clear I couldn't speak, 'Miss Norris gave in her notice last term. She left to look after her mother. Only, um … Gladys?' She gave me a sharp jab with her elbow. The next part was my story to tell.

I took a breath which didn't seem to reach my lungs, left me still with that tight sensation of breathlessness. 'Only now I'm not sure whether she's left or not. I think there's been some mistake. Something's happened…I don't know what.' I felt hot and close to tears.

Miss Nimmo's welcome smile had become tense. She cut across my flounderings. 'We will talk about this later in my study, Miss Strachan, Miss Hazel. For now, we have a term to plan.' She looked sternly at her staff, whose faces betrayed a desire to question, gossip and conjecture. Some whispers had already begun, but Miss Nimmo quelled them with a rap on the table. When she had regained silence, I saw her breathe slowly and deeply before she began the business of the meeting.

In Miss Nimmo's study, both Amy and I responded like children caught out in some prank. All we could do was to repeat what we knew, or thought we knew, of Nina's plans.

'She told me she'd given in her notice,' I said.

'She told me that too,' Amy backed up.

'Did she not confide in any other members of staff?'

'It would appear not, headmistress,' Amy said. 'Everyone else looked completely surprised by the news she had left.'

I took a deep breath and described how I'd found our room. I displayed the unmarked exercise books, which Miss Nimmo took from me, and hesitantly proposed that Nina might have changed her mind, that perhaps her mother had died and she intended to carry on with her teaching. But I ran out of steam. The whole story I'd told myself depended on Miss Nimmo's knowledge of it. The fact that she was in the dark meant that Nina had lied – to me, to Amy, and by omission, to everyone else. The knotted snake in my stomach uncoiled and travelled up into my chest. My breath came short and panicky.

Miss Nimmo laid a steadying hand on my shoulder. 'Try to put this out of your mind, both of you, if you can, and leave it to me to find out what has occurred. I shall let you know when I have learned anything certain. For now, it is imperative that you do not encourage chatter of any loose kind, amongst the girls or other members of staff. Can I rely on you?' She turned and looked long and hard at both of us, until our eyes dropped. Then she dismissed us.

The moment we were out in the corridor, Amy turned to me, her face animated. 'Something's happened to her. I just know it. Didn't she love to walk around the slum areas? Anything could have happened to her there. Maybe she's had an accident. Is her bike still at your lodgings?'

I hadn't checked, but if Nina had visited the slums, which was a possibility, she wouldn't have used it. I told her so. 'I suppose she could have gone down for a farewell visit to the Club, but she hadn't been for ages.' My mind toyed with the new idea, however, and began to build that up into a likely scenario. Hadn't *I* been caught up in a street fight? Perhaps something bad *had* happened to poor Nina, preventing her departure for home.

Amy received these thoughts with a sort of frenetic energy, which had her juggling my simple and open-ended scenario into scenes of dark deeds that became more and more lurid. 'She could have been knocked over by a horse and cart, or run over by a tram, or … but then some one would have seen… but no, if it happened in the slum areas, they'd have covered it up, concealed the body…'

'Amy, shut up!' I couldn't bear it. 'This is Nina you're talking about, our friend. How could you?'

Amy did stop but she didn't look contrite. After a bit she said in a brusque tone, 'I was just being realistic, Gladys. You have to admit that something's happened to Nina. Must have.'

I hated to see the high colour in Amy's face, the interest bordering on enjoyment that she appeared to be feeling.

'It's not enjoyment,' she countered. 'Of course it isn't. I feel the same sense of something awful as you feel. It helps me to toss ideas about like that. Even awful ones. It helps me accept what may come, so that whatever the reason for Nina's disappearance, it won't be such a shock.'

I still looked at her with horror. 'But to imagine her death! And in such horrible ways.'

'She could *be* dead, Gladys. It would explain everything.'

I thrust the idea away, anger taking the place of confusion. 'No. Absolutely and definitely, no. She'll be with her mother, you'll see, and all of this will turn out to be some kind of mistake. Things like you've imagined don't happen to normal human beings like you and me. And Nina. They just don't.' I turned my back on Amy and, since I didn't feel like fielding questions from the rest of the staff, went straight to my classroom.

After school I sat on my bed, staring at Nina's. There was a slight indentation in the bedding in the centre, made by her reclining body. My mind kept churning: *a mistake, some kind of mistake.* I gnawed on it obsessively but could make no progress. The best sense I could make was that Nina simply could not bring herself to hand in her notice, either to Mrs Cartwright or to Miss Nimmo, for that would have meant facing up to reality. I could understand how someone might keep deferring unpleasantness, hoping that something might happen to render it unnecessary. And perhaps something did. If news of her mother's death occurred she might have been so distressed that contacting the school, or telling Mrs Cartwright, was forgotten. She could have left in a hurry. That made sense. I squashed the idea that she would surely have sent a telegram later.

The more I weighed up this scenario, the more I liked it. She'd been able to tell both Amy and me. Perhaps that was a kind of trial run for telling Miss Nimmo, after which she would have been committed. Had putting those unpleasantnesses into words for her friends made them more, or less, real to her? Obviously not real enough to face up to the people she needed to tell. Most of all, why hadn't she confided in me if she had a problem? I heard the echo of her answer: *Look deeper, Gladys.*

I hadn't looked deeper into Nina's misery. I hadn't seen how she was finding it difficult to cope. Worse, I knew in my heart that I *had* seen, and had brushed it aside and not helped her as I should have, as any true friend would have.

My thoughts were taking such a dark turn that I could no longer stay in that room. I checked Nina's bicycle was there. It was much better than my own, so I took it and rode off to the canal, where we often went together. Maybe I thought that just riding there, fitting my body over the shadow of Nina's own, would help me find answers. Of course it did not, and with a heavy heart, a sense of something coming that would change me for ever, I returned home to Mrs Cartwright's thin-lipped comments as I sat and ate my evening meal in the residents' dining-room. Nina's empty chair on the other side of the table vibrated with her absence. I fancied this was palpable to everyone, since whenever another resident approached it, he veered away, as if pushed, and sat elsewhere. Loneliness was my only companion.

Usually, Nina and I had managed to eat before the gentlemen residents returned from their work and filled the dining-room with their grey presence. Today, they sat, masticating their food around me, their knives scraping on the plates, creating a background of sly noise that had me gritting my teeth to stop a scream funnelling out and blowing them all away like dry leaves. I was aware of their sidelong looks. I fancied that their unspoken questions clamoured for attention. Certainly the air felt heavy with them, along with the waves of disapproval emanating from Mrs Cartwright's upright figure in the doorway. Usually Annie was left on her own to serve us all, but today the Cartwright stood there like a black candle that shed no light. The silence from her, and from her male tenants, made me certain that suppositions about Nina had been already tossed around the room. Only my presence prevented this grumbling complaint and conjecture from continuing. I resolved that I would never again eat there, but would ask for cold cuts in my room until the day I left. And it was evident that, as soon as the Nina situation was clarified, I must leave.

The first few days at school were difficult. They would have been worse without the girls, but they were still hard. I could not put my usual zest into what I did. The girls responded by withholding their energy. Their written exercises were done in a sulky silence. I often caught eyes looking at me, their expressions puzzled, when they should have been bent over the page. Their recitations droned along without spirit and were not criticised, as they would normally have been.

The children may have heard rumours about Nina, I supposed, but if so no one dared ask me anything directly. More likely, they were just responding to my lack of animation with their own minor form of rebellion.

Amy and I sat in the staffroom and could find nothing to say. Here was another place where all eyes looked at us and, when we met their gaze, slid away. When the first weekend came, we met up in Chamberlain Square with relief. It was good to be able to talk, free of the weight of silence imposed on us by the headmistress.

It was a raw day, the air heavy and damp with unshed rain. Dark clouds lowered the roof of the sky. By mutual consent, we headed for the shelter of the Museum and Art Gallery.

I remembered the last time we were there, with a Nina who was shocked I had never visited the city centre. We found a seat opposite a vast painting, full of draped fleshy figures, which neither of us did more than glance at. The room was empty. Its size and high ceilings echoed with the murmur of voices from the main hall.

'I'm surprised we haven't heard anything,' said Amy. 'I wonder how Miss Nimmo is going about the task of finding out what's happened.'

'I expect she's contacted Nina's mother. Oh! How that will upset that poor lady. It doesn't bear thinking about.'

'She'll already be pretty upset, don't you think? With Nina not returning? She must have been trying to find out what has happened too.'

'Think of all the people this thing touches. Whatever happened to Nina it has huge ramifications. Look how it's affected just us. We can't function properly. Our minds are caught up in the web of this mystery and until it's solved we can't get on with our lives.'

'Do you miss her?'

I looked at her, surprised. 'Don't you?'

'We weren't close.'

'Of course I miss her. We shared a room. That's becoming unbearable, by the way. I can't live there any longer than I have to. The other lodgers stare at me. Mrs Cartwright wants me to pay Nina's half of the rent, and I can't. I told her I was leaving at the end of the month. That doesn't give me much time to find alternative lodgings.'

'I'll help you. And if we can't find somewhere in time, you can always stay with my family for a while.'

'That's so kind, Amy. Thank you.'

'In fact,' Amy leapt to her feet. 'Why don't we start looking now. We're in the area you've always said you'd like to be and it would distract us nicely. We shan't do anything otherwise except talk Nina, Nina, Nina all day long. I wish I could push her out of my head.'

'Don't, Amy. I feel the least I can do is to keep her in my thoughts. She's been a good friend to me.'

'She was always rather difficult, though. You must admit, Gladys. She could bite off your head. I always found her prickly company.'

'Oh, Amy!'

'Well, it's true. You had to tiptoe round her, being careful of what you said. And of course I know she could be enormous fun too. But don't sanctify her, Gladys. I'm just trying to keep her real.'

'Then stop consigning her to the past. As if she were dead.'

Amy just looked at me. She opened her mouth and closed it again. Turning her back on me, she began to walk out of the room, her feet clacking on the polished floor.

I ran after her. 'She has a good heart. A wonderful laugh. A big laugh. That's what I like to think about.'

Amy stopped walking, so fast I nearly bumped into her. She

turned to face me. Her expression was solemn as she adjusted my hat. 'Look at you,' she said. 'Your hair's all escaping. You look like a wild woman.' She slid her gloved hands down to my shoulders. 'Dear Gladys, I listen to you and admire the way you try to keep Nina alive but I think we must face up to the fact that the mystery may never be solved. She's disappeared. Maybe she isn't dead. Maybe she just wants people to think she is. She didn't want to go and nurse her mother. She couldn't bear the thought. Perhaps she simply ran away.'

'Taking nothing with her? None of her clothes?'

Amy shrugged. 'Who knows? Perhaps she'd found a friend to shelter her, whose clothes she could borrow.'

I began to churn yet another scenario over in my mind. I seized on it as another possibility. It was an escape from the dark thoughts that gathered around me when I sat alone in the prison of our shared room.

Amy continued to look at me with an anxious frown creasing her forehead. ' Come on, Gladys.' She finally broke the silence. 'Let's find you somewhere to live.'

Just around the corner from the Square was Paradise Street. My spirits plummeted further as I followed Amy's jaunty grey coat with its high fur collar, past Christ Church with its tall spire. This street would be wonderful of course. It was central, much further from the school but still only a tram ride away. It was close to New Street Station, the General Post Office, the Town Hall – which was both concert hall and theatre – the Council House, two other theatres and all the amenities of Chamberlain and Victoria Squares. But, and it was a giant 'but', just because it was central, it would surely be unviable for my limited finances.

Amy pooh-poohed my qualms. 'You said you could manage a little more than you pay the Cartwright – not as much as double, of course. You made that clear. But we're only looking for a room, remember. These big houses often have an empty maid's room at the top. It's worth trying and you may be surprised.'

I continued to follow as she scanned the houses on the left-hand side of the road. My heart was rebellious, however. I didn't want a tiny maid's room, even if I could have it to myself. I dreamed of the kind of comfort offered by my father's study at Rowstock, only with the addition of a bed. That this was an unrealistic aspiration I knew in my inner heart, but I still clung to the vision.

It wasn't long before we saw a notice in the window of Number 33: *Room available. Professional gentleman preferred.* The house looked gracious and charming. I felt it reach out to me, as if we recognised each other.

I turned anxiously to Amy. 'What do you think they'd feel about a professional lady?'

'You can but ask,' she said. 'It looks a nice place. Good location.'

'Yes.' I felt a thumping in my chest. I hadn't even seen the room but the area was just what I'd envisaged. And a room for a professional gentleman would surely not be one normally slept in by a servant.

I looked up and around, at the grandeur of the buildings, listened to the hum of people from the nearby square. Behind me I could see the columns of the Town Hall. This was all I had dreamed of. Where was my courage? The daring I'd had as a child? I could hear Jim's voice in my ear. Nothing ventured…

I swallowed hard. Just looking at the house, I knew I wanted to be here so much that I'd rather starve than not be able to afford it. 'It'd be worth paying a bit more,' I said, fighting impulse with a show of caution. 'If it's a nice room, that is.'

She laughed. 'You haven't seen it yet. It's probably full of mouldering furniture and overrun with cockroaches.'

Her attitude lifted my spirits further. 'Don't be silly.' I indicated the height and grandeur of the buildings all the way along the road. 'No bug would dare to invade this area.'

My heart still banged and threatened to close my throat with nerves as we went up the three steps to the front door.

'Very clean,' observed Amy approvingly. 'And the door's been recently painted.'

'Mmm.' My voice had deserted me. My hands were still by my side. I just couldn't bring myself to knock.

Seeing this, Amy gave me an impatient look and rapped for me. The lace curtain tweaked aside from the window nearest the door and a young woman's face looked out, handsome rather than pretty, with wavy golden hair in a neat chignon.

It was a maid-servant who answered however and ushered us into what was clearly the parlour. 'The Misses Strachan and Hazel, Ma'am,' she announced to the lady I'd seen through the window.

After we'd explained our purpose, Amy doing more of the talking than myself, the lady explained that she would show us the room but that she'd have to ask her husband, who was in London for the day, whether he minded housing a young woman, albeit a professional lady.

'Personally,' she said, 'I'd like it very much indeed. It'd be company for me, especially when James is away.'

My heart sank a fraction. I wasn't sure that I wanted companionship so much as a place where I could be on my own. I asked to see the room.

'Of course. And oh, I'm Sophia by the way. Mrs Sophia Cox.'

We followed her upstairs, admiring the wide staircase and ornate banisters.

'It was my husband's family home. But it's expensive to run and so we thought we'd rent out our spare room to help with costs. Oh!' she stopped suddenly. 'I shouldn't have said that.

James would be mortified to hear that I'd spilled out our financial troubles in the first five minutes. It's not at all the done thing.'

Her confession had made me warm to her and I followed her into the room with a lighter heart.

What a room!

I stood in the doorway, sniffing appreciatively at the rich scent of recently applied beeswax. The furnishings were comfortable and included a dark oak table by the window, where I could already imagine myself sitting with a notebook, whose pages would quickly be covered by poetry. The bed was massive, a four-poster with heavy brocade curtains. I was a little intimidated by it, but the rest of the room reassured me. There was a bookcase and a large wooden wardrobe and chest-of-drawers. A thick maroon rug, heavily patterned in navy and cream, covered most of the floor. There was flock wall-paper, also maroon, with cream chrysanthemums picked out on it. It was beautiful and intimidating at the same time. I wanted it and knew it would be beyond my reach.

The tall window, flanked by heavy maroon curtains, looked out over the road, so that peering to the right I could see Christ Church with its tall thin spire, which blocked off the whole end of the street. To the left I could just see the junction at the end of the road and a jumble of further buildings. There were none of the red-brick houses which characterised my present lodgings. Everything here was on a grander scale.

'It's a wonderful room, Mrs Cox,' I said. 'How much is it?'

Behind her I saw Amy crossing herself and raising her eyes up in mock prayer. 'Please call me Sophia.' She paused and looked hard at me. I felt her taking in my prim clothes, the garb of the school-mistress. I itched to polish the smeared toes of my boots on the back of my stockings.

'I shall have to discuss it with my husband,' she said, 'but we'd thought perhaps six pounds.' She must have seen the tension in my face because she took a step closer. 'Is that all right? I'm sure there's room for negotiation.'

My voice came out tight and breathy. 'Six pounds a week?'

'No, of course not. It's only one room! Six pounds a month.'

And as I let my breath out in a sigh of relief I heard her jabber on about the fact that I could join them for meals, and washing my clothes wouldn't add too much to the burden of the servants, but that six pounds a month would make a considerable difference to them until her husband's writing began to sell better. 'I'm sure James will agree,' she said. 'He's back tonight and we'll be able to discuss it. I know it's Sunday tomorrow, but perhaps you could come by in the afternoon?'

On the steps outside, Amy and I hugged and we both did a little dance all the short way up the street towards Christ Church.

'I have a really good feeling about this,' she said.

'Me too. Paradise Street! It describes my present feelings exactly.'

It was Sophia herself who answered the door when I returned, without Amy, but with her encouragement ringing in my ears: *Hold firm, Gladys. Convince the husband of your good sense and quiet character. Win him over.*

Sophia, talking non-stop, ushered me into a gracious room with a large piano dominating one end and such a quantity of chairs scattered around that I wondered if the room was used for concerts. Striped wall-paper of sage green and a dull gold reflected light from the many windows, flanked with gold-coloured curtains. It did not look like a room that suffered from lack of means for its upkeep. Quite the opposite, it reeked of privilege and wealth.

Mr James Cox rose politely as I entered and came forward to shake my hand. He was so tall that I found my eyes travelling up and up the closer he came. He towered over me, but it was a weedy towering. Like a plant grown in a dark cupboard, he looked stringy, starved of light and sustenance. Even his beard and moustache were patchy, as if they grew on unfertile soil.

His eyes, however, large and dark and fringed with lashes any woman would have ached for, were luminous and liquid. All of the life of the man appeared centred in these pools, which now looked warmly at me in my Sunday best, with polished boots and a clean white blouse.

'Welcome to our home, Miss Hazel. My wife has told me all about you and done a good job of winning me over already. I would like, however, to find out a little more about what you do.'

So, under his gentle probing, we sat and I talked about my life at the school. When he found I taught English, he leaned forward from his place on the sofa and his face became animated. We spent a happy few minutes talking about Yeats and other current poets, some of whom were unfamiliar to me.

He leapt up and strode over to a bookcase, from where he extracted a thin calf-bound volume, which he thrust into my hands. Fired with literary enthusiasm, his frail frame took on strength and harmony. His long slender fingers caressed the volume as he passed it to me. 'Take it. Read it,' he said. 'It may change your life.'

I turned the volume over in my hands. It was called *The Ballad of Reading Gaol* by Oscar Wilde.

'I can't take this away,' I stammered. 'It's too precious.' But already my own hand caressed it, appreciating the softness of the cover, the gold of the lettering. I opened it up to admire the marbling on the inside covers.

'You can read it here,' he said, his angular face warming into a smile that quite transformed him and lent his skin a healthy flush. I glanced at Sophia, still seated on her side of the sofa and caught her eye. She too was smiling, her teeth caught on her lower lip.

She rose quickly, with a rustle of her skirts and came over to clasp both my hands.

'The oracle has spoken,' she said, 'and you will be our first lodger.'

I looked from one to the other, brimming with happiness. 'When can I move in?' I asked.

'As soon as you like.'

'I shall put the book on your bedside table,' said James, as he instructed me to call him. 'It will await you there and I shall be interested to discuss it with you when you have read it. Be warned. It is not a happy journey. This is a darker Wilde, such as we rarely see.'

With their kind words putting a new swing into my step, I felt more able than usual to face the ghosts in my Aston lodgings.

———⬲———

The following morning, before either of us had started our first class, Miss Nimmo called Amy and me into her study. The summons caused a flutter of interest in the rest of the staff, who followed our exit with greedy eyes. Even as we closed the staffroom door behind us, we could hear the voices begin and grow shriller as we walked, with a sense of dread, behind the headmistress.

'I am very sorry to tell you both, that the police have found Miss Norris.' Her gaze roamed slowly over both of our faces. 'I advise you to sit down.'

I began to shake and Amy touched my hand reassuringly.

'It seems that a young woman was found in the canal just

before Christmas. The police had no idea who she was. When she didn't come home for Christmas, Miss Norris's mother sent a representative, the local vicar, to find out what may have delayed her, because she was too sick to investigate on her own account. Mrs Cartwright – who runs your lodging-house, Miss Hazel – was not at home. So the vicar went to the police-station.' Miss Nimmo bowed her head, her expression grim.

'I knew she shouldn't have spent so much time around the slums,' blurted Amy into the silence.

Miss Nimmo raised her head. 'Why would she do that?'

I explained about the Club and the elementary school, about how we wanted to help the poor who had the misfortune to live in those warrens. As I spoke, I watched Miss Nimmo warily, uncertain of how she might react to the news of this use of our time when not teaching. Might she not be angry, or at least concerned, that we might be skimping our first duty to our paid positions?

Her face showed nothing but puzzlement and I took heart from that. Momentarily I had worried that I might be dismissed for dereliction of duty.

'You three all did this on a regular basis?'

'Not me,' protested Amy virtuously, shifting her chair the slightest fraction away from mine.

Miss Nimmo looked at me. 'Perhaps that is the reason then. Miss Norris's concern for others overwhelmed her so that she could no longer cope.'

'Surely it was an accident,' said Amy. 'That was what I meant when I told you she visited the slums. It can be dangerous there…' Her voice faltered as Miss Nimmo turned to face her.

'The police found no reason to think it was an accident. The Reverend Mr Bond was told that they believe that Miss Norris took her own life.'

Amy gasped and I felt sick.

'I am relieving both of you from duties today,' Miss Nimmo continued. 'I hardly need to remind you that what you have just learned should not be talked about with anybody at all. I do not want the girls upset. I shall make an announcement to the staff myself, with the same injunction against idle gossip. I advise you both to go home now and clarify your thoughts, ready for a resumption of duties tomorrow. This is a very sad business indeed.'

'Will there be a funeral?' I asked as we rose to leave.

'I understand that that will take place in her home church. The Reverend Mr Bond has it in hand. Neither of you need attend. Writing a letter of condolence will be quite sufficient. Here is her mother's address.'

She handed me a note. I looked at the address, barely registering it. This is what I should have had before Christmas. Nina's withholding of it was a clear sign that she had never intended to return. Why had I had no inkling?

As I cycled back to Mrs Cartwright's, knowing that I must face her to tell her of the imminence of my own departure, I remembered how I had read about the young woman discovered in the canal in Papa's newspaper. My eyes had seen it but I had felt no chord of recognition. For some reason, that upset me more than anything. I should have known. I should have seen, in my last conversation with her, how tightly she kept herself locked away, how she had said goodbye to her feet, how her face, against the light of the window had been blanked out. Now I could see that already she had been beyond help. She had made her decision. How long before, I did not know. And I knew that all the signals had been there, on that morning, and I should have looked deeper and recognised them.

13

Guilt rode me for a long time. The sniping of the Cartwright and Nina's sad spirit felt a just punishment for neglect and self-absorption. I bore it because I must; I had paid for these lodgings until the end of January and could not afford to pay my kind new hosts until the beginning of the next month. Luckily, they were content to wait until then.

'We have managed so far,' Sophia had said, 'and you are our idea of the perfect first lodger.' She suggested that I started to move some items prior to that. But there was little to move and I could easily manage what there was in one journey, so I declined the offer. In truth, the contrast between the two dwellings would only have tormented me further. And perhaps, too, a little part of me wanted to feel the pinch of guilt. Escaping too soon would have encouraged forgetfulness and I didn't want to forget Nina, or what she had taught me, even though I could not yet face either Miss Derris and the school, or Violet and the Club, both of whom would have expected full explanations of Nina's fate.

My journeys to work through the grey month of January, when Nina's bike slid on the icy roads and crackled through the frozen puddles under an unforgiving sky, were a necessary torture. I wore the poisoned cloak of my guilt and it ate into my mind and soul, until Amy told me, rough with irritation at my wallowing, to snap out of it.

'How can I?' I answered, equally irritated.

She rolled her eyes. 'You're like one of those flagellants who walked the streets in medieval times, whipping themselves and wearing hair-shirts next to their skin to stop the wounds healing. I bet they had no friends. You've probably no idea how patient we're all having to be with you, but honestly, Gladys, enough is enough! It's time to move on.'

I deliberately misunderstood her and explained how I had to wait till the beginning of February to move lodgings and she cast her eyes upward again.

'Will you remove that hair-shirt of yours then too? Even the girls are talking about how dull your lessons are now.'

That stung. One thing I'd always prided myself on was my rapport with my pupils. Amy was watching me with a tight little smile. All right then, perhaps I wasn't putting as much effort into my lessons as before. I'd try harder. A few days later, after an afternoon spent hearing recitations and enjoying the lilt in the voice of one of my stalwarts who, like me, had discovered Yeats, I rode the bike home with *Had I the heaven's embroidered cloths* steeping my brain in the luxury of language. My thoughts were seamed with the gold and silver of Yeats' words, that lit the dull January day with their beauty. I threw myself on my counterpane and only then, in the presence of Nina's empty bed, did I realise I had not thought of her for the whole afternoon. Amy was right. I must immerse myself in other things. It was time to move on.

So it was a relief, at the start of February, to move out to Paradise Street. No more crimped lips from the Cartwright. No more whispers in the dining-room. The longer journey to work, by tram rather than bicycle, was more than compensated for by the pleasant surroundings I now lived in and the warmth of my hosts. I wallowed in my new-found luxury, pushing aside for the present all thought of the slums. And Nina? When she intruded, it was at my invitation, as I gradually came to terms with my own feelings of guilt about her, dipping into it in small doses.

Time passed pleasantly. I threw myself back into teaching, completed the spring term, enjoyed a holiday with my family, and returned at the beginning of the new term refreshed. The room in Paradise Street embraced me on my return, on a beautiful day which held the promise of summer. I looked around with joy at the warmth of the wood in the sunlight and the dust-motes dancing on the air. Sophia had placed a bowl of daffodils on my table and I drank in their perfume as I prepared my lessons for the new term.

I had planned to introduce my class to the poems of William Blake, which I fancied were easy for learning by heart and thus useful for their recitations. Of course I would concentrate on the *Songs of Innocence*; my pupils were too young for the *Songs of Experience*, but reading the latter had brought up afresh all that I had put behind me. Blake's poem *London*, in particular, resonated of the Birmingham slums. Like Blake, I remembered seeing in the faces in those streets 'marks of weakness, marks of woe' and the verse about 'youthful harlots' conjured the faces of Sarah and Millie. The poet activated my guilt again, not about Nina so much – I thought I had laid her ghost to rest – but about all she'd showed me. I had neglected the Club and the elementary school. Now I felt strong enough to resume there and I knew that Miss Derris and Violet needed to know what had happened to Nina.

It was fresh April, a period hovering between spring and summer, where one day could lend, even in Birmingham, a bounce to everyone's step, while the next tipped sleet onto our hats and drove us shivering off the pavements and into the shelter of shop doorways. It was one of these colder spells when I returned to the elementary school.

Miss Derris, I knew, would be the hardest to tell and I wanted to get it over with first. Nina and she had established a strong bond of mutual respect.

I arrived as the girls were leaving, pelting in their inadequate clothing through the falling sleet. One or two of them grinned up as they passed me on the pavement by the gate, but the weather did not encourage more and they ducked their heads and ran shivering on. I did not see Ada among them and Miss Derris herself was out of sight from this angle. Perhaps Ada was helping tidy up in the schoolroom.

Abruptly the sleet stopped and a watery sun came out from chasing clouds. In a rapid succession of sun and shadow I saw the door to the boys' classroom open and Mr Keane's angular body emerge to line them up.

Avoiding his ironic eyebrows, I shuffled past the tense line of boys, whose feet pawed as at a starting line, held back one at a time by their teacher's grip on their narrow shoulders. Then the last boy's name was uttered, with each syllable dwelled upon. As always Mr Keane's whole tone and manner suggested that there were things about this boy that if only the world knew of them, would confine him to the deepest dungeon for life. I had suffered this whole pantomime too many times in the past to want to indulge, yet again, Mr Keane's desire for an audience. So I pushed slowly past, my nostrils full of the smell of boys, quite different, somehow more feral, than that of girls. With relief, I pushed at the familiar scuffed door to the girls' classroom and entered in.

The last time I had been there it had been six months ago, just before Christmas. Nina had been alive but, I now believed, had already chosen her course. The room was quiet.

I stood, unnoticed at first, watching a sharp-elbowed child with a tunic so big for her that the bony wing of a shoulder kept being revealed as her dress slipped sideways. She was not Ada. She collected the slates from each desk, her movements creating a syncopated rhythm: lift the slate, wipe it with a duster, sneeze as the chalk tickled her nostrils, wriggle to realign the shoulder of her tunic and on to the next slate.

The rhythm broke as the child saw me and Miss Derris looked up from the tidying of her desk. Our eyes met and I felt the prickle of tears.

'You can leave now, Lizzie,' she said, her eyes still on mine.

'But, Miss…'

'Thank you, Lizzie. Miss Hazel is here, as you see. We can manage.'

Reluctantly, Lizzie left, with one more hitch of her tunic as she stood framed in the doorway. Miss Derris followed her and shut the door firmly.

Meanwhile, to avoid thought, I picked up the remaining slates and, in a haphazard fashion, piled them on the desk, wiped them with the damp duster and, remembering past observations, collected them in groups of five to stow them on the ledge around the room. I only stopped when Miss Derris put a hand on my shoulder. Then I looked anywhere but at her. Specks of chalk dust floated in the air, illuminated by the sun through the long main window. I couldn't see the dull brick of the privies or the smoothed cobbles of the yard; the bright sun eliminated them and lent to the schoolroom a softness I had never noticed before. Miss Derris had filled two vases with green branches of elder and the sharp heavy scent of their lavish white blossoms hung in the air. The cloying perfume of the elderflower reminded me of death. Elders were flowering all along the canal too.

At last I spoke, the words dredged up through a shroud of

memories of Nina here in this room, her voice, her kindness as she helped with a young person's reading. My words came out in hiccoughs between long silences. Miss Derris, without speaking, guided me to a chair by her desk and sat down with me. Gently, she rested her hand on the back of mine. The solid feel of the wood under my palm calmed me. Like wax near a flame, the soft warmth of her hand on top of mine began to release the words. They started to flow, at first as if negotiating clogs of leaves and twigs, but soon as if the build-up of water thrust these barriers away and tumbled through and over them in their need to pour out. By the end of my tale, both of us were in tears.

For a while, Miss Derris was silent. I stared at the ink-stained surface of her desk. At last, she cleared her throat and spoke. 'It doesn't seem possible, does it, for someone so competent and brisk to be hiding so much turmoil inside herself?'

'It doesn't. But it's new to you. You've had no preparation and the shock must be enormous.' I looked at her, a person who was used to self-control, and noticed a bend in her shoulders, as if something inside had warped her bones into a new shape. 'It sounds heartless, but I have spent so long thinking about her I must try to move on. Is it awful that I feel so much better now I've told you the whole thing?' I explained that I probably would come to the school rarely now, because of my desire to concentrate on the plan to document as much as I could about slum dwellings, with which to confront the Council.

Miss Derris looked doubtful. 'Will they listen? You're just a woman after all.' She accompanied this with an ironic tone and a quirk of her lips which took the sting out of her remark.

'I'll find a way.'

'Good luck. Have you visited the Sanctuary, by the way? Get someone to take you there.'

I had heard of the Sanctuary, a successful venture aimed at helping women and children from the slums, located in the St Mary's area of Birmingham. Violet would take me, I felt sure.

Thinking of Violet made me long once more to busy myself in a place which really needed and appreciated any effort I made, big or small. I got up to go but remembered Ada. Her avid little face swam into my mind. Where had she got to?

Miss Derris clenched her lips. 'Her mother's had a new baby. Ada is acting as nursemaid to her other siblings. It's a tragedy. She's fourteen, but I doubt now whether she'll ever come back. Like so many others, she's sucked into the caring role, the role expected of women.'

'Like Nina.'

She nodded. 'But unlike Nina she has accepted her role.' She rose to accompany me to the door. 'Good luck, Gladys.'

I eyed her. If it were anyone else I would have asked if she needed my company home, or at least that I should stay longer until she felt better. But Miss Derris was used to the habit of control. Like Nina, like Violet, her strongest feelings were reserved for anger at injustice. I wondered at my own tears, so frequent and easy nowadays, after a childhood trying to quell them.

I didn't want to talk about Nina in front of the greedy eyes and ears of our Club members. Instead, I asked Violet to take me to visit the Sanctuary, and I told her as we made our way there. She received the news in grave silence. Her only sign of emotion was to grip my wrist and squeeze it as we walked from the tram-stop towards St Mary's.

'It must have been hard for you,' Violet said as she squeezed. 'I can see why we haven't seen you for a while. But Nina would approve of your new determination to confront our problems.'

I nodded, my heart full, and we walked on in silence until we saw the square tower of St Mary's Church.

'I'll be interested to see what you think of the Sanctuary,' said Violet as we approached. 'It's good to have their example. They've made a real success, particularly with helping the children in this area, but...'

'But what?'

'I'll let you make up your own mind. At least you'll see that our Club is not the only one of its kind, and that we're not lone voices in the wilderness. You'll notice straightaway how very well run this one is.'

She was right. The Birmingham Sanctuary for Women looked smart and clean. I observed the fresh green paint on the doors and window-frames, the whitened steps, the smooth cobbles. Pots of daffodils flanked the entranceway. There were several buildings, all part of the complex, all uncannily neat. Surrounded by slum dwellings, which spidered out in every direction from its hub, it was as startling as a bandage on an unwashed limb.

It was quiet too. Some children were playing in a corner of the first room we entered, under the eye of three smartly dressed women. Meanwhile their mothers, I presumed, waited at a table and talked in low voices. The rattle of their teacups on saucers only emphasised the lack of the kind of din we were used to at our Club. There, only the evenings were quiet, a place for those like Millie and Sarah who sought refuge from the prowling dark. I started to approach the group of tea-drinkers, but was cut off by a woman in a grey skirt with a crisp pink blouse who had been sitting at a desk at the back of the room. She greeted Violet as an old acquaintance and I was introduced as someone interested in the workings of the place.

'Welcome, Miss Hazel. I am Mrs Devine. Do please call me Coral.' Her voice was brisk. I could imagine her making lists, juggling figures, but not putting an arm round a person in distress, not waiting for hours of the evening to encourage a thirteen-year old child to feel safe. 'I'll be delighted to show you around. This room here is where mothers and their children come first. There are plenty of donated toys, and our volunteers organise the childrens' play and make sure they get along nicely with each other.'

She paused to allow us to admire. Two children, watched by a middle-aged woman, took turns placing coloured bricks on top of each other. A small group sat on the floor and listened to the tale of the *Sleeping Princess*. I wondered what they made of the talk of palaces and court life. Not that I felt that children shouldn't be stretched and offered vistas of other worlds and lives to enrich them, but the language of the book was aimed at much older children than these.

I smiled at the woman monitoring the brick-play and noticed with a kind of relief that, as she looked away, the younger girl of the pair knocked over the tower and stuck out her tongue at her partner. Hiding my smile and leaving the helper to sort it out, I turned back to Violet and Coral, who were by the admissions table, looking at the lists of attenders and the rota of volunteers.

'So this is where we decide what help each woman needs,' Coral was explaining, ' and, if it's their first time, we take the children to visit the doctor for a thorough examination. Appropriate treatment is then given, or suggested. Follow me.'

We walked down a scrubbed corridor and into another room where, behind dark green screens, I could hear the murmur of voices as women and children were examined. 'We are so lucky to have the voluntary service of a number of doctors and trained nurses, on a rota basis.'

They were indeed lucky. There was only harried Dr Hayes prepared to come to our Club, when he could. Coral Devine whisked us on, out of a door and into a courtyard flanked by other buildings. These had been stripped and were roofless. Good bricks had been stacked on one side for reuse and a mountain of rubble and rubbish was being moved bit by bit by men with barrows.

'As you can see,' she said proudly, 'We are in the midst of change. We have reclaimed this slum courtyard and are in the process of cleaning up the buildings here into a proper kitchen, where food will be available all day, a room in which disabled children can safely play and even a public house where only soft drinks will be served.' She looked around at Violet and me with triumph. 'Recognising the importance of the public house life for the menfolk, this is our attempt to keep that sense of fellowship going, but to encourage the men away from wasting their money on alcohol. In time, we hope that non-alcoholic public houses will spread throughout the City. To identify problems and then tackle them head-on – that's our motto. No more evasion or sweeping unpalatable facts under the carpet.'

I saw Violet's eyes roam over the rubble and the piles of brick, the men who built and altered, with shovel and pickaxe, to create an idea of how to live with poverty. In contrast to the rooms we had passed through, this area teemed with robust life. Comments and laughter flew between the men and banter, loaded with swear-words, ripened the air around us.

A few paused when they noticed us and 'ello, Ladies,' called out one, his teeth startling in his sooty face. His eyes shifted to me and he leant on his pickaxe. 'I'm 'appy to show a pretty young woman like you 'ow a man works.' Coarse laughter greeted this remark and I blushed as Mrs Devine told the man to keep his eyes on his work and glared around at the laughter of the other men on the site.

'Who finances all this?' Violet said as we moved away.

'There are many good men and women who share our vision,' was the rather huffy reply.

Violet's face was unreadable. I wondered if she was jealous. Her own vision, the Club in Aston, was so disadvantaged compared with this.

We went back into the first room where a young woman had come in, a boy of about four in her arms. Stick-like limbs protruded at odd angles from the folds of his mother's shawl, but the child's face under its peaked cap was bright and his eyes focused.

'Who have we here?' Coral swept to meet them in a rustle of skirts.

Violet and I held back, out of politeness, and watched as Coral took down details and then indicated a chair near the group of mothers.

She returned to us, shaking her head. 'Poor child. Another victim of malnutrition, I fear. We see so many here. The doctor will assess him shortly and we will give all the help we can.'

Shortly after, a group of older mothers, accompanied by a noisy pack of school-age children, barrelled in. The children shoved and jostled towards the empty tables. It seemed they had come to take advantage of a free lunch. Under the cover of the din we quickly thanked Mrs Devine and took our leave. Our last sight was of our guide, who moved determinedly between tables, separating children and creating order out of chaos.

Violet and I walked in silence for a while. Eventually I broke it. 'It's wonderful what they're doing, isn't it? They're obviously very successful.'

'You don't sound very sure.' Violet's voice was neutral.

'Oh, I am sure that it's an excellent venture. It has backing – far more than we have at the Club – and many more volunteers. But... I don't know, I feel that somehow we're all, with the best intentions in the world, going about things in the wrong way. Instead of fighting for real change on a large scale, we are accepting the status quo.'

'Oh, idealist Gladys. There's always going to be poverty. There's always going to be the kind of sickness that has deformed that young boy and that kill so many.'

'But there needn't be, surely? Oh, I know what you're saying. We need the Club and the Sanctuary for the present, I'm not denying that. As long as we don't accept such sticking-plaster solutions as the whole answer.'

We plodded on in further silence for a while. I pulled my collar up against the wind that grabbed at us as we rounded a corner and pushed us down a street full of smart-fronted shops and small businesses. The bustle of this prosperous area, so close to the warren of slums, stirred me up further. I looked at the jewellery tastefully arranged on navy velvet in a window, knowing that behind this very building was the maze of slums we had just passed through. No slum-dweller could afford such pretty luxuries. Nor the tailored dresses and coats in the shop next door. Were the proximity of such things a constant smart to the poor? Or did they just duck their heads and hurry by?

Seeing my expression, Violet pulled me away. 'I know what you're thinking,' she said. 'Tear your mind away for the moment. I want to know what you thought of Coral Devine.'

I didn't answer straightaway. I wasn't sure what it was about the Sanctuary that had me so disgruntled. They were doing good work, compassionate work... And Coral as much or more than anyone. But I hadn't taken to her. She had struck me as cold.

'Well?' prompted Violet as we left the bright shop-fronts behind us.

'I suppose ... oh – a bit pleased with herself. Riding the

wave of her own virtue, I suspect. No, that's cruel, I'm sorry. She's a good woman and she's not sitting at home surrounding herself with the frivolities of the well-to-do. And it was good to see so many volunteers, rich women, who want to help, but … there were just so very many of them. When we arrived there were more society women than there were slum dwellers. They've swamped the spirit of those women and children- suffocated it …'

Violet interrupted. 'Of course they haven't.'

I remembered the girl who stuck out her tongue. 'No. The spirit is there, but the people aren't showing their true selves. They're cowed by the sheer number of society knobs, I suspect. On their best behaviour. Give me Elsie and her lip any day! At least she's real!'

Violet laughed and linked arms with me. 'You're right, Gladys, in some ways. Our Club recognises differences, while that lot there treat everyone like patients arriving at a hospital. It's efficient. It will work and will give genuine relief to far more people than we can, but I too prefer our place and the ebullient characters of our visitors. Here's to Elsie!'

'And Millie and Sarah!'

'Ellen! Mary! Katie!'

Our footsteps increased in pace and fairly rattled along the pavement towards the tram-stop as we shouted out names like hooligans. Like runaways throwing off their fetters.

We made our way straight to the Club, but sitting on the tram I fell once more to brooding on my reactions to the Sanctuary. It seemed to me, I said, that those good women had missed the point. They were not offering answers, but, as Violet had said on an earlier occasion, they were simply putting salve on an open wound, a wound which would keep seeping because their efforts did not begin to touch the real problem, which was, still and always, the housing. Miles of it. In every area of Birmingham. Often hidden behind the exteriors of successful businesses and shop-fronts, like the ones we had just seen for ourselves. A vast spider's web of misery and disease.

'I can't exclude myself,' I concluded. 'Now I live in one of those areas too, where the pillared facades of the rich conceal the courts of the poor, sweep them out of sight, so that we can get away with never thinking about them.'

'So you live in a place where everything is easy. There are servants to oil the machinery of your life. Mine too. How do you think I have time to devote to the Club? I have a cook, a scullery maid and other servants who keep my home running like clockwork, so that my husband might have nothing to complain about. Don't feel guilty about it, Gladys. You are prone to embrace guilt at any excuse. Think of it this way. Living as you do gives you the strength to fight on behalf of others. How would Elsie, or Mary with her nine children, find the time or energy to fight their own cause? They are so worn down by the circumstances of their life that all their strength is consumed by the effort of making it through each day. We need to be strong, you and I, because who else have the poor got to fight for them?'

'But my Paradise Street conceals their Hell Row.'

Violet laughed. 'Your Paradise Street replenishes you so that you will go from strength to strength. Because you are the kind of person you are.'

I had to concede her point. Thank goodness for Violet, who could always slice through my dramatic emotional excesses, to expose the core. She looked at me curiously as we made our way back to our own familiar Club, where, as we entered the door, we were greeted by loud-mouthed Elsie shouting, 'I've been waitin' for yow two, this last 'arf 'our. Did yer fall in the privy, or wot?'

Violet and I exchanged a look and burst into laughter – healing laughter, laughter which swept away the sorrow over Nina, and the contrast between here and the over-organised Sanctuary. No, not swept away. Rather, caused a shift in my inner being, from helpless reactor, tossed this way and that by emotions and outrage, to honed weapon, focused and certain: a sword, as my name suggested. But it would be better if I were an arrow, which might be less clumsy and more far-reaching than a sword.

I leave Truda with the latest pages but cannot bear not knowing how she reacts to them. Is it well-written? Clear? I have been honest about my own short-comings. Will Truda think I am wallowing or being too hard on myself? So I hover, coming in and out of the drawing-room where Truda sits at the round table and turns each page over in a slow steady rhythm without comment, just the occasional nod or sigh. Finally, 'You've never mentioned Nina before,' she says as she puts down the last sheet.

It's strange that it has come to matter that I have done justice to the story as a piece of writing. As if it is fiction when everything is as true as I can remember it. As if it will one day be open to the public eye and I will be judged.

Laughing, I say something of this to her instead of encouraging conversation about Nina.

'Who will judge you?' she responds. 'There's no need. Look how you are judging yourself. For not seeing Nina's state of mind. For your perceived inadequacies on a social level, as a teacher, as a friend.'

I hang my head. 'Is it well-written?' I whisper.

'Why does that matter? The truth is many-faceted,

awkward, lumpy. It cannot be honed into palatable shapes; if that is what you are doing then you are not writing from your heart. You are not exposing your soul for you are too busy making the prose pretty.' She looks at me and her face softens. 'Of course it is well written. But is it the truth? Have you the courage to tell it, all of it, how it is?'

I don't know, I think but cannot say aloud. For soon there is Michael and a lot more that I have hidden away. There are things I have never said to anyone, not even Truda. Do I want her to know that part of me?

'I am so ashamed of how I was,' I blurt.

'You forget that how you were is just how I first loved you. You're no worse than anyone else and mostly a lot better.' She puts her gnarled old hand with its knotty veins over mine; I notice the raised veins in mine too, my flesh darker than hers from the garden. 'Go on as you are,' she continues. 'Let it come out just as it wants to. Ooh, and let's have a cup of tea, shall we? With scrunchies?'

I grin. Scrunchies are my version of flapjacks, hard on the teeth, very oaty and sweet. Peter loves them too. I have some in a tin, left over from his last visit – too short a visit because he was waiting, so excited, for his first child to be born. He was restless, wanting to see me but not wanting to be away too long from his wife, Rosemary. Only a few hours and he was off in his unsuitable old Lagonda, not a car for a baby to travel in I told him, Truda and I waving through the roar of the engine and the smell of exhaust that lingered long in the lane outside our house after he had turned the corner. A baby. Not long after that and Jenifer was born, taking Peter even further away from me. The kettle boils for our tea. I wipe my eyes before loading up a tray with our refreshment.

14

It had taken me a long time to begin reading *The Ballad of Reading Gaol*. It was there, as promised, on my bedside table and, in the months of recovery from the shock of Nina, I would riffle through a couple of stanzas and recoil appalled from the grimness of it.

In the first few weeks of my residence in their home Sophia, who knew about Nina, protected me from stress by keeping our evening meal together light and cheerful. James had to resort to other means to extract an opinion on his loan. He waylaid me often, darting from the drawing-room like a lizard from its hole when he heard my footfall on the stairs. I would explain I had barely begun the book.

'Why?' he asked, genuinely bewildered that I wouldn't race to finish and then enjoy a scholarly discussion of its merits.

I explained about the preparation needed to fulfil my school obligations. He wrinkled his brow, blinked and left it a few weeks.

Then he pounced again, gangly limbs almost tripping themselves up in tangled haste, to prevent my escape up the stairs. At least by now I felt more capable of objective criticism. I had progressed with my reading of the long poem and wondered at the sea-change in Wilde, who had until then always struck me as flippant. I realised that once again I had not looked deeper, at the beating heart below the surface wit.

Standing there on the stairs I explained to my kind host how I was attempting to document the hardships of the poor, most specifically the conditions in which they lived. This meant that I saw the whole idea of imprisonment through the lens of the slums. Weren't the poor in a prison as dark and depressing to the spirit as Wilde found his gaol? To myself I added: hadn't Nina faced a prison too, one as confining and depressing as any?

Delighted that I had at last ventured an opinion, albeit not a literary one, the conversation over the dinner table, a few hours later, ranged around this comparison of mine. In what way were the Birmingham back-to-backs prisons? James listened courteously, his brow deeply lined by an increase in his bewilderment and his attempts to understand my point-of-view.

Some days later, I arrived back from school with a pile of correcting and was half-way up those wide stairs. This time it was Sophia who chased after me. She followed me into my room. I placed my books on the oak table by the window.

'Have you much to do?' she asked tentatively. 'Only… we have a guest for dinner.'

'Oh,' I said, 'that's fine. I can eat up here and leave you to enjoy the company in peace.' This happened quite often. Both Sophia and James had family and many friends. Then there were the times I was out late and ate cold cuts in my room – far superior to those that the Cartwright had laid aside for Nina and me.

Sophia eyed my exercise books. 'Are you very busy or can it wait? We have a particular writing friend of James's here today. We want very much for you to dine with us. We thought that you and Bradley would find much in common.'

Was this an exercise in match-making? Such a thing had not happened before. I hesitated.

'Bradley is a journalist,' Sophia continued. 'He has had articles published in many newspapers in London as well as locally. In fact he is doing rather well.' She laughed lightly, not without a wistful envy. 'Much better than James. Poor James, he is fixated on tackling a novel. Have you read anything by Thomas Hardy? He is the latest in a long line of idols. Now it's a tragic love story, unfolding in a Dickensian kind of city, that James has turned to.'

'I thought he wrote poetry.'

'Yes, he does. But he is turning, he says, to something more commercial, since his poetry makes little money. Plenty of critical acclaim, but that doesn't put food on the table.'

Poor Sophia sounded very bleak. When I first moved here I might have been less sympathetic, taken in as I was by the outward show of wall-hangings, carved wood and the size of the sombre pictures. But, under her tutelage, I had seen how the wall-fabrics had worn thin, how the pictures were drowning under a patina of ancient grease that resisted anything as cheap and easy as the cloth or duster. The wood of the banister was chipped and you had to watch carefully which of the chairs you pulled out to sit in, for many of the legs were broken, and the velvet seat-coverings were frayed. As for the glorious piano, I had tried it myself, with Sophia's encouragement. Even with my lack of musicianship I could hear the tinny tone of the keys. If only Rita's Bill, so skilled a musician, could have visited and given the piano the new lease of life it wanted. But Bill was far away, in Canada. Though I was fond of him part of me still wished he wouldn't come back, for then Rita would be lost to me too.

I turned my thoughts away. I still had Mama and Papa. We wrote to each other with our news, but infrequently. The ties that bound us together had loosened. Now it was the outer world that had bitten hard into me, as it had into most of my siblings. It was shaking us all, as a terrier does a nest of rodents.

'Like you,' said Sophia, 'Bradley is concerned with the conditions of the slums.' She waited.

I looked at the pile of books. They suddenly appeared less important. A man. And a journalist. Now, what if I could make him into the arrow I needed to break through the armour of the City Council?

Bradley turned out to be a rather over-weight but twinkly young man, with round Pickwickean spectacles. Behind those spectacles brown eyes blinked anxiously at me, and his rather feminine, rosebud mouth smiled with a downward curve, which added to an impression of diffidence. He was taller than me, but not by much, and his clothes bore the rumpled look of someone who slung them over a chair at night without much regard for their welfare. When gangly James came to stand by him, I couldn't help laughing at the contrast between the two friends.

My delighted laughter broke the ice and the first impression of diffidence melted quickly away under the flood of cultured conversation, washed down with wine. I couldn't help noticing that James drank two glasses to every one of Bradley's. As for Sophia and me, we sipped slowly and made our glasses last. The more he drank, the more James's words soared in elaborate flights of fancy, underpinned by Bradley's more worldly and astute comments. I had never seen my host inebriated, and wondered at it. Perhaps it was just the enjoyment of the moment.

They told me of their meeting at Oxford. Both at Corpus, both on the same staircase, both reading English.

'I had to take pity on him,' said James. 'He would never have survived without me.'

Bradley laughed. 'And there was I thinking it was you who had to be dragged, kicking and screaming, into the modern world.' He turned to me, brown eyes U-shaped with mirth. 'You'd never credit it, Gladys, but James wouldn't read anyone who came after the Metaphysicals. He was a Jacobean through and through. He dressed in black, with floppy silk cravats and had perfected a series of melancholy poses. Oh, and he was much given to looming at the sides of rooms in the shadows, from where his hollow voice would suddenly boom out, at most inopportune moments, frightening all others in the room. So, you see, I just had to drag him into the light.' He raised his glass to James. 'You became my mission, dear friend.'

'You cured me or I'd never have won such a fair lady as my Sophia.'

'That's true. Though you did woo her with poetry of a strained and tortured kind. I can't imagine why you fell for it, Sophia.'

'No one else would have thought of writing me poetry at all. It is flattering to be the subject of such sighs and tears.'

'Don't you dare quote them, dearest! Those poems were a young man's splutterings and not for general consumption.' I was surprised to see how anxious James looked.

Sophia blew him a kiss down the length of the table. 'Never fear. They will always be precious to me. Now, the only thing we ought to consume is cook's good food. Bradley, you'd make a better job of carving this meat than James. Will you do the honours?'

I enjoyed the conversation and seeing how the two friends bounced ideas off each other but, as the steaming pudding arrived, I grew anxious that we'd never get to the subject of the slums.

'I hear that you're concerned with the plight of the poor...'
I began.

'Not now,' said Sophia. 'Wait till after the meal, Gladys, if
you don't mind. I can't bear to spoil the food with earnestness.'

'Nor I,' said Bradley, wiping his spectacles free of steam
and replacing them. 'No earnestness when confronted by jam
sponge. Absolutely my favourite!' He applied himself with
gusto to the dessert but smiled reassuringly at me before he
tucked in. It was a promise and I gave in gracefully.

Once again the conversation reverted to literature, but in
a more serious fashion. Why was it that James's poetry hadn't
taken off with the public? Was it too old-fashioned?

'I am still a Jacobean at heart,' confessed James, finishing a
bottle. 'I believe the reader should work at a poem to uncover
its meaning.'

'And the public is too lazy to work at it. They want the
lyrical nothings of such as Tennyson,' said Bradley.

'Tennyson is not nothing,' I protested, still in love with the
Morte-d'Arthur and *The Lady of Shalott*, which had excited my
younger years.

Both men looked at me and waited. Bradley's eyes gleamed
behind his spectacles. 'I mean, that his craft is second to none.
The way he uses alliteration ... his rhythms ...' Under their
gaze I fumbled to a stop.

'As I thought,' said James. 'Tennyson is a woman's poet.' He
struggled with the cork of another bottle.

Sophia put her hand over it. 'Don't you think you've had
enough, dear?' James grinned back at her. 'What d'you mean?
We're celebrating.'

'Celebrating what?' asked Sophia.

'Bradley's sell-out as a word-hack, of course.' His grin at
Bradley took any sting out of the words. 'Bradley has decided
to forget our efforts to start a new revolution, to put muscle

and rigour back into literature – all the things we talked about as students.' He slapped the table and the glasses rattled.

There was a tiny pause. Bradley grimaced apologetically at me. Sophia successfully pulled the bottle from James's grasp and replaced it with a glass of water.

'What could I do?' Bradley finally said, his tone light and humorous. 'Faced with your obvious superiority, I had to embrace the lower road. Unlike you, I had no cushion of inheritance from my parents...'

'A very small one,' slurred James.

'Small, but enough to allow you to keep to the high road, dear friend. Especially with the ability to use your inherited house to make money, through lodgers as utterly charming as Gladys.' He dipped his head in my direction. 'Lacking your advantages, what recourse had I but to use my facility with words in another way?'

'To sell yourself to the highest bidder.' James shook his head in maudlin disappointment.

'Not so,' Bradley countered. 'I may adopt the kind of style the public like to read, but I choose the subjects that interest me.'

Was now the time? I opened my mouth but caught Sophia's eye. She gave a little shake of her head. I knew that soon I would have to go to bed. There was school tomorrow. But it would be rude to move before my hostess.

We sat amongst the debris of our meal. Jane, the little serving-girl – the only member of the house-staff apart from the cook – arrived heavy-eyed to clear the table.

'Let's retire to the drawing-room,' said Sophia. 'Just clear away and then go to bed, Jane. You needn't wait up.'

'Thank you, ma'am.'

Bradley waited until the door had creaked shut behind her before he said, 'You know how I feel about servants. Why do you still have any?'

In answer, James threw his arms wide, to indicate the size

of the house. 'It's too much for Sophia to do on her own. As it is, Jane cannot manage either. Once a season, Sophia's mother sends a posse of servants from her house to clean the place from top to bottom. And that will have to do.'

'I predict that in twenty years time there will be no servants or large houses like this for the middle classes. The world is changing.' Bradley looked at me. 'You're a member of those classes, Gladys, what do you think?'

'I suppose I am middle class, but a very poor one. We never had servants when I was a little girl in Ireland.'

'Aah, well, Ireland! What do you expect?' James was showing the results of his drinking. His long spine had begun to collapse forwards, as if unable to maintain the effort required to keep his head balanced on his neck.

'You're Irish?'

'Not at all,' I said, and laughed at myself as I slipped automatically into an Irish lilt. Our roots, I thought, are never very far away. 'We've lived in England since I was ten. And over here we do have a cook and general help to my mother, who comes from the village every day. Sometimes, her son helps in the garden and the farm labourers do any outside heavy work and keep our orchards fruitful.'

'You see. You have a grand estate – land! Farms!'

I liked Bradley. I was pleased that he had reached a point in the space of a single evening where he felt he could tease. It reminded me of home.

As we moved into the hallway to go to the drawing-room, Sophia excused herself. She was tired. She looked at me, expecting that I would accompany her upstairs but now I was having too good a time, and said so.

'I'll come up soon,' I said, watching her ascent of the shallow bright wood stairs until she disappeared into the shadows at the top.

'You'll be too tired to face your classes tomorrow.' Her face appeared briefly, a disembodied mask, leaning over the top banister.

I laughed and she shrugged good-naturedly and disappeared. 'Don't talk all night.' Her voice floated down.

'You're a teacher?' asked Bradley, immediately interested. 'From what you've been talking about this evening I thought you were another writer. How do you find time to document the slums?'

'You know about that?'

'Sophia told me. It's one of the reasons I'm here tonight.'

So I needn't have worried. I stood there, in the hallway, with the front door behind me, the stairs in front. Between was the expanse of the wooden floor, with its large oval table in the centre and its arrangement of dried flowers and grasses – all browns, gold and russet. In the warm gaslight the hall looked shining and grand, but I knew that was an illusion. In daylight, cobwebs linked the brittle stalks of the dried flowers and the parquet floor was chipped and pitted with careless use.

We never got as far as the drawing-room. There in the hallway, I told Bradley about the Club, about the elementary school, and about Nina who had started me on the road. Bradley went still. His eyes were on me.

'Is she the one who …? I wrote about her in my Christmas piece.' He turned to James. 'That article I sold to the London Gazette, remember, James? I showed it to you. After Christmas, I followed the story up.' He came to a stop.

Both men were now looking at me, as I swayed on legs that had turned to rubber. 'You're – *that* journalist?' I finally managed, through lips stiff with shock. Bradley leapt forward and caught me as I tottered. James pushed up a chair and I sat. From there, I spilled out Nina's story, hinting at but not dwelling on my own feelings of guilt.

'The important thing,' said Bradley, ' is that you are following where she pushed you. You are doing something about the conditions.'

'But I'm not, don't you see? I'm not getting anywhere. I blunder about like a beetle, observing, seeing, making mistakes, but the people I most want to help just continue suffering, dying, succumbing to hardship. They don't even expect any better. That's how it has always been for them, for their parents too, and their grandparents.'

'And so on ad infinitum.'

'Yes, Bradley. That's just it – and so on ad infinitum. Nothing changes.' I felt a huge weariness wash over me. 'It's our helplessness, as women, that feels so overwhelming. No one else cares.'

'On the contrary,' Bradley knelt by my chair and looked earnestly at me. 'There are many of us who do care. I think you'd be surprised how many good men feel as you do.'

He looked towards James, who had collapsed on the bottom stair, and started to smile. It became a gentle, ironic laugh, as a snore emerged from our host, his mouth dropped open and his head fell to one side with a thud against the banister support.

'I was going to include James as one who does care. He does, though he is not yet as aware as he might be. We can do something about that, can't we, Gladys? We'll bring together what I can investigate and combine that with observations of your own, and present it together to the City Council. What do you think?'

'I think it's a wonderful idea.'

We made plans to meet up here at the weekend in a month's time and I went to bed with a lighter heart. Something was beginning. Something good.

15

I hoped to add to the odd jottings I already had in my journal so, on my next afternoon off, I took a pen and notebook with me and boarded a tram. My intention was to gather more material, to impress Bradley with my diligence.

I travelled down to the Bullring, from where it was an easy walk into Digbeth and over the River Rea, via the canal bridge, into Deritend. I paused on the bridge to look over at the river, whose sparkling waters I'd sat beside on many occasions in its northern reaches. The contrast couldn't have been greater. Here the water moved sluggishly, as if weighted down by its surroundings. The sides of buildings towered over it and stole its light. The current churned and threw up silt and filth and the air smelt of soot and mud.

Deritend I knew contained some of the worst areas of slum housing but it was an area I had not previously visited. I filled a notebook with sketches and my own observations, but if spotted, I was seen off.

'Wot yow 'anging about 'ere for?' said one, blocking her doorway with her body to shield it from my probing eyes, while another set a squat dog with massive jaws onto me, who chased me out of the court and halfway down the alley.

The worst incident was when a furious woman, wearing rusty black and a man's peaked cap jammed over her ears, gave a piercing whistle that brought more women out from every door in the court.

'Wot yer doin', Mrs Nosey-parker? Spying for the landlord? You should be ashamed of yerself!'

'I'm just trying to help...' I began, but the rest of the women drew together in a threatening group.

'We doan't want help from the likes of yower kind. Get on out of 'ere.'

One of them advanced on me with a broom, whacking the cobbles in front of her as she approached. Another woman broke out of the group and threw the filthy contents of a bucket in my direction. My skirt was spattered, but fortunately most of it fell short. I wanted to run, but the alley was filled with other women and their children, attracted by the noise. A group of young boys, no older than four or five, pushed through their mothers' skirts and chased after me, whooping and hollering.

'Bugger orf outa 'ere,' they yelled and threw stones, like a shower of hail, luckily with no great accuracy. Their efforts, however, opened a pathway through the crowds, which I was quick to take. Picking up my skirts, slipping and sliding on the wet and uneven cobbles, I ran, pursued by coarse laughter.

My hair was falling around my face and my clothes sticking to me with the humiliating sweat of fear. Fancying that a more public place would be safer, I made my way to nearby Smithfield Market.

Here there was a jumble of open-air stalls and street-sellers, with anything from meat and vegetables, to second-hand clothes and household items. The noise was incredible: the rattle of carts over the cobbles, the stall-holders shouting their wares, the strident ringing of a hand-bell as a market-seller sought to outdo the competition. Smells assailed me from all sides: fish, old meat that my mother would have walked past in disdain, coal, wood, dust, dirt, ammonia from the buckets tipped to wash down the cobbles – each in turn caught and snagged on the unwary throat.

I saw children scrabbling in the cobbles around the stalls. They filled bags with tiny pieces of coal – little more than dust – dropped paper, ends of wood: fuel for their fires, I guessed. I lingered as close to particular stalls as I could, to hear the haggling and the prices, noticing how many of the poorly dressed women were content with lumps of fatty gristle, or bacon bits. Good vegetables heaped onto the stalls were passed over by these women, who settled for the outer leaves of a cabbage or potatoes past their best. Some of these treasures, turned over by richer customers, ended up on the floor and were collected up by the children, who stuffed them in their pockets.

All too soon, once more my observations began to be noticed. Under a rain of abuse from both stall-holders and customers, I had to leave. My determination and desire to find out more, though, was not in the least bit dampened. I would just have to go about my researches in a different way.

Frustrated at the lack of success of my first weekend's research, I persuaded Violet to accompany me the following week. She did better still. She spoke to my old nemesis, Elsie, who insisted on coming too. This meant we were closer to the Club, in the slums of the Lozells area, which bordered Aston.

'You'll want a body wot knows 'er way around,' she bellowed. 'You can cum to my court.'

I found myself taking a breath as we plunged into the long terrace of houses leading to Elsie's home.

As if we were explorers entering the jungle, and she was the native guide, she pointed dramatically down the terrace. 'Ower grove,' she said and clattered in on her noisy wooden clogs.

'Grove?' I asked, trotting to keep up.

'Wot we call our alley.'

'If there were a single tree,' I commented to Violet, 'I could understand it.'

'If you were a bird and looked down on the terraced streets with the branches of the courts leading off, perhaps then it would make more sense,' said Violet. 'I imagine on a map laid on the town planner's desk, the tangle of the roads reminded the council of woodland.' Her mouth twisted. 'Those people don't have to live in them, of course.'

'I wonder if they thought conferring the names of flowers and trees on these hell-holes would make the inhabitants view them in a better light.' The narrow 'grove' we walked down now was squeezed between the two rows of brick houses with their grey slate roofs. The cobbles were rough and uneven underfoot, with large gaps where stones were missing. I was glad it was not a winter evening. Gas-lights were few and far between and the route would be treacherous.

Elsie waited for us impatiently. 'Cum on, yow two,' she yelled. 'We're 'ere. Honeysuckle Court. And 'ere's my home, number 3.'

First we walked into a tiny downstairs room. Greyish washing hung over the backs of chairs, arranged close to the blacked grate at one end. Above the meagre fire in this grate hung a pot, and a kettle with a large handle stood near the hearth.

'Is this all…?' I managed before Violet interrupted, drowning out the rest of my sentence and giving me a painful nudge.

'I told you, didn't I, Elsie, how Gladys is hoping to find out as much as possible about back-to-backs like yours. She and a journalist friend are going to tell people about your homes and what changes you'd like to make. Then they will try to get something done about all those hardships you have to put up with.'

Elsie glowered at me and folded her arms across the shelf of her bosom. 'I don't want no trouble from the landlord,' she bellowed. 'Wot yer sees, yer can see fer yerself. You're not getting any mower help from me than bringin' yer 'ere.'

I took the hint and looked around the rest of the room, keeping any further questions locked behind my teeth, while Elsie planted herself at the bottom of a narrow bare staircase leading upstairs and firmed her lips into a pleat. The walls bloomed with mould, interlaced with cracks in the plaster, like the contours on a map. The low ceiling bulged with damp. A hole in the glass of the single window was stuffed with rags against the draught.

Upstairs were two rooms, one no more than a boxroom, filled entirely by a single bed. Here, Elsie explained, her husband and herself slept, "Cept when he's had a jug of ale and fallen asleep afore the fire.' The larger room had a rickety bed in it, piled with coats and a couple of stained blankets. Where had I seen something similar before? Yes, Ireland. The O'Connor children had all slept together under a heap of clothes and blankets, with no sheets to lie soft against bare skin. But in that room there had been light and, outside, the continual wash of the sea. Here, the peeling walls, covered with a watery white distemper which helped to glue the hair and dirt plaster together, were stained with black soot marks from candles and the blood-filled bodies of squashed bugs.

Avoiding a bucket at the top of the stairs, which Elsie explained was because the younger children had difficulty finding the outside closet at night, we made our way back down. Our visit had created interest in the court and the lower room when we returned was full of children, while outside a herd of women jostled at the open door.

Once Elsie had explained why we were there, she puffed out her chest in pride to be the centre of attention, and bossed the others with strident commands.

'Ag – you tek 'em in and show the work you do at home...' Her eye roved over the rest and turned to us. 'You won't want to tek notice of the rest. Their houses're the same as mine.'

She over-rode the protests that greeted this comment. 'Wot's the point?' she bellowed. 'There's only so much a body can tek in of the way we 'ave to live. It's the same wherever you go, ent it? Norf, Souf, East or West.' Her arms flew in wide gestures. 'This lady 'ere,' she gestured to me, 'is goin' to tek ower story to the papers. Then it'll go to the King hiself, prob'ly. Ent that so?'

I nodded feebly, unwilling to disillusion Elsie or puncture her standing with her neighbours. Somewhere between my entry into her front room and my descent from the bedrooms I had obviously changed status in her eyes, from an ignorant, clumsy busybody to something of a celebrity.

We were taken round the court itself, shown the standpipe for water in the centre and the tin bath hanging on the wall, which was for everybody's use. A younger woman, with a baby tucked sideways under her arm, wrapped so tightly in a cloth that it resembled a sausage roll, insisted on showing me the closets along the back wall, from which such a noxious reek emerged that it was hard to control a reflex to vomit. Each one was shared between three to five families, she explained. Holding my breath, I saw a square box with a large round hole in the top. There was a nail in the wall on which bits of newspaper were fixed.

'The littl'uns 'ave to 'ang on tight,' said my guide, ''cos the 'ole's too big for 'em. I remember fallin' half down there and my big sister 'avin' to haul me out.' She chuckled. 'Mrs Hathaway puts all 'er bills on the nail. She says they might as well be of some use. Better wipin''er arse than worryin''er on the kitchen mantle.'

'I use me bills for lightin' the fire. Best place for 'em.' This came from a woman who had piled in behind me, blocking the exit.

Slowly I let the stale air out from my lungs and took in an experimental breath. The stench was unbelievable. I knew I would disgrace myself if I had to linger any longer.

The young woman grinned, clearly enjoying my discomfort.

'Over 'ere's the wash-house,' she said. 'Beginnin' of t'week, first person rolls their dirty clothes over in the maiding-tub and fills the copper wiv hot water and soap. We like *Rickett's Blue* soap powder, 'cos it makes the clothes a lovely blue.'

'Better than grey, which the whites turn into after a while,' agreed another.

I looked around at the equipment in the wash-house, recognising the dolly which we also used, at home, to agitate the washing in the soapy water. In a corner there was an ancient and rust-stained mangle. I learned that, soap-powder being expensive, the same soap and water was used by every household and had to last the whole day. I couldn't bear to think of how dirty the water must be by the end of the afternoon.

'Yow wanta see my little business at home?' interrupted the woman Elsie had called Ag.

She led me into Number 7. It couldn't have been more different from Elsie's, which in comparison was homely. This was all the room contained: a long table, which stretched to within an inch of the grate at one end – the only warmth in the room – and nearly blocked the access to the stairs at the other end; a sofa, jammed against the wall and with its front half concealed under the table; four wooden chairs on two of which a couple of ancient women sat bent over, their noses almost touching the table's surface. On the table were piled garments of a heavy material such as I imagined factory workers might wear, and the old women moved their matchstick fingers to wield their needles in and out, in and out. They were sewing button-holes. Each push through the heavy cloth was an effort, and I could see that the ends of their fingers were blistered and calloused by the repetitive action.

The room was dark, lit only by a couple of candles in jars, one by each of the workers. There was a gas-light on the wall but it was rarely used, Ag explained, since it was expensive. Pennies in the meter released the gas, but few could afford to use their hard-come-by cash in this way. It was a luxury kept mainly for special occasions.

'How can you see to stitch?' I asked one of the old women, whose nose hovered an inch above the cloth she was working.

Ag folded her arms and glared at me. 'You 'ere to cause trouble?'

'Not at all,' I hastened to reassure her.

Ag explained that the two workers were her mother and her mother-in-law. They could no longer manage factory-work in their old age. There was too much competition from younger women for those kind of jobs. They could, however, do piece-work at home and this brought in much needed pence for the whole family.

Behind the table, from the dark shadows, came a squawk. I shifted my gaze in that direction and saw that two children lay in the gloom of the battered sofa, their bodies partly concealed by the table. The flickering candle-light showed the dark hollows of their eyes and the pallor of their cheeks. One rested his head on the other one's lap, and both looked listless.

I don't know what it was about this particular room that haunted me. I wrote of it to Mama and Papa, as well as putting down every detail into my notes to share with Bradley. The dankness of the air, the shadowy dark, the unnatural quiet of the children, the twiglike wrists and fingers of the old people, all worked a kind of horror on me that I could not shake off.

Even going back to Elsie's house, where tea was offered all round in chipped but loved cups, even the obvious camaraderie and mutual supportiveness of those who shared this court, could not undo the sight of that cheerless room and its occupants. They etched themselves on my retina and accompanied me back to the Club with Violet, and thence to my comfortable home in Paradise Street.

16

Bradley and I met up in due course, under the interested eyes of Sophia and James. We pooled ideas and Bradley offered to weave it together into a coherent document. 'We need pictures, too. Photographs of the interiors of these homes, or at least good illustrations. I have a photographer friend.'

He also promised a campaign of snippets from our findings as newspaper releases. These, he explained needed to be the first advance. A few months of stories about hardship and images of the living conditions and public opinion would be roused. This in turn would work to shame the Council for its neglect.

For my part, I wanted to approach the Council straightaway. But Bradley advised against it. Such tactics would only put their backs up. They needed to be softened up first.

I sighed. 'How long will all this take?'

'Years probably.'

I closed my eyes. 'Isn't there a quicker way?'

James chipped in, speaking to me gently. 'We all know how hard you've worked. But just think how long it would take even if they agreed to make changes straightaway. You're talking of building new houses, of destroying their present homes and starting again.'

'It'll be very expensive,' said Sophia.

'You can't just go in wielding a sledgehammer and create immediate change. It's not going to happen,' agreed Bradley. 'People need to be made aware first.'

I thought for a bit. 'You're right,' I said finally. 'We have to change minds. I had no idea how dreadful things were until Nina forced me to look. Most people will have as little idea as I did.'

'Exactly,' said Bradley with a smile. 'Our stories in the newspapers will rub people's noses in what they don't want to see. They will be uncomfortable about it, but a significant number will begin to ask for reform.'

'No marching into the Council offices with our document of demands then,' I said, ruefully. I had rather fancied myself as a Valkyrie, wielding my flaming sword.

'That's not how it works.'

'You met Bertie Foster-Smythe Bradley, when you interviewed him for that article you wrote at Christmas,' said Sophia. 'Isn't he on the Council? You could try presenting the document to him.'

'I've met him too,' I said, and told them about my visit to the theatre. 'I cannot forget how he called his workers animals. Personally, I wouldn't want to see the man again.'

'He's at least getting rid of slums near his factory,' said Bradley.

'Only so that he can expand his business.' Nothing would convince me that the man who'd shown his lack of respect for women by fondling my knee when his wife was out of sight had any good in him at all. I saw his smug expression, his wet, too red mouth and shivered.

'We need to start somewhere,' said Bradley, after a pause

in which he looked at me with a puzzled frown. 'All right, Gladys, I might approach the man myself but will you write some of the articles for the paper? I'll try to put them in under your name but they may not accept them. You're not a proven journalist, as I am. And you're a woman. But I'll do what I can to make the editors accept you as a new voice.'

This idea perked me up, despite Bradley's assertion that it was still difficult for women as writers to be taken seriously, and despite the time it would take. It was hard to accept that change wouldn't happen overnight. That those two ancient women, working till they dropped of exhaustion in the cold and damp, would probably never see the benefit of what we were beginning. That Ada would spend her life in the slums, without the escalator of education to carry her out of them. That Millie and Sarah's young faces would become hard and bitter as they sold their bodies for pennies. But something had to be done. And Bradley and I would work together to do it.

Not for a moment did I believe that it would take as long as Bradley said. But three long years of frustration followed, years in which Bradley and I tried to batter down the portals of the wealthy. I closed my eyes and thought of the foot-slogging grind of it, the crushed hopes as those who might effect change resisted, even when faced with incontrovertible evidence. It was a difficult and depressing time.

By the end of 1908 the division between school and my work at the Club and as an occasional journalist had become easier to manage. Bradley's name was accepted without question when we sent articles to newspapers in Birmingham and beyond. He was a well-known journalist. More importantly, he was a man. The issues we wrote about, the lurid phraseology we sometimes used to capture attention, were not considered the province of a woman.

I wrote about prostitution, disguising the names of Sarah and Millie; talked of the difficulties of educating the poor, using my own experiences in the elementary school; spoke of how difficult it was for a girl born to poverty to rise out of it. I cited the pressures of caring as something that pulled women away from useful work and raged against the need for a married woman to give up her career. None of these were popular subjects. In fact, they were considered too shocking and radical to have been written by a woman. After the first rejects, I took Bradley's advice and began to use my initials, GMH, rather than my full name. Let them think I was a man, if that made them happier; the uncomfortable truths were still reaching the breakfast tables of the wealthy and, I hoped, disturbing their rest. But the hovels of the poor remained and it seemed change was as far away as ever. Everything was too slow for my impatient spirit.

Then, in late January 1909, Violet told me that there was to be a large meeting of the suffragists at the Town Hall. Would I accompany her there? The last time she'd asked me to such a meeting I had not even heard of them. Now no one could be unaware of their cause as their campaign hotted up and thousands of women flocked to support them. I had declined the last time Violet asked me, some years ago, but things had changed. I had changed. I had experienced for myself how women were marginalised and not listened to. Perhaps suffrage would give us more clout. It was worth going, at least, to make my own judgement.

When I mentioned it to Bradley, he was keen to be included. 'You mustn't wear your reporter's hat,' I said.

'I always wear my reporter's hat. It's what I do. What do you mean?'

'I mean that you shouldn't go with any pre-conceived notion like I'm always reading in the papers – a lot of hysterical women, that sort of thing.'

'I wouldn't dare!' he teased.

Bradley and I arranged to meet Violet on the steps of the fountain in Chamberlain Square, but we were early. It was a surprisingly mild day, the sky low with layers of cloud, but no rain. The steps, the raised area around the fountain and the space between that and the high podium, on which the Town Hall's Corinthian pillars rested, were milling with people. Scarves, hats, heavy coats and muffs, in the dark shades of winter wear, jostled around each other. It could, from the air of excitement, have been a group of people waiting for a treat: the start of a parade or the arrival of royalty.

There were a lot of women, as one would expect, but a great many men too. Some of the older men, dressed in their dirty working clothes, were clumped together, laughing and pointing at the women. Roving bands of youths, peaked caps pulled low on their foreheads, threaded the crowds. There were one or two well-dressed gentlemen, escorting women, but I was puzzled by the presence of the working men and, especially, the adolescents. Why were they there? It could only be to cause trouble, or to take advantage of the crowds in some way.

'Watch out for pick-pockets,' I said to Bradley, who always kept money loose in his gaping coat pockets.

'I think they've other things on their mind,' he answered, and he directed my gaze towards the porticoed front of the town-hall.

There, animated groups of young men were filling up the spaces between the arches, all but blocking the arcaded entrance to the building.

'Is that their plan, do you think? To make it difficult for us to enter?' I asked.

'It's possible. Just keep watching.' His hand reached up to his top pocket for his notebook and pencil.

A gang of boys ran through the crowd like starlings, scattering the knots of women. There were cries of protest, but the children moved too fast. They were heading towards us, running and jumping, as if this was all some great game. Hopscotching over some older men, who were seated on the steps, and pushing through some women who were beginning to make their way down towards the hall, they flew up the steps towards us by the fountain. Now they were close, I could see that their hands were covering their pockets, all of which bulged suspiciously.

Bradley and I moved aside a little to let them by, and watched as the boys jumped onto the low wall surrounding the pond, which contained the water from the fountain in front of the Chamberlain Memorial. They teetered there. One fell backwards into the water, causing shouts of mirth from the others.

'First bath you've 'ad in a month!' I heard, as the boy pulled himself out and stood dripping. His face was woebegone, as he began to check the contents of his pockets. They were full of pebbles.

I had cause to remember gangs of boys with stones, from the night that I discovered Millie and Sarah in the alleyway. I looked around at the bulging pockets of the other youngsters, poised the length of the wall.

'I think this could get rough,' I said, nudging Bradley. 'I wish Violet would get here.' I told him about what I'd learnt from the women at the Club about gang warfare, for which stones – usually larger than these, and chipped to give them a sharp edge – were the weapon of choice, as each gang patrolled the perimeters of their own particular 'manors'.

'You're right. Trouble is in the air. You can almost smell it.' Bradley was scribbling hard. 'Keep close to me and you'll be all right.'

I'd like to have believed him, but Bradley's rather portly stature and his kind round face, didn't advertise strength.

Where was Violet? Had she been delayed? Even with the crowds milling round the square she should be able to see us up on the raised area.

People were beginning to go into the hall, but they were not finding it easy. The youths we'd seen lining up in the arcade had relaxed into more casual groupings. It would be hard for anyone to accuse them of deliberately blocking the entrance, but I was sure this was the truth of the matter.

We watched as other young men, working together, pushed between women as they talked to each other. They used elbows and shoulders to shove them roughly aside. With dismay, I saw one woman stagger and fall to the ground under this treatment. Her friends helped her up and I could see she was not hurt, but she was shocked. Her group looked around for the perpetrators, but they had moved elsewhere.

A stone was thrown from our left. It whirred past me and straight into a group moving towards the hall, catching the back of a man's neck. His hand flew up to investigate and he turned and looked straight at me with a frown. Then his eyes shifted to the boys on the wall. I saw understanding cross his face and he marched away from his group, into the arcade, and came back with a couple of policemen. As soon as they saw the police, the boys jumped down and ran to the other side of the square. The police shrugged and returned to the arcade, despite remonstrations from the man, joined by his whole group of women.

From my vantage point I could see that the boys had not run far. They were the other side of the square, in front of Josiah Mason College, where they entertained themselves, throwing pebbles up into the air and catching them.

'Why do you think the police seemed so indifferent?' I asked Bradley.

'I expect that they were charged with seeing there is no trouble at the Town Hall itself and couldn't leave their posts.'

'They didn't look at all concerned about that man.'

Bradley looked at me sympathetically. 'You still don't get it, do you? The victim may have been a man, but he is clearly a supporter of suffrage. The police are not. Their sympathies are, for once, more on the side of the troublemakers than those who have come to the meeting.'

'Oh, surely not!' I had great faith in the police who, in Birmingham, had a difficult and dangerous job controlling the many gangs and intervening in their battles.

'You'll learn,' was Bradley's cryptic reply.

As if to support this cynicism, the boys on the other side of the square suddenly crossed the space between us and ran up one side and down the other side of the steps, brushing so close to me that I staggered against Bradley. They dodged large groups of women but knocked individuals aside in their flight, leaped over a group of young men seated on the ground between one of the arches, and disappeared into the building.

'What are they up to?' I asked.

'Trouble of some kind. I've no doubt we'll find out.'

'Will the speakers at the meeting be safe?'

'The police won't let anyone be hurt, wherever their sympathies lie. It'll be all right.' He didn't sound certain.

The hubbub of voices in the square made it hard to hear anything. Was it my imagination, or had the quality of the sound changed? When we arrived, there was excitement in the voices of women greeting each other and exchanging news, but now it was punctuated by staccato shouts from some of the working men. From their faces, distorted by hatred, it was clear they were hurling insults. I saw a stocky middle-aged man spit straight into an elderly woman's face and felt sick. A more orderly group of older men linked arms and chanted,

'Women, Home, Women, Home.' Did they mean *Go home*, or were they linking the two words to suggest that home was where a woman belonged?

The crowds of women, many wearing purple, green and white bands on their hats, which Bradley explained were the colours of the W.S.P.U., or square brooches on their lapels, began to move purposefully towards the main door of the Town Hall. The time had approached for the start of the meeting. At last I spotted Violet, looking around for us.

'Sorry to be so late,' she said breathlessly. 'You'd think the whole world was heading in this direction. So many people and cabs blocking the streets. My tram was held up and in the end I just got off it early and ran! It wasn't like this the last time I came to one of these meetings. I suppose it's because Mrs Pankhurst is here this time.'

'Mrs Pankhurst herself is going to be here?' I filled up with excitement. Sophia and James sometimes left the newspaper for me to read, and this lady's doings were often reported.

I looked around for Bradley, to introduce him to Violet, but he'd moved closer to the porticoed entrance to the hall and was scribbling still harder.

Before we could reach him, a young man patted Bradley companionably on the back. 'Good on yer, mate,' I heard. 'Glad to see you're writing down wot those bitches're up to.' He didn't wait to hear what Bradley had to say, but moved rapidly past. Still, I waited till he had disappeared in the throng before I pulled Violet forward and introduced her.

Most of the large groups of women had gone in before we made our own way. Now I could see for myself how the young men seated on the ground, or lounging against the sides of the arches, sought to humiliate those who passed. They moved aside for some, but closed in on others. In front of us were a group of women wearing the green, white and purple colours.

A couple of the loungers straightened and bent threateningly over the women as they passed. One flicked at the brooch on a woman's coat. Another knocked off a hat which displayed the W.S.P.U. ribbon. They jostled them in an elaborate pantomime of pretence: stepping the same way as the women, and then as their victims tried to evade them, moving to block them again. Their faces were straight, or pulled into masks of exaggerated apology, and their timing was impeccable. Just as their victims became incensed, or those behind them looked as though they might intervene on their behalf, they cleared a passage, flourished a bow of exaggerated and false politeness, and the women passed through. Each incident only lasted a few seconds.

We moved ahead slowly, as the police made a show of stopping each person who entered. Yet I had clearly seen those boys earlier run into the arcade and not out again. Had they been allowed access then? They must have been. Or perhaps the police had been elsewhere and they'd slipped in unnoticed. My stomach churned with questions and anxiety. What was going to happen in that hall? If we couldn't trust the police – and there were only two of them, it seemed – then who was there to trust?

Just as we thought we were nearly through and into the arcade, a young man seated on the ground by the pillar, leaned forward and pulled at the skirt of the young woman nearest him. She screamed and kicked out at him with her foot, landing him a good wallop on his shoulder. His response was to put his hand up inside her skirt.

There was a second's frozen shock and then everything happened at once. Another member of her party yelled for the police to come. Violet and I pulled the young woman away. Bradley punched the offending youth. Two other youths moved in on Bradley but a fierce looking woman began to belabour them with her umbrella. Everyone was shouting, but we took the shocked young woman aside and comforted her. Violet brought out her hankie and the girl – she looked about eighteen or nineteen – mopped at her eyes.

'It's all right. It's just the surprise,' she said. 'How dare he!'

'How indeed,' sympathised Violet.

'It's not the first time I've suffered indignity from a hater of the Cause,' the girl said, as she handed back Violet's hankie. 'Last time it was a policeman, who felt my breasts as he dragged me away from a hall where Winston Churchill was due to speak.'

The shock of this left me speechless. I looked around to see what the police were doing to sort out the problem. Bradley was arguing with them, his face and neck an unhealthy red. The youths appeared to have vanished. More policemen were visible inside the main door. Earlier this would have reassured me, but now I wasn't sure. Nothing any longer appeared quite as it had. My view of the world had shifted again as I began to see what Bradley had meant. It was time to say farewell to my blind acceptance of the goodness of authority.

The girl we'd helped was made of stern stuff, already a hardened campaigner for suffrage and, from her conversation, an ardent adherent of the Pankhursts, particularly of Christabel. We moved calmly now into the building, said farewell to our new friend who, with her party went into the lower part of the hall, where friends were saving seats for them. We followed her, but we were too late to find seats there. It was packed and abuzz with excited conversation. A little disappointed, we made our way upstairs.

The last time I'd been to the Town Hall, it was to see a rather lacklustre version of *Hamlet* with my older pupils. Then the audience had been quiet. Even before the show began, there was a kind of polite expectancy; people spoke in hushed voices. Now, the packed hall, both up and downstairs, was full of calling, shouting individuals, both women and men. The air was electric with anticipation.

Women's voices predominated, but whole rows had been taken over by youths, perhaps the very ones that had heckled the women on the way in. Town Hall officials, in smart dark-green uniforms, paraded up and down the aisles, eyeing the audience sternly. I felt reassured. Surely they would keep order if it were needed.

Meanwhile Violet and I sat back in our seat and looked about us, enjoying the atmosphere. I caught Bradley's eye. He looked tense but smiled reassuringly. He gestured to his notebook, which I could see was already covered with his looping scrawl.

All at once, there was a hush. A ripple of whispers ran round the hall and a small figure, holding herself very straight, came onto the stage and walked serenely to the front, where a lectern had been placed for her use. She pushed it aside, stood at the very front of the stage and ran her gaze over the whole auditorium, slowly. As she lifted her face to take in the circle, where we sat, I had a startled moment when I felt she saw me, had picked me out from the crowd. I drew in a sharp breath and Violet asked me if I was all right.

'Absolutely fine,' I whispered. 'How small she is.'

'But quite beautiful, I think,' Violet whispered back.

'Yes,' I agreed. 'Though older than I realised.'

And suddenly the woman on the stage stopped the roaming of her eyes and began to speak. At the same time, the young men in the audience began to shout her down.

I caught the first few of her words, no more than greetings to us all, and then from behind me male voices drowned her out. I looked over my shoulder. A whole row of youths, standing now, shaking with venom, yelled insults. Their language was of the worst gutter-sort. They accused that frail-looking woman down there of being a bitch, a whore, a man-hater, a traitor. There was no crime, apparently, that Mrs Pankhurst had not committed in their eyes.

Everywhere, women rose in protest, but Mrs Pankhurst gestured to us to remain seated and, reluctantly in some cases, we obeyed. She herself was unmoved. She stood there as the insults flew at her and moved not a muscle of her calm face. Violet was right. She may have been getting on in years, but she was beautiful. Her face was full of quiet determination and courage.

A group of young men near the front of the auditorium began to scramble over the backs of seats, pushing the women seated in them aside and even using their heads as supports. They were making for the stage. The protests of women began once more to fill the air. From somewhere at the back of the lower level, a stone was thrown. It hit the front of the platform and bounced back into the front row of seats. More stones, small but hand-picked for flight, rattled onto the stage.

At last the officials began to intervene. I saw a young man restrained as he reached the stage and escorted to the door, but others were now pulling themselves up the front of the platform. What would they do if they reached their target? What if a stone hit her face? I did not realise how scared I was for that indomitable lady until Violet pulled her hand away from mine. I had been wringing it like a dishcloth.

Still Mrs Pankhurst did not move. Her dress, which would have betrayed the slightest tremor, might have been carved in stone. She barely blinked.

It wasn't until the men had made it up onto the stage, where they grouped together and hesitated, unsure what to do now they had successfully reached their objective, that a large group of officials came in from behind the stage curtain and escorted her out. Others took hold of the youths and marched them down the stage steps and out of the door. Order was restored.

The auditorium buzzed with talk. What would happen now? There was a general milling of officials, bolstered by members of the police-force. I looked around to see if there were any more rowdies but there were none visible. Perhaps now Mrs Pankhurst would return.

Indeed, it looked as though that might be the case, for the stage-curtain moved, but it was another woman who came out and stood near the front.

'I am the other Emmeline,' she said in a warm, humorous voice. 'My name is Emmeline Pethick-Lawrence.'

There were a few male bleats at this, but no real anger.

'My friend and colleague, Emmeline Pankhurst, has been taken away for her own safety. She has left the building. We are so sorry for your disappointment but she will be back…'

One or two jeers…

'… soon. We will get word to you, and next time she will be heard. In the meantime, ladies, keep the faith. Raise money and awareness for our Cause, for we have need of every one of you – every single one from factory maid to fine lady.' With a last look around and accompanied by one or two isolated catcalls from the remaining youths, she pushed her way through the back curtain and disappeared.

Everyone began to leave, full of talk and surmisal, but we sat on. I looked around at the red velvet seats. Relieved of their human burdens, they looked cold and empty. I too felt empty, with disappointment. The lights on the stage were turned off. Uniformed officials were checking the rows of seats for forgotten possessions. They hadn't started on the upper areas yet, but soon they would. I got up and leaned over the wooden balustrade. What was I hoping for? A glimpse of Mrs Pankhurst?

I remembered the feeling that her eyes had picked me out. I began to tingle all over.

It wasn't over. She would return.

Violet was up now, fishing under her seat for her coat. Bradley was still seated, scribbling so hard that his pencil had pushed through some of the sheets in his notebook. I went to look over his shoulder and saw he had sketched some of the incidents in a cartoon fashion.

'Not bad,' I approved, leaning over to look.

'Hopefully I can get some artist at the paper to make proper drawings from these, to accompany my write-up.' His face was quite pink with excitement as he wrote the last observation with a flourish, and pushed pencil and notebook back into his top-pocket.

'Let's go, shall we?' He took off his spectacles and polished them with a rather grubby handkerchief.

Violet already stood at the end of the aisle, adjusting her coat. Bradley and I joined her and left the empty upper levels with their mute rows of seating, darkening now to ghosts as some of the lights were turned off. Downstairs there were still small knots of women, standing quite still in the area by the entrance to the auditorium and staring at the stage, as if they expected this was all a trick and Mrs Pankhurst would appear once more through the curtains.

I hoped very much that it would not be long before she returned. Excitement and a kind of apprehension still bubbled in me. I felt on the brink of something, something as yet unknown, that would lift me quite out of my ordinary existence.

And it wasn't long. The news had been passed through suffrage channels, via offices scattered through the city, and leaflets passed from woman to woman. No newspaper carried the news. Bradley said that newspapers were only interested in suffrage when it caused a riot.

Violet had come to hear of it from a suffragist friend. The network of women, members of both the main suffrage groups for the main part – the Pankhursts' W.S.P.U. and the N.U.W.S.S., whose president was Millicent Fawcett – had supporters among all classes of women. Violet had spent the intervening time, as I pestered her with questions, filling me in on some of the workings of the present suffrage groups. She herself was a member of the N.U.W.S.S. and she advised me to join, but I still saw Mrs Pankhurst's face in my mind. Her eyes haunted me and I itched to hear more of what she had to say.

The comparative secrecy shrouding this second visit to Birmingham Town Hall meant there were few rowdies present. A small number were scattered outside the hall, but there were police around and they confined themselves to the occasional shout. Bradley wasn't with us this time, having an assignment from a newspaper he could not miss. His instructions to me had been to take everything down, for later discussion.

This time, however, could not have been more different. Violet and I sat in the main body of the hall, as close to the front as we could manage. I fiddled around for the notebook in my new satchel – a present at Christmas from the family. There were a few men in the audience, but they were older and clearly escorting a woman. Family men. Husbands. It was good to see that there were men supporting the Cause. Would my father? Jim and the boys?

The atmosphere was more relaxed this time, though still expectant. Gloved hands around the auditorium waved at friends elsewhere in the hall. I sensed such fellowship from this assembly, a camaraderie that I found exhilarating. I wanted very much to be a part of it.

Mrs Pankhurst spoke effortlessly, without appearing to strain her voice in the least. Yet it carried easily, and filled that large space. She told us of the years of peaceful campaigning to gain suffrage through Parliamentary persuasion, how that had failed. She told us of the many petitions that had been made to prove to Parliament how many thousands supported suffrage for women.

'Time and time again,' she said in her slightly accented voice, 'petitions have been presented. Eight years ago, in 1901, twenty-nine thousand, three hundred and fifty-nine signatures from the Lancashire cotton-mill workers and others from the North-West – my own part of England – were presented. The petition was so large – the size of a garden roller – that it took several women to carry it and it took over a large part of the train-carriage, by which means it was transported to London. We applaud Esther Roper and Eva Gore-Booth for this effort, which has shown the kind of support there is amongst women of all classes for our Cause.

'Yet it failed.

To date every petition, all our lobbying of individual Members of Parliament, has likewise failed.'

Quietly, Mrs Pankhurst's eyes roved over her audience. Not a sound could be heard in the whole hall.

'It is time to change our tactics. We have tried peaceful means. We have tried campaigning to promote candidates sympathetic to our rights to serve as Members of Parliament. They have taken their places and forgotten us, forgotten all we did to help them to their positions. Or so it seems. If they have worked for our Cause, there is nothing to show for it. They have failed.

'We have tried petitions and targeting Cabinet Ministers for support. That too has failed.

'So what to do now?'

Again there was a long silence.

'Now, dear friends and comrades, it is time to leave peaceful means behind. A number of us have already shown the way. My daughter, Christabel, and her loyal supporter Annie Kenney, a mill-worker herself, who gave up her livelihood to work for the Cause, devised our banner.'

Here women in all parts of the auditorium stood up and, in pairs, shook out white banners with 'Votes For Women' written boldly on them. Two of these climbed up the steps of the stage and unfurled their banner behind Mrs Pankhurst.

The auditorium exploded into applause. I found myself cheering and clapping with the rest. Such a feeling of fervent hope and excitement filled me as I had never experienced before.

Mrs Pankhurst raised her arm and kept it raised until we had fallen silent. 'Christabel and Annie interrupted the Foreign Secretary, Sir Edward Grey, and Winston Churchill on our home turf in Manchester's Free Trade Hall. What happened next I'll leave to Christabel to tell.'

The clapping and cheering began again. I looked around. I'd heard of Christabel, Mrs Pankhurst's firebrand daughter. Bradley often commented on her activities, not always with approbation. I wished he were here this time; he'd be sorry to have missed this event.

Christabel proved to be one of the banner holders, standing, with her friend Annie Kenney, behind her mother. They gave the banner to Mrs Pethick-Lawrence to hold and stepped forward, holding hands. Smiling, they raised their held hands up, a token of solidarity and friendship, before Christabel moved to the front of the stage to stand next to her mother. She didn't look much like her. Her face was rounder and her body stockier, but both women stood proudly and confidently, shoulders thrown back and both had the same straight-lipped smile.

'There we were,' she began when the applause had died down, 'in the Free Trade Hall, near enough to the front to be able to make ourselves heard. And make ourselves heard we certainly did. We interrupted the speakers with this question...' Here she scanned her audience with a merry look. 'Our question. The question we insist on and will keep insisting on until we get an answer: Will you give votes for women? And just in case they were all deaf we backed the question up with a banner, with those words clearly inscribed on it. Well, we kept interrupting. The distinguished speakers could not deliver their speeches. They scarcely got out more than three words together before we waved our banner at them and shouted our question. I don't think they could have had any doubt what we were asking for, do you? But that event was four years ago. You'd think, wouldn't you, that after four years of asking this question again and again, someone in government would have heard. But it appears not.'

She leaned forward, embraced the audience with her eyes, as if speaking personally to each one of us. 'You have my word that we will continue to ask that question for so long as we are denied suffrage. Nor is there any likelihood that we are just going to melt away. We are not.'

Here again I found myself cheering with the rest.

Christabel raised her arms again for silence and resumed. 'Back to that day in the Freemason's Hall. With their speeches in tatters, Churchill and Grey were incandescent with fury. We were evicted from the Hall. We talked instead to the crowds that had gathered outside, until we were arrested, taken to court and fined. We refused to pay the fine and were imprisoned.

'When we were due to be released from Strangeways prison a week later, a large gathering of supporters met us.

It was touching to see how many there were and it bolstered our spirits. *We have made history*, I told them. We were swept along to a meeting at the Free Trade Hall – the same place from which we had been thrown out a week previously. In the very place we had been silenced and from which we had been brutally evicted, we now spoke freely. We described the treatment we had received, the roughness of the police officers, and it lit a fire in all the women there.

'How fitting that this fire of rebellion should have been started in the hearts of women at St Peter's Field, Manchester, where the Free Trade Hall is situated – the very site of Peterloo, where three-quarters of a century before, large numbers of men and women calling for the very same right, the right to vote, were attacked and trampled to death by armed and mounted militia. How fitting!

'What was revealed by us then is what our path must be now. No more peaceful campaigning. It has failed. We are no longer mere suffragists. We are an army. We are, as the Daily Mail called us – meaning it as an insult – the suffragettes. We are proud to adopt that name. Because it is a military sounding name. The name of an army. And this time we shall not fail. We will provoke and interrupt, we will harass Ministers at their private homes, we will invade the Houses of Parliament and interrupt debates. In short, we will make a thorough nuisance of ourselves until we are granted the vote.'

I clapped until my hands hurt. Christabel Pankhurst moved back to join Annie Kenney and both together raised the banner high. Mrs Pankhurst moved up to join them. Finally, when the clapping and cheering died down, which it took a long time to do, all three women sat down, and another young woman, very pretty and dressed in a light-blue suit with a large blue hat supporting green, purple and white ostrich feathers, stood up and we fell quiet to listen to her.

'It's hard to follow that, isn't it? I have only important bits of information to tell you, so listen carefully. For those who don't know me, I am Gladice Keevil and I am the Society's District Organiser for the Midlands, based here in Birmingham. She proceeded to tell us how to join the W.S.P.U. and the many ways we could take part. We were told of fund-raising activities and asked to subscribe to the suffragette newspaper, *Votes for Women*, which would tell us of all that was happening to achieve suffrage country-wide.

'Since those events of 1905 that Christabel has just described,' she finished, 'there have been many changes to the W.S.P.U. No longer is its headquarters in Manchester. Our own Peterloo brought attention to our cause far and wide, throughout the British Isles. Now our main office is in London, but we have other offices in many major cities and we are looking for more volunteers, people who will help to disseminate information and to encourage women of all classes to support us. If there is anyone here who wishes to join up today, please wait in your seats.' She gave us a dazzling smile and sat down by Mrs Pankhurst.

The hall broke out into excited chatter. Violet got up and began to ready herself for departure. Automatically, I began to button my coat and started up to join her. Mrs Pankhurst's words and those of her daughter jingled in my head. They were a call to arms, to all women. Why was I leaving? They called to me too.

'I'm staying,' I said to Violet with sudden decision, and I sat back down.

17

The staffroom buzzed as I entered in the next morning.

'What are you wearing?' asked Amy, coming close to peer at the little square badge fixed to my collar. Then she stood back with her head on one side, taking in the rest of my apparel. 'Is this wise? In school?' She tipped her head to indicate the gossiping crowd of older staff around the table.

'I look clean and smart,' I protested. 'Just different to my usual black, that's all.'

'Black is somewhat more practical, don't you think? And doesn't advertise rebelliousness.'

'So you recognise the colours.' I was wearing a white blouse, a wide purple belt around the waist of my usual black skirt and a green, white and purple scarf draped around my neck, all items I had purchased at the Town Hall after the meeting. 'I've become a suffragette.' I felt my shoulders straighten with pride.

'I can see that,' hissed Amy, pulling me over to our usual quiet seat by the window. 'But seriously, Gladys, do you want to lose your job? The little brooch is one thing – but the full regalia? Isn't that a bit dramatic?'

'Look around,' I said. 'We're all women here. I've been asked to recruit new members.' I turned to smile broadly at the disapproving looks, which had settled on the faces of many of the oldest there, then smiled back at Amy. My stomach fluttered. I wasn't feeling as confident inside as I wished. 'Remember Freddie? She was a friend of yours, I believe. Why should she have had to leave work just because she married? What if you want to marry one day?'

'I sincerely hope I do.' Amy replied stiffly. 'I'd be happy to leave and devote myself to a husband and family. Husbands need the support of their wives, need to know their home is smoothly run and their children are cared for.'

'Amy!' I was so shocked, that my shout of protest rang across the staffroom and caused an abrupt hush.

'It's the truth,' said Amy defiantly. 'And I hope it happens soon. Marriage, I mean. If the likes of the Pankhursts get their way, there'll be chaos and I don't want any part of it.'

I got up from the window seat. I wanted to separate myself from Amy's views. Stomach churning, I wondered if I'd lost my one remaining friend on the staff. The bell rang for the start of school, and I made my way to morning assembly feeling very self-conscious.

As I walked down the corridor to my classroom, Miss Nimmo tapped me on the shoulder from behind.

'I see you've joined the suffragettes,' she said in a friendly tone.

'Yes, Headmistress,' I said. 'I went to the meeting at the Town Hall and joined up straight afterwards.'

'I shall be happy to talk about it with you soon. Something needs to be done to further women's education and improve their lot.'

'Oh, I'm so glad you feel like that. I was afraid…'

'Not afraid enough to stop you flaunting the suffragette colours in public.' She leavened this remark with a little laugh. Then her face straightened. 'I support your choice, Miss

Hazel, so long as it doesn't interfere with your excellent work as a teacher. Is that understood?'

'Absolutely, Miss Nimmo.' I felt light with relief. I hadn't realised that by wearing my outfit to school I was sounding out the feelings of my colleagues. When I made the decision to come in my uniform, for that is what it was, I was proud, nervous, with a jumble of unacknowledged feelings hidden beneath: the desire to challenge, to provoke those I worked with into disclosing their own attitudes. My respect for Miss Nimmo was such that her approval was paramount. If she supported me and the Cause, then others would follow. Even Amy would rethink.

Buoyed up by pride and hope, I bounced into the classroom and drank in the gasp of surprise from my class.

'So how was your first day as an out-of-the-closet suffragette?' Sophia greeted me in the sunny hall.

Her mother's team of servants had recently cleaned through the house from top to bottom, so that now the tall windows let in buttery slabs of late spring sunshine and the parquet floor gleamed with polish. Sprays of pink and white blossom nuzzled newly greened branches in a lavish display on the hall table. I drank in the smell of the flowers, the clean fresh scents of my Paradise Street haven.

'What would you think if I joined too?'

'Do you mean it, Sophia? I'd be delighted of course.'

'I think James and Bradley are interested too.'

'I'm not sure they can be actual suffragettes, but there are lots of male supporters. The more the merrier, I think.'

'Bradley's back from London. He's coming to supper tomorrow to find out about the meeting. He'll love your new regalia.'

'Won't he just!' I gave a twirl, using the scarf as a banner over my head. 'Wish I could have afforded the hat.'

'Never mind. I'll trim your old straw with the right colours for you.'

'Would you really? That's so kind, Sophia.' I gave her a hug before running up to my room. It wasn't until after supper that I remembered my bag, full of exercise books for marking. I found it under the hall table, but by then it was too late to deal with them.

I'd hardly eaten a thing as I described to Bradley what had been said at the meeting and the profound impression Mrs Pankhurst and Christabel had made on me. James and Sophia had heard it all the evening before, but were indulgent and prompted me if I left something out. Certainly my excitement meant the words tumbled out any old how and Bradley had to interrupt and ask for clarification.

'So,' he said finally, leaning back in his chair to survey me more clearly. 'Gladys has found a cause.'

'No,' I contradicted. 'I'd already found a cause – the conditions of the poor – but I have found a possible way to do something about it. If women can influence government, which they will when they get suffrage, who knows what changes can be achieved?'

'Dear Gladys,' Bradley beamed at me affectionately. 'So carried away. So full of hope.'

'There is always hope,' I snapped, not liking the patronising implication of Bradley's tone.

'Despite the petitions that have failed, the lack of interest in Parliament?' put in James.

'Yes,' agreed Bradley. 'I've investigated some of the history of women's attempts to achieve suffrage. They've been trying since the 1860s.'

'Exactly,' said James, 'and they haven't got very far.'

Anger filled me. 'It's different now. More and more are

flocking to the Cause. Thousands. We will be a tidal wave!'
I half rose from my chair, knocking it over behind me. The
crash checked my feelings and I apologised.

'It doesn't matter,' said Sophia gently. 'But you won't be
much good to the Cause if you don't eat. Look at your plate.'

I mumbled another apology and obediently pushed some
food into my mouth.

'You know that we are behind anything you do,' Bradley
said. 'James and I will support you and your Cause in any way
we can. And, by the way, I love it when you're fired up. You
look like Joan of Arc. All that flaming hair escaping round
your head like bolts of electricity. Into battle with you, Gladys.
We'll follow!'

I smiled round a crammed mouthful of pie. Now my initial
excitement at telling Bradley about the meeting had passed, I
realised how cross-currents of emotion had been riding me
ever since. I was fizzing with undirected energy, and ravenous.
Food was fuel and strength. Sophia was right. I should look
after myself. Sometimes it might be hard to remember that,
when I wanted to start the fight immediately, wanted to taste
the achievement I was sure would follow.

'What's the next step?' James asked.

'I'm to be briefed at the Birmingham office of the W.S.P.U.
next week, in Ethel Street. It's quite near here. They want me
to be an assistant organiser.' I felt again the rush of pride I'd
experienced when complimented on my education by Mrs
Field, who had talked to me after the meeting. She was
delighted to hear of my involvement with the Aston Club and
with the elementary school too.

'I myself assist Miss Keevil – there are two or three of us.
But we need more, especially educated, committed people like
you,' she'd said and then asked if I could fit duties around my
teaching job. I'd been sure I could, citing the outside school

activities I'd already done as proof. Why should my role as an organiser interfere any more than the Club had?

'What does being an organiser entail?' asked Sophia.

'Assistant organiser,' I corrected, then had to admit that I didn't know yet. Next week, after my meeting with Mrs Field and, hopefully, Gladice Keevil herself, I would have more information.

'Be careful,' warned Sophia. 'You can't risk losing your post at the school. Some of these suffragettes get into all kinds of trouble.'

'She'll be careful. Won't you?' Bradley smiled. 'Necessity first, the W.S.P.U. second.'

I didn't want him to be right, but I knew he was. It was then I remembered those exercise books. Once they would have been the first thing I dealt with. They would have been begun before supper and finished before I slept. Now I was too drained by excitement to contemplate anything further that evening.

As the train took me towards Didcot, I could hardly wait to get home. I was wearing all my suffragette bits, including the colours on my hat, thanks to Sophia, and couldn't wait to show it all to the family. How I wished I could talk to Rita, but she'd written excitedly that she'd be away visiting a school-friend who lived in Paris. 'Now we're definitely settling in Canada, I've got to get used to far-off places,' she'd enthused. 'I'll be there for three whole months! Imagine!'

I couldn't.

Mama would be especially proud of me I thought, as I fingered the brooch on my collar. The others? I didn't know, but I'd convince them.

I was enjoying the looks from my co-travellers too. A girl of around ten, sitting with her mother, kept glancing at me out of the corner of her eye. Her mother stared out of the window at the passing fields, the soft greens of Berkshire.

I leaned forward and smiled at the girl. 'Do you want to know what this brooch and the colours mean?'

She nodded shyly and glanced anxiously at her mother, but that lady's eyes were now closed and her head rested against the window.

I took off the scarf and handed it over to her. 'The colours were chosen to represent the suffrage movement. Do you know what suffrage is?' The girl shook her head and I explained about the vote and how important it was. Did she think that women were equal to men?

She put her head on one side and thought for a while. 'Men are stronger than women. Daddy always lifts our cases for us.'

'That's true,' I agreed. 'Women are usually physically weaker than men.' Then I thought of Elsie, built like a house, and some of the others who did presswork, turning the heavy handles of the machines used to stamp out metal components. Men's work, usually, but eagerly sought by the girls because the money was more – though always less than the men.

I had ascertained the child's name by now – Francine – and was careful to keep my explanations simple. 'That scarf you're holding, its colours are symbolic. Purple stands for dignity, white for purity and green for hope. Because we continue to hope that women will be allowed to vote like men. Maybe, when you are a woman, you will live in a changed world because of what we suffragettes are doing.'

A middle-aged man in brown tweed, wearing a cloth cap, was listening from his side of the carriage. 'Careful my missis don't get to hear your twaddle,' he said. 'Votes for women indeed! I'd sooner give my chickens the vote. You lot run around squawking – I've heard you – woman standing on a box last market day. Like chickens without heads – no sense at all. Putting ideas into people's heads what they shouldn't hold with.' He leaned over and shook Francine's mother. 'Wake up, and stop this firebrand burning her nonsense into your daughter's head.'

The mother's face was bleary with sleep and with something else. Sorrow it looked like. Her eyes had the lustre of someone who has not long stopped weeping, and her hair spilled from under her hat, as if she didn't care for herself. Yet Francine was clean and well turned-out.

Once she'd ascertained from her daughter what kind of 'nonsense' I was filling her head with, she gave me a watery smile. 'Thank you for your kindness. You can return that scarf now, dear,' she put a hand on her daughter's arm. 'And don't tell Daddy.'

'It's all right, Mother. I'm used to not telling Daddy things. But it doesn't matter. I didn't really understand what the lady was saying. Except about the colours. And something about voting, which I don't expect I'll ever want to do.'

I opened my mouth but was silenced by a look from the mother.

'You're right,' she said to Francine, but with her eyes turned to me like black holes. 'There's no need to know more. When you're married, as a pretty girl like you will someday be, there's no reason to vote. Your husband will do all the thinking for you, and handle your money, and keep it safe, and give you only what you absolutely need.'

The bitterness of her words were counteracted by the saccharine tone in which she spoke them. I could only guess at the unhappy relationship that lurked in the background.

We were slowing up for Didcot, the rhythm of the train changing from its regular clackety-clack to a rattle interspersed with huffs of steam. I reached up for my bag, above the head of a man whose face had been concealed throughout the journey by a newspaper. Occasionally there had been a crackle as he turned a page, and once I thought there was the kind of silence you notice when someone is listening with attention. Now the newspaper lowered and he stood to reach my bag for me.

'Thank you,' I said.

'Good luck to you,' he answered with a meaningful emphasis, and a flash of teeth from under a lavish moustache.

I descended to the platform, where I could see a porter was lifting down my bicycle from the luggage car. There was a lift in my heart from that gentleman's well-wishes. I knew he referred to the Cause.

18

'What's all this?' Kay was the first to greet me.

'I'm a suffragette now,' I answered proudly.

She didn't comment, but took me into the house to see Lina. Papa had walked to the village to play chess with a crony and Mama had popped over to the farm to pick up some eggs.

'I'd take those off now,' Kay suggested. 'No need to be confrontational.'

'That's exactly what I need to be, now that I've joined up and have been made an organiser.'

'It's a bit showy-offy don't you think?'

'And not very suitable for traipsing round to see the animals either,' said Lina.

'Have you more orphans in the barn?' I asked her.

'Sadly, no. I have a couple of dear rabbits and a little dog who had his leg caught in a trap, but I've been busy with other … things.' She dried up suddenly and looked away.

'She's been spending a lot of time up at the rectory, reading,' supplied Kay.

'Well, that's nice,' I said, rather at a loss.

Looking at the floor, Lina spoke in a rush. 'I've read all the classics, especially the ancient Greeks, and novels of course – I love George Eliot, she's so wise – but the Brontes' books are rather cruel, I feel, and turbulent, and I've read the whole of the Bible.'

'She's read it twice,' Kay said. 'And she's amazing. She remembers whole chunks of everything she's read – I tested her once – she's word perfect. Her memory is just incredible.'

'Perhaps you have a photographic memory. Lucky you, Lina. With all this knowledge you could train to teach, like me.'

'No,' said Lina firmly. 'I'm not strong enough for that. But one day perhaps I could look after a child in his own home, and maybe tutor him too.'

'Or her,' I said. 'Girls – as you've just proved, Lina – need nurturing and educating just as much as boys.' I looked at Lina, her twisted spine which now she was twenty gave her a pronounced hump, her narrow clever face and fine eyes. Her hair was luxuriant like Rita's. I had consistently seen Lina as a child, but she was far from that. Trapped in that frail body was a sharp mind that needed feeding. And she'd found a way to do that herself. 'I'll send you things from school when I'm back. Poetry, some wonderful essays I've discovered by an American called Ralph Waldo Emerson ...'

Kay was chewing her lower lip in the way she'd always done when she felt left out. 'Go upstairs and take those things off before Mama and Papa see them.'

'I want them to see them. They need to know who I am now.'

'Well, introduce it all gradually then.' As I hesitated, she shrugged, 'Take it or leave it. That's my advice. You always have to go at things like a charging bull. I think you'll find tiptoeing is best. Especially with Papa. Come on, I'll help you up with your bag.'

I took Kay's advice, reluctantly, and left most of the suffragette regalia on my bed. But my hands hovered over the brooch on my collar and rebelled. A small brooch wouldn't cause a fuss, might not even be noticed. Then I could bring up the Cause when the time felt right.

I heard the chatter of voices downstairs and then a shriek. Mama! She pounded up the stairs, burst into my room and hugged me so hard I could scarcely breathe. Then she stepped back to look at me properly and straightaway saw the brooch.

'New?' she asked. Her face was puzzled. Her eyes squinted as she came closer. 'There's writing on it.'

I'd forgotten how short-sighted she'd been getting recently. She had spectacles but rarely wore them, usually because she'd left them somewhere the last time she used them and couldn't remember where. Her face was longer, thinner, but her hair, so like mine, was as wild and full of electric life as ever. The walk back over the fields from the farm had mussed it into a wispy halo.

'Votes for Women,' she read. 'Oh! You've become a suffragist. Gladys, darling, you are someone after my own heart. If only I had the energy, I would have joined myself.'

She hugged me again, holding me longer this time, as if thinking about this new knowledge. Then she withdrew a little, but kept her hands on my shoulders. Her eyes looked straight into mine.

'Go slowly with Papa,' she advised. 'We've talked a little about it, because their exploits are so often in the newspapers, and I'm afraid he's with Lord Curzon, rather an anti-suffragist. He's an old-fashioned kind of man, as you know.'

A few weeks ago I wouldn't even have heard of Lord Curzon's views. To prepare me as one of the organisers Mrs Field and others had given me a condensed education of the history of suffrage up to the present time. I had been appalled at my own ignorance. Me, a woman who educated the women of the future, and I'd known almost nothing of the long struggle for female emancipation!

'Wouldn't he let you join? Is he really so anti, when he has such a parcel of girls of his own? And he let me go to University. While you, Mama, you've always seen to our education. You made no difference between your girls and the boys. It was your love of literature that ignited the flame in me. I believe you have the same greedy mind as I.'

Mama laughed ruefully and sat down on my bed. 'Once, maybe. Before it was all worn down by children. Just you wait, Gladys. There's nothing like having a family to change your view of things.'

'Do you regret it?' I tried to keep an objective tone. A conversation with my mother, adult to adult, was a rarity and to be treasured, but inside me Gladys, the needy child, dreaded her answer.

She sighed. Her fingers had found the suffragette scarf left on my bed and were kneading it. I held my breath.

'Of course, I don't,' she said finally. 'Look at you all. What mother wouldn't be proud to have produced such a range of interesting and worthwhile people.' She smiled at me, held the scarf up and looked at it. 'Oh, you've bought it all.' Her eyes roamed over the other bits. 'Do the school mind?'

'Not a bit. The head is a wonderful woman and completely for suffrage.' I looked at her sitting there. Despite what she'd just said, there was something sad about the droop of her mouth. What did she do with herself now that most of her children had gone?

'Mama, why don't you join the movement? It would give you something to do with your time. I expect Oxford has an office. You could see Aunt Louise, spend a little time with her, and help the Cause too.' I was excited. A recruit from my own family! Why hadn't I thought of it before? Mama was an obvious choice. Maybe Lina and Kay would be interested too. Or Rita – but with marriage probable next year, and then departure from this country, it wasn't likely.

Mama got up and brushed herself down – little, fussy movements that meant she was thinking something through. She moved over to the mirror on my chest-of-drawers.

'Goodness, is that really me?' She ran a hand over her hair, which did nothing at all to tame it. Then she turned back to me, one long fine hand still held to her head, as if she were keeping a lid on what it contained.

'I have enough to do, Gladys, running this large house.'

'You have Kay and Lina to help you. And Nora of course. You didn't have anyone in Ireland and ...'

'I was younger then. It may have escaped your notice, Gladys, but things take longer when you're older. I have my books. I have my garden. And there's your Papa. He needs my company.' Mama sighed. 'When we left Ireland he was glad at first, but he's a Naval man first and foremost. He always missed the sea...'

'So did we,' I whispered.

'There's never been enough for him here. That's why now he's as needy of me as a whole parcel of little children.'

'Oh, Mama. I didn't realise.'

'Well, you're not here. And even when you were – young people don't notice these things. They have the business of growing-up to attend to, and it's a time-consuming business – I remember it well – full of new awakenings of the body and the mind. It makes young people self-absorbed. They can't help it.'

'Are you unhappy?'

'No, darling. Not a bit. Your Papa is a good and kind man. He loves his crosswords, his newspaper, and he's become a passionate grower of roses – you'll have to admire them. Of course he always loves to talk things through with me, reads out letters to *The Times* – that sort of thing. We discuss. And I read, of course. Nothing will take that from me. And we love our daily walks. Sometimes we take the trap and go exploring – take a picnic. Lina usually comes with us. It's a full life. A happy one.'

She looked at me as if daring me to argue but I just went over and kissed her. She was taller than me, so I stood on tiptoe and wobbled a little against her cheek. That made her laugh.

'Just keep in touch,' she said, her hands holding my face between them. 'You don't write enough. Now you're a suffragist, I want to know all about it.'

'You'll just be living it at second-hand.'

'It doesn't matter. It'll be a link with you. I'll treasure the connection.'

Supper was a quiet affair. I still wasn't used to the family minus the boys. Jim was rarely seen now that he was fully trained as a Marine. He was somewhere at sea and wrote, just scribbled notes, very occasionally. Last time I'd been home Duncan was still there, learning about farming from our tenant farmer, Joe, but now I heard he'd joined Edgar in London and was in training for the East India Company. Edgar was to take over a tea plantation somewhere in the Northern hills of India and Duncan hoped to follow him there. The vagueness of it all upset me. Before supper, Papa and I had puzzled over the pink map of India on the globe in his study, but it wasn't much help. All that could be seen was that it was a great distance away.

When I grumbled a little about this at the supper table, surprised that Duncan wasn't following his original dream of being a farmer, Mama explained that probably the home farm wasn't exciting enough, and anyway it was natural that he and Edgar should want to stay together. She paused, as a shadow crossed her face, before rallying and saying cheerfully that she'd always known that her boys would fly away. Thank goodness that girls stayed closer to home. Except Rita.

'That's what's expected of men,' said Papa. 'They have to go out in the world and make a living, so that they can support a wife and family.'

'Perhaps that will change,' I ventured. 'Once women have the vote...'

'Which is by no means certain,' put in Papa, throwing me a sharp look.

Kay glared at me. Was this my idea of tiptoeing?

I gritted my teeth. 'Once they do, they will try to redress that balance. Why shouldn't women continue to work, even after they are married?' I glanced over at Mama, but she ducked my gaze.

Papa thrust his unlit pipe into his mouth and clamped down on the stem. 'If your mother had done that, where would we all be? You'd have been brought up by a nursemaid, and I doubt whether whatever Katherine earned, clever and talented as she is, would have been more than the wage I would have given out for your care.'

'You'd have been deprived of my constant love and attention,' said Mama gently. Her eyes settled on me with kindness, but I fancied I saw a touch of reproach there too. 'You lot were a handful I wouldn't have wished on any stranger. You'd have run rings round a nursemaid and turned into complete wild things.'

'Exactly what we were accused of being by Aunt Mary,' said Kay. 'We *were* wild things, Mama, there's no getting round it.' She looked at Lina, sitting quietly by her side. 'All but you – you were just a baby.'

I was happy to accept Kay's diversion. For now. 'Do you remember Ireland?' I asked her, surprised. 'You were only four, and Lina just two.'

'Of course I do. I remember the sea. And Jim's tests.'

'Tests?' Papa asked.

'Jim set us all tasks which we had to do to test our courage.' Kay tipped back in her chair, as if she were a child again.

'What sort of things? Why didn't I know anything about it?' Mama sounded as alarmed as if those tests had happened yesterday, and not nearly twenty years ago.

I glared at Kay. No one was supposed to know about the courage game and all the challenges Jim put us through. She'd be mentioning the badges next. My fingers felt the little badge on the left shoulder of my blouse, which Papa had not even noticed.

Kay tossed her head. 'They were good for us. They taught us to be brave and not to complain. Jim was very much a sort of parent to us, Mama, you remember. You were too busy.'

At Mama's insistence, we related some of the milder tests and she screeched in horror. 'All this going on behind my back and me with no knowledge of it. Well, thank goodness I didn't know, or I'd have locked you all up in your rooms for sure.'

When we'd finished eating and clearing away, we sat back at the dining-room table with small tots of port each in tiny glasses. To celebrate my home-coming for the holidays, explained Papa. The table, which easily seated all our friends and relations, was too long for so few of us. Its shining dark wood stretched into the shadows, haunted by the ghosts of our absent loved ones.

After a toast from Papa, Kay and Lina excused themselves, but Kay shot me a warning look as she left the room.

'Where are they going?' asked Papa. 'What's more important than family?'

'Lina will be bedding her animals down for the night,' said Mama gently. She reached over and patted Papa's hand. I looked at that hand, its swollen veins, its prominent joints. When did he start looking so old? Of course I knew he was much older than Mama, well into his sixties now, but still – I hadn't noticed before. How unobservant we can be of ones we love.

'What about Kay then?' asked Papa petulantly. 'She hasn't got animals.' He looked out at the light evening sky, scarcely visible through the profusion of roses around the window.

'Kay has friends in the village,' said Mama. 'She'll be out visiting, I expect.'

'Alone?'

'She's quite safe, Papa,' I said. 'I wander around alone in Birmingham, where anything could happen. Kay will come to no harm in quiet old Harwell. She's twenty-one and can look after herself.' I was sure I was right, but I did wonder if Kay had found another boyfriend.

For now, I returned to the question of suffrage. I judged the time was right and drew attention to my little square brooch with the hand-written *Votes for Women* printed across its centre. I explained I had been made one of the assistant organisers. This much was news to Mama too.

Both parents listened with attention and without interruption, except to ascertain that my work would not be affected.

'On the contrary,' I answered. 'Miss Nimmo congratulated me. I have her full support.' And I went on to relate how I'd worn the colours to school, to show to my class.

Papa's eyes narrowed a little, but there was no explosion.

Mama leaned back in her chair. 'It's good this is happening. I think it has to. There are a lot of unfairnesses for women as things are.'

'Such as?' Papa asked. His voice was tight.

I told him about the difference in wages between men and women for the same work, about not being allowed to work when pregnant, which put such a burden on the poor. And I described, as I had done that Christmas four and a half years ago to Jim, the realities of slum life. This time, I related it in a matter-of-fact way, uncoloured by emotion. 'That's my real reason for joining the suffragettes,' I finished, after explaining about the need for strong female voices in Parliament.

Mama and I both looked at Papa when I'd finished. He bent his head over his pipe, tamping some tobacco down into the bowl with a fierce concentration. We watched as he went through the whole process of tamping, adjusting, adding more tobacco, tamping again and then fishing in his pocket for matches. When he was done, there were a few puffs on the pipe to check that it was drawing well, his lips parting with a wet smack of satisfaction. The ritual of this we had encountered a thousand times over the years, but never had it appeared to take so long. He leaned back. His mouth elongated around the pipe stem in what might have been a smile. Then his blue eyes sharpened and looked at me. With a sigh, he removed his pipe and placed it in the ashtray. I knew this ritual of old. He would assuage his temper with a few puffs, then address himself to the issue, his initial ferocity caged behind the calming smoke.

'I want to tell you what happens when you fight for a cause and get all het up about injustice. It's the way wars start. And then there's blood, and fighting, and tears, and none of it's any good. No war I've ever heard of, or experienced, has gained much except further hardship for those very people – the poor – that you're so concerned about.'

'But you were a customs officer in Ireland because there *were* no wars.'

My diversionary tactic made Papa's eyes blaze. 'Not then. Not when you were children, but before. There was the Crimea. You've heard of that, I suppose?'

'Of course I have. I didn't know there were naval battles though.'

Papa subsided a little. 'There weren't. But the whole thing was about Sebastapol. The Russians wanted it, since none of their ports are any good in winter. The fighting over the port was on land, but the Navy carried the men and horses over there – so many horses in the belly of the ship, terrified and screaming when storms hit us. Many of them broke limbs and many more were lost when we unloaded them onto the rafts.' Papa's own eyes looked through us as he talked. He shook his head to clear the vision. 'We carried the wounded and dying too. Our ships were often no more than floating hospitals. The waste of life, Gladys, men and beasts. The stench. I shall never forget it. Usually in the Navy we kill from afar. A ship's cannon takes out another ship at some distance. At the Crimea all of us Naval men were brought face to face with death at its most ugly.' He groped for the pipe in the ashtray and pushed his seat back. 'Will you excuse me?' He rose. His shoulders were stooped and his hands grasped the edge of the table as if it were a rock above a precipice. We watched, appalled, as he straightened his back before he let go of the table's support and left the room.

'I must go to him,' Mama said, her eyes accusing. 'For years he had nightmares about the Crimea. They were getting fewer...'

'I wasn't the one who brought it up,' I defended myself. 'I don't understand how women's suffrage can be likened to the carnage of mass warfare.'

'You used the word suffragette. Papa does read the newspapers, remember? He knows the suffragettes are itching for a fight.'

I opened my mouth to argue the point, but 'Later,' said Mama. 'We'll talk later. And this time *I'll* prepare the way.'

Days passed in which Papa was careful to see me only in the company of others. Time was spent pleasantly enough. Lina and I talked about literature. Kay disappeared for hours at a time and I was almost sure she was still seeing Harry, though she denied it.

'I do have girl-friends too, you know,' she declared hotly, the one time I found her in the barn, dismounting from her bicycle. 'It's just that I like to visit them away from home. Mama monopolises them if they come here. She lands on them as if starved of company. It's very tiresome.'

'She misses the days when the house was full of young people,' I said mildly. 'Do you cook and help with the household?'

'Of course! Who do you think I am?' yelled Kay and stomped out of the barn.

If it hadn't been for Mama, and Lina's appetite for learning, I'd have gone back to Birmingham early. It was surprising to be at a place I loved so much and to feel lonely. I missed Rita and had devoured all the letters she'd sent home from France. My body and mind crackled with inactivity and could hardly wait to be used constructively once more. I lay awake at night planning speeches in my head to sway people to the Cause. My efforts with Papa were a warning and a fuel for these orations, which sounded wonderful in the dark as I lay sleepless in my bed, but in the sobering light of morning were seen to be full of flaws and a nasty grandiosity that I knew I must avoid.

At last it was the day before my return for the new term and I looked forward to leaving as never before. Mama and I had had many talks and I felt closer to her than usual. Gone was that feeling I had grown up with that I was the naughty child, the dark shadow to Rita's perfection. I drank in Mama's approval as a tonic. I gave her much more detail about the suffrage movement and in return she filtered this information into an acceptable form for Papa. He began to cool down. So, on the morning of this last day I went into his study to pick up the baton once more. I resolved to be careful.

Papa sat in his comfortable chair, his back to the window with his newspaper held up to its light. He tapped the newspaper sharply and laid it open on his knees.

'Listen to this, Gladys. Here's an article in which Lord Curzon ...'

Papa had pre-empted me and all my resolutions flew out of the window. 'Oh, I can guess what he says...' slipped out in a sharp tone which I was unable to prevent.

'Don't interrupt. You were never brought up to be so impolite.'

It was already going wrong. 'Sorry, Papa. Tell me what the honourable gentleman says.'

Papa leaned forward over his desk and fixed me with an acid stare. 'Watch your tone, young lady. I'll pass this over to you for your consideration... since I cannot trust you to listen without interruption.'

I received the paper humbly but didn't look at it. 'I don't want to fight with you, Papa. I'd much rather you were on my side. Curzon will only be re-iterating the things he's said before, that it is unnatural for women to be in the public sphere, that our brains are different to men's and not capable of intellectual analysis...'

'And here he says that giving women the vote would be a danger to the British Empire...'

'Why? What reasons does he give?'

Papa blustered, puffing his cheeks out and beginning sentences without finishing them. Then he admitted there weren't reasons given as such, except that women's bodies and minds were less strong than those of men. There were many jobs that they could not do physically and many, such as governing the country, they would be mentally incapable of managing.

I laughed. 'You have a clever wife and your girls are not stupid either. You really believe that nonsense?'

'Could you drive a bus, or build a house? Would you be able to make tough decisions in time of war? Would you be able to construct a solid argument in Parliament and impose it on the loud voices of opposition?'

'I believe so. I'll send you copies of some of the articles I have had printed in the papers. You know I can formulate an argument, Papa. I am accepted by clever men like Bradley and James, on an equal footing. Maybe I am lacking in physical strength – but there are men who are small and weak in body also. And women – ' I was thinking of Elsie – taller and stronger than most men. It's not a war with men, Papa, our quest for suffrage.'

'Indeed not. There are many women against it too. Queen Victoria for one.'

'The most powerful woman in the world! That's laughable. You do know she's dead, don't you?'

His answer was a glare. 'How can you be so disrespectful? The old Queen made our country the great nation it is today. Despite that, she always put her children and the home first. That is what women should do.'

I turned to go. This would only end once more in a full-blown row. How could Papa be married to Mama and still hold the views he did? Didn't they talk to each other?

There was an abrupt sound behind me, something between a sob and a sigh. 'Don't go, darling.'

His tone was softer but I didn't turn round. I felt tired of the merry-go-round of women's place, women's strength, women's minds that surfaced in so many conversations with men. Thank goodness I had James and Bradley in my life.

'I'm leaving tomorrow, Papa.'

'I know. Your teaching post.' I heard him get out of his seat, the rustle of his paper as he laid it aside. 'I don't mean to be hard on you, Gladys. I'm just worried about where all of this will lead you. I do so admire what you're doing. Educating the young – isn't that the best way to change the world? – slowly and without fighting.'

I shook my head, but turned to face him. 'I'm educating girls and, yes, that may help – but not if the men they marry insist on the status quo. Men must be educated too. Especially the men with the power to change things.'

'You'll never change the minds of Parliament.'

'No more, Papa, please. I don't want to argue with you, especially before I leave for a whole term.' I hurried through the door, full of a despondency that weighed heavily on my spirits. If I couldn't persuade my own father what good would I be out in the streets, at rallies and meetings?

The next day, as Joe was lifting my bicycle and bag up into the trap to take me to the station, I hugged Lina and Kay. Lina cried noisily and Kay took her back inside to comfort her. I resolved to be true to my word and send books and letters to her, to everyone. Especially I would keep Mama updated.

Mama came out with Papa to see me off.

'Your Papa is worried about you. We've talked. We just want to extract some promises from you – is that all right?'

I nodded.

'Stick to the paperwork of an organiser and don't get yourself into trouble. That's the first thing.'

'I will have to go into town to pass out leaflets and stick up posters. I'm not going to be sitting at a desk.'

'Well, avoid trouble, that's all we're asking. Don't endanger your position as a teacher.'

'I won't.'

Papa was itching to speak, I could tell. He broke away from Mama's restraining hand.

'I don't want you having anything to do with those Pankhursts. There was something in today's paper about them. They are nothing but harridans, simply after creating trouble. One of them has been in prison! Can you imagine? Women have chained themselves to railings to please them! They regularly get into unseemly scraps with the police...'

'That's because the police have orders to block our campaign whenever they can.' I told Papa about the woman I'd met when I first went to hear Mrs Pankhurst, how she'd been molested by the police, how she'd said that that was a common occurrence.

'Then these women should try behaving like ladies. I have no sympathy. They've brought it on themselves.'

'So you wouldn't be angered if I were molested by a police constable?'

'I would be ashamed, because it would only happen if you were not behaving in the way you have been brought up.'

Our voices had risen. We faced each other, breathing hard. Mama tugged at his arm. 'James, dearest. You promised.'

Papa turned to go back into the house. Without a goodbye. Without a hug.

Mama looked at me with such sadness. 'Do try, beloved daughter. Keep out of trouble. Any conflicts with the law would break our hearts. Write your articles for the newspapers and make them as incendiary as you like. But don't put yourself on the front line and in danger. You promise?'

'Papa didn't even say goodbye.'

'I know. He'll be waving from his study window, I'm sure. We both love you so much. Dear child. Remember that and don't be angry with him. He's a bit old-fashioned; he's not going to accept change easily, but he will in the end. He's a good man. Let me work on him. When you come back in the summer things will be different, I guarantee. So long as you don't provoke him and keep out of trouble.'

'I'm a suffragette, Mama. You know that. It was the Pankhursts that inspired me.'

'He doesn't realise that… But still, you don't have to behave badly, do you? You know that Papa says, and here he is right, that the increased militant activity of the suffragettes is turning Parliament further against suffrage. That's the last thing you want, surely? You may want to look into the activities of other groups. There are plenty out there. You don't have to give up your ideals, but there are other ways of attracting attention to the cause. Just promise me you'll think about it.'

'I will. Thank you for this holiday. It was you, darling Mama, who have made it special. I'll write, I promise.'

'Mind you do.'

She kissed me soundly. Kay and Lina, red-eyed, came out and joined in the hug. I heard the door open and Papa stood there too. Instantly I forgave him and ran over to kiss him goodbye. With farewells from my reduced family filling my heart, everything felt possible and rosy. I turned to stare at their diminishing figures as the trap rattled out of the drive. The sun was high, bleaching detail from their faces. Only Mama stood out, slightly shadowed by the copper beech. Her face flickered as the leaves above moved in the breeze and her bright hair was quenched.

All the way down on the train and as I rode my bicycle the short distance from New Street Station, I thought how good it had been to be in tune with her. That final image of her face passing in and out of the light, as a candle gutters in the wind, became my solace every night before sleep.

19

Throughout the summer term my duties as an assistant organiser were easy and no threat to my teaching. I had given up my help at both the Club and the elementary school so my two free afternoons were available. In addition I spent weekends working there with a team of helpers and all of us went out on the streets disseminating our newspaper *Votes for Women*. My team included Violet from the Club and sometimes, at weekends, Miss Derris too, who I soon learned to call Charlotte. Then there were my Paradise Street friends, who helped occasionally. So I had a good core team and inherited others who had been working at the office for some time.

Gladice Keevil, our District Organiser, was efficient and full of ideas. One of these was the Cycling Scouts entrusted with distributing our newspaper and leaflets in the outlying villages of Birmingham. As summer progressed, I found this a pleasant way to spend a warm day. There were a few grumbles, mainly from the farm labourers, who could not see the relevance of suffrage to their women folk, but I found it easy to parry their banter. From them there was none of the aggression I had seen from men outside the Town Hall.

Miss Keevil was often away spreading the word in other Midland towns, so a few of us, who met with her approval, were given other tasks in her absence, principally a variety of money-raising activities. Early in the summer, there had been a huge bazaar in London, and all of us had been busy drumming up goods for the stalls. Any left-over products were offered for sale at the weekly *At Homes* and brought in much needed funds.

One day Miss Keevil witnessed me talking to a group of women who hovered on the edge of joining. This was at our Ethel Street headquarters. There were often little knots of women, mostly of similar background to myself, nibbling at the idea of joining but worried about commitment. I was giving them reassurance, while at the same time firing them up to feel the kind of anger at injustice that fuelled me. It wasn't difficult and that particular knot of women all paid up and joined. I had not noticed Miss Keevil watching. She stepped forward and congratulated me.

'You have a gift for persuasion,' she said.

My face felt hot, but I was pleased all the same. Gladice Keevil's talent for public speaking was well-known. She had come to prominence in London and had been appointed to her present post at Christabel Pankhurst's suggestion.

'I'd like to see you out in the streets more,' she continued. 'We need to reach more of the working women. A few years ago Catherine Osler of the Birmingham Women's Suffrage Society visited the nail makers and chain makers where they worked in their own homes. We could do something similar.'

'I'm familiar with the slum courts,' I said, 'and have seen some of the women who work from home.' I remembered the ancient pair, bent over their button-holes. Then I told her of the Club, the women I knew there who worked at home and in the factories. Glancing anxiously at her – she looked so pretty and neat – I talked of the prostitution that so shocked me.

'I can see you are exactly the kind of person we need,' she said without a blench, putting a warm gloved hand on my shoulder. 'There was a fire in your belly as you spoke just now. Get out there, Gladys. Aren't we both warriors, both with the same name?'

'Similar,' I laughed. 'Your version sounds posher.'

'My mother likes France.' She gave me her winning smile. 'That's her excuse. Now – next week-end. Take a couple of friends and supporters and a stool or box to stand on. Have with you a heap of our newspapers and go to somewhere like Deritend. Somewhere which needs us and where anger is simmering under the surface. Time to spread the word and find some angry women for our cause. Anger is the best fuel and we need to tap into it.'

'Look what the cat brought in!'

Elsie's mocking voice was the first to greet me.

'Got too high and mighty fer us, 'ave yer? Wheer's them newspaper articles wot were going to make us all famous? Wheer's all those changes to our housin'?'

'Hold on, Elsie,' said Violet laughing. 'You haven't seen Gladys for months. Is that the way to welcome her back?'

'Got too big for 'er boots, I shouldn't wonder.' Elsie's voice had dropped to a growl. 'A bite at fame and fortune and we're all brushed under the rug.'

Others had gathered around now, smiling and excited. Seeing this, Elsie dropped into the background, glowering.

A young woman brought over a cup of tea. I looked at her, looked again. It was Millie. We fell on each other's necks like old friends.

'My, how you've grown,' I exclaimed. 'What are you doing now? Where's Sarah?'

Millie showed me her hand, which had a nasty burn all down one side, puckering the skin. 'We both got work,' she explained. 'In t' same factory. We're makin' iron parts for beds. I just got in t' way of the solderin' flame. So I'm off work for t' moment, helpin' with the babbies at home.'

'But no money while you're off?'

'Course not. Won't be for much longer though.' She showed me the reddened skin of her hand again. 'It's stopped seepin' now.' A crust had formed round the edge of the wound. 'I'll be back next week.'

No good advising her against going back too soon. I knew the machinery at metalwork factories were too heavy for most women, but the pay was good. The two girls had done well landing such employment. Their families must be delighted.

Mrs Hardy, still in her widow-black and starched apron, came round with cups of tea for all. She hovered as I began to tell everyone there about the work I was doing now for the suffragettes. I wasn't in full regalia, but wore my badge and hat with its coloured ribbon. Violet's first loyalty was to Catherine Osler and therefore the Birmingham Women's Suffrage Society but I was pleased to note that several women there sported our badges. Violet was quite happy to belong to both societies. 'After all,' she said, 'everyone is working for the same ends.'

'I can see I'm preaching to the converted,' I said, beaming around at them all.

'Preaching!' scoffed Elsie in the background. 'Oo does she think she is?'

'Elsie's right though. I did talk big and promise to grab the Council's ear with my newspaper articles. Maybe some of those helped a bit, but change takes time and what will help more is for we women to get the vote. Then we can start to change things from the very top. From the Houses of Parliament even, where, once we have the vote I have no doubt there will shortly be female Members. Maybe one day there'll even be a female Prime Minister!'

This sally caused howls of mirth.

When it had died down, 'Has Violet already given you pamphlets to hand out?' I asked. 'I have some new ones here if you can pass them on to friends and neighbours.'

'Know wot I'd do wiv 'em! Hey, girls – wot do you usually do wiv bills and papers? Hang 'em on the hook in the toilet and wipe yer arse on 'em.'

There was laughter at Elsie's remark but many women took a few pamphlets from me all the same, and those who could read began spelling out the words for the others.

'That's sommat I can do this week,' offered Millie eagerly.

An idea had come to me. 'There's more you can do. I'd thought to make a practice speech here today, just to test the water – see how it went down. But it looks as though Violet has already been doing that. I don't mind telling you I'm very nervous. My District Organiser has told me to get out and start spreading the word. Millie – I don't suppose you could take me to the factory gates where you work? That would be an excellent starting-point.'

Millie looked doubtful. 'There's mostly men workin' theer. Only a few girls like me.'

'Never mind,' I said staunchly, though my heart quailed. 'I've got to face men sometime. I've been told to go out into the streets and drum up interest. Where better to start?'

To me the factory looked like a prison. The huge red-brick building – long and wide, though no taller than an average two-storey house – had a brick courtyard and an entranceway of spiked iron gates. Time and weather had stained the original brick with sooty daubs and the front yard, where two large carts and their patient horses were standing, looked slick with a wet black moss. As Millie and I watched, the wide front doors opened and a group of men carried out some large packages, loosely wrapped in brown paper. Grunting with effort, they loaded up the carts and turned to go back inside. One young man, seeing Millie there, called over to her.

'Comin' back soon are yer, chick?'

But before she could answer he was pulled inside by his companions.

'Is he your young man?' I asked, looking at Millie who had bloomed with more plentiful food and hard physical labour into a strong young woman with pronounced features: a wide mouth and large soft brown eyes. Her dark hair was disobedient and framed her face in a wild frizz.

Now those eyes hardened. 'He'd like to be. But he ent good enough for me. He'd likely drink and hit me and say he were sorry and drink again. That's the pattern of ower lives in t' courts. I wanna get aht of that, and if I work 'ard and keep away from men, mebbe I'll afford summat better.'

We stood aside as the gates were opened by the janitor and the heavy horses pulled their loads out into the street.

'What yow waitin' fer?' asked the janitor and was told to mind his own business by my young friend.

We waited until he'd crossed the yard, shooting black looks from under his brows at Millie.

'He gave you such a stare, Millie. Will you be in trouble for that?'

'I don't care. He's nowt' to do with hirin' and firin'. He's jest a dirty man.'

Her look was so full of hate that I surmised this man had propositioned Millie in some way. I wasn't surprised. Millie had changed. There was nothing of the tentative girl in her now. She would make anyone look twice. I wondered what had happened to alter her so.

'If only you'd stayed at school,' I said. 'Education is what gets you out of this sort of life.'

'If you're lucky. They pull yer down, them courts. I've seen it again and again. A woman struggles to make 'er house better. She covers the walls with paper to 'ide the cracks wheer the bugs live. She nails up pictures of grand ladies and houses. She puts money in the caddy above the fireplace. But then the babbies come. Soon enough that paper peels off in t' damp and drippin' clothes hang from them nails. Sumtimes I feel like runnin' away. But wheer? Sarah says the only way is to go to London to be a ladies' maid or summat. What do yow think?'

'I think running away is more dangerous than staying. There are other ways to escape. I'll see what I can do.' In my mind was forming an idea. Millie's coherence and anger were just what the cause needed. I would ask if she could be taken on as a paid worker with the W.S.P.U. There were many working-class women who worked with us. The Kenney family were the most high-profile. Ex-cotton-mill workers from Lancashire, Annie was Christabel Pankhurst's right-hand aide and one of her many sisters, Nell, had been District Organiser right here in Birmingham until recently.

Millie had latched on to my tone and thoughtful expression. She opened her mouth to ask another question.

'Just wait,' I said, and at that moment the bell, housed in its own little sentry box on top of the roof, began to ring to signal the end of the day's work. Its deep clamour summoned the janitor once more, who chewed his moustache in suppressed fury and spat in our direction.

We stood to one side of the gates and I climbed up onto

my wooden chair. As the first men reached the gate I began to speak.

Most of the men gave me a quick glance and kept going, their strides long and purposeful. But by ones and twos, a few started to gather and listen. Perhaps they had stopped for a cheap laugh, but Millie had their measure. Any signs of disrespect and she laid into them with her sharp voice and quick remarks. She spoke their language, so was more able than I to turn their attempts at humour – at my expense – back on themselves.

The group of men concealed me from the women as they started to leave work. They must have had to come from further inside the long building. They emerged from its dark throat, blinking in the light and, knotted together for support, they began to hurry by. Seeing this, Millie pushed through the men to fetch them.

'Mek way fer the ladies,' said one mocking voice. He made a sweeping bow as the bewildered women followed Millie to the front of my audience.

The beginning, with just men for an audience had been hard. I had stumbled and repeated myself, despite having practised my opening lines in front of Sophia and James. James had wanted to hone my words into a more rhetorical and poetic shape, but I knew that the direct approach was best. Nonetheless, my assertions that women had rights like men had caused much merriment among most of my listeners. Now I had a little cluster of young women to talk to. If there were any among them like Millie, I'd be lucky indeed.

I began by talking generally about suffrage. Some didn't know what it meant, so I explained as clearly as I could.

'You're one of them mad lot,' came the interruption. 'Don't listen, ower lasses. You don't want to 'ave anything to do wiv that lot. Always in trouble with the pinchers – wanna lose yer jobs?'

'Get out of it,' yelled Millie. 'This ent yower business. This business is women's business so leave us to it. What we do wiv our lives and wiv ower jobs is up to us.'

'Hear, hear!' called out one or two of the women and my heckler retreated.

'Just joining the W.S.P.U.,' I quickly said 'will not threaten your work. You can wear one of the badges and show support for us women fighting on your behalf. Every one of the badges bought brings money in to help our cause. And it's not just my cause and that of women like me. It's your cause too. The cause of all women. Because we're all in the same boat, all of us marginalised, all of us ignored. We want to change that.'

One or two of the women drifted away, but four stayed, and a small group of slouching men, pretending indifference, listened too. I began to feel better.

I explained some of the other ways people could help in their free time. I included the men, who shuffled, embarrassed, but still stayed. I stressed the friendliness of all the women I'd met since I'd joined. By the end, these four said they'd come to Ethel Street to find out more, if Millie accompanied them. One of the men asked if he would be welcome too and I assured him he would.

I couldn't help it, I felt a sense of satisfaction unlike anything I'd received from teaching. This was harder, but I'd succeeded. And Millie would prove an asset, I was sure of it. What better way for her to rid herself of her slum-forged shackles than to ally herself with the ardent, vocal, intelligent women I had met from all classes and walks of life since I had joined the suffragettes?

Though I'd spoken many times now in streets, market-places and outside other factories, I still spent the night before with my stomach in knots and a lump in my throat that threatened to stopper it from emitting any sound at all. Millie had been accepted as a paid worker, after a few days in which Miss Keevil set her a variety of tasks. She had had to organise paperwork, make up piles of leaflets for distribution and copy out rotas of tasks for the daily work of the movement to run smoothly. She was willing and tried hard to please. Better still, she was my own fierce supporter, more valiant and constant than my other helpers, who, with their own busy lives, were unable to commit themselves so completely.

I suppose I began to be blasé. Though always nervous about the act of speaking, once I had begun my tongue took flight. I had encountered no real trouble to date. I decided therefore, one Wednesday afternoon, to go to an area new to me. The gun quarter, as it was known, around Snow Hill Station, was famously populated by many Irish. With memories of my childhood, softened by the sentiment of time, the idea of an Irish neighbourhood was attractive. I would appeal to them through my own love of their homeland.

Millie was caught up at Ethel Street, helping get ready for the weekly *At Home*, to be held that evening in a large house in Edgbaston. James, Bradley and Sophia were in London, where James had just published a slim volume of poetry, to great acclaim – from other poets. Charlotte Derris would be teaching and Violet was always at the Club on Wednesday afternoons. Despite the lack of support, I decided to go ahead alone. I ignored the warnings I had had drummed into me from the start, that I should not put myself unnecessarily at risk and should always be accompanied by one or more helpers.

Snow Hill was a pretty name. I found myself thinking of the apple blossom in the orchards at home but of course the reality was far from that. I emerged from the station, carrying a sturdy orange box this time, and climbed up the steep hill which led from the underground platforms. Though it was only one stop from my own station at New Street, the surroundings had none of the municipal grandeur to which I was accustomed. Instead I found myself surrounded by a maze of hardware shops, inter-leafed with back-to-backs. I could see the spire of a church not too far away and decided to head in that direction.

Soon I passed a group of boys playing on a street corner – some obscure game which involved throwing pennies at a wall – and lingered there to watch. The sun was warm on my back and high above the sky was threaded with wisps of cloud, but with wide acres of blue. More than enough to make a whole ship's worth of sailor's jackets, as Mama would say.

The boys didn't notice me until one penny bounced far back off their wall and landed at my feet. Suddenly a row of fierce eyes glared at me.

'That's ower penny.'

'You spyin' on us?'

'She's been sent by t' School Board.' The speaker rose to his feet, eyes like knives. 'En't yer?'

I started to splutter a denial, but the boys all rose and fled down the nearest alley. Even a hint of the School Board, whose methods of forcing absentee children into school were draconian, as I well knew from Mr Keane at the elementary school, sent them like rats into their holes.

I couldn't blame the children for wanting to be out in the fresh air on such a rarely beautiful day. Refusing to be downcast by my first encounter with the local residents, I carried on in the direction of the church, or so I hoped, though the spire was no longer visible. I had plunged into narrow streets whose tall brick buildings masked it from sight and narrowed that joyful blue of the sky to a ribbon. The heat was exhausting too and whoever would have thought that a box in which oranges had once been packed could prove so heavy?

At last I came out on a wider street with more promising shops on each side and a couple of large public houses. Avoiding the latter, and failing to see any sign of the church I had hoped for, I decided that this place was as good as any for my purpose. My box, laid at one corner of a crossroads, occasioned a few glances but little more. Only when I climbed up on it, gripping a sheaf of pamphlets in my hand, did one or two of the shoppers pause and eye me curiously.

As usual, my stomach swooped sickeningly and my voice emerged in a panicky squeak. I did what I usually did: repeated a few phrases designed to attract attention, until I had enough interest to warrant launching into the speech. The well-worn phrases, practised so often in my room at Paradise Street, allowed my voice to settle until I made a passable impression of confidence and knowledge. A small cluster of women, some with children, began to listen.

All might have been well if it hadn't been nearing the end of the day for some of the men. A spill of them came past at a leisurely lope, heading for the Gunmaker's Arms up the road. My little crowd of women, all so far with the air of having nothing better to do rather than the kind of interest I wished for, took up a fair section of pavement and forced the men to take a detour around us. Like cruising sharks around a shoal of fish, the men changed direction and began to push through the group of women, shouldering them aside. The women didn't take kindly to this, but belaboured the men with whatever they had to hand: hats, or rolled up bags of potatoes and other vegetables. Soon the air between the sexes bloomed into colourful insults.

Others began to join and the knot of people surrounding my frail platform lurched one way and then another, as others joined the fray, pushing and shoving with the happy abandon of those who love a fight without caring much what was the cause. I felt like a sailor in a storm-tossed ocean. No one took the slightest bit of notice of me; they were all far too busy exchanging insults.

One woman stood up beside me for a moment, to get her bearings before, without affording me a glance, she jumped down and waded into the fray, laying about her with her fists. Her face, beetroot-coloured with glee, was afire with a spirit that would have been the envy of Boadicea and her daughters. Potatoes flew through the air and chunks of coal. I had time to notice that one or two of the women hung around the fringes and squirrelled away these treasures as they rolled out of the centre, before I was knocked flying and found myself in the midst of stamping boots and flying skirts. I could do nothing but cover my head with my arms and try to wriggle through to safety.

My body would be black and blue tomorrow. I was tripped over, stepped on and kicked, not with any particular malice but a blithe disinterest in me and my plight. I curled up, made myself as small as possible, my arms wrapped round my head and waited for it all to pass.

There was a sudden splintering sound and a swathe of curses. I opened one eye and peeped from under my elbow. So much for my stalwart orange-box. It was in fragments. Two or three men had used it as a vantage-point from which to sight those they wanted to target and their combined weight had proved too much.

A couple of long dusty skirts were backing towards me. I cried out to announce my presence but the noise was too great. The occupants of those skirts lost their balance, brought up short against my body, and fell over on top of me. I saw the beetroot face of the female warrior, her hat bent over to one side, her hair loosened into snaky greying locks. We lay briefly eyeball to eyeball before she began to use me as a platform from which to lever herself upright. A filthy hand pushed down on my cheek and a finger poked my eye.

I screeched. Whether that had briefly, by its very indignation, cut through the hubbub of oaths and insults, or whether something else had thrown a blanket of calm over the proceedings, I could not tell. I was doing the best I could just to come out from this whole and with my clothes intact. Certainly my dignity was a lost cause.

Out of the melée a large strong hand seized mine and pulled. Somehow, I found myself eased out of my predicament and standing next to a tall burly man. He took hold of my shoulders and pushed his cap back on his head. Now a pair of blue eyes looked into mine.

'Are you all right?'

I nodded, for the present incapable of speech. In front of me a knot of people still struggled together. I was surprised how few there were of them. From my position on the pavement I had feared I might be swamped by a heaving crowd of hundreds, whose feet threatened to do me serious damage. Perhaps some had left, but there were only a couple of women and half-a-dozen men still half-heartedly exchanging shoves and words.

'I'm sorry,' I said. 'It felt worse than it was. From down there.' I indicated the ground.

The man's mouth twitched. Blue eyes regarded me with humour. 'I gather you were not there for the view. It's Gladys, isn't it? What were you doing out here on your own?'

I was struck dumb. He used my name. Bewildered, I squinted up at my saviour. A man in his early thirties at a guess. Not handsome but his eyes ... his hair ... 'Michael?'

'The very same.' He swept off his cap and swept a mocking bow. 'Come to England as promised and looking you up, also as promised.'

I was so confused by this revelation that I could not even formulate questions.

Stuttered beginnings – what? … how? … but … when? – were all I could manage.

He smiled down at me. I took in the changes to his appearance. His hair appeared closer to brown than the dark blonde of my memory, eyebrows thick and well-shaped over those intense eyes. They were unchanged, blue with darker rings around the iris. I remembered how they altered according to his mood as stormclouds will alter the colour of the sea.

By now the fighters had moved on. We were alone. He saw my hat, very crumpled and torn, and picked it up from the pavement.

'Do you want it on?' He was shaking it and brushing at it with his hands, before settling it very gently on my head. Those big capable hands. Now they reached out and touched the little badge on my collar. 'Gladys the fighter. That hasn't changed then.' Now he took my elbow and started to steer me down the street.

At last language returned to me. 'What are you doing here? Why aren't you in Ireland?'

'I told you I would be coming to England.'

'So you did. But how could you know I was in Birmingham?'

'Shall we walk? There's a place we can have a cup of tea near the station.'

On the way he talked about the difficulties he'd had at first settling down in this country. He was more educated than most of the Irish who came here. They came as labourers, on building sites, roads or railways. For a little while Michael had done that too, first in Liverpool and then in and around

London. One day there had been an accident when a building was being demolished and he had witnessed it. He wrote up the story for a local paper and it was printed. The money was more than Michael had earned in a week of manual work. So he wrote some more. Short pieces about the countryside, pieces of local history.

By now we were sitting in the dark interior of a little tea-house. It was shabby, and the cakes they offered had been out too long in the air. But I was talking to Michael, my Michael, who had so often jumped into my mind over the years, especially when I'd first come to England. The time he'd complimented my hair had fed my thoughts throughout my early teenage years. I'd imagined him as my secret admirer and, when Rita was being particularly irritating about her many admirers, brought a picture of him into my mind to feast on.

'Gladys? Are you listening?'

I was not. I was lost in contemplation of his face, but my staring was not appropriate, as I knew, and I ducked my head to gaze at the tabletop on which his hands rested. They were whiter than I'd remembered, but strong. Fine dark hairs sprinkled them and disappeared into the sleeves of his shirt.

I gathered my wits. 'What a strange co-incidence that you were there today.'

Now it was he who looked down at his hands on the table-top. 'I have a confession, Gladys. I followed you from your headquarters at Ethel Street. I've been there a few times in fact, hoping you might be there, with no luck until today. I'm sorry. I should have revealed myself but I didn't know how to approach you, whether you'd remember me, whether you'd be frightened. I never forgot you, Gladys.'

There was a rushing in my head, a kind of panic. 'You've been following me?' I shook my head again, not sure whether to be angry or not. 'And how did you know where to find me, or that I was a suffragette?' I took a gulp of cold tea to clear my thoughts.

'I was sent up to Birmingham by a London newspaper, to cover the meeting at the Town Hall. That's where I saw you, in the audience. It was totally unexpected, but you were unmissable, unmistakeable – your bright hair straying in all directions, your lovely face alight. My heart almost stopped beating. I knew then that I had to be here, in Birmingham, hoping to see you again and meanwhile covering the doings of the suffragette cause. I work now for the *Birmingham Post*. Much of what I am asked to do are sycophantic articles about wealthy factory owners, who like to see their stories of success in print. But that's not what I want to do. Suffrage is the important issue of the time.'

I was struggling to make sense of all this. I wanted to keep the conversation safe, impersonal. Caught off balance, I found his admiration more frightening than flattering. And he'd acted surprised when he'd picked me up. For a moment. He'd been convincing. He was a good liar. I needed to think about that…

For now, journalism was safer ground. 'You always could write.' I took a deep breath. 'Have you come across Bradley?' And I described how Bradley – who he was aware of but had never met – had been writing articles to attract attention to the plight of the slum-dwellers and, latterly, the struggle for the franchise of women. Modestly I told him that I'd written some of these articles myself and published them under Bradley's name.

'What a remarkable woman you have turned out to be,' said Michael softly. 'Didn't I always know you'd be something special?'

My face felt hot. I fanned it with my gloved hand, noticed

how the road I had fallen on had left its filth there and, instead, thrust one of my leaflets at him.

He cast an eye over it, eyebrow cocked. 'Were you hoping to hand these out?'

'Yes. And I've wasted the afternoon. Not one handed out and no converts.'

'Will I take you to a more likely place?'

He paid for my tea, escorted me out onto the pavement, where the bright sun dazzled and beat back from the surface of the road to create an arc of light which embraced us both. Despite myself I was melting under his charm. It felt like a dream – this strong man matching his steps to mine and taking me to a place of his choice. Ironically, it was by the very church which I had failed to find. Without my box to stand on, he found a stone platform outside a side-gate to the churchyard and offered me his hand to help me up.

I suspected this was the platform on which coffins were rested on the way to their burial and hoped that my tongue, dazzled by the bright day and the added brightness of this encounter, would not fail me.

Michael approached small groups of women, most of them older, or carrying infants, and courteously brought them to meet me. With this orderly crowd and Michael standing by, his eyes warm and encouraging, the words spilled out like honey.

Afterwards, Michael congratulated me, told me that I'd converted him as well as several of the women there, and, listening as I gave the women directions to Headquarters in Ethel Street, asked if men also were welcome. Then he looked deep into my eyes and asked if he, specifically, would be welcome. I felt suddenly shy and looked away from his too probing gaze.

'Will I walk you home?' The Irish phraseology, and the

faint accent which still coloured his speech made me feel comfortable. It took me back to a time where I felt safe, nurtured. Having found him again, I realised I didn't want to lose him so soon, so I told him my afternoons off from teaching, when I could be found at Ethel Street before I took to the streets. I would welcome his protective presence, should he ever find himself able to accompany me.

'What do you do on the streets? It sounds dangerous. Speaking like you did today perhaps?'

'Yes. Or putting round fliers, finding ways of advertising rallies. There's always lots to do.'

His eyes became unfocused and stared over my head. I took the opportunity to look up at him again. How tall he was. He seemed to come to a decision, looked down at me again and sought my eyes with his.

'I think it would be a good idea for a journalist like me to have someone on the inside of the Women's Social and Political Union to focus on. Someone exactly like you. Your travails as you fight for your cause would make a good story. The personal element. That sells newspapers. I've decided. For the foreseeable future, I shall devote myself entirely to you.'

The way he said this was laden. I knew he meant more than writing articles. I felt giddy with a mixture of pleasure and alarm.

'I don't want my name to be used in your stories. That would worry my family.'

'I can give you another name… Does that mean you like the idea?' He took hold of my hand and held it firmly.

'I like it very much.' I tried to remove my hand from his but he raised it to his lips and kissed it. I felt the heat of his breath through my dusty glove.

The day ended by Michael walking me home to Paradise Street. I had come on the train, but in truth the distance was not far and seemed nothing at all, so easy was it to converse with him. It would have been simple enough to ask him inside to meet James and Sophia, but something stopped me. I didn't want to share this new-found friend so soon. I wanted to keep a halo on the day.

20

It has been a few days since I've written anything. Coming face to face in my mind with Michael has stirred up so much feeling. There is the necessity to live it again as if for the first time, to not allow what happened later to distort my memories. Yesterday I made a start and suddenly my whole old body began to ache, my breasts, my thighs; my stomach tightened in that old never-to-be-forgotten remembrance of desire and there was a throb between my legs that I never thought to feel again. Oh, Michael.

Then there is Truda. She is eager to read it all, to know me from the inside out. Do I want to be known that way? Aren't there some things that need always to be secret? Especially what happens between a man and a woman.

This morning, at breakfast, when she asked why she hadn't heard the rattle of the typewriter for a while, looking at me with that quick birdlike glance over her spectacles, I explained something of this. It's about secrecy, I said, and intimacy, stuff that should never be shared.

'Do you not think I haven't heard it all before from all those women in my clinic?' she said. 'I may not have ever known a man myself – well, not in that way – but I ran a clinic to help women prevent those multiple pregnancies that have blighted lives for centuries, and often I helped Bessie with her venereal disease clinic. There's not much I have not heard or seen.'

But nothing of the sweetness of it, I thought, the rush of desire, the stroking, the soft greed of lips, and the tender aftermath. Nothing of that.

She saw the doubt on my face and shot me a shy look. 'I know what you're thinking. And of course there's no need to spell out the details. That's between you and him. But do remember that I met him, that I knew from the start what you were to each other ...'

'We did try to conceal it in your house.'

She laughed. 'Not very successfully! There was a creaky floorboard on the stairs that was rather a giveaway.'

'Oh!' A hot blush steamed up my face all these years later, as if I were a youngster caught out by a parent.

Truda poured me a hot cup of coffee which I sipped gratefully. 'Weren't you shocked?' I asked once I'd calmed down.

'A little, at first,' she admitted. 'Because of your class and status, I suppose, and because of the respect you were held in by the suffragettes I knew. But I also know that part of what the suffragettes were about was breaking old taboos and shackles. Young women of all classes were going about unchaperoned, challenging men in their own domain. Of course traditional sexual boundaries would be breached as well. So I quickly accepted it, though I hated to see you hurting, even back then when our friendship was new.'

Still I could not begin writing again. Instead I worked in the garden, pruning and preparing it for the spring to come. The labour freed my mind to think about those early days with Michael. I saw him again, still young, just into his thirties, powerful from the heavy work he had done when he first came to England, his hair the colour of wet hay, not quite blonde not quite brown, which streaked and lightened in that first summer of our love, so much of which was spent out of doors. And those eyes, their directness, the crinkles around them when he smiled. His slow smile. His large workman's hands with the fine tapering fingers…

Ahead of me, Michael wobbled along on a bicycle veering from one side of the lane to another. He ended up steering straight into a bush and threw himself off, shouting, 'Every man for himself!'

I was helpless with laughter at his clowning, but another in our party, Edith, was not impressed.

'Fancy a man not knowing how to ride a bicycle,' she snorted through her nose.

Michael rolled his eyes at me. 'Fancy a woman not knowing how to take a joke,' he muttered so that only I could hear.

I waved everyone on. 'We'll catch you up. Meet at the village green.'

It was a beautiful hot day, the air heavy with meadowsweet and buddleia. Butterflies flickered from blossom to blossom. The grasses at the side of the lanes were weighted with seedheads and attendant beetles. Swallows dipped and wove across the deep blue of the sky. A hawk wheeled and mewed a little distance away while, crouched in the foliage, small birds twittered and rustled.

We watched the backviews of the Cycle Scouts as they disappeared round the corner.

'Perfect,' said Michael. 'Now I've got you to myself.'

Gently he took hold of the handlebars of my bicycle with one hand and tugged at my arm with the other.

I resisted, laughing. 'We've got to catch up with the others.'

'Not too soon, I hope.'

'We need to assess the area – it's new to us – and make a plan of campaign. Then …'

'Then?'

'When we've got rid of all the papers…'

'We can have some time to ourselves?'

'It's Sunday. I think that would be permissible.'

'I think it would be compulsory. A necessity for the good health of mind and soul.' His voice deepened and he took a firmer grip on my wrist to pull me closer. 'I need to kiss you, Gladys. It's the first item on my own plan of campaign.' He manoeuvred round the bicycle and shifted his free hand up to my cheek. Firmly he stroked and explored the outline of my face.

I closed my eyes and tipped my head back. The sun, beating down on my eyelids, dazzled my brain and stoppered the channels of thought and care.

The bicycle fell to the ground between us. I could hear the whirring of the spokes until the sound slowed and died. He lifted me over my fallen steed and held me against him. Then, slowly and soundly, with a thoroughness that had every pore of my skin singing, he kissed me.

'Hrrmph.'

I opened my eyes to Edith's disapproving expression. Behind her were three other cyclists, young women, whose expressions were full of a delighted excitement.

'Millie has taken a group on to Springfield,' said Edith, trying so far as possible to face me and turn her back on Michael, a feat not entirely successful, as we still stood close, though not as close as we wanted to be. 'There weren't many houses up ahead. Nothing but a little hamlet really. We gave out newspapers and Millie gave a short talk to a couple of labourers and a milkmaid. I said I'd find you – er, both – and we'd go on to Moseley before heading back.'

Michael stepped naughtily into her line of sight and, keeping hold of my hand, suggested that he and I might go to Kings Heath – since it was a lovely day, from where we might take the train back.

'Do you think that is entirely proper?' said Edith. She pulled me away from the rest and spoke in a furtive staccato: 'I must say, Miss Hazel, I hadn't expected to feel it necessary to chaperone one of the organisers, as you are – a post that should be treated with respect. An approach of such – frivolity – brings into disrepute our cause, in my opinion. Miss Keevil will hear of this.'

Guilt caught me by the throat, but I was determined not to give her the satisfaction of showing it. 'I imagine Miss Keevil has better things to do than to worry about such trivialities,' I murmured. 'The papers are being distributed. Millie will have said as much as I would have done.'

'But to risk sullying the Cause, just when so many men, in the newspapers and in government and other high positions, are arguing that women's minds are trivial and hysterical and unsuitable for the honour of the vote.' Her voice had risen until touched by that very note of hysteria she feared.

'I am truly sorry to have upset you…' I began.

'It's the example you're setting, and you a school-teacher too.'

Michael hovered behind her shoulder and pulled a comical face. I glared at him.

'Do you need help, Gladys?' he said, ignoring my look.

Edith wheeled on him. 'No, she doesn't. And nor do any of us. I should be happiest, I must confess, if you took yourself back to Birmingham immediately and left us to promote the cause of women without you.'

I pulled myself together. 'Michael is a journalist, who is covering our cause from a more intimate perspective, that of the ordinary woman. We need someone on our side, rather than the kind of reports that usually appear in the papers, full of scandal and exaggeration. Miss Keevil has approved him. That's why he is here.' This had the benefit of being the truth.

Edith's lips wrinkled into tight creases.

'Dear Madam,' Michael took over. 'I apologise for my frivolous behaviour. I was led astray by the beauty of the day. Gladys may not have told you that I have known her since we were children. Our families are friends. There is nothing unseemly in our behaviour, nothing our friends and family would not approve.'

I was struck dumb by his bravado and outrageous words. If only they were true. Would my family approve of him? I very much doubted it. Though educated and literate now, to my parents Michael would always be that Irish boy from a poor background and a much lower social rank. And yet – if they met him, if Mama could see him for what he had become…

'I promise to behave,' Michael continued. 'Gladys and I will cycle together with you until we have fulfilled the agenda of the day.' His eyes slid sideways to me, searching for approval.

Freely, I gave it.

Later, as he escorted me to Paradise Street and left me outside the door, I laughed with him, a kind of hysteria filling us both, at my use of the word *intimate* to dragon Edith.

'*Michael is covering the cause from an intimate perspective.*' He mimicked my voice in a ridiculous squeak. His voice deepened suddenly and his eyes hooked mine so that I stood on the doorstep, in full view of the windows of Paradise Street, and stepped close enough for my skirt to brush against his trousers and to cover the toes of his boots, with their dusty reminder of dry August lanes. 'Oh, how I wish,' he whispered and dipped to kiss my ear under my hat-brim.

It had been too sudden, too soon; no time for thought – I was simply overwhelmed. There were other cycling Sundays that long hot August, and many other days with no school to bind me down, when we roved the countryside, sometimes in company and sometimes – as my co-workers became used to his presence – we managed to go our own way, so that those days blurred together into one long slow unfurling of our love. It was nothing like the girlish crush I'd had on Bill Waterfield. This was real and was fed by touch, though always, always, just as I ached for more, Michael would suddenly draw back, get up from our bed of grass and walk away.

'Why?' I asked.

'I respect you too much.'

A frustrating answer because it could not be faulted, it was what a gentleman should do, and yet I knew there was more to it.

Once, I dared to challenge it. 'Things are different now. We women are different, or soon will be. When we have won freedom for women along with the vote, we will throw off the past, where to experience anything at all we had to be shackled to fathers and brothers. Already we suffragettes walk without chaperones, and go boldly into company and speak our minds without invitation. I'm proud to be one of these bold new women, who can challenge the rules of society. Your drawing back may be out of respect, as you say, but the implication is that you have to think *for* me. And you don't. I can, and do, think for myself.'

I'd been addressing Michael's back, some feet away from me, where I sat up on the dry grass. His face, as he turned towards me, was dappled with light from the shifting leaves of an oak. I noticed the brown edges of the leaves. Autumn gathered and threatened our outdoor courtship.

'Gladys, don't you know how much I love you? It's not something I expected. But – I must take care of you. Caring is so much a part of what I feel for you. We mustn't be rash and allow our feelings to carry us away.'

'Why not?' I felt mutinous, as if I was talking to a sensible parent, not the man I adored and with whom I already knew I wanted to spend the rest of my life.

His face hardened. Instead of answering, he strode over to his bicycle, thrown next to mine by the hedge. 'Come on. It's late. If we're not careful it'll be dark by the time we're back.'

'So?' I struggled upright and fished my hat from its perch on the grass stems. Where we had been, the long stalks were broken and flattened. I kicked rebelliously at the patch where we had rolled and kissed and parted, just as our breath had become ragged and … oh, how I ached for him. And I knew he wanted that too. So why?

'What if I took you to meet my parents? Next weekend perhaps?'

'I'm in London on the heels of a story. It's a commissioned piece.'

'Then the weekend after.'

'Gladys, no. I'm not coming to meet your parents. You know what their reaction would be. Michael Allen, the lad from Ireland, struggling to make good perhaps, losing his Irish brogue – almost – but still soiled by the bogs he came from.'

'They're not like that,' I said, but with less conviction. He was right. That is exactly how my parents would see him. And Mama might perhaps be brought round, but not Papa.

We were silent as Michael examined my clothing and removed stray seeds and whiskers of wild barley. We were still silent as we rode back to town, each buried in our thoughts.

For a short time this conversation kept us apart. For a few days, I didn't see him at all but one evening, as I made my way up Paradise Street after a hard day of tedious but necessary paperwork at the office, there he was, outside the house waiting for me. Delight filled me and I ran the last few yards to be caught in his arms. We held each other as he whispered apologies into my hair, until the door abruptly opened and Sophia stood there.

'You'd better come in,' she said, 'unless you want the whole neighbourhood gossiping.'

Once safely inside, she eyed Michael critically. 'So you are the reason we barely see our Gladys any more.'

'I am.'

I pushed in and introduced them.

'Perhaps you'll join us for supper,' said Sophia graciously. 'So that we may know something about you.'

'Will Bradley be there? I so want Michael to meet him, since they're in the same line of work.'

'You know Bradley,' said Sophia with what I deemed to be unnecessary emphasis. 'He drops in at any time.' She paused and cast a look at Michael again. 'Mainly to see you, Gladys, as you very well know.'

Of course I cared what Sophia and James thought but I could have lived even with their disapproval if they did not find Michael up to scratch. Bradley, however, was a different matter. He was more than a friend. I had relied on him completely for the last couple of years, as a mentor, a co-worker, a kind of surrogate brother.

'Michael is an old friend,' I explained, taking a leaf out of Michael's own book. 'Our families know each other. We were close neighbours.' I caught Michael's amused glance.

Sophia eyed me keenly. Then she beckoned me away into the drawing-room. I saw Michael stiffen as he was left behind, before wandering off to look at the pictures in the hall. I knew he felt judged and that he was angry, but holding it in.

Sophia closed the door behind us. 'I have seen your ... friend. He's walked you to the door before. I saw him ... you ... through the window.'

I blushed suddenly, unable to help myself. She had watched him kiss me. We always lingered in the shadows by the entrance steps.

'Yes,' I said, not meeting her eyes. 'Is it still all right? To have him to supper?'

'Of course,' she suddenly said. 'Any friend of yours... Well, sorry about my greeting. I suppose I was hurt. I thought *we* were friends. I imagined you'd tell me things that were important to you. As I can see this man is.'

'Oh Sophia,' I hugged her. 'Of course we're friends. Always. What is happening between Michael and myself is so sudden, so ... well, I've kept it secret from everyone.'

'Even your parents? If he's an old friend and neighbour?'

There was something in Sophia's face that made me think she didn't entirely believe that story.

'It was back in Ireland, when we were children,' I confessed. 'And it's still too new. That's why I haven't told anyone yet. It was a surprise meeting him again. And maybe nothing will come of it.'

'Forgive me, Gladys. You left Ireland when you were ten. What do you know of Michael since those days?'

'I know enough. I know I love him.'

Her face didn't soften.

I blundered on. 'And he's a writer too, like Bradley and James. I think Bradley might be able to help his career along. What do you think?'

' I think Bradley is very protective of you.'

'I know. He's been like a brother to me.'

'James and I have often wondered if he'd like to be more.'

I was so startled I couldn't speak. Was this another instance of not looking deeper?

Oh, Nina, I thought. Will I never learn?

I dragged myself back from the brink of those thoughts, made myself contemplate dear tubby Bradley. Had there ever been any clue? I thought not.

'There's nothing like that between us,' I said with certainty. 'There's never been a sign of it.'

In the event, supper was an eye-opener for me too. I hadn't realised how well-read Michael was. The priest in Ireland had given him a classical education, one to one, not dissimilar from that James and Bradley had received from Harrow. That same priest, as I remembered well, had also fired him up politically. He was wise enough to present the argument for Irish Home Rule in a balanced way, citing the words of Parnell and others to back up his points. But when the conversation turned inevitably to poetry and James's latest book, Michael wanted to hear some of it immediately.

James pushed his chair back so suddenly that it fell over and Sophia laughed.

'Look how excited he is! The thought of reading his poetry to a new audience!' She got up to lift his chair from the floor but Michael beat her to it. For the first time I saw her smile at him with genuine pleasure.

James came back carrying another decanter of wine in one hand and some type-written sheets in the other.

'These are the drafts,' he said waving the papers in the air. 'Full of crossings-out and arrows in every direction. That's because the fair copies are still with the publisher.'

He slopped wine into every glass and danced over to his chair.

'Have you finished eating, Michael?' said Sophia anxiously. 'Before you start, James, and our guest feels too polite to take another morsel.'

Michael grinned and said he'd eaten more than enough and James, striking a pose, began. There was something old-fashioned about his usual poems, but these were different. They were about new beginnings – 'I wrote most of this collection as the old century gave way to the present one,' he explained – 'about hope and the joys of family life.' At the end of the first of these he got up and kissed his wife. 'Now they sound prophetic. You see ...' he began.

'No, James, no. Not in front of our new friend.'

But James reached out for the wine decanter and poured some of the rich red liquid directly into his mouth.

'James!' Sophia struggled to rise, but was pushed down by her husband.

'My wife – my darling Sophia – I know you good friends will want to know – is having a baby.'

I caught her eye. It was apologetic. I had been so often away that I was not party to my friend's most important news. Why was it that I could never concentrate on more than one thing at a time? Why was I so neglectful even of people I loved or admired? Sophia, Bradley ... Mama.

Around me Michael was adding his congratulations, James was crowing and Sophia was weeping, I had no idea why. Suddenly the door opened and the wide-eyed little maid put her head round. She could not get a word out, however, for hot behind her was Bradley, his spectacles gleaming in the candle-light as he added his congratulations – it was obvious he already knew. He was introduced to Michael and took my hand solemnly before he lifted it and kissed it.

The old-fashioned courtesy undid me and I found myself rushing over to Sophia and hugging her, wiping her tears with my handkerchief, and hugging her again. In truth we were all, except Bradley, more than a little intoxicated.

'How I've longed for a family,' declared James, though I'd never heard him mention it before and Sophia had often worried otherwise, especially with their financial difficulties.

'Are you a family man?' asked Bradley, turning to Michael.

Michael hesitated.

'He has numerous younger brothers and sisters,' I supplied eagerly.

'Not unlike Gladys then,' said Bradley, still gazing intently at Michael.

'He's wonderful with children,' I ran on and described my first sight of him, surrounded by siblings and carrying a newborn baby in his arms. 'He'd make a good father.' Immediately I blushed and ducked my head as everyone fell silent and looked at me.

Sophia covered. 'Come on, Gladys. We've much to talk about. Let's leave the men to their port and cigars.'

I glanced at Michael as I obeyed. Was I leaving him in a lion's den? Bradley hadn't taken his eyes off him. But Michael gave me a strange little smile and I had to be content with that.

21

Dearest Gladys,

Papa and I were so very sorry that you were too busy with your suffrage duties to come home for the school holidays. You haven't answered the last couple of letters and Papa is sore about it. Now he is threatening to write himself! Good heavens, you will say! Papa to write a letter! Perhaps the rarity value of such an event will prod you to scribble just a little note. We would both love that so much.

You have been sorely missed. Jim has been here and brought with him a young lady! Her name is Ida Dixon and he seems very smitten! She stayed for a weekend and was then delivered back to her family in London. Time will tell what will happen there! To me she appeared very young and rather earnest. Lina liked her, despite Ida's distinct aversion to smelly animals, but then Lina has a generous heart and is prepared to like everyone.

You will read between the lines a certain lack of enthusiasm for this young woman and I suppose that is so. Put it down to every mother's wish to keep her sons as the dear little boys they all once were. No woman is ever good enough to pass muster with a boy's mother, says Papa, and he is probably right. I dare say I will bow to the inevitable in the end.

Now to you. I so enjoyed your letters back in April and May – full of news and detail about your work as an organiser. I am sure that you have not told me of how difficult speaking to people in the streets really is, and how fraught with danger. I have an imagination, remember! Do please keep safe, darling girl. You tell me that you always have people with you to make sure you're safe from hecklers, so I suppose I must cease worrying.

Does the fact that I have not received a letter since the end of May mean that you have nothing to report? Or are you just too busy? I repeat, do please drop your loving Mama and Papa a short note to tell us you are all right.

Papa scans the newspapers every day to read what they say about the progress of suffrage and about the woman at the head of your organisation, Mrs Pankhurst, who he sees as something close to the arch-fiend! Of course I have not told him that you are a suffragette; he thinks you're working for one of the quieter organisations, who seek the franchise through more peaceful means. However, both of us are glad that very little militancy has happened over this summer.

Take care of yourself always, darling. Keep safe.

Your loving Mama.

Dearest Mama and Papa,

I am well and very happy. Of all people to meet once again, who would have expected to see Michael Allen, here in Birmingham! You will remember him, I expect, from Ireland…

This and many other drafts went into the wastepaper basket. I could not crease my thoughts into any other pattern. Michael filled my heart and mind. I so wanted to shout about my feelings but I knew I could not. Michael as a young boy had been right. They would 'patronise' him at best, be horribly false and kind to his face but then forbid me to see him again. And that I could not bear.

Finally I scribbled what amounted to a list of my duties. Mama was right, nothing very exciting had occurred over the summer. This I told them, knowing they would be pleased to hear anything and be reassured by the obscurity of my tasks.

... My time is mostly spent compiling rosters of those who will hawk our newspapers. Some of these will go out into villages around Birmingham. We call them the cycle scouts. But not all of them have their own bicycles, so it falls to me to find any shortfall. I also have to arrange the weekly 'At Homes', book the venues, make sure there are refreshments and, most importantly, find inspiring speakers. Where possible, I find speakers from Headquarters in London. But these must be found a bed for the night and that also must be organised. So you see, it's all very mundane and not at all dangerous! But I do think it's necessary. The work of informing and welcoming new and old members at the 'At Homes', is vital to keep up momentum for the Cause. The selling of papers and news-sheets and speaking wherever possible to new audiences is also vital. Every new member, every sale, furnishes money for our cause – not much, because we want to attract women from all classes – but if there are sufficient numbers, it all adds up.

Thank you for news of Jim and his lady-friend! How

I wish I had been there. I'd certainly have given you my honest opinion of her. Jim deserves the very best.

Give me news of the others too, please. Is Lina still studying? Has Kay got a young man? Will Duncan go to join Edgar in India as he threatened?

I will try to keep writing, really. I do mean to. It's just that there's so much going on, not to mention the wonderful friendships I am making through my work here.

Your loving daughter, Gladys

August pushed further towards its inevitable end. Blackberries hung heavy in every hedgerow, tangled with beads of white bryony, and scarlet rosehips. Michael continued to come as a cycle scout with me. Often it was just the pair of us. It was a blissful way of spending a Saturday or Sunday afternoon. I basked in his admiration as I spoke to small clusters of people on village greens and he helped hand out the papers. With his approval I blossomed and became a confident speaker. On good days, I experienced that wonderful feeling of words taking flight. At those times I knew I became inspirational for some who listened.

And word got back to Miss Keevil.

'Didn't I know you had the gift of persuasion? I spotted it from the start,' she said approvingly one afternoon at Ethel Street. 'I want you to be the speaker at the next *At Home.*'

Most of these gatherings were in the houses of the wealthier members of the organisation, in such places as Edgbaston, but I had reason to know that the next one was to be a bigger affair, at the Assembly Rooms. I'd drawn up the roster of helpers there myself, and organised who would be supplying the refreshments and other necessities.

I gulped. I had sent out invitations to many wealthy local families, including those of my school colleague and erstwhile friend Amy Strachan and her friends Bertie and Eveline Foster-Smythe. It had been bad enough knowing that I would have to be polite and friendly to dreadful Bertie, who would no doubt look at me in that mocking way of his and find a way of reminding me of my own naivety. But to speak in front of those people – all the great manufacturing families of Birmingham – would be more than daunting. I began to feel sick to the stomach.

'You can do it, you know,' said Miss Keevil. 'Speak as you do when you're out and about and address the men first.'

'You'd do it so much better,' I muttered.

'That's as may be. But they've got tired of hearing it from me. A fresh face and a new voice will work wonders. You'll see. Oh, and I've heard who's coming from London to speak to us. It's Dorothy Evans – very well thought of by Headquarters.'

Millie was hovering in the background during this conversation. She had collected the latest editions of *Votes For Women* from the printers and was employed at the office table, sorting them into piles and tying them round with string ready for distribution.

When Miss Keevil had disappeared from sight she added her own belief in me to that of my District Organiser.

I looked at her thoughtfully. 'How would you feel about speaking with me?'

'Oh, Miss … Gladys, I cain't, I really cain't.'

But I was warming to the idea. 'You could, you know. Those factory owners – I bet they've never set foot on the factory floor. What do they know of what it's like for a woman to work there? Nothing! I've heard you, Millie, sorting out those hecklers. You've a good quick tongue and your gift for repartee beats mine hands down. I always think of what I wish I'd retorted half an hour later!'

'But that's because thoose people are my kind. I know 'ow

to handle them. I woon't 'ave the first idea with them fancy folk.'

She began to back away but I caught hold of her hand. 'I'll help you. We'll practice together – we've got a few days – but there's no one can tell them better than you, who have experienced it, what it's really like – the conditions, the pay. Tell them what the difference is between the work you do and the work of the men. Do you really manage less than the men?'

'Noo. There's not much in it at all.' She sounded calmer. 'Sum of ower women have muscles on them like the men and they manage them machines just as well if not better. They're less careless too.'

'You see?' The thought of Millie by my side and, perhaps, Michael somewhere in the room, made me feel a whole lot better.

'So you've found a cause, Gladys,' said Bertie, his mouth glistening wetly through his curled moustache. 'I'm not surprised.' He bent close enough for me to smell the pomade on his hair. 'Still a little firebrand, are you?'

I smiled noncommittally and slid rapidly out of reach. The man had the persistence and unwelcomeness of a slug. Did he really not see how much I disliked him?

Carrying a plate stacked with little cakes, beautifully iced and each with a tiny flag stuck into it bearing the suffragette colours, it was easy to make my way to the further reaches of the room. All the while, my eyes roved around, seeking a head of sleek taffy-coloured hair, bleached by our days in the sun, but all I could see were nodding hats, bedecked with a forest of feathers and flowers. I waved at other friends. Bradley was there, escorting Sophia. I wondered briefly where James was. A number of helpers were clustered around Miss Keevil, who had just entered in the company of a slender young woman, with dark hair under a flamboyant hat, who had a determined look about her. This must be Dorothy Evans.

Reminded of my forthcoming speech my stomach twisted. It was one thing addressing a class of eleven-year-old girls, quite another to speak to hundreds at a big meeting. I remembered how nervous I'd been before my very first class but how quickly I had become used to being the centre of their attention. I breathed slowly, deeply, to calm my nerves.

'Gladys,' a voice interrupted.

Millie stood beside me, jostled by crowds making their way to a seat.

'You've been standin' theer for ages,' she said, 'And look, sum of your cakes will slide onter the floor if yer not careful.' She took the plate from me to save them.

'Oh, Millie,' I groaned. 'Look how many there are!'

'You're s'posed to be comfortin' me! 'Course I can see how many are 'ere. And few of my kind among 'em. But it's not like yow to be sceered.'

'Millie, I'm always scared. Every time I have to speak, whether it's at a street corner, or to a group of suffragettes at Ethel Street. I think it's just the way I'm made.'

'But you doan't show it.'

'You learn ways of coping. Are you scared?'

'I doan't know why. But not really. They're just a bunch of toffs who doan't know a thing. I'm ready to tell 'em so they can't pretend they doan't know ever again.'

'That's the spirit,' said a familiar voice.

And there he was. Michael. His broad form blotted out the room and the noise.

Everything in and around me calmed.

I saw Millie's measuring look travel from me to him. But then she took the plate and we were alone in the little island of peace he had created.

Michael took me by the elbow and steered me to the side of the room. 'Do you want people to stare at us?'

I didn't really care, but taking my cue from him, I left him leaning against a wall at the side, under a civic painting of some great Birmingham industrialist. Perhaps it was not a good idea after all to have invited him. Not that I worried for my reputation; I didn't give a fig for that. But because he filled my mind so completely that it was hard to think straight.

I needed to gather my thoughts. The speeches would come soon, but Miss Evans would be the primary speaker and that would give me time to rehearse in my head what I had already rehearsed countless times.

We had a low dais at one end of the rectangular room. Miss Keevil and the newcomer from London were already seated there. I beckoned Millie and we took our places on the other side of the table with its arrangement of flowers and ribbons in green, purple and white. Behind us was propped a white banner, with *Votes for Women* in huge letters written across it.

Miss Keevil leaned over her neighbour and introduced us. Close up, Dorothy Evans was striking. Her features were just too large for prettiness, yet the impression she gave was of beauty nonetheless; that large wide mouth with its slightly drooping lips, her huge grey eyes. It was a face that compelled attention. She smiled and it was a smile of such fun and mischief that I found myself almost laughing in return. I liked her immediately.

It was Miss Evans' task to report what was happening around the country. She stood up as Miss Keevil introduced her and began straightaway on Headquarter's frustration with Prime Minister Asquith. The Chancellor of the Exchequer, David Lloyd George, had proposed a controversial new budget, which he called the People's Budget. Though the Liberals had a huge majority in Parliament, they were struggling to get this budget adopted, so Asquith had not allowed the usual summer recess.

Having given us the background, Miss Evans turned to how our leaders, the Pankhursts, had reacted. Parliament's obsession with the budget had pushed any consideration of female suffrage out of the door.

'This was promised us, as it has been so many times before,' declared Miss Evans in ringing tones, her eyes travelling around her audience. 'Asquith said that this summer there would be a proper discussion of our latest petition and a vote taken. But what has happened? Nothing. Not a blind thing.

'How can this be when suffrage is now the principal item of news in every newspaper around the country? Suffrage societies around the kingdom have proliferated and membership exploded. We are not going to go away. We are not dust to be scraped under the rug. We are not something shameful that must be banished to the attic. Or the kitchen. Or the parlour where we should make polite conversation – about what? Nothing at all. For that kind of empty-headedness is what this government expects of their womenfolk.'

A spatter of applause greeted this: enthusiastic clapping from our members, but also the polite gloved applause of a fair number of our guests. Good. They were on our side.

Miss Evans had paused to sip at some water. She took a deep breath: 'So we invoked the Bill of Rights.'

Though we had read about this in our weekly reports from Headquarters, couched in angry terms in our newspaper, it was quite another thing to hear it ringing out over the silent room. She was an excellent speaker, this Dorothy Evans, fiery and strong. She explained clearly what taking this step meant. There would be many wives of manufacturers and industrialists here who would know nothing of all this.

The Bill of Rights was an ancient seventeenth century law that said all subjects had the right to petition the King. Therefore, a large deputation of suffragettes, led by Mrs Pankhurst, had gone to the Houses of Parliament to insist that they had a right to see Asquith face to face, as the representative of the King.

'The result was as we have come to expect,' continued Miss Evans, her voice low but tense with controlled anger. 'Once again we were met by a large line of police, who forced us down the steps of the building. As usual, we were made to feel not just second-class citizens, but criminals, when all we were asking for – and in terms that were by no means forceful – was to speak gently and persuasively to the leader of our country, as is our right.

'We were manhandled by a huge number of police, who forced us down the steps of the Houses of Parliament. I was thrown so violently that I landed at the bottom of the steps in a heap and, though this occurred back in June, I carry the bruises still.'

As her hands ran over the parts of her body affected, there was a smattering of shocked response throughout the assembly. Worried that too much emphasis on the police and violence would be counterproductive to recruitment, I glanced at Miss Keevil. Her face was impossible to read, but her gloved hands were clenched together in her lap.

'Anger at this refusal to hear our peaceful demands has had many consequences,' Miss Evans continued. 'W.S.P.U. members will have heard how individual women have taken it on themselves to make their own protests. Thus Marion Dunlop, an artist, made a two-foot square rubber stamp protesting our legal right to speak to the Prime Minister and stamped the message on the outside wall of St Stephen's Hall, a part of the Houses of Commons. Some days later, knowing she'd be recognised from the first occasion, she disguised herself and went inside the Hall, where she stamped her message again in indelible ink.

'Other women protested by breaking the windows of Government offices, the Treasury, the Home Office, the Privy Council...' She broke off as the unrest that had been steadily growing in the body of the hall threatened to drown even her loud, clear voice.

Chairs scraped back as husbands and wives rose to make a shocked exit. A man with a jutting black beard strode towards our podium.

'How dare you,' he hissed. 'You think we will join an organisation that promotes violence and puts our own womenfolk in danger?'

Another man had joined him and turned to address the body of the hall. 'I came along because I believe in the rights of women to vote, but not if such methods are encouraged. We already support the Birmingham Women's Suffrage Society, which is a part of the NUWSS, so we follow the legitimate approach advised by Millicent Fawcett. My wife is an old friend of Catherine Osler, the President of the Birmingham group. All of us are dedicated to female suffrage, but not by means that demean women. We will lend our support to Parliamentary lobbying and to petitions, but that is all. I am taking my wife away and I invite others here to follow my example.'

There was a ragged cheer at this, interrupted by Miss Evans, whose face had remained calm and intent. She raised her arms for quiet, and looked at the rest of us on the podium to help her. So we stood up too, not without some qualms at the way the evening was turning out.

'All of these women...' she cut across the subsiding noise. 'I repeat, all of these women I have mentioned, acted of their own initiative. Our organisation, the W.S.P.U., did not suggest it.' This she emphasised, separating each word. 'I am here to assure you of that.'

Miss Keevil shot a meaningful look at Dorothy Evans and whispered, 'Save the rest of your speech for tomorrow, when you speak to our own members only.'

I stood there, sifting through the content of my own speech in my mind. I would have to ditch most of what I had been going to say immediately, which had also been incendiary, in its own lesser way. After such a speech as Miss Evans had given, supporting the W.S.P.U. had suddenly become dangerous. I looked sideways at her. Her mouth remained firm and her chin was up. She swivelled her eyes at me. There was an amused gleam in them. To me it looked very much as if she was enjoying the ferment she had created.

I saw Michael mouthing something at me from his place against the wall. He made soothing gestures with his hands. He could tell that the noise in the hall was too great for my voice to penetrate.

But Miss Keevil had remained standing and she nodded sternly at me. Obeying that look, I sat myself down again. I glanced at Millie, sitting quietly on my other side. She laid her hand on my shoulder and leaned in to whisper.

'Phew! I never wanted to speak any'ow.'

That made me smile and my stomach slowed its roiling.

Miss Keevil wasn't supposed to speak now, but I guessed she would do something to prevent the men leaving, taking their wives with them. Her voice was strong, with a commanding edge. Within seconds, the noise died enough to hear her and those standing turned to face her way. She made them laugh about how often they had heard her speak. Her tone was, as usual, as if she were a nurse speaking to naughty children. I had seen her many times using this very ploy. Something about her attractive face, which contrasted sweetly with her fierce tone, mesmerised men. Not for the first time, I marvelled at how successful a gambit this was. Here were some of the most powerful men in Birmingham, melting like wax in her hands, their faces softened into boyish enjoyment, their eyes emptied of anything critical or even intelligent. How did she do it? I wished I had one half of her gift.

'You're contemplating an exit now. But don't,' Miss Keevil said, once she had waited, sternly raking the audience with her pale slightly protuberant eyes until the last naughty boy had fallen quiet and sat back in his seat, pulling his wife down beside him. She wagged an admonishing forefinger at this penitent rebel and a ripple of laughter travelled round the hall.

'Well now. Isn't that better? I hadn't intended to speak, but here I am like a teacher with an unruly class. Miss Evans, as you could see, was carried away by her own fierce anger. And I have to remind you that you have seen and heard me just as angry. We women are all angry to be still, after so many years, having to find new and better ways to attract attention to our cause.' She looked gravely around, her face wiped of its former humour.

'Miss Evans has emphasised how those women were acting of their own volition. Supporting our union of women is not in itself a dangerous act. But, I will not hide it from you, it is daring.' Again she paused and her eyes raked the audience. 'But who amongst you is not daring? Which of you hasn't defied convention to build their business and make it successful? The women Miss Evans talked about are spirited, unafraid, and yes, we need women like them: women with firm opinions, women who know they deserve better in modern Britain. But there are many ways of supporting our cause and not all of them mean that you have to put yourself at risk.

'And we need you men too. Without support from their

menfolk – husbands, fathers, brothers – women find it harder to assert their rights. We need you all. If you have any sympathy for the rights of women. If you see women not as inferior beings but as people with intelligence and the capacity to make judgements, like yourselves, then stay and give us your support.'

Then she smiled around at the quiet crowd and introduced me.

I took a deep breath and opened by praising the city of Birmingham for its place in the world as a great manufacturing city. I flattered the municipal giants who were there and watched them relax. I described how the goods made: the jewellery, the bedsteads, the metal works for ships and carriages, the guns, the watches and clocks, all of which had made the city famous, could not have come about without the workers, both men and women, who were the lifeblood of the factories. I talked of the smaller industries, the work farmed out to women in their homes: the makers of buttons, and of the smaller metal parts which fitted onto the greater ones produced by the factories.

Having prepared the ground, I handed over to Millie. She would relate what it was like to work on the factory floor. She would point out in her no-nonsense way the discrepancies between how men and women were treated. And she would finish with an account of what it was like to live in Number Four, Sycamore Court.

Her story was delivered with the minimum of emotion but the bald facts spoke for themselves. I saw one wealthy woman hold a lace handkerchief to cover her mouth and nose, as if she could smell the court yard, with its stench of night soil, emptied daily on the cobbles from every household's buckets.

When she had done, I appealed to the wives and women there to help their husbands right such wrongs and I invited everyone there to meet any one of us members – easily identified by our badges and hats with the suffragette colours – who would describe the variety of tasks the women might feel they could help with. Despite what had seemed at first to be turning into a fiasco, we had turned things around and an unprecedented number joined the society.

I saw Bertie sliding out of the door with Eveline and collared them. 'Going so soon?' I said sweetly.

'I shall send money to your union as soon as may be,' Bertie blustered. I didn't believe him. His eyes had the trapped look of a cornered rat.

'I found it most interesting.' Eveline suddenly said, her voice a startled pipe rather than its usual society drawl. She pulled away from her husband's possessive grasp. 'I shall certainly see that a considerable amount is sent. You deserve it.'

'And *you* deserve it,' I said, catching hold of her gloved hand. I felt a flood of warmth for her. As our eyes met, I noticed something there that had been previously hidden, a frightened flash of defiance. 'You can always come to our social evenings. The next *At Home* is at Mrs Newton's house in Edgbaston. You'd be very welcome. I think you'd be surprised how friendly it all is.'

'Come along, Evie,' Bertie interrupted. He took hold of her shoulder.

She smiled at me, a genuine smile without artifice, pulled away from that grip and, turning smartly on her heel, she preceded her husband out of the door.

Pockets of people left slowly, talking vehemently among themselves. There was a queue of those who wanted to join there and then. Millie and I fielded these while Michael, Bradley and Sophia lingered, waiting for me. As I looked at the numbers signing up a thrill of triumph filled me. A near disaster had turned into a resounding success. I longed to share these feelings with my friends.

'How soon before you're finished? I want to spend some time alone with you,' whispered Michael in my ear.

'No chance this evening,' I said ruefully. 'There are too many others here.' I gestured towards Sophia and Bradley as I wrote another name down on the growing list of new recruits.

Michael sighed but began to stack chairs with Bradley while Sophia, already a member, though a haphazard one, began to help with plates.

Miss Keevil and Dorothy Evans were in a close and intense conversation near the dais. It wasn't an argument – at least neither looked angry – but a difference of opinion certainly. It broke up when a group of young women clattered up the platform to collect the suffragette banner and decorations, which would be used again. Miss Keevil engaged them in a series of instructions which rendered Miss Evans temporarily obsolete. Some of the helpers, listening to their District Organiser while looking sideways at the glamorous visitor, looked disappointed to see her drift away. Miss Evans headed determinedly towards Millie and me and our queue of would-be suffragettes.

It took a little time, as first one, then another new suffragette clustered around her to ask questions. I noticed how the younger members in particular hung on her every word. She was charismatic, this woman. I had not been unaware of her appeal myself.

'I was interested in your talk, Gladys,' she said, as the last hero-worshipper left her. 'Interesting to hear more about Birmingham, especially as it is possible I will be taking over from Miss Keevil at some time in the future.'

'Really?' My first reaction was alarm. Miss Keevil had been a rock. There was something unsettling about Miss

Evans. I wasn't sure she would offer the kind of support some of the younger members might need. She would certainly fire them up, however. I looked at her, trying to see below the surface attraction. Despite my initial alarm I felt a stirring of excitement.

Miss Evans was still speaking. 'I hope very much you will be a support to me, as you have been to Miss Keevil. When it happens – not till after Christmas, I have heard – I hope that you and Millie will be my guides to the region and, more than that, friends too.' She gripped my wrist and gave it a friendly squeeze.

'I'll do my best,' I said.

'We're moving into new times,' Miss Evans said, her voice increasing enough in volume to attract others. Heads turned. She waited. Soon a crowd of young suffragettes had gathered round her.

I realised she was determined to finish her speech. Being silenced earlier had left her, perhaps, with a sense of incompleteness. I could understand that. Now, however, it wasn't so dangerous. Those that remained were all suffragettes already; only a handful remained in the queue to join the movement, and all of these were young. Miss Evans might be just the kind of person, with just the kind of message, that these wanted to hear. I remembered how excited I had felt when I first heard Mrs Pankhurst and Christabel. It had lit a flame in my heart that had never been dampened. Others deserved to experience that passion too.

Miss Evans rose to the occasion. Miss Keevil was within earshot and, casting a glance at her, Miss Evans began with reassurances that she wasn't aiming to 'seduce the wives of municipal dignitaries into neglecting their duties as helpmeets, mothers, household managers…'

There was a little shocked giggle from one or two at the

word 'seduce'. Her voice became more ironic. 'And as you can see …' – here she shot a flirtatious glance at Michael, passing by and loaded like Atlas with an impossible number of chairs – 'there are many ways that men too can help the Cause.'

He paused to listen despite his burden and I saw again that twinkle in her eyes of pure mischief, but delivered with such charm that no one could take offence.

'I assume that all who are still here are staunch supporters. So listen to what I must say, for all of you to consider.

'You will have read in the newspapers of the events I described – the breakage of windows, the defacing of public buildings – but such stories are usually reported for their shock value and expose the women as scandalous traitors to their sex. The full story, as I have explained, is somewhat different.'

By now everyone left in the room had gathered to listen and she cocked her head at them and paused to catch the eyes of as many as she could. I noticed how Millie and some of the other younger members appeared to hold their breath as her glance netted them in, one by one.

'If we are ignored,' she said, 'and treated as criminals, what recourse have we but to behave like criminals? Marion Dunlop was arrested and imprisoned for damaging property. So were the window-breakers. All of them asked to be treated as political prisoners, as is their right. Our cause is political after all. We are just ordinary women, from every social class. All we want is what men already have: the right to vote. You'd think we wanted something outrageous: the right to rob and steal, or the right to go about naked…'

Again, this idea was greeted by a nervous squeak of laughter. Miss Evans' smile broadened.

'Now, things are hotting up. They have to. Sent into ordinary prison cells, denied the rights of political prisoners to have certain privileges, Marion Dunlop went, of her own accord, on hunger strike. After ninety-one hours, the Home Office instructed the prison to release her. What courage that woman had and what a risk she took! But what a weapon against the Home Office and these unjust imprisonments she has discovered!'

She stopped suddenly and allowed that last idea to sink in. 'Is this it? Is this the weapon we need against the Government? Is this brave action one that will change the game in our favour?'

Everyone around her appeared to have stopped moving. They were as if frozen, as each one of us considered the implications of what she had said.

'Now you see what I was leading up to! Now you understand what exciting times we live in. This is the moment when a tidal wave of women, righteously indignant, will carry all before it! And we will use the weapons given us by these pioneers. They have shown the way, for all those with the courage to take up the cudgel. And, though Headquarters did not promote such methods, they now fully endorse them. Any who embrace militancy will have the backing of the Pankhursts and the rest of the team in London.'

She looked around triumphantly as her audience buzzed, some with consternation others with excitement. Then she turned to me. It was as if a light had been suddenly turned down, for her face had fallen into exhausted creases and, without her merry smile, her eyes were ringed with darkness. I saw what energy she had put into her speech and how, now it was all over, it had drained away. 'I'm tired now,' she said. 'It's been a long day. Would someone mind taking me to my lodgings?'

Miss Keevil scooped her up and swept her off, leaving many frustrated, their questions and concerns unanswered.

The woman knew how to leave people interested. Many would think further over the night and come to separate decisions. Nearly all would be guaranteed to reappear at Headquarters for Dorothy Evans' follow-up on the morrow.

Would Ethel Street, a place of efficient organisation and predictable duties under Miss Keevil, really become her headquarters too? And what would her arrival mean for us? Certainly there would be more militant activity. I felt a mixture of excitement and apprehension as I finished packing up the meeting and joined my friends to go home.

22

It was a tired but happy band that made the short walk from the Assembly Rooms to Paradise Street. We staggered along, our arms around each other, swapping delighted reminiscences of the evening. But soon I noticed that Sophia was flagging. Concerned, I dropped back with her.

'What's wrong?'

'It's nothing.' She made an effort to look happy. 'I'm a little tired – but nothing in comparison to what you must feel. All that build-up and your speech. What luck that it's still school holidays.'

In front of us I could hear Bradley's tone of voice change. It became intense and strained, but I failed to hear what he was saying. Michael began to increase his stride, Bradley trotting to keep pace. Were they arguing? I heard my name mentioned once, clearly, but nothing more as we came closer to Christ Church, at the end of Paradise Street.

Here all conversation had to cease, drowned by the twittering racket of the starlings as they landed in wheeling masses on the church roof, the trees and all over the bird-spattered statue of Robert Peel which stood in front of the church portico. The shadow of the tall spire threw itself over us. Beyond, the dusk pulled its own shadows behind it. I shivered. It was hard not to feel a sense of frightening change, pulled towards us in the train of the evening.

Some kind of speaking look passed between Bradley and Michael as we moved out of the cacophony of birds. Bradley claimed Sophia's arm and marched determinedly on towards Number 33, while Michael fell back with me. The voices of the starlings fell to a comfortable murmur and a soft rustle of feathers as they settled for the night.

My mouth was open on a question. What were he and Bradley arguing about? But Michael diverted me by kissing me on the top of the head.

'I was so very proud of you this evening. You spoke marvellously.'

I glowed. 'Did you make lots of notes?' I had seen Bradley scribbling in his usual battered notebook, but every time I had looked up at Michael, I had met a pair of blue eyes and his hands had been stuffed in his pockets. 'You're supposed to be following the campaign, reporting on it.'

'I'm following you,' he said, squeezing and twisting my fingers rather too hard. It hurt. Did he mean to?

I pulled away. 'What's wrong? You're in a strange mood. Is it something Bradley said? You looked as if you were having words.'

He didn't answer directly. 'I have to go soon.'

'Go? Why? What do you mean?'

He turned his face away.

'Where must you go?'

He kept his face averted, so that I had to crane round to see his expression. It told me nothing.

'Gladys, I'm so sorry. There are a few troubles back home. I shall have to leave here for a while.'

'Go back to Ireland?'

'Yes. But not for long.'

'Is it your parents?' I was prepared to lavish sympathy. Perhaps someone was ill.

'I can't say, darling. Not now. I'll tell you. I promise. After I'm back.'

'Why did you say nothing earlier? You've not even hinted at this before.' Hadn't he said something about wanting to be alone with me? What had changed?

'I didn't want to upset you before your big night.'

It sounded plausible. Just. Perhaps that is what Bradley and he were arguing about. Bradley, always protective, may have been angry that Michael hadn't told me before of his impending departure. And yet... There was something else. I could feel it. Had I been too caught up with arrangements for the evening to notice? Perhaps Michael had been trying to tell me for some time and I'd just kept blithely on, not letting him talk, not giving him any opportunity, always taking his love for granted.

My mood suddenly deflated and I must have let out a small sound, because the others, by the steps to Number 33, turned to look behind and waited for us to catch up.

'You will be back, though?' My voice emerged thick with emotion.

'How can you doubt it?' But he still sounded strange, as if he were holding back something more.

He drew apart from me and we walked awkwardly towards Sophia and Bradley. My head felt jumbled, full of questions and fears. I felt as if I were wrapped in a hard casing that kept me separate from everybody, as if I had no connection. Even my feet sounded strange to me, clopping on the pavement in their serviceable shoes.

Sophia searched my face anxiously. 'You're tired, Gladys.'

'Not surprising,' said Bradley. 'It's been a big day.' He looked not at me but straight at Michael.

Now I felt as though filled with boulders. Every part of me was heavy with the dread of something unknown. With an effort I dragged my awareness back to the present, to Michael, standing back from the rest of us, to Sophia whose face was streaked with tears. Dear Sophia, who was always there for me. I gave myself a mental shake. She deserved my attention.

'You never told me what the matter was,' I said. 'I'm sorry, I'd forgotten your condition – is it something to do with the baby? Have you overdone things?'

She laughed shortly and shook her head.

'That's a relief.' I was dragging concern into my tone when all I really wanted to do was to curl up into a ball of misery, or shout at Michael – *why, why?* And demand an answer. 'Well, then,' I laboured on, 'is it James? I did wonder why he wasn't there this evening.'

She nodded and burst into tears. I fumbled in my purse for a handkerchief and she took it gratefully.

'James had a bad review,' Bradley explained. 'He can never cope with criticism.'

'But he has had so many good notices. And his publisher loved this new collection,' I said.

'Yes, I know. But try telling James that. He was the same at Oxford. For him, all the praise is as if it's never been as soon as there's one word against his work. Then he can think of nothing else. It eats at him like a maggot.'

'It's because he never really believes the good things,' Sophia choked through layers of handkerchief. 'I worry what he'll do one day. And I can't seem to get through to him.'

'Then we must all go in and comfort him,' I said, looking up out of habit to Michael for support. But he hovered at the edge, his expression unreadable in the dusk. I went over to claim his arm, but he remained stiff and uncooperative.

'Will I leave now?' he muttered, as if arguing with himself. 'Maybe it's best.' He looked at me and his hand reached out to remove my hat.

'The torch of your hair,' he said, stepping back, and I could have sworn his voice, like Sophia's, was full of tears.

'Only a short time ago, you were looking forward to being alone with me. I don't understand. What's changed? Is it something Bradley said?'

'He brought me to my senses, shall we say. Truth is, I haven't been thinking. Or rather, I have, but only of my own self. I have... responsibilities ... that I've neglected.'

'To your family. I understand that.'

He was silent, ignored my proffered hand. His face was bleak. Again, he turned away from eye contact. 'Tomorrow morning I shall be on a train to Liverpool and I have a lot to do before I leave.'

I was more prepared to forgive now that I knew it was something to do with his family. Wouldn't I drop everything if I knew one of my beloved parents or siblings was ill and needed me?' I wish you could have prepared me for this a little, that's all.' I tried to keep blame out of my voice.

'The news was sudden. I just tried to pretend... to defer the inevitable for a little ...' His voice caught as if choking and suddenly he pulled me into his arms. For a brief instant he held me so tight I could scarcely breathe, before he let me go and strode back off towards the end of the street. I watched him until his shadow merged with the darker shadows of the church wall, before I turned back to the others. My thoughts had frozen.

My lungs were tight and the stone in the centre of my being had grown to monstrous proportions. I could hardly lift one foot after another.

Gone. The word accompanied each reluctant step. How would I manage without him? I knew that I was tired, not looking at things sensibly and I gave myself a few stiff words of advice. It wasn't for ever. He would return. He'd said he would. As I reached the bottom step, where the others still stood with Bradley holding Sophia, I dragged my attention to what was happening there.

'The thing is,' Sophia was saying, her voice so subdued I could hardly hear her, 'he's probably drunk. When I left, he had a bottle of wine in his hand and another waiting on the sideboard.'

I remembered the way James had poured the wine straight from the bottle into his mouth as he crowed the advent of their child and pulled myself together. Time to brood on Michael later. Now I had to attend to my friend, who needed me.

Bradley and I took one arm each and helped her to the front door.

'I'm sorry,' she kept saying. 'I feel so wobbly. And so emotional. Perhaps it's the baby. Mother told me that she felt quite incapacitated throughout carrying me and kept bursting into tears for no reason.'

'You have plenty of reason,' I said as Bradley pushed the front door open.

James was sitting across the hall, a few steps up from the bottom of the staircase, long legs sprawled in front of him. There was a bottle clamped between his thighs and all around him a swathe of shattered glass, twinkling like jewels in the gaslight.

Sophia shook us off and ran over to him. She stopped a few feet away and shrieked,' What is this? What have you done?' She had frozen like someone caught in quicksand.

'I pelted the bastards. They won't treat me like that again.'

I saw the little maid's frightened face peering round the corner of the kitchen corridor and went over to her.

'Bring a couple of brushes and dustpans, Doris. No need to be frightened. Just some broken glass, that's all.'

She pulled me into the corridor. 'The master stood on the bend of the stairs, Miss, and threw all the best glasses one by one at that newspaper on the hall table. I didn't know what to do.'

'Of course you didn't. It's all right now. We're here.'

Doris and I swept up the glittering shards while Bradley and Sophia sat on the stairs, one each side of James, and listened gravely as he explained how he had lobbed heavy crystal at 'that bastard critic – what does he know about poetry?'

We agreed that the critic wouldn't know the difference between a sonnet, a villanelle or his own arsehole, that he had as much poetic sensibility as a goat and probably less charm, and that he was the son of a harlot and a boar.

'I'll remind you what poetry should be,' James said, staggering to his feet. He struck a pose ready to declaim, but stepped forward, lost his footing and slid down the remaining steps to land in an angular heap on the hall floor.

Doris, who was shifting broken crystal into an over-full dustpan, squeaked as one of James's shoes sent her pan skittering over the polished wood. She gave me a look of frightened appeal.

I rescued the pan and handed it to her, gesturing that she should wait until James left the hall. It wouldn't be long. A loud and fruity belch ascended from her recumbent employer, followed by a long rippling snore. Sophia took the offending newspaper from the table, where it had received the inaccurate slings and arrows from James's outraged vanity, and crumpled it up. I took it and gave it to Doris for disposal.

Bradley and I, with Sophia alternately helping and being told to keep back for the baby's sake, manipulated James upstairs and deposited him, with some difficulty, fully clothed on his bed.

'Where's Michael?' asked Sophia suddenly.

'Never there when you need him,' I joked, my heart bleeding. 'He had something important to do. Apparently.'

'Oh,' said Sophia.

Bradley looked at me solemnly, his mouth unusually stern. We left Sophia, calmer now James was unconscious, grappling with his shoes and such clothing as she could manage, and went back downstairs. There, the lowered gaslight caught freckles of missed glass on the floor and under the hall table, while on it, the display of Michaelmas daisies with yellow and white chrysanthemums held more flecks, like dew, nested in their petals. A phalanx of unopened bottles stood to attention against one wall. James had been gathering his troops for a long night.

'We need to talk about Michael,' said Bradley.

At which I joined the general emotional frenzy with some tears of my own, that rained down my cheeks and stung my eyes as sharp as glass.

It was an hour or two later. I had calmed down and deferred conversation by rousing poor Doris. She and I had completed the clear-up of glass and bottles and finally she had gone to bed, armed with a soothing mug of cocoa. Bradley made us both tea in the kitchen and we slumped there, exhausted by the evening's events.

The scrubbed oak of the table was reassuring and reminded me of the kitchen at Rowstock. The green tiles of the walls, the big cream range and the oak cupboards, stained with years of use, under the gaslight turned down to its lowest gave off an atmosphere of quiet gloom, like being underwater. Bradley and I sat on the solid chairs, hands appreciating the warmth of the cups. Neither of us broke the welcome peace.

As I rose finally to wash the china, Bradley spoke to my back.

'What did Michael tell you?'

I didn't trust myself to turn round, but applied myself with an attempt at fervour, to the soap suds. 'He has to leave for Ireland. Something to do with his family.'

I heard a sigh. 'He said nothing more?'

'What more is there?'

'It doesn't matter. At least he's gone and that's for the best,' he said.

Instantly I wheeled. 'What do you mean?'

'Michael leaving. I found out a thing or two about him that made me very uneasy, but he told you he was going to Ireland. That's something.'

' Of course he's going. That's where his family lives and that's where we met. In Ireland.'

'And you know that the Irish question is of great moment now.'

I just gazed at him, bewildered. What did politics have to do with Michael and me? I still held a wet cup in my hand. Automatically I reached for the tea-towel and began drying.

'Has suffrage so filled your head, Gladys, that you're unaware of anything else? We both listened to a speech this very evening which explained how the Chancellor's budget had shoved out all debate about your cause.'

'What is the point you're trying to make?' I slammed the poor cup onto the draining-board. 'The only issue I can see is that Asquith promised us a full hearing this time and he reneged on that promise.'

'He had reasons. Forgive me. You know how much I believe in your cause. I believe the government is getting there slowly and that suffrage will come. But this time more important problems have taken priority. Ones that you care about: the terrible poverty in our country and especially the poverty in Ireland, that has caused the death of millions over the last decades.'

I spat at his 'more important', but I was tired and scratchy of temper. With an effort at being reasonable I drew out a chair and sat facing Bradley. 'So, explain. How will the budget help and how is Michael involved in all this?'

'Forget Michael for the moment and listen.'

'No! Forget Michael? Do you know what he is to me? Have you any idea? Even if he never returned I could not forget him.'

'Oh, Gladys.' Bradley's voice was gentle now and he slid a hand across the table towards mine.

I pulled away and turned my face from him, so that he could not see the hot tears of rage and misery forcing themselves out of my reluctant eyes.

Bradley spoke gently. 'In short, the People's Budget ...'

'I don't want to hear!'

'Gladys!'

Childishly, I put my hands over my ears. 'Talk to me about Michael and why you sent him away. You did, didn't you? It was something *you* said.' I glared at him.

He had stood up, his face creased with distress. 'The last thing I would want is to hurt you.' Gently he removed my hands from my ears and held them, his thumbs caressing them. 'Nor do I wish to see you hurt. Please, dear Gladys, just bear with me for a little. What I'm about to explain concerns Michael. But I have to give the background first.'

I gave in and nodded. My head spun with weariness and distress. We sat down, Bradley drawing a chair around to sit closer to me.

'You need to understand the significance of the People's Budget, as it is inspiringly called. It aims to tax the rich in order to create a welfare fund to help the poor. It's a revolutionary idea and I'm not surprised that the Chancellor's had opposition from the wealthy who, if it comes about, will see a proportion of their money being redistributed to the needy.'

Despite myself, I began to focus more closely on what he was saying. It was indeed a revolutionary idea and I could not help responding to the enthusiasm in Bradley's voice. 'Is that why Parliament was not given its customary summer break? Because of the opposition to the budget?'

'Exactly that. Because of the large liberal majority, the budget was passed in the Commons, but the House of Lords blocked it.'

Now I was caught up and beginning to understand the importance of what Bradley was telling me. 'Because the Lords are full of wealthy people.'

'Yes! And more particularly – now we're getting to the Irish problem – the budget proposed land taxes.' He paused to watch me understand the implications. I still had not quite got there. 'Who owns the majority of land in Ireland?' he prompted.

'The English. Huge estates ... tenant farmers who have to pay rent to the landowners... evictions when the crops fail ... famine and starvation.'

'You have it. And, of course, many of these landowners are members of the aristocracy and thus of the House of Lords.'

I remembered a childhood conversation with Michael. How he'd tried to explain his family's hatred for the English, that he'd wanted them all out of Ireland. 'You think Michael is involved in some way? That he's not just visiting his family?'

'I'm not absolutely sure of his involvement. But he frequents a public house, popular with the Irish, which is known as a place where revolutionary plots are formed. Recently a number of guns were discovered leaving there in the hands of known troublemakers. British army guns, stolen by Catholic revolutionaries like the Sinn Fein and about to be smuggled to Ireland.'

'You think Michael is part of that?' I could not keep the

horror out of my voice. 'Is that why he's going to Ireland? To take weapons with him?'

'Oh, Gladys. I don't know. I'm so sorry.'

'You have no proof.' I pulled myself together. My Michael of the gentle hands. My Michael wouldn't do such things. 'All I have to do is talk to him. He'll tell me. There are are no secrets between us. And I'll explain about this budget, how Parliament is trying to help. That we're not abandoning Ireland. He should support the liberals and what they're trying to do, just as we suffragettes have been doing. Oh, Bradley, this is positively good news. Now that I know, I'll be able to bring him round – not that I think he's involved in what you say.' I shot him a fierce look. 'Why, he's never mentioned Ireland to me, not in any political way – just talked about his brothers and…' I stopped. A memory surfaced, of Michael telling me what a rebel his brother Patrick was, the one next down in age to himself. He had been in some sort of trouble, setting fire to hayricks or some such. Michael had made light of it, but I remembered that brother, the way he'd looked at me as a child, with such hatred, as if he'd shoot me dead if he could. The way he bullied little Duncan. The memory brought a doubt in its wake, a small doubt certainly, but for the first time I wondered about the truth of what Bradley suspected. Could he be involved? My Michael? I shook the thought away. Absolutely not. Most likely Patrick was in trouble and he'd gone to sort it out.

Aware that Bradley was looking at me and that my face had probably reflected that doubt, I switched on a smile. 'Even if he does live in Ireland, Michael chose to come here years ago. Even at fourteen that was his plan. To live, get an education and work over here. He likes the English. When he's back I'll encourage him to write pieces about this budget, pieces he can send to the newspapers in Ireland, to help the people over there understand what it could mean for them. That's something you could do too, Bradley.'

'I already do. Don't you read the newspapers any more? I know, I know, you've been too busy preparing for this evening. It's consumed all your time.'

'Will the budget get through?' I asked. 'Will it be re-presented?'

'I hope so. For now it is blocked and that is a great shame. Lloyd George and Asquith are talking about reducing the power of the House of Lords. That will be another fight worth reporting.'

The fizz of excitement was draining out of me. I was simply too tired to take in much more. 'It's a bother that such a crisis should occur when we women were getting so close. The Pankhursts and Headquarters are not going to let up. Well, you heard Dorothy Evans. Militancy will increase.'

'I know.' Bradley looked at me with concern. 'Don't get too caught up in it, Gladys. Keep your good mind open to other things that are going on in the world.'

'Too late for that. I'm already caught up.' I looked at him defiantly. 'And Michael with me. That's the only battle he's involved with, I'm sure of it.

'But you don't have to be militant. There are different ways.'

Bradley wasn't the first to suggest that. For a moment I contemplated a different path. Could I leave the suffragettes and move over to a more peaceful society like the NUWSS? It would please my parents. I looked at Bradley, his whole plump face creased up with care. 'I know you're only saying this because you're fond of me. I'm fond of you too. You're probably my greatest friend. After Michael. All I can promise is that I'll think about it – not being so involved. But now I just want to go to bed. My head's spinning. There's much to think about.'

Bradley got up. 'I should go home myself. It's late.'

'Too late to walk the dark streets full of hooligan gangs of rebel Irish,' I teased, but he didn't smile. 'I'm sure Sophia and James would want you to stay in the guest room. It's always made up for you. Good night now.'

He opened his mouth to say something more. I could see the anxiety in his face. 'Gladys…' he began.

'Enough,' I said. 'Go to bed.' And I left him standing there.

23

There wasn't much time to mourn Michael's absence after all. A new term was beginning, and a new school year. I had a fresh set of faces in my classroom and one or two changes in the staffroom too. Amy was there, of course, and greeted me more cordially than she had of late. News of the *At Home* and her friends' reaction to it had thawed her somewhat.

'I still couldn't do what you do, Gladys, but Evie was full of praise for you.'

'And Bertie?'

'Well …' she laughed. 'You know Bertie. He appeared surprised at Evie's enthusiasm, kept calling her *the little woman*. "*The little woman wants to spend all my money on supporting the Pankhursts, would you believe it?*" You could tell Evie didn't like it. It's the first time I've seen her interested in something other than her appearance so, good for you, Gladys.'

'Does that mean you might join up too?'

'Good heavens, no. Mother and Father would have a fit. And so would Jerome.'

The coyness of her tone alerted me. Obediently I asked who Jerome was and received a flood of love-struck words. Despite myself I sympathised. Hadn't I fallen in love myself? I hoped Amy would not encounter the kind of obstacles that I had, but of course she wouldn't. Amy's course in life had been set out for her from the moment she was born. She had never rebelled, except perhaps by becoming a teacher. And that honour she would cast aside as if it were nothing, as soon as Jerome proposed.

I congratulated her, noticed that she asked me nothing about how I'd spent my summer holiday, and listened as she prattled on about a journey to Brighton to enjoy the sea air and how much Jerome had missed her when she was there.

'Let's meet up next weekend, Gladys,' she said, linking arms as we set off down the corridor to our separate classrooms. 'We used to have such fun, didn't we?'

She didn't wait for an answer.

A letter came from Headquarters warning that the Prime Minister, Herbert Asquith, was coming to Birmingham's Bingley Hall to speak. It said we should be prepared to interrupt his speech and find any other means of making our presence felt.

The prospect of some real action had Ethel Street buzzing with plans and surmisals. We must not let Headquarters down. We needed to show of what stuff the Birmingham suffragettes were made.

Miss Keevil took charge with her customary efficiency and charm. My task was to organise others to spread the word and to drum up extra support. In addition, I had to find places for the many suffragettes who would come to stay in Birmingham from all over the country. This was no mean task. There would be large numbers.

A list of willing house-owners was available, and these

were contacted, but we were still short. At my wit's end, I asked Sophia and James if they would be willing to help. They had room enough. For my sake they agreed, though disappointed that there would be no money forthcoming for the trouble. These people would have to be fed after all. But Headquarters were very strict about expenditure. Only if nothing else could be found would payment for lodging be approved.

The weekend cyclists were diverted to handing out leaflets in shopping areas, outside factory gates, and from door to door wherever they could. Others chalked notice of Asquith's arrival on pavements and put up posters inviting supporters to gather outside the railway station, where Asquith would arrive. No matter that these were often torn down; there were plenty of volunteers to replace them.

He was speaking on a Thursday, a school day. I went to Miss Nimmo to ask her for the day off, which she kindly granted me, so long as it didn't happen too often. Thank goodness she was a supporter, although one who could not, by reason of her position, be active.

Amy grumbled. She had lost her free afternoon to cover for me. Annoyed, I told her that she was doing her bit to support other women and to fight against the kind of injustices imposed on our sex. 'Remember Nina,' I said. 'Look around at the spinster staff. How many of them might have liked to be married and have a family, if they could have done that and remained as teachers?'

She looked. 'I doubt it. Look how hideous they all are.' I sighed. Amy really was a lost cause.

Our temporary guests were arriving on Wednesday morning by two separate trains, one from London and the other from

Manchester. There would be two women for our lodging on each train. Instructions from Headquarters were that all women travelling to the venue must look respectable and not obviously members of the W.S.P.U. This is because a few women had already made themselves well known around the country as agitators. One or two had been imprisoned. The police would be on the look-out for such dissidents.

Many had already arrived, from Bristol, Leicester, Oxford, even as far as Newcastle and Penzance. These women were used to travelling and were either unencumbered by the need to work, or, in the case of a select number of courageous women, were prepared to put themselves at risk. The latter were paid by London as agitators for the Cause.

Of course I could not ask for another day off work, so Sophia met our four guests and I would find them, well settled in, when I returned from school at teatime.

I entered Paradise Street in a high state of excitement. The whole build-up to Asquith's arrival had been tremendous and there was not one of us that wasn't sparking with the energy of having something certain and important to do. Walking through the hall I noticed to my amusement that Sophia had arranged the central flowers on the hall table into the colours: white chrysanthemums, sprigs of green leaves and the green vase wrapped round with purple ribbons. Clever Sophia! I could hear the buzz of conversation from the drawing-room and ran upstairs to deposit my school bag.

To my surprise, my room contained another bag and a flamboyant hat was flung onto the bed. I recognised that hat. Hadn't it graced the head of Dorothy Evans at our recent *At Home?*

It had. There she was, sitting easily next to Sophia, talking to three other women.

She smiled as she saw me in the doorway and rose, 'Gladys!

I hope you don't mind that I've taken the liberty of sharing your room. It's a big enough bed, I noticed, for two, and I told our lovely hostess what friends we'd already become.'

Behind her I noticed Sophia's raised eyebrows, but her mouth smiled. 'Come and join us, Gladys. Tea and cake.' She cut a generous slice, which I devoured while being introduced to the other three guests.

The two from Manchester were long-standing members of the W.S.P.U. They had joined when the society had been based in Manchester, home to the Pankhursts. One had been a cottonmill-worker with Annie Kenney and spoke glowingly of the inspiration that young woman was. Her name was Ivy and her friend, Constance, a shop-girl, also knew the Kenney family. It took a little time to get used to the Manchester accent, so different from the flat elongated vowels of Birmingham to which my ear was attuned.

Dorothy's companion, Marion, happily not also ensconced in my bedroom, was usually a secretary at Headquarters. Dorothy had admired her sense of adventure and persuaded Mrs Pethick-Lawrence to let her come. Marion had left a comfortable home in Surrey, defying her parents. They had wanted her to marry an army officer who had served with her father in the Boer War. 'So old!' she said, 'And very very dull.'

It was a jolly tea-party. Our giggles attracted James in, who enjoyed playing host to a bevy of attractive and adventurous women. The time passed easily until we needed to go to Ethel Street to receive instructions for the big day.

Early on Thursday morning Dorothy and I made our way to New Street station under a cloudy sky but, fortunately, no rain. The other three were heading straight to Bingley Hall. They explained, rather mysteriously, that they already had their own instructions, from Christabel herself.

Neither Dorothy nor I had slept much. It was strange to have someone sharing my bed again, someone who wasn't Rita, who was taller and a less comfortable presence. It gave us an impression of closeness, without the real intimacy of knowing each others' minds and feelings. If anything, the unknownness of Dorothy Evans loomed even larger and more mysteriously. There had been no whispered secrets. Both of us had decided to try to sleep, to conserve our energy for what was to come. But I had been aware of her restless shallow breathing, the little shiftings of her body, which told me that she was awake. Yet I could not intrude. I lay there, listening and wondering, before my mind drifted outwards to touch Michael's spirit, wherever it lay, and I dozed fitfully.

When we arrived at New Street station a huge crowd had gathered, mainly of women, sporting the suffragette colours and waving *Votes for Women* banners, though there was a smattering of men. The noise was subdued as yet. Being short, I struggled to see over the hats and feathers of the many women that had gathered, and had to rely on Dorothy's reportage of events. The numbers were unprecedented, even given that our local suffragettes were swelled by members from all the other societies in Birmingham. Dozens more had arrived from other regions. All around me I could hear snippets of conversation in different dialects.

The City Council had been busy overnight, to prepare against us. Steel barricades had been put up at the station and along the route Asquith was to travel. 'What do they think we're going to do? Murder him?' said Dorothy scathingly.

'Pr'haps that'd be a good idea. I wonder noo one's done it already!' Millie had spotted me somehow and fought her way through the racket to join us. 'They've put them fences all along. Yer can't even see over them. Sit on me shoulders, Gladys. 'Ave a look if yer can.'

Dorothy helped me onto Millie's strong shoulders and supported me there so that I could see the barriers for myself. Recognising me, some of the Birmingham women made a passageway so that I could get to the front of the crowd.

'Must be nine, ten feet at least.' I was breathless with suppressed excitement and fear. 'Even on your shoulders, Millie, I can't see over.'

'What d'they think a pack of women're goin' ter do? Shows they're sceered of us, doon't it? I'm goin' ter tek a look further on since he ent arrived yet.' Millie stooped to allow me down and soon I saw her perky little bonnet with its suffragette ribbons bobbing through the crowds.

'She's a plucky one,' said Dorothy. 'Useful.'

'You're thinking of when you take over here, after Christmas. Is that definite?'

Dorothy smiled sideways at me – a look I was already getting to know – it had a laziness to it, only employing one side of the mouth. It made her look sly, mischievous. She was prevented from answering by the arrival of a young woman, her face flushed and eyes feverish.

'If we all pushed at the barriers, we could knock them down,' she suggested.

'They're going to do that at the Hall,' said Dorothy, 'But by all means try. Have a go anywhere along the route. Are you armed?'

The girl revealed a bag full of stones. 'Go on then. Do your worst!'

'But don't hurt anyone,' I warned. 'Aim for the car, if you can.'

'She'll never see the car behind the barriers,' Dorothy pointed out.

'Well, maybe not, but try to throw over the top of the barrier.'

'Where you'll hit a policeman or two, if you're lucky.' Dorothy was grinning.

'Oh dear! Save them till we're at the Hall itself,' I began to say, but the girl was gone before I'd finished.

'We mustn't hurt any person,' I turned to face Dorothy.

'Even a policeman? They hurt us readily enough.'

'It'll get out-of-hand. We shouldn't put ourselves on the level of the street-gangs.'

'The police fight dirty too, Gladys. Wake up.' She moved away from me.

My heart pounding, thoughts jumbled, I watched as the girl and some equally over-excited companions fought their way through the crowd, further down the route that the cavalcade was to follow.

The sound from the crowd suddenly changed. It rose from a medley of disparate voices to a concerted shriek. A man's voice hollered, 'He's here! He's getting into the car!'

'They're peekin' through the cracks in't fencing,' Millie came back, hat awry and wiry hair mussed, to report in my ear as a racket began to drown all other sounds.

They were beating on the metal barriers, a noise like hundreds of theatrical thunder sheets all being shaken at once. People were lobbing stones over the fences and everyone was shouting. It was possible to chart Asquith's journey by the movement of the crowd, which, like a vast many-headed monster, jostled its slow way along the route.

The car Asquith was in was no faster than a horse-drawn carriage, but considerably safer from stones because of its roof. Safer too, since even horses of the best temperament would have been terrified by the noise that accompanied the entire journey. I noticed that many had brought tin trays with them, in order to make more din.

'Where are the police?' I yelled. I would have expected them to be dispersing the crowds.

'Linin' the route inside the barriers. That's why noo one's

bin able to push 'em down,' Millie shouted back. 'I saw 'em tekin' their positions when I first got 'ere.'

'I expect they're knee-deep round the hall too,' I muttered grimly. 'They were certainly expecting trouble.'

'Them wot expects a fight gets it,' Millie added with satisfaction.

'Absolutely,' said Dorothy, her face mirroring Millie's.

We were pulled and pushed by the crowds heading the short route to Bingley Hall. The cavalcade had to pass Christ Church at the closed end of my street before turning left towards the hall. I grabbed Millie's hand and called Dorothy to follow.

'Come on, we'll cut through past my house and get to the Hall faster.'

The sudden quiet of Paradise Street was a relief, but our blood was up and we ran as fast as we could down its length and turned right towards the Hall at the far end. Even at this distance, we could hear the roar of the crowd. It had a hysterical sound to it, like a vast farmyard where the chickens had turned on the fox and were screaming defiance.

As we drew nearer the sound began to congeal. It took shape, became more organised. Now the words 'Votes for Women' could be heard and we raised our voices to join the cry and pushed in until we too were part of the mob. To our right, we could hear the women following the route of the cavalcade begin to take up the refrain and could see the white banners waving. Only a few startled onlookers stood, mouths open, at a short distance from the mass. The combined voices had cleared the area of pigeons and starlings, who perched on rooftops a little away, or wheeled with alarm against the cloudy sky.

The Hall was clearly visible. I didn't at first realise why. There were large objects strewn all along the edge of the road.

People were picking their way among them: some women but also a number of police constables. Both sets of people were laying their hands on the objects and arguing. Because of the noise of the crowd, I couldn't hear what was being said, but it soon became clear as woman after woman sat down on the objects. They were the barriers which had been pushed over, as promised, allowing an unencumbered view of the hall entrance.

A couple of constables took hold of one of the seated women and lifted her under the armpits. She kicked out and was seized from behind by her friends. More police ran out to help their colleagues but something stopped them. They must have received an order, for they abandoned the task of removing the women and instead moved back to block the hall doors.

I could see Miss Keevil, standing on a box. She was waving her arms rhythmically, conducting the women's voices. In front of the low structure of the Hall, there was now a milling of black uniforms, lined up to guard the entrance, and all had drawn their truncheons out from their belts. They held shields in front of them, against which the occasional stone bounced.

The three of us pushed further through, the crowd willingly giving way to us as they recognised Millie and me. Now we stood facing the Hall, with our backs to another building. We were close to Miss Keevil on her frail platform, herself ringed round with a bodyguard of suffragette faithfuls, who kept her from being jostled or from police interference.

All at once a number of constables broke away from guarding the hall entrance and began running around like disturbed ants. Some of them were looking up at the building opposite the side of the Hall and holding their shields up against a volley of stones that were being thrown from there.

Millie shouted in my ear, directing my gaze up to the rooftop. 'Look, sumeone's up there.'

Indeed there was, and not just one person. Somehow, a

few women had climbed up onto the roof and were throwing stones. One of them bent down and began to remove slates, which, being sharp edged would make an even deadlier weapon. Now some of the constables were making their way along the side of the building, looking for a way up, while others ran off down another side street.

All the excitement was interrupted by an increase in sound, a huge concerted howl, like the wail of banshees denied the gates of Heaven. The rhythm of 'Votes for Women' changed to 'Give us the Vote' under the lead of Miss Keevil, a faster and harder rhythm, that pounded and broke against the black car as it drew to a halt, as close to the entrance of the Hall as possible.

Now I could see why Bingley Hall had been chosen for Asquith's speech. The grander venues had steps to negotiate. In front of this hall there were none. The car could draw so close to the entrance that all Asquith needed to do was to get out and, protected by the car and the police who had made a double-rowed fence of their bodies around it, enter the hall. One step in the open. One step where he might, if very unlucky, suffer assault. But of course none came except the assault of sound, which we delivered until we were hoarse.

Once the Prime Minister was safely inside, there was a sudden cessation of movement and the volume of sound decreased. All of us watched and waited to see what would happen next. Much of the crowd began to disperse and soon we saw why. There were mounted policemen off to our right, their uniformed torsos visible over the heads of the spectators. Slowly and steadily they proceeded down the road towards the hall, driving people in front of them and off into the side roads.

'Cor, lummee,' whispered Millie. 'Never 'ave liked 'orses.' She moved her feet restlessly, anxious to run.

'Don't worry,' I said. 'Be afraid of the men on top of the horses if you like, but a horse will never willingly hurt you.'

That memory of Lina in her sand-hole had surfaced, the way the galloping horse had twisted sideways to avoid harming her, had come shivering to a halt.

Millie's voice broke in. 'How d'you know?'

'Just trust me,' I said. 'They're gentle giants.'

'All right,' said Millie doubtfully.

Quickly and efficiently, the mounted police cleared the crowds away until only we, the dedicated few were left.

'Stand your ground,' called Miss Keevil. 'There's still a chance to get in and interrupt his speech. And lift those banners.' She began the chant of 'Votes for Women' once more and we all joined in.

We were quieter now, expecting at any moment to be moved on, but the mounted police halted some yards away, a line of shining horse-flesh, like statues but for the sudden shake of a glossy head and the champing sound of their teeth working on their bits.

I was struck with admiration for their beauty and discipline, so missed the first part of what happened next. When Millie nudged me I turned and saw that in front of the Hall was a line of carriages and the occasional automobile, disgorging Asquith's audience before moving out of the way. Most of these were privately owned; smartly dressed drivers and shiny horses marked the difference from the few hackney cabs with their weary animals and drivers. Amongst the back views filing into the Hall I recognised what may have been the tall figure of Bertie, accompanied by a lady in a stunning green hat, who could only have been Eveline, always at the forefront of Birmingham Society. One of those shuffling towards the entrance turned and scanned the onlookers with his eyes. It was Bradley, portly and familiar. Millie and I waved until he saw us and grinned in return. He held up a notebook and tapped it and I nodded my understanding.

'Couldn't he at least have smuggled in a banner?' asked Dorothy, breaking off mid-chant.

'No!' I laughed. 'But he's a journalist and on our side. If there's a chance to ask questions, he'll make the case for suffrage.'

Both of us then joined the chant until the last cab had disgorged its occupants and begun to move away.

The police were busy again. Because we were quieter and fewer, they had not bothered us, being more concerned with helping the audience in and guarding them from trouble. In any case, the mounted police stood, threatening in their stillness.

Some of the hansom cabs remained, the heads of their horses drooping. A smaller barrier of constables stood and blocked the Hall entrance. Miss Keevil and a few of the senior suffragettes began to pack up. She came over to me.

'Stay if you can, Gladys. There is no other way into the Hall – we've checked – so there's nothing more we can do. We've made our point. But it would be good if some of us remained to help rescue those brave women on the roof. Unless you're frightened of the mounted police, of course. Don't put yourself at risk. We need you.'

She had no sooner left than a horse-drawn fire truck appeared from the other side of the Hall and the firemen in their brass helmets, aided by the police, began to unravel fat lengths of hose. Then, to our horror, they aimed the nozzle at the rooftop. A jet of water soaked the women there, the gush so fierce that it knocked one over, so that she began to slither down the sloping tiles. Her companions grasped her by both hands and heaved her back up. But the jet was relentless, forcing all five women into a huddle, where they stood with their arms round each other. When the water was turned off we saw that policemen had arrived on top of the roof and had laid hold of the sopping women. In short order they were brought down to ground level and hustled into the waiting hansoms and away.

'At least they're not in a Black Maria,' breathed Millie. 'Me uncle was teken off in one of them.'

'Taken where?' I had no idea what a Black Maria was, but there was no time to ask.

'They'll go to prison, of course. But they'll be charged first, I dare say,' said Dorothy, a gleam in her eye.

'With what? They were making a protest.' I was full of righteous indignation. 'They threw a few stones, but with no intention to hurt anyone, I'm sure. Our instructions were clear about that. Maximum annoyance, no threat to the living.'

'That's not wot they'll say though, is it?' Millie was wise in the ways of the world. 'And I 'spect there'll be police who 'ave been hit. Too many of 'em not to be.'

'Cuts and bruises,' scoffed Dorothy, 'but they'll make a meal of it and an example of our women.' She turned and gripped me by the shoulders. 'And if they're imprisoned they'll know what to do. They'll use our latest weapon.'

'They'll hunger strike!' I'd caught her fervour.

'Look out,' cried Millie suddenly, grasping me by the arm and giving a sharp tug.

Dorothy and I turned to see the mounted police beginning once again to move forward. I took a few steps towards them, beckoning those who remained to follow. 'Spread out into a line and stand firm. The horses won't hurt you.' I stood in the centre of the road and faced the oncomers, pleased to see that to the right and left others also lined up and stood.

Dorothy stood to my left. 'The horses might not hurt you, but the police have truncheons,' she whispered out of the corner of her mouth.

'We're women, Dorothy. What are they going to do? Swat us like flies?'

'I wish I had your faith.'

The line of horses with their stony-faced riders paused. Behind me I could hear shouting and screaming, interspersed with angry male voices, but all my attention was on those horses. Suddenly the rider in the centre shouted a command and the horses surged forward, no longer walking but charging. The change was so sudden that it took me by surprise. From standstill to canter in a heartbeat. I took hold of Dorothy on one side and Millie on the other but first one then the other pulled free. I was alone.

I could smell the sweat of the animals as they approached and the shouts of the men to clear off and then they were upon me. Like a cresting wave, one minute they loomed above me, so close I could see the flecks of sweat flying from their mouths and their rolling eyes and hear the tremendous clatter of their hooves on the cobbles. And then they parted, snorting, stepping sideways, brushing against my skirt with their strong legs, and cantered past.

I stayed frozen for a moment, staring at the near empty street ahead of me, where a few onlookers remained, their mouths open in consternation. I watched as their faces changed and their hands lifted and came together. They were clapping, a sound I could not hear for the booming of my heart, that matched the hollow sound of hooves on stone.

As the sound of hooves faded, I heard clapping and cheering from the remaining suffragettes behind me.

'You did it, Gladys!' Millie ran up to me beaming.

'We're proud of you,' said Dorothy. 'That took courage.'

'Where's the badge?' I joked, thinking of Jim's game, but of course no one understood.

'Come on, now. Time to go home. You don't want to be arrested like the others.' Dorothy took my arm.

'More arrests?'

'Yeah,' said Millie. 'While the 'orses were chargin', cops were pullin' us out of the line from be'ind. Doon't think they thought them 'orses would do as you said. But they did, Gladys, they did! It were wunderful!' Her eyes were sparkling.

I turned to look at the Bingley Hall and the row of hansoms in front of it. The police were bundling more women into the cabs and being kicked for their pains. I saw one woman being lifted and pushed head first into a cab as if she were a log. Her hat fell onto the ground and a black boot stepped on it.

The mounted police waited further down the street, looking at the little knot of women who remained. None of us wanted to test my theory any further. We hurried away, before we too were picked up.

'What's next?' I panted.

'We return to Ethel Street and wait to hear whether they've been charged.'

'They'll goo to prison, won't they?'

'Probably they'll be offered a fine, which they'll refuse to pay. So then they'll be imprisoned. That's the usual pattern.'

'Not if the women have offered violence. It's different from the early days,' I said.

'That's true.' Dorothy was thoughtful. 'It's a whole new game now. We'll have to wait and see what happens.'

'They'll goo to Winson Green, I 'spect. Wheer me uncle went. It's a 'orrible place,' she shivered, 'with high walls like a castle.'

'What had your uncle done?'

'He stole coal from t'rail yards and sold it on. 'E didn't charge much, but still most couldn't afford the price. Businesses bought it though, and ower family got it fer free.'

'How can thieving – sorry, Millie but it is – and political protest be judged in the same way? We're not criminals.'

'It's not going to change now,' Dorothy sounded impatient.

We've always been treated like criminals – didn't you listen to my speech, Gladys? – so now we'll behave like them. We'll keep making a nuisance of ourselves, keep getting imprisoned and – now – keep hunger striking.'

Millie had chimed in with the end of this refrain. Her voice was awed. 'Then we'll 'ave won. Who'd 'ave thought it? It's soo simple really. And I'm a part of it! Oh, thank you, Gladys.'

'It's not me,' I protested, pleased. 'I asked you to join because of your strength, Millie. I've never made a better choice.'

24

The following day at Ethel Street Miss Keevil congratulated all of us on our efforts. 'I don't think Mr Asquith is ever going to forget his visit to Birmingham,' she said.

Most of the visitors had gone, so our offices were crowded mainly with our own supporters, weary but pleased with themselves.

'Miss Evans and I will attend the Court in the morning and find out what sentences each of the nine get and where they are to be held. Then we'll plan a campaign of how best to support our brave ladies.'

'Who were the five on the roof?' asked one. 'I didn't recognise any of them.'

'I've heard that only one came from Birmingham. The others were volunteers from elsewhere, used to protests of this kind.'

'Mary Leigh was one,' volunteered someone from the floor. 'She's an old hand. She'll know what to do.'

'She'll hunger-strike,' Dorothy chipped in. 'She's done it before and was released.'

The atmosphere was highly charged. Everywhere I

saw young women with flushed faces and sparkling eyes. A volunteer called Clarice, who worked part-time as a secretary for us when she could be spared from her parents' grocery store, had an arm round Millie's waist.

Millie herself looked younger than her sixteen years. Her wiry unmanageable hair was all over the place and there was an urchin streak of dirt on one cheek. At a glance from Miss Keevil, she went into the kitchen to make tea for those who wanted. Obeying a gesture from Millie, Clarice accompanied her.

'Will it be all right if I stay at your lodgings again?' Dorothy asked. 'I don't think I could face the journey back after all the excitement. But London duties call so I'll be gone tomorrow. In any case, it would be nice to have a chance to get better acquainted with each other, and with your charming landlords.'

'Since the others have already left, I'm sure that you could have the room Marion was in. And Sophia and James are more than my landlords, by the way; we're good friends.'

' As I hope we will all be soon. I'm going to ask for you to be co-organiser with me after Christmas.'

'I'll help, of course,' I said cautiously. 'But remember, I'm still a full-time teacher.'

'I hope that works for you,' Dorothy said. ' You'll find it difficult, even with the support of your headmistress. Wait till your name surfaces in the newspapers. Your school board won't like it one bit.'

'What do you mean?' I was alarmed. I loved my work, though it's true it had recently taken second place to the W.S.P.U.

'I'm just saying that that's what happened to me. You know I taught Physical Education, hockey and such. I lost my job soon after I joined the suffragettes. One report in the paper that had me as a stone-throwing harridan and that was it.' She mimed slitting her throat. 'The end of respectability. The end of my safe little post at a Kentish school.' She paused dramatically. 'The start of a new way of life. New horizons! The call of adventure! I've never looked back.'

I contemplated a future without teaching. It was also a future without the approval of all that I knew and loved. Despite Dorothy's warning I was sure I could juggle everything successfully, as I'd done so far.

The nine women were sentenced to prison, as Miss Keevil had assumed would be the case. Most, including our Birmingham member, were given three months. Mary Leigh, as a repeat offender, was given four. They were sent to the gaol at Winson Green. No one expected them to be there for very long.

Even with the sure knowledge that the Home Office would capsize under the emotional threat of hunger-striking, it would take courage to refuse food. Mary Leigh was there to hold them to their resolve. Miss Keevil and I would keep their resolve up from the outside.

A number of us decided to go to the prison building and to sing loud stirring songs to encourage those inside. We sang *Hearts of Oak*, with the word 'boys' changed to 'girls.' We sang *the British Grenadiers*, with the syllables 'W.S.P.U.' fitted in instead of the title words. Two young women had brought their father's hunting bugles, which made a fine noise ripping through the dusk and drowning out the shouts of a couple of prison guards to move us along. We felt happy and light-hearted as we sat on Clarice's family grocer's cart behind their long-suffering shaggy cob. That first evening we sang until we were hoarse, sure that we could be heard by those inside.

The second evening we were greeted by police, who would not let us linger but chased us on and frightened the horse.

We comforted ourselves that our shouts and yells would have reached those inside and told them they were not alone. Someone had brought along a violin and was attempting to play Brahms' *Cradle Song* 'to soothe our friends' spirits,' she said.

The third evening we went in sombre mood. That day we had heard that the Home Office were not going to release the hunger-strikers. Instead they were to be forcibly fed. We had no idea what this would mean, just that it sounded horrible. Ethel Street, where we met every evening before going to cheer up those at Winson Green, was rife with rumours.

'They'd have to hold your nose, so that you can't breathe and when you open your mouth to take a breath then they'll push the food in,' said one.

'That woon't work, you'd just spit it aht again,' Millie whispered in my ear.

'They'd have to get the food past your oesophagus,' said another, who worked at a chemist's and had some medical knowledge, after which the ideas became wilder still.

'Up your bottom,' said one giggling girl, whose understanding of anatomy was notably lacking. All the younger members found this extraordinarily funny.

Most imagined that they would have to lie you flat and then pour it somehow down the throat.

'You'd shake your head from side to side,' surmised one.

'Yes, they'd have to hold you still, wouldn't they?' said another, and suggestions spooled out from that thought: clamps, harnesses, weights – there was no end to their ghoulish invention.

I listened with growing concern, but most of the younger members were big-eyed with the excitement of it all. The implications had not struck them. They were so fresh and innocent, I hoped it never would. Not that I had any better idea than they how forcible feeding might be achieved, but I was sure that it would be uncomfortable and painful.

Miss Keevil tried to calm the suppositions down. 'I dare say we will find out in due course how it is done. You can be certain that, by whatever means, it will not be pleasant. But I have every confidence in those inside; whatever is done to them, they'll learn to bear it as they must.' Then, with a lighter tone, 'Now, on to your chariot of war, young Boadiceas! Go and cheer up our captured warriors.' And the laughing girls spilled out into the dusk, for it was all a great lark to them.

And so our evenings continued, long enough to cheer the prisoners with our high-spirited noise, but always cut shorter than we wanted by the police. I noticed that, every time, Millie and Clarice would meet shyly at first. Millie's bright face, usually full of animation and laughter, fell serious as their eyes met. I was glad their friendship had had a chance to blossom. Both were there every evening, because Clarice's father drove his cart over to pick us up. Then he took us all over to the gaol. I noticed how close together the pair of girls sat on the cart, and that often they held hands. It gave me great pleasure to see that Millie had made such a good friend, since Sarah had refused to join up. She valued her job, she said, and both Millie and I could understand that. Jobs were precious.

'How lovely that your father will do this for us. And that he'll let you be a suffragette,' I said to Clarice, a blonde waif-like girl who looked younger than her seventeen years.

'He didn't let me be a suffragette. We fought over it and I won.' Her chin lifted and face hardened. 'He knows when he's beaten.'

Father had heard the interchange and threw over his shoulder, 'I'd rather see her safe by being here with you all. That one knows no fear, never did. It's no good arguing with her. Never was.'

Clarice greeted this speech with a delighted chuckle. 'Joining the suffragettes is the best thing I've ever done, and the most exciting. Where else would I be able to make such friends for life?' She took hold of Millie's hand and squeezed it.

Rowstock, September 1909

Dear Gladys,

Papa and I were anxious to read in the news that the Prime Minister was treated so disgracefully when he came to Birmingham. The scenes of anger and violence that we read about sounded truly dreadful. We do both hope you were not involved. Write to us with some reassurance. We want to know, precious daughter, that you're safe and well and particularly that you're not involved in such frightening events. At least, I comfort myself, it was a school day. Papa pointed that out. So you would have been safely behind your desk, promoting a love of literature in your pupils. Thank God!…

I put the letter down with exasperation. Each letter that came made me feel more isolated, when I should have felt closer. Even the trivial news of Lina's latest wounded animal, suspicions that Kay had not after all broken off with her unsuitable village boyfriend as she should have, descriptions of a picnic in the lovely September weather with Jim on a brief visit, this time without Ida, did not feel more, but less, engaging. How could this happen? My family, which had been all in all to me for so many years, appeared in my mind like a distant cameo, unreal and frozen in time.

I took out a pen to find some answer and laid it aside. How

could I send them reassurance, when we were still rallying the prisoners every evening? How could I tell them what was real and important to me when it did indeed involve violence? And I could not lie. So I sent no reply at all.

There was more trouble too. Catherine Osler, for many years the leader of Birmingham Women's Suffrage Society, now an old and very much respected icon of the Cause and of many other good causes that she had championed, had come to Ethel Street to denounce the methods of the W.S.P.U. Violence, she had stated, was not to be tolerated and military tactics would in the end be self-defeating. She begged Miss Keevil to withdraw herself and our whole membership from such a strategy. Miss Keevil refused and Mrs Osler withdrew her support from anything we may undertake in the future that was not by peaceful means.

I arrived after work on the fourth day to find Ethel Street in ferment. One of our top administrative helpers was also a member of the B.W.S.S. and, obeying Mrs Osler's wishes, was withdrawing her help, taking with her many other senior members, Violet amongst them. They had been the backbone of the voluntary workers, happily straddling the needs of both societies. Suddenly our remaining volunteers looked very young, inexperienced and many of them rather silly – apt to be carried along by the excitement of the moment and to behave thoughtlessly.

'Can you help?' Miss Keevil asked, her face drawn with exhaustion.

I suggested that Millie was capable of much more responsibility than she had hitherto been given, and that her friend Clarice would work well with her. I hoped that Clarice's father would allow her to leave the family store but, remembering his wry remarks on the cart, knew that Clarice would jump at the chance and would get her way.

For myself, I could do no more than I was doing already. I came every day as soon as my teaching had finished and, after Ethel Street closed its doors for the evening, I went back home to mark my pupils' work into the early hours of morning and to prepare my lessons. With the extra time spent supporting the prisoners, sometimes I did not fall exhausted into my bed until two in the morning. Once, I woke up as the starlings left the trees at the end of the road and took their noisy flight through the grey dawn, to find I was slumped over the exercise books on my desk. The side of my face was imprinted with a crease like a scar from the side of a book. It did not fade for hours.

Such a busy September had kept my mind off Michael, but eventually our evening exploits stopped as the prisoners, one by one, were released. The horrors of forcible feeding quickly became apparent. Each one was met by Miss Keevil, in a member's private hansom, and given a hero's welcome but all were wobbly and weak while Mary Leigh herself, who'd survived the longest under this torture, was so ill when she came out that she had to be taken straight to a nursing home. Nevertheless, she raised a gallant hand to wave from the window of the brougham, loaned to us for the occasion by one of our members.

Ethel Street was full of rumours about what the prisoners had undergone, each one more unlikely than the last. The older members sought to quell the fears of the younger ones, but those with vivid imaginations were feeding off the attention they received and thoroughly enjoying themselves. Whenever more than two or three were working together on a task, hands would slow, eyes would widen and mouths would gape as they contemplated the latest hideous idea.

'At this rate noo one will ever hunger-strike or even risk

imprisonment. They're scarin' each other aht of their wits,' said Millie.

'Something will have to be done,' I agreed. 'Forcible feeding must be shown to be what it is by someone who's sensible and not out for creating a melodrama out of it. Hunger-striking is still, as Miss Keevil says, our most potent weapon.'

Millie looked at me thoughtfully. 'Would you hunger strike?'

'If I had to,' I said staunchly, though my heart quailed at the thought. 'It's still a way of reducing the sentence after all.' None of the nine prisoners had served more than three weeks of their time.

A few days later, Miss Keevil called us to a meeting. The sister of one of the prisoners was to speak to us about the realities of forcible feeding. This would finally put to sleep all those silly rumours.

Mary was a plain young woman who worked as a shop assistant in Perry Barr. Her sister Alice, a secretary in the same area of Birmingham, had been the only local suffragette arrested. After a warm introduction from Miss Keevil, Mary stepped forward, a sheet of paper in her hand, which shook so hard she could scarcely read from it. After a few attempts, she put the paper down and blinked at us through her heavy spectacles.

'My sister could not come today. She is still finding it hard to speak. Her throat has been scraped so sore by the insertion of a tube, you see. It was through this tube they tried to feed her.' She stopped abruptly.

'It's all right, Mary,' inserted Miss Keevil gently, while the younger members behind me shuffled and whispered. I turned to glare at them which made Millie, between Clarice and I, stifle a snort in her hands.

'Very schoolmarmy,' she whispered.

Mary lifted her head again and cleared her throat. 'Alice wrote it all down for me, exactly as it happened. And it happened three times a day for the whole time she was there. I want to read it to you, but my eyes got all swimmy for a bit and I've never spoken to so many people before.'

'Do you want me to read it for you?' Miss Keevil got up and put a hand on her arm.

Mary shrugged it off. 'No. I'll do it myself. If Alice can go through this for what she believes, reading what happened to her, and to all the others there, is the least I can do.'

She returned to the paper. It still shook as she lifted it, but she began and, though her voice faltered and lacked strength, the silence in the room was complete as she read the bald facts of how this torture was performed.

'I was taken into a special room where there was a prison bed with pillows and not much else. I was put onto the bed and propped up against the pillows and held upright by two wardresses, one each side of the bed. Apart from holding me up these two women also pinned my arms and legs down. Another wardress helped them in case I fought, which the first time I did. I did not fight after that because it is useless and makes the pain of the procedure much worse. A fourth wardress helped the two doctors, who attended each time. One of the doctors listened to my heart before the procedure began.

'A towel was put around me. A doctor and a fourth wardress stood behind me with towels around their necks and forced my head back. The wardress then held my head while the doctor forced my mouth open. The other doctor, from the front, then pushed a tube down my throat. At first it tickled and I felt like sneezing. Then, as the tube went further down I felt as if I would choke, and then I just felt stunned with shock. The tube had to go down eighteen inches. When it was there the doctor behind me forced my mouth further open, and the other doctor pushed the cork gag down in between my teeth, to keep it open.

'The top end of the tube has a funnel attached, made of china. Into this, as it was held high over my face, about a pint of fluid, a liquid food they call Bengers, was poured in. While it was being poured down, one of the doctors took my pulse.

'After the food had gone in, a basin of hot water was brought and the tube was pulled out. A lot of stuff came up with it, mucus, I suppose, and remnants of the food. The tube was rinsed in the basin. I was laid back and a blanket put over me. I felt horrible, dizzy and sick and with a deep pain in my chest. I could not stop wanting to spit for some time afterwards. Finally, the doctor listened once more to my heart and I was supported back to my cell.

'The wardresses spoke to me after that and begged me to take the food from a cup in future. I would not. Once or twice, perhaps because my throat was so sore, they tried to feed me from a teaspoon. They dropped the stuff between my teeth and then held my nose and forced my neck back until I choked. This method hurt just as much but in a different way.'

Mary stopped. There were tears streaming down her face, which she swiped at carelessly with her sleeve. She gave the paper to Miss Keevil. 'My sister says that she would do it again. Yes, it was uncomfortable, it hurt, but she is recovering. She is very brave. I hope I would be as brave as she. I've come to tell you that I want to join now. A cause must be worth something if people are prepared to go through so much for it.'

'Why do you think some doctors agreed to do such a thing?' I ask Truda now. 'I've always wondered.'

She shrugs, still reading through the sheaf of papers. 'Money, I suppose.' She thinks further. 'Or power. Maybe they thought by helping the Government they would further their careers.' She takes a sip of cooling coffee. 'Or maybe they just hated women. Or feared them.'

"But don't they take an oath? Mustn't they do everything they can to heal and not to hurt?'

'That's the Hippocratic oath, yes.' She puts the papers aside. 'I met a doctor once, after the war, who had participated in forcible feeding. He was a wreck. He'd tried to make up for his guilt at hurting women by going to the Front. There, as he sawed off limbs and drowned himself in the stench of blood and fear and guts, he would weep himself to sleep when he could snatch rest, which was seldom. He was in Hell, he said, and deservedly, for hadn't he broken his oath by torturing women? That was the time I had gone to seek help for a patient who was so stunned by the War, the constant din, the deaths of his comrades, that I felt he would never recover. I was floundering, couldn't help him. By that time this doctor had turned to helping people with psychological problems, mostly men with shell-shock, like my patient. He was still paying, you see.'

'Did you manage to help that poor soldier?'

'No. It was beyond me. I could not know what he had gone through; it needed someone who had been there. So I sent him to that doctor …' She was quiet for a little. 'You see, not all those prison doctors were monsters. Perhaps some were just obeying a directive they couldn't refuse. Perhaps they were as trapped as you were.' Then, with a visible shake of her body to throw off such shadows, she speaks brightly, 'I enjoyed the passages about your friend Dorothy Evans. She came to Leicester once or twice to speak and she always managed to fire everyone up. I dare say some of the daring deeds done by the suffragettes of Leicester would not have happened without her.'

'Yes,' I agree. 'She had a power about her, a dangerous influence that was very attractive. I was just one of many young, rather naive women who succumbed to it. But I liked her too, though I never completely trusted her. She could change, like stormy weather. Sometimes after an adventure with Dorothy I'd feel so shaken up that I didn't recognise myself. But we had laughs too, fun – well, you'll see when I get to that part.'

She hands me the pile of paper with a smile. 'I can hardly wait.'

25

Once the excitement had died down and Bradley, using Mary's transcript, had written a report for the national and local newspapers, I had time to miss Michael more sharply. Bradley's report had stirred up a good deal of public feeling against the Home Office for the forcible feeding policy, especially from the medical profession. Many doctors wrote to the newspapers citing the dangers of pushing tubes down the throats, whether by mouth or through the nose – which was the chosen method in Newcastle, the next place to try the procedure on suffragettes. Either way could cause serious damage and if liquid food went by mistake into the lungs rather than the stomach, it could have even more serious consequences.

At night in bed I wondered about those doctors who would continue to use these methods under Home Office instruction, wilfully hurting other human beings. I ached to talk through everything with Michael. Bradley would be a second best, but he was busy pursuing the stories of militancy around the country and reporting on them.

Where was Michael now? It was six weeks since I'd seen him and I hadn't heard a word. Was he still in Ireland? I conjured up the house his family lived in, which stood away from the edge of the lane and faced the sea. I saw again the harbour beach near his house and my mind travelled down the well-remembered route past the O'Connell's, past the spiky grass and the dunes that marked the beginning of our stretch of beach, to our home. Who lived there now? I imagined that our spirits were somehow stamped on the air of that loved place and that we walked it still, up and down those warped stairs, along the sloped and creaking floorboards into our bedrooms. My spirit hovered over the diary I had left hidden behind the wainscot there, before flying back to the Allen's house, where Michael was, translated in my half-sleeping state to the teenage boy with his intense blue eyes and his hair the colour of wet hay.

It was nearly Christmas before I saw him again.

Term was ending. There had been a further flurry of letters from Mama, and one terse one from Papa, in the wake of the increasing news reports of militancy and forcible feeding. I knew that going home for Christmas was becoming impossible because of the barrage of worry and criticism I would receive from the family. Even Jim had written briefly, telling me news of the ship he was being transferred to and eulogising on his lady-friend Ida Dixon, before asking me to keep in closer communication with the family, who were understandably concerned about what I might be up to. For Jim to interfere there must have been considerable pressure from all at Rowstock.

No, I did not want to return home, though never in my life before had I missed a family Christmas. I was tired – more than tired – worn out: the end of term tests, the marking of papers, rehearsals for a little play I had written for my class to perform and, in the late afternoons, evenings and week-ends, the constant demands of my role as an assistant organiser. It was with relief that I accepted Sophia and James's invitation to spend Christmas with them.

'Bradley will be here too,' Sophia said. 'We can pamper you a little.'

'So long as you receive some pampering as well,' I said, mindful of the growing life in Sophia's womb.

'Oh, I'm fine,' she said. And indeed she was. For a while she had been sick in the mornings and often, at the smell of food, in the evenings too, but now she was past that. Her face glowed and even her hair, usually a pale gold, appeared more vibrant. Compared with my pallid skin and deeply-circled eyes, Sophia looked like an advertisement for Pear's soap.

I wandered the streets after the end of term, looking for presents to give to my friends and trying not to feel guilty that I wasn't choosing for the family. I would buy them something when I next went back, whenever that might be. For James I found a beautiful copy of Palgrave, easy to slip in a coat pocket and bound in red Morocco with gold tooling. For Bradley there was a new notebook, also leather-bound. The blank pages made my mouth water with the desire to write in them. So I bought another, a secret pleasure for my own use. Sophia was easy. I found some rose-scented soaps and a face cream with the same delicate perfume. I had just come out of a shop where I'd bought green tissue and red ribbon for wrapping when I saw him.

Almost as soon, he saw me and stopped in his tracks. For a strange moment or two we simply looked at each other. His face was a mirror of my own doubts and questions. He chewed his bottom lip until an expression of distress crossed his face and he turned abruptly and started to stride away. Heaving my bag with its packages onto my shoulder, I gave chase.

It didn't take long to catch him up but the strength of my own emotions had tied up my breath, so that I panted as if I'd run a marathon. I pulled at his sleeve and he stopped, his face averted. Christmas shoppers broke around us like colourful waves around a rock. Some gave us curious looks.

I manoeuvred to face him. 'What's happened? Were you trying to avoid me?'

At last he looked at me. He turned his mouth down ruefully. 'You took me by surprise. I wasn't ready for you.'

'Come,' I said. We needed to talk and the crowded street was not the place.

Obediently he trailed after me and we found a place that was not entirely full which sold tea and cakes. I led him into the warm, sweet-scented interior, full of large-hatted women chattering over their presents. There were children there too, excited at the build-up to Christmas, stirring glasses of hot chocolate with long spoons. There was a table in the far corner, just vacated, that would suit our purpose. I ordered tea for us both, waited as the thin-lipped waitress wiped a desultory cloth over the crumbs left by the previous customers, and then fixed Michael with my eyes.

He had had time to gather himself; he met my gaze steadily. 'Tell me,' I said, and waited.

'I'm just back from Ireland.'

'I realise that. You've been gone a long time and not a word.'

'There was nothing I could say.'

'To me? Nothing?' I tried to keep the anger out of my voice. No, not exactly anger, though it had the same bitter taste in my mouth and roiled in my stomach just so. This was the man I loved. Who had said, not just once but many times, that he loved me. Who had held me and claimed something of my inner spirit from me that could never be returned. I had been changed by him. I, the awkward child, so often unsure of my place in the family's affection, had never felt uncertain with him. Until he left me.

I watched him turn his cup around and around in its saucer and willed him to look at me.

Finally: 'It was a family matter,' he said. 'Private.'

'Was it trouble with your brother?' Bradley's doubts about Michael jiggled inside, demanding attention.

He looked up suddenly, surprised. 'Which brother would you be meaning?' Since he'd returned, Michael's Irish accent was more obvious. 'I have three.'

Cautiously I said that I remembered that his next brother down was troublesome, bitterly against the English. 'I wondered if he'd done something unwise perhaps.'

His face relaxed a little. 'Patrick will always do something unwise – he was born to it. No, it's not him, so far as any of us know. He ran away long ago to join the Sinn Fein. He might be alive or dead but he's better away from the rest of us, where he cannot draw down the law on our necks.' He paused and gave me a measuring glance.

Something about his attitude frightened me. I waited, scarcely breathing.

'You see, it was … *her* I had to go to. She was ill and there was none to care for her.' He shot me a quick awkward glance. 'My mother, you see, is too wrapped up with my father, whose arm never healed properly after it was broken in a storm at sea.'

There was a pause. Michael fiddled with his cup and did not meet my eyes. 'Michael?' I had to repeat his name. He didn't look up. 'Who are you talking about? Your sister was ill?'

'No, dear. My wife. It was my wife who was sick.'

The last part of this speech I heard as if through cotton-wool. It arrived distorted and muffled into my ear like a buzzing insect, after those two words *my wife*. There it lodged and buzzed in a continuous loop.

'Your wife?' I finally managed.

'Yes, dear. Did you never wonder? I am four years older than you – thirty-three. Of course I have a wife. But we have been apart these few years, while I made my way in this country. I sent money back for her and the children.'

Children too! The buzzing in my ears became unbearable. With a cry that I could not stifle, low but still loud enough for people to glance around from their happy chatter and stare, I scraped my chair back. My whole body shook as I got to my feet and hurried, stumbling over shopping bags and feet, pursued by cries of outrage or concern, I did not know or care which.

The cold air outside greeted me with a welcome slap. I leaned against the tea-shop wall, where Michael found me and put an arm around my shoulder. Which I shook off. I was never lost for words, but they failed me now. Michael looked at me with concern. 'I'm sorry. I truly am. If I was free I'd marry you for you are my true love, you honestly are. I wish I'd met you before I met Nuala.'

'You did,' I spat. 'I fell in love with you as a child and there has never been anyone else for me. I never forgot you.'

'Oh, Gladys,' he said and reached out to touch my hair, spilling out from under my hat in its own separate wild reaction. 'I too never forgot you. But how could I know we'd meet again? It didn't seem likely. Seeing you that day at the Town Hall was like a miracle, like the sun had suddenly surfaced through the grime and cloud. I fell in love with you all over again and my wife was so far away, so unreal...' He faltered to a stop.

'I want to go home.'

'Of course you do, and I'll see you there safe.'

'No. I'll go on my own.'

Listening to him, though the honeyed words dropped into my ear like balm, I wanted to be alone. I needed to confront the problem head on, to pull it into me and make it my own. I didn't know whether I could ever face Michael again. Michael, who was all to me, and whose ache in my body was like the onset of a disease.

When pressed, I said something of this to Sophia, who was appalled but seemed strangely unsurprised. I tried to contribute to the Christmas they so kindly arranged but I must have been a dull guest for the most part. I couldn't help thinking of my family and missing them sorely. It was a hard effort to banish them from my thoughts, especially when, on New Year's Eve, I taught some of our well-worn family parlour games, when Sophia's parents joined us and her younger sister. For a time the familiarity of the games and their competitive fun lifted my spirits from thoughts of home and of Michael. Until Bradley, who had remained throughout the Christmas period, caught me just as I was going to bed and invited me into the kitchen to help wash up, followed by a cocoa.

We had taken our turn to tidy up after the guests, allowing both Doris and our hosts to go to bed early. James was rather the worse for an indulgent evening of mulled wine and Sophia was exhausted with her pregnancy, as she often was. Bradley was easy company and we chattered inconsequentially as we set about our chore, squabbling like brother and sister about who would wash since neither of us wanted the task of drying.

Then, out of the blue, he said: 'Michael's back then.'

'I don't want to talk about him.'

'So he's told you.'

'It's not about the guns at all. I don't think he has anything to do with that.'

'Not even if I told you that Patrick Allen is in Liverpool and suspected of arranging for a shipment of dynamite to be taken over to Ireland? He's being watched and will be arrested before he has a chance to sail.'

'Oh!' I was shocked. 'But not Michael? He won't be arrested, will he?'

'Not if he's not with his brother at the time. He's only a suspect. Nothing has ever been found on him.'

'So he may be innocent. He told me he hadn't seen Patrick for years...' Why was I defending the man who had lied to me over his marriage and may well be lying about his brother too? ... Because I loved him still and I must not. Must not.

'He may not be involved, Gladys. I hope so, for your sake. So if it's not about the guns, what are you so glum about?'

I had had a little to drink. The warm spicy wine churned inside me, flew to my brain and my tongue. 'He's married,' I blurted.

Bradley froze for an instant then flew to my side, relieved me of the tea-towel and caught me around the waist. From there he escorted me, trembling like a loose sail in the wind, to a kitchen chair. Once again, I stared down at the pocked surface of the scrubbed oak. The floor was dotted with crumbs from the mince-pies and spilt sprinkles of sugar. I gazed at them, making maps out of the shapes to keep myself from thought.

Bradley hovered over me. 'I think better of him for telling you.'

I looked up. 'You knew?'

Bradley nodded. 'I was concerned about you. I set some investigations in motion. It seemed unlikely that a man of his age, a Catholic, would not have ... family ... at home.'

I remembered how Sophia had received my news. Bradley must have shared his concern with her. Doubtless James too. Tears welled up. Was I the only fool in the world? Or just the biggest one? I hadn't looked deeper than the surface Michael chose to show me. The same mistake I kept repeating. I closed my eyes: oh, Nina!

Did his lie make everything we did and all we were also a lie? Perhaps he did, as he said outside the shop, love me a little. Perhaps he hadn't been able to help himself, any more than I could.

I smiled shakily up at Bradley. This roller-coaster of feelings went beyond words. I could not speak of the disappointment, the realisation that we would never marry after all, the betrayal of the trust I had put in him – the stupid, unthinking trust – the trust of a child, as I had proved myself to be.

26

Soon after Christmas Miss Keevil left us for Exeter, where she was to take up her next post as Organiser. A General Election was in the offing and Miss Keevil's role was to encourage support for the Liberal party under Mr Asquith, since Birmingham was already a safe Liberal stronghold. Having worked so long on Asquith and his ministers, to have to switch horses at this stage would have set us back years, or so the thinking went.

The party for her leaving was warm and regretful. Miss Keevil had been much admired as an Organiser. Towards the end of the gathering, rather breathless, Dorothy Evans arrived and Miss Keevil welcomed her as the new person in charge. Dorothy's lustrous eyes roved warmly around the assembled suffragettes and came to rest on me. Her smile became a beam.

Within a few days the first crisis surfaced. The owners of No 14 Ethel Street required their building for other purposes. We needed to find fresh headquarters. With an idea blooming in my mind, I made my way home.

Over supper I approached the idea with Sophia and James. 33 Paradise Street would make a credible headquarters for the

W.S.P.U. if they agreed. They had both enjoyed housing their suffragette visitors and, with Bradley, were all supportive of the Cause. The large drawing-room would be wonderful for the smaller *At Homes* and, best of all, they would be paid quite handsomely.

James, despite some good reviews for his latest volume was not bringing in much money and I knew, with a child pending, this was an anxiety for Sophia. They said they'd think about it and talk it over and, the very next day, they agreed.

'What will it actually mean? Will there be hordes of women taking over the whole house?'

'You can designate which rooms we can use. No one but I will sleep here, so it's only a daytime thing. *At Homes* happen in the evening and are weekly, to pass on news, encourage new members and make plans. But don't worry, we have several houses we use for these, so they need not impact on your home too much. We would need a room or two for office work – a couple of the smaller rooms upstairs perhaps – and the ability to make tea and so on to keep the workers happy.'

Sophia brightened as she thought this through. 'It may be fun. I do get lonely sometimes, especially as James…' She stopped and made a grimace.

I knew what she was saying. James was often drunk these days, though it rarely showed until the evening. I had seen him start after breakfast, removing a bottle of wine from the cabinet there and returning it, towards the back of the cupboard, behind the unopened bottles and the sparkling empty decanters. We both hoped that taking the money worries from his mind would help reduce this habit.

Dorothy quickly made her mark. The younger women, especially, loved her and hung on every word. Sophia enjoyed having her around and quickly made herself indispensable, busying herself with some of the endless paper work and introducing some of the recruits to the kitchen and to Doris, who became more mouse-like by the day under the onslaught.

Dorothy was slap-dash about the weekly diary and the accounts that Mrs Pethick-Lawrence at London Headquarters insisted were sent every Friday to London to be checked over. It was a lot to ask. Dorothy went up to the desk in my bedroom on Friday morning, answered the door as gruff as a bear when refreshment was brought, emerged wild-eyed around teatime and finally exploded out of the front door 'to get some air,' hurling her reports, to be sealed in an envelope and posted, into someone's arms as she left.

Sophia and I looked at each other in concern. After only two weeks in which we observed these struggles we saw how Dorothy's spirit appeared quenched and, like a light seen under tumultuous water from a ship sinking beneath the waves, her energy sputtered and was in danger of being lost altogether. Tentatively we offered to help. Sophia was good with figures so she took over the accounts, while I wrote up the diary, after which a much sparkier Dorothy scanned it over and approved it for posting off.

In this way I became, as promised – or threatened, as I sometimes thought – co-organiser with Dorothy, which was ratified shortly by London Headquarters. Because I was still a fully salaried person, however, I received no financial reward for my increased labours.

With the extra work the days flew by and I had no time to dwell on Michael. Our principal task was to prepare for the General Election at the end of January, making sure that for politicians and the electorate the subject of women's suffrage was always in the public consciousness. If the Liberals increased their majority we had high hopes that this time, surely, votes for women would happen. Indeed, Asquith had promised as much. If a reform bill was introduced, he said, then it would be subject to a free vote in Parliament.

While Headquarters worked on the wording of such reforms, and rallied those in Parliament to our way of thinking with promises of support in the run-up to election, we prepared our own rallies and meetings to promote our liberal candidate, to increase our membership and keep ourselves in the public's eye – a harder task without the headline-grabbing shock tactics of militancy. Promoting the Cause through violence was halted for the duration, by order of the Pankhursts.

But the relentless raising of funds had to continue. Income had to be more than expenditure in those weekly accounts. To this end, we had a succession of American Teas, as we called them, where people brought items with them to sell, as well as enjoying cake, a gossip and inspiring talks from a series of speakers. Another successful venture was to rent a shop where we could sell suffragette related goods and craftwork. Dorothy and I had argued strongly for this idea, convinced that the talents of our artistic members, whether it was paintings, jewellery, clothes or toys, would easily outweigh the expense of the rent.

More cautious members were worried. The treasurer, Mrs Pethick-Lawrence, was a stickler for making sure that expenditure was less than profit. They needn't have worried. Though the shop had a slow start, it soon became a money-earner, with the added advantage of proving to be a good place for advertising events too.

When the Election occurred the Liberals did remain in power, but with a smaller majority than before. I wondered if this was due to the unpopularity among the landed classes of Lloyd George and his People's Budget. Bradley thought that was likely and warned that a beleaguered government would be likely to shelve suffrage for the moment.

'Mrs Pankhurst won't allow that,' I said.

'The trouble is that Asquith is now having to rely on the Irish Nationalists and Labour party to get anything through Parliament and both of them have other issues on their minds.'

I sighed. 'Home Rule again.'

'Exactly. And there are eighty-two Irish Nationalists in the house. Female suffrage is not of any interest to them at the moment.'

'The Labour Party is strongly for us though. I know many of the suffrage societies around the country have high hopes of them.'

'That's true, but there are not many of them and there is a lot of industrial unrest at present. Suffrage is not high on their agenda either. I think you'll probably have to be patient.'

'Again. That will mean militancy once more. The Pankhursts won't put up with another wait.'

We all waited for the news from Headquarters at the beginning of February, expecting to be told to encourage militancy wherever we could. Instead, the weekly newspapers and the accompanying letter to the organisers instructed the very opposite. Millicent Fawcett had persuaded Mrs Pankhurst to halt militancy until a new Bill had been considered. This Bill would be drawn up by a Conciliation Committee, consisting of Members of Parliament with women from all the suffrage societies. The wording of the letter was hopeful. Nothing should be done to upset the government, though naturally efforts to increase our support base and money-making enterprises should continue. The public must not be allowed to forget us.

After the excitement of Asquith's visit, some of the younger members were disappointed. They had enjoyed the drama. But the day-to-day routines, and escapades into the surrounding villages to spread the word, the social events and the soap-box speeches in shopping centres or outside factories, continued and were not without drama or that thrilling sense of freedom, previously unknown to most well-brought-up girls. The outdoor speeches in particular invited heckling and danger; women were manhandled, pulled off their boxes, spat upon, had buckets of water thrown over them, or were pelted with stones.

In the Easter holidays, I resumed this kind of duty, always with trepidation, not so much at the thought of speaking – many had reassured me that I could now handle a crowd capably – but at the unknown possibilities from passing strangers, some of whom liked nothing better than to humiliate a woman. Since the police were always strangely absent from such events, no help would be forthcoming from them. Indeed, one young acquaintance of mine saw two police constables coming down the street as she was pulled down from her box and her skirt ripped. She shouted for help only to see them look at her, before turning quite calmly to walk off in the opposite direction.

One fine April day it was my turn to be subjected to such an assault. My speech had started quite well, with a band of men and women appearing to listen, when a couple of young labouring men, grimy boots and caps pulled down low on their heads, broke through the audience and laid hold of me. One, a man with a narrow, greenish-white face, ducked behind me and reached under my arms to lift me.

'Bitch,' he shouted in my ear and placed both his hands over my breasts and then painfully twisted them, pulling me up and backwards, while the other man, small, with crooked teeth, kicked the box from under my feet and then grabbed my legs, pushing my skirt up as I kicked and screamed.

Millie, who was handing out leaflets, ran to help and was kicked in the stomach for her pains. Groaning, she bent over double while my erstwhile audience made haste to leave, not wanting to be involved I suppose, though one woman, crying 'Shame on you,' hit the smaller man with her umbrella. This at least freed my legs for a while.

I fought it – the pain and humiliation – kicking out and trying to claw at them with my stupid short nails, as the man behind pulled me into him and slid me slowly down his body, close against it, until my feet were on the ground. One hand worked downwards towards my groin, while the other still cruelly crushed one breast. He was thrust unpleasantly up behind me. I could feel the hardness of his muscles, like ropes, and smell the pungent sweat which was released every time he moved.

I gritted my teeth. My mind separated itself from my body, a ploy I'd learned when, as a child, I was locked by Jim in that dark shed, for me by far the worst test of the courage game all those years ago. This separation of mind and body switched off the thoughts which invented horrors and kept me sharp and rational. I would not give my aggressors the satisfaction of thinking they could treat me like this because I was a woman. My hands flailed, seeking to gouge and hurt wherever I could make contact; my feet kicked. I could hear grunts when I met tender flesh.

Goodness knows what would have happened, here in the open street at the end of a blue spring day, if a powerful figure hadn't appeared from nowhere and grabbed hold of the men. I like to think that I would have prevailed, that calling on the strategies of Jim's game I would not have given in. But I cannot be sure.

My saviour pushed the smaller man aside with such force that he fell face-first onto the cobbles and then grabbed hold of the other by that very hand that was pressing through my skirt. I heard the man scream as his arm was twisted. He immediately released my breast and I stumbled into Millie's waiting arms.

It was Michael – for the second time my saviour. In my heart I'd known straightaway it was him and relief filled me as I watched him wrestle with my assailant.

'You don't lay hands on my girl,' he snarled as finally he threw the man on top of his friend. Then he began to kick both of them, so that they tried to rise, fell over each other and finally stumbled off, limping and hurling swear-words over their shoulders.

'Are you all right, darling?' Michael's eyes were still blazing, but his voice was soft.

I nodded, still dazed, still separated from discomfort. Blinking, I looked at him. 'How come you were here?'

Michael ducked his head. 'I try to keep an eye on you.' Millie and he exchanged a look.

Breathing deeply, I pulled my clothes together. I was shaking with shock and the aftermath of relief.

'You've been following me? Again.' But though my tone was sharp I couldn't help myself; I felt flattered that he couldn't stay away from me. Since the last time I saw him I had fed the embers of my shock at his lies until I had built up a righteous anger. But I still missed him, every day. That had never gone away. So that now what was uppermost in my thoughts was the fact that he'd cared enough to want to look after me. He must really love me, as he'd said – though I hadn't believed him. Deep down I have never felt I was lovable.

The turmoil of emotions, horror and fury at my assailants, frustration that I'd been too weak to fight them off myself, relief that the incident was over, though that green-white face was imprinted on my sight and I knew would revisit me in my dreams, all this boiled up from my insides and spilled out onto the pavement at my feet. The shame of being publicly sick made me turn away. Over my shoulder someone passed me a large white handkerchief. Michael.

Millie came round and touched my arm. 'Good 'e were 'ere, eh? You know 'ow much 'e cares fer yow.' She shook my shoulder. 'I doant know what's come between yer, but I meant it fer the best.'

I looked at her face, so full of concern, and nodded ruefully. I couldn't blame Millie; I had not shared Michael's betrayal with her or with any of the regulars at Paradise Street, not even Dorothy.

My breasts hurt where they'd been manhandled and the sickness, or the violence of the assault, had left my legs weak. Millie held me round the waist, but it was Michael I looked for.

'Don't leave me now,' I said. *My girl* resounded in my head, but it wasn't possible. I knew it wasn't. 'Thank you.' Our eyes met. 'Can you perhaps just see me home? Both of you. I don't think … My legs feel …'

'Of course,' he said, stepping to my side. We stumbled along together, each with their arms around me, until Millie drew away.

'I doant think yer need me no more. You'll be all right wiv yer fella. Me mam's expectin' me back fer tea, see.'

And before I could protest that I did not feel up to being alone with Michael, that my feelings were all of a jumble, she had melted into the crowds and disappeared.

That episode undid all the months of effort to push Michael from my mind. I had tried to forget him – to immerse myself in work, at school and as Dorothy's helper. I thought I'd succeeded. Bradley had often been around, keeping my spirits up when they might have flagged. Sophia and James, clearly under instruction, had also tried to distract me, but as the spring progressed they had had other things on their minds.

Throughout those weeks Sophia had bloomed but found it hard to move for the weight of her belly and the clumsiness of walking. Her mother had arrived with a cradle, bedding and napkins. Sophia was rarely seen without knitting needles and quantities of white wool. The parents-in-waiting spent more time in their own private rooms, away from the bustle of the office workers. James could sometimes be found wandering around with a bemused expression, as if caught unawares by something surprising and wonderful. His pockets bristled with scraps of paper, covered with spidery writing and crossings-out, and the ends of his fingers and his mouth were stained with ink. He appeared to have stopped drinking.

Somehow, the time had passed without Michael, though he was always waiting there, at the back of my mind. But now, just when Sophia was due to give birth and Bradley was in London on an important story, there was no one to warn me against myself. This rescue, the walk back with unconscious feet, the heat of his arm – it was as if we had begun again, met for the first time. We talked and talked. This time there were no barriers or lies between us while Ireland, with his many responsibilities there, drifted far away, became conveniently unreal.

Michael admitted that he'd taken to shadowing me, whenever he could. Millie had been a willing accomplice, informing him of my commitments. He knew when my school days finished and had sometimes followed me home. His heart, he said, was full of such a weight of longing he could barely carry it around in his chest. 'I've been like a love-sick youth, my eyes diverted by every gleam of red hair, or pulled towards voices that I mistook for yours.' He grasped my fingers. The warmth of his hand travelled up my arm, suffused my neck and face with hot blood.

I was giddy with this love, this desire. Something about the wrongness of it all, the consciousness of transgression, fed that desire. I could not help myself. Neither of us could. Now that we both knew what barriers separated us our love for each other took a new turn, a more sinister one because of the mutual knowledge of our guilt. Our kisses became longer and lingering. I became bolder with him, and he no longer drew away. We knew what we wanted but could not see it through for we had no place to go and the weather was cold and wet.

At night I burned for his touch. My hands mimicked what I wanted his to do, but only fed the flames. Those cycling days of the previous summer, when we had rolled around in the long grass and barely touched flesh to flesh seemed haloed in innocence, sweet and almost laughable. I was on the cusp, sweating in my white sheets, my innocence aching to be broken, to be forged into something new.

In the midst of this obsession, at the very end of April, Sophia's baby was born. A boy! And perfect, said the proud parents, in every way. He was to be called Alfred, after Lord Tennyson of course, but from the start his baby name was Freddie. I had to count each finger and toe, exclaim with them on the quantity of dark hair covering his head, on the darkness of his eyes, 'Like mine!' exclaimed James, while I, who remembered many small siblings and how their eyes and hair changed colour after the first weeks, agreed with everything they said and joined in the besotted applause at each hiccough, facial contortion and dribble of wind.

To me small children were still a source of distaste. Yes, I had learned now to conquer my feelings and I was too wise to show anything but pleasure when invited to cuddle the creature. Sometimes I even wondered whether a child of mine, a child made with Michael, would convert me entirely. Perhaps. But I knew that must never be. Unless ... And I would stare at the window and allow my eyes to drift up to the sky and imagine finding freedom in another country, as Rita and Bill would do when Bill next returned from Canada and they finally married. In a new country there would be no taboos to chain us down and no one to know of Michael's ties in Ireland. I dreamed, the warm weight of Freddie in my arms, until he became in my mind my own child, mine and Michael's, and I watched the clouds drifting like ships to who knows where, until guilt tripped my thoughts and chill reality lodged like a bone in my throat.

What I was thinking was wicked. It was against the laws of God and of our country and I must not contemplate it. Yet thoughts cannot be trammelled by guilt and, like birds in a net, they fluttered and sought for escape. A Lyons Corner House just around the corner from Paradise Street became our second home, where we talked, planned, argued, fell out, were reconciled and, in short, manoueuvred our way through the many twists and turns of a love affair.

As the season blew towards a reluctant spring and the chatter of the Paradise Street starlings increased in volume and urgency, Dorothy was surprised at how eager I became to take to the streets. I visited small businesses in people's homes, where three or four women laboured in dim light over precision work, and large ones in the business quarters. I spoke on street corners, outside factory gates and outside churches, as they disgorged their congregation on a Sunday. I was tireless and Michael was always with me, writing down my speeches and reporting on the incidents, the successes and failures of my campaign. Though he did not use my name, these reports were remarked on by Dorothy, who knew very well who was the subject. Never easily taken in, she guessed at our love. I became the object of some teasing, once in front of little Doris and another time in front of Sophia who, babe against her shoulder and cooing, luckily missed what she said. For I knew that, despite their fondness for me, neither Sophia or James, and certainly not Bradley, would condone my love for Michael. How could they? I was beyond the pale.

Unable to talk to my close friends and bursting with the need to tell someone, to share the burden of guilt, to reassure myself, I suppose, that starting up with Michael again did not make me a bad person, I chose to confide in Dorothy.

'Dear girl,' she said. 'Is it that handsome fellow I saw you with the first time we met?' I acknowledged it was and then, to cut short her cries of delight that were causing heads to turn in the room we used as our main office, I took her into my bedroom and explained the truth of the situation.

'Married?' she said thoughtfully. 'And with children. Hmm. You are in a pickle aren't you? What are you going to do?'

This of course was the crux of the problem in any case. Having explained that I could not, would not be without him, I professed a helplessness as to how to proceed.

'People do divorce sometimes. But it's a wretched business and follows you afterwards for ever. I know one couple who married after she was divorced, and they had to live abroad. They were ever so lonely, I gather. Is that what you want to do?'

'He can't divorce. He's a Roman Catholic.'

'Aah!' For quite a long time she was silent. She paced around the room, picked up a book lying open on the desk and put it down again and gazed at the view down to the church from my window. Finally, she turned. Her face was stretched into a cheerful smile, which didn't quite ring true. 'Enjoy it while it lasts, Gladys. Wring what you can from it, but be careful not to fall pregnant. It'll burn out I expect. It must do. Because eventually you'll have to end it.'

I could not see how I could ever do that. Dorothy was far more worldly than I. My eyes filled up with tears.

Instantly she ran over and sat beside me on the bed. 'Oh, Gladys. You can do it, you know. You are strong and brave, you've shown me that already. Men are far weaker than we are. He will hang on to you as long as he can, his need will be greater, so it must be you who is strong enough to finish the miserable affair, because it's not going anywhere, is it? It can't.'

Now the tears overflowed and she stayed to comfort me but my weeping was not just for my predicament with Michael, but because I had just found another friend who could not show me a way to be with him, an easy solution. Since she, too, felt I must end the relationship, I felt I'd misplaced my trust. I should not have been such a silly fool, to let my secrets dribble out like oil from a rusty engine. And if I could not confide in her any more, did that mean I would lose Millie too? Dorothy was so often with the girl, she would be bound to talk to her. Such a secret was irresistible fodder for gossip. Millie approved of Michael, but she did not know his circumstances. Would that make her feel differently about me too? I realised how much I relied on Millie's admiration.

I could not be the subject of scandal and conjecture amongst the other suffragettes. It would be unbearable. Breathing hard, I asked Dorothy please, please not to tell a soul. I explained how shocked Sophia and James would be and she nodded.

'I am sad, Gladys, that you'd think I would tell anyone. I thought we were friends. Have you listened to what I've advised? I think you've only heard what you feared most.' She turned my head so that I could not fail to look at her. 'What I advised was to enjoy it while it lasts. I think he's a gorgeous creature and I don't blame you one bit for falling for him. *I* would if given half a chance. He's welcome, so far as I'm concerned, to accompany you to our meetings and *At Homes*, even if he can't be seen here in Paradise Street. Sophia never comes any more now she has other things to think about. I won't say a word. But the loneliness of your position, the hopelessness of it, will finally finish it. Trust me on this. And when that happens, you will find the strength to draw it to a close. Meanwhile, make hay! Why not? Isn't that part of what we're fighting for? Our freedom as women, to express ourselves, to live life as we wish?' She gave me another long look, patted my head once and let herself out.

So I'd been wrong. She wouldn't betray me. I had at least one arena of my life in which I could be myself and in love. My spirits lifted a little. I thought over what she'd said and knew she'd underestimated my feelings for Michael. I could no more deny what was between us than fly. How could I ever end it?

The summer gave our mutual desire more opportunities. Armed with leaflets, we would cycle out of Birmingham every weekend, sometimes with the cycling suffragettes, sometimes on our own. Our kisses were our food and drink and there were many grassy hollows dented by our clutching bodies. For yes, as concealing grass grew taller in the fields, dotted with poppies and cornflowers, we did indeed make hay.

The first time I was so frightened. What if, as Dorothy warned, I had a baby? Michael, as he pulled me to him, said he'd be careful. Tenderly he undid the myriad tiny buttons of my blouse and caressed my breasts. I winced at first, remembering the harsh treatment of my loutish aggressor, whose green-white face still haunted my dreams, but Michael showed me how sweet love can be. He did not hurry me, but kissed each part of every limb until my whole self was water, was flowing towards him, was merging.

Even after that first time, when I brushed away the fallen

snow of hawthorn that decked us, and marvelled over every part of him, over the clean lines of his body, his broad chest, the softness of his skin which, I don't know why, I expected to find so much coarser, even then I felt entirely at peace. I trusted him. Somehow we'd find a way to be together.

27

That summer Bill came back from Canada and asked Rita to marry him. The wedding was planned for August. Naturally, and not without some trepidation about my long silence, the lack of answers to their many letters, I was there, along with most of the family. I arrived the day before the wedding, which was to be in Harwell Church.

Jim had managed to get leave, for he was between bouts at sea. 'Just luck that I happened to be here and not due to sail again for another few weeks.' Duncan was arriving on the train later that day, but Edgar was in India. Lina and Kay were to be bridesmaids and were off somewhere to cut flowers. I had not seen them yet.

Mama and Papa were also absent when I arrived, by bicycle, from Didcot station. 'They're at the church, making things ready,' cried Rita, flinging herself at me and knocking my hat off. 'Why did you never write?'

I started to form an answer when Jim and Bill came round the corner of the house and there were more greetings, a little cool from Jim. I had not answered his letter either.

After the wedding, Rita and Bill would sail for Canada and travel to Nakusp, where Bill and his cousin Horace had cleared some forest in order to create a small-holding. Bill boasted of the wooden house he had built with his own hands. He held them up so that we could admire his calluses.

'Your piano-playing hands!' I exclaimed.

'Indeed. There is a piano there already, and a kitchen – a bit plain, but Rita can say what she wants when we're there – a living-room and two bedrooms. One for when you come to visit, Gladys.'

When teased by a disbelieving Jim, he admitted that he'd had help with the erection of what would be his and Rita's first home. First they'd built the house for Horace and Elspeth and a shack for Bill, then they'd all worked on expanding Bill's, about a quarter of a mile higher up the hill from his cousin.

'My goodness it sounds civilised. I thought you had chosen a god-forsaken spot in the middle of the wilderness,' said Jim. 'What's the plan for you and your cousin?'

'English fruit,' said Bill dreamily, expounding on the acreage he had bought. He waved his hand as if to conjure up the green and pleasant land he envisaged. 'Apples, pears, plums.'

He was tanned and his hair had lightened to a russet brown. Rita clung to his arm, dwelling on every word. He had always had charisma. Everything he said was spoken with an authority that defied contradiction. However ridiculous, you just had to believe him, but I did wonder about soft English fruit high up amongst mountains.

The sky spilled a sudden shower, sending us scurrying into the house for shelter. Despite it being August, the weather was cloudy and cool, which had Rita pouting briefly before her happiness reasserted itself. The shower, like Rita's mood, was shortlived.

'Bill looks well,' I commented as we walked off into the orchard arm in arm.

'He's very fit. Nothing like wielding a pickaxe all day long to toughen you up, he says. I will like Elspeth, Horace's wife, he's sure, and her children. Apparently she's taken to the hard life out there as if born to it. And she's the daughter of some high-up army officer, brought up in Hampstead. I should find the change much easier than her. At least I'm a country girl and used to animals.'

I looked sideways at her. I didn't think Rita was particularly tough. I wondered, and worried a little, how she would take to hardship, real hardship, with no water or electricity – recently installed at Rowstock, with enormous pride – no big kitchen ranges for the cooking she loved to do. Nor was she noticeably fond of animals, at least none but those which were fluffy and sweet and preferably in adorable babyhood. But looking at her glowing face I hadn't the heart to voice my doubts. I knew what gave her that glow; I recognised it.

I clamped my teeth against the words bubbling up to be spoken. I could not tell her, no not even Rita, for she would tell Mama and then where would I be? I'd have to produce a suitable man out of a hat for everyone's delight, and Michael was not that. The pain of this realisation dulled the day for an instant but Rita was oblivious, chattering on about what Bill had advised her to take on the ship with them: serviceable clothes and a bolt of hard-wearing cloth to make more, strong boots, cooking utensils, bandages – the list was endless, and endlessly related as we walked around the orchard.

'I wonder when I'll see all this again,' she said. 'Probably not for years.' She hugged me. 'I can't wait to see Nakusp. Say the word, Gladys. Doesn't it just sound so exotic? And the Colombian River, the Selkirk Mountains, the Arrow Lakes. Her tongue rolled round the syllables, trying them out, tasting their strangeness. Did you know, Bill is even taking his grandfather's telescope out with him this time? He's made sure there's a house in Nakusp that is suitable for it. Apparently, he's paid for the roof to be removed and altered so that it will be under cover, with a glass window which it'll poke through on clear nights. He'll have his own little platform from which to watch the stars. We'll watch them together.' Her voice had grown dreamier and her smile could have engulfed the world and every incipient trouble within it.

By the time we returned to the house, Mama and Papa were there and, just as the questions began, but after the cautious hugs, the trap turned up from the station with Joe driving and Duncan in it, carrying his top hat in his hands and already part-dressed in his wedding finery, all but his tails which he carried in a battered gladstone. Duncan at twenty-six looked much older than I expected. He'd grown plump and his hair had started to recede. He favoured Mama's family in height, rather than Papa's, whose genes had created lanky young men with long faces out of the other two boys. But as soon as Duncan grinned and jumped down from the trap, his cheeky dimple appeared and he was our little boy again.

'Why didn't you bring your good clothes in a suitcase?' scolded Mama.

'Too much packing,' said Duncan, and received a playful cuff. 'Where's the bride?' He was engulfed by Rita and emerged red-faced and happy.

Bill had gone home with strict instructions from Rita to be at the church in time, or else. Kay and Lina had turned up with bouquets of rosebuds from our own wall, beautifully wired together. Now they were fussing about preventing them from wilting before the next day. There were angry words, for Kay had insisted, against Lina's wishes, on making the clusters today rather than getting up early the next morning.

'What if there'd been a storm in the night that stripped the petals off or something?' Kay glared round. 'Well, it's possible. Look at the weather!'

'There's no problem,' said Mama consolingly. 'They can go in the sink in the pantry. I'm sure they'll be absolutely fine.'

'They look gorgeous,' added Rita. The beam on her face had remained. I'd never seen her look so pretty.

The rest of the afternoon, before a scratch supper, was a flurry of trying on dresses – 'I had one made for you. You didn't think you wouldn't be a bridesmaid too, you silly? I'm sure it will fit – you're about the same size as Kay. Try it on and we've still got time for adjustments.' Rita was good with a needle.

The dress was a pale pink, which looked shocking with my hair, but I didn't say so. Rita must have noticed however. 'Never mind, there's a little circlet of pretty wax flowers to wear on your head, white with yellow centres. That will flatter your colouring and I expect it will cover up most of that hair.'

Somehow this speech did not help. Rita had a way of saying something that was meant to comfort but which concealed a shaft of something else. I knew of old that she didn't think much of my looks or figure.

I stared at myself in the fly-spotted long mirror in her room. I saw a dumpy woman, no longer young – I was thirty – with a pale rather round face, full lips and that hair. Like the best kind of sunset, Michael always assured me, but what I saw was what I'd always known, that my hair was wild and orange and untameable. Who could love me next to Rita, shining with the radiance of the chosen bride? Then I smiled. Michael did.

'Oh good,' said Rita, misinterpreting my smile. 'I knew you'd like those circlets. Mama found them in Oxford and they're perfect.' Suddenly she stopped. Her tone altered. 'What do you think of Mama? Do you think she is well?'

I looked at her. What I'd seen of Mama was what I expected to see – how she always was. Rita looked at me, a worried frown creasing her forehead. I thought again. Was Mama thinner? Now I thought perhaps she was.

'Not just thinner,' said Rita. 'She's got a cough, especially in the mornings. It's dry and it goes on and on. Of course, she makes light of it and Papa's not worried. Or he says not. Please keep an eye on her, Gladys. Don't keep away so long. It's not too far to come back from Birmingham. Promise me.'

I promised.

The wedding was gorgeous. Even the weather smiled in the morning, though it was still unseasonably cool. Rita wore a dress like the sheath of a Madonna lily, of a creamy white material, with raised shapes of roses in cream. The bottom of the dress flared out like the opening of petals and the material shared the lily's waxy sheen. Bill, standing tall beside her, looked as though he'd swallowed a pot of ambrosia. His eyes, as she arrived beside him in the church, devoured her and none of ours were dry. Rita, our beloved Marguerite, the first of us to marry. Like Edgar, also lost to foreign realms, we all felt that Rita was travelling into a dark unknown, from which she might never return.

Conscious of this, when all was done and the guests, including Bill's difficult, arrogant family, had drifted away on a hospitable wave of food and drink, we girls gathered around a red-eyed Mama. Grouped together, each of us holding onto a part of our mother in love and sympathy, we watched the couple drive away, surrounded by trunks with important labels on them. We waved frantically as the trap disappeared round the corner with Joe, unusually smart and sporting a shiny bowler worn far back on his curly head and an elderly Bracken, wound around with honeysuckle pulled by Lina from the orchard hedgerows. No sooner were they out of sight when Mama staggered slightly and we supported her back into the house.

She made light of it. 'I'm fine. Don't fuss.'

Lina made her a brew of foul-smelling leaves, which hung to dry from a hook over the kitchen range. 'Ivy and thyme,' she said. 'Very good for clearing the chest.'

'Ivy!' I exclaimed. 'Has she seen a doctor?'

'Of course I have,' said Mama. 'Lina's teas may smell vile but they're far more effective than anything the doctor gives me.' She looked gratefully at her youngest daughter. 'Thank you, dear.'

I watched her sip the tea, how she tried to hide her grimace at the taste. After draining the cup she coughed, great heaving efforts that reached down to the bottom of her lungs. Lina handed her a bowl and Mama obediently spat a mass of mucus into it.

'She needs to do that,' explained Lina. 'Her chest is full of phlegm.'

'It's nothing to worry about,' Mama repeated. 'I get it every winter, when it's damp.'

But it's August I thought and met Kay's eyes.

'Of course, you haven't helped,' Kay said as soon as we were out of the kitchen, leaving Mama and Lina together. 'Staying away for so long and not answering letters.'

'I know. I'll try to do better.'

'Mind you do. She's so proud of you. I think, if she hadn't married, she'd have liked to have been a teacher.'

'She taught us well in Ireland. You're right.' I thought of Nina, of the unknown Freddie whose place at the school I'd filled, even of silly Amy who would throw away her teaching skills to be a wife. 'Why can't women have it all?'

'Whatever do you mean?' Kay's voice was dismissive. She left me in the hall and stalked out of the front door.

'I mean,' I whispered to myself, and for the spirit of my mother, 'that women should not be marginalised into being merely mothers, wives, carers of the sick. We have so much more to offer.'

'Eh? What's that?' Jim had come up behind me and planted a kiss on the back of my neck. 'Still in the pink,' he teased, knowing how much I hated the colour.

I grinned up at him, so tall and smart in his uniform with each leather and brass component polished half to death.

'Can't wait for you to meet Ida,' he went on. 'Mama wasn't too warm to her when they met …'

'She'd be like that with anyone. Mothers and sons. No one would ever be good enough.'

'But Ida is – good enough, that is. She's the girl I'll marry.'

'Oh, Jim. When?

'Well – I haven't asked her yet. But we've talked about it. She's not too sure about being a service wife. I talk of my adventures and she already knows I'm away a lot of the time. But that way we wouldn't grate on each other's nerves, would we? Like Mama and Papa do nowadays.'

'Really?' This news emphasised more than anything else how absent I had been. The Mama I thought I knew was kindness itself to Papa. What had changed?

'Papa has got very old since he gave up the Navy. His work in Ireland was paltry compared with those sea-dog days, but at least it was something. It kept him agile in body and mind. Now all he does is prune his roses, read the newspapers and get angry about everything that is reported there.' He looked hard at me. 'Visits from you would stimulate him. You challenge him and make him think.'

'You mean I give him something else to be cross about and deflect his attention from irritating Mama.'

Jim laughed agreement. 'Absolutely.'

'What does he make of Mama's illness?'

'She's not ill, is she?'

'Rita thinks so. And the two girls.'

'Papa has not mentioned it. Perhaps he hasn't noticed.' He read my expression. 'You're worried. Don't be. It'll be nothing. Mama is much younger than the old man. She'll outlive him by years.'

'Gloomy, gloomy, gloomy.' Duncan's voice broke in. 'What are you doing with long faces when we're here for a wedding?'

'The wedding's over,' Jim pointed out.

'Yes, but there's a lot of food left, and drink. Do you think we can tuck in to the remains?'

The remains were on the lawn where we used to play croquet, in a long tent loaned by Harwell Church. The tables of patries and sandwiches, little cakes and strawberries from the garden, had been hauled free of the tent and sat in bright sunshine on one side of the lawn. As the day progressed, the sun had driven away the chill air of the previous day. Willing villagers were dismantling the tent, luckily dry after a wet night but a hot cloudless day. We watched from by the table as the tent was heaved onto a farm wagon. Duncan, munching a bun decorated with pink icing, went over to pet the shire horse hitched to the wagon.

'He's never got over his love for horses, has he?' I remarked. I was an inch away from relating my adventure with the mounted police, but instead I just reminded Jim of Lina's childhood adventure.

We watched as Duncan divided up the remains of his bun and allowed the horse to taste it with gentle whiskery lips.

'He should have been a farmer,' said Jim.

'Won't it be something like that when he joins Edgar in Darjeeling?'

Jim screwed up his face. 'I don't think so. So far as I can tell from my travels to similar regions, a tea plantation doesn't use animals at all. It's natives who pick the leaves and carry them in baskets and take them to be dried. Nothing really for a plantation manager to do except manage people. And money.'

'And the heat.'

We looked at Duncan again. He had loosened his collar and removed his jacket. He was sweating profusely. The horse had lowered its head and our brother was scratching its poll between the ears. The enjoyment of both parties was evident.

'Actually,' said Jim, 'I don't think Darjeeling is that hot. It's mountainous you know.'

'Still.'

'I know. If Higher Farm had been free, perhaps. But Papa would never turn out tenants as good as Joe and his family, that have been there for so long and done so well with it. And then there's Edgar. Between farming here alone and joining his brother out there there's no real contest. Duncan has not been himself since Edgar left England.'

'He's got fat.'

'A little chubby perhaps. Nothing that won't wear off when he's happily reunited with his other half. And I hear that life is pretty good out there for the English. In India they're the upper class, rich, with servants and plenty of leisure time. I could almost envy them – a life-style we could never have in this country.'

Lina and Kay joined us. Lina collected the little vases of rosebuds strung along the centre of the tables and, when this was done, Kay slowly shook and lifted the pink tablecloths for the wash.

'She's thinking of her own wedding,' Duncan whispered as he ambled up, having seen off the horse and observed Kay's dreamy expression.

'Is there to be one?' I asked.

'Only in her mind,' laughed Duncan and quietened as he saw Lina's disapproving look.

'She still thinks of Harry, you should know,' said Lina *sotto voce*. 'It was cruel to split them up.'

'He wasn't suitable,' said Jim. 'It wouldn't have worked.'

Immediately I thought of Michael and bit my lip.

'What?' said Jim to me. 'You disagree? A village boy. With no education or prospects.'

'No, no,' I said hastily.

Suddenly Mama and Papa were there, chasing the wasps from the remains – which had all now been piled up on a single table – and helping us collect the plates. There was a flush on Mama's face and no sign of a cough. She chatted and laughed, revisiting the day, its successes and those little moments that make memories: Rita's veil slipping, two old village men sharing a joke in the corner of the tent, one of Lina's cats – she had adopted five – escaping from the barn and leaping into the middle of a plate of meat paste sandwiches. She looked bonny and well now, the old Mama, as did Papa. I observed how, once the last remnants had been taken into the house, our parents linked arms and wandered around the garden perimeter, as they always had done on warm evenings. Maybe Rita was worrying needlessly.

On the journey back to Birmingham, I revisited a brief encounter with Mama, when she'd questioned me closely about my involvement with the suffragettes. It had left a sour taste in my mouth. It was just before I left and I was packing my carpet-bag in my old bedroom. She had come half into the room and leaned against the door-frame. 'There's not been enough time to talk, but I wanted to say that I don't like what's happening in that movement of yours. Have you considered other societies, as I advised?'

I repeated my commitment to the Pankhursts, and described how I'd felt personally chosen by Mrs Pankhurst, the first time I'd seen her.

She gave me a long look. 'Call it a mother's intuition if you like, but I have a bad feeling about this. You don't write. That speaks of guilt to me. You are uncomfortable with the choices you've made – aren't I right?'

I couldn't look her in the eye.

An expression of pain crossed her face. She closed her eyes. 'I've always known that it would be you who broke my heart.'

A protest formed in my mouth but she raised a hand to quiet me. 'Yes, Gladys. For it is you who have the most power to do so. Because you are the most like me. And I *know* you.' She fixed me with a hard look. 'I recognise your impulsive heart, because it is *my* heart too. You rush into things. You make mistakes.'

Suddenly the colour drained from her face and she steadied herself against the door-frame. I rushed to her side, but she shook her head. 'It's just tiredness, and emotion. My two eldest girls …'

I made a move towards her but she kept me away with an impatient flap of her hand. 'Nothing to worry about. Now let me go on. I must speak, while there is a chance and you are here.

'Is it really too difficult to let me know what is going on in your life? Is it just your Cause, or is it something more?'

Again that look from her. Again my eyes slid away.

She nodded wearily, as if I'd spoken volumes. 'You are treading a dangerous path, my girl. Thank goodness your Papa knows nothing. I've made excuses for the lack of letters and kept my concerns to myself. But I fear for you.'

Bewildered and uncomfortable – it was as if she had dived into my mind, rooted around in the dark silt, and found all my secrets: Michael, my increased involvement with the suffragettes, the dangers I was encountering – that man with his green-white face like a malignant spirit…

'I must go,' I stammered, aware that I'd miss the train if I delayed further.

'Yes, go. But don't return until you decide to make a clean breast of all you're up to. There must be honesty in a family. I won't settle for anything less.'

I watched as she gathered herself, pulled herself upright, giving the door-frame a pat as to an old friend, and left with her back firm.

Was this the aspect of a sick woman? If so, she was putting a good face on it. In the wake of her words, said mildly but with a contained anger propelling them, I too felt bitterness. Here I was once more, out beyond the pale, even further than Rita on her way over the Atlantic Ocean.

28

Once back in Birmingham I was swallowed up by events and, despite all my promises to Rita, I gave little thought to Mama, the rest of the family, or even to Rita and Bill with their new exciting lives. I found Paradise Street in ferment.

'It's too much,' cried Sophia, standing alone in the middle of the hall and clutching Freddie so tight that he bawled. 'All these people filling my house and spilling into every room. There's no peace anywhere.'

'What's different?' I asked of a passing volunteer.

'Nothing that I know of,' she said with a shrug. 'Miss Evans has us all re-organising the paperwork and she's bought some more cupboards for filing and keeping things in and we've moved stuff around to fit them in. We're busy shifting things around now.'

'This is a home!' howled Sophia spotting me, and the volunteer scampered off.

I took Sophia by the arm and led her into the kitchen. It didn't help that the kitchen also was full of young women jabbering like parrots. They fell silent as I came in and glared at them.

'Give us a moment,' I said, indicating the door and they shuffled off, big-eyed.

I sat Sophia down and relieved her of her son, whose cries had increased in fury to the decibel level of a ship's siren and whose face had undergone an equally violent transformation from rosy pink to purple. I jiggled him madly against my shoulder, an activity he found so startling that he was shocked into silence.

'This is a home,' repeated Sophia in a quieter tone.

'I know, dear. It must be difficult for you. But you did agree and the money is helpful, isn't it?' Against all odds, the infant had fallen asleep against my upper arm. A milky bubble formed from his open mouth.

'I agreed before I had a child. It's impossible with Freddie. Too much noise and he wakes and then he cries. And I can't sleep. He's awake all night. So I try to catch some sleep in the daytime but I can't. Oh!' And the tears came.

'We'll tell everyone to keep as quiet as we can. I can see that this is getting you down. Poor Sophia.' Really it was hard to see what the problem was. It was a big house and solidly built. Difficult to believe that you'd hear anything in their rooms at the far end of the upstairs corridor. Today perhaps, but not normally.

'Thank you Gladys. I missed you. Was it a nice wedding?'

That was the first of many such episodes. The workers crept around, mostly, but there were noisy moments when they shared news or greeted each other. It was becoming impossible and Dorothy began to make noises about finding somewhere else. 'Though this is so perfect.' She rolled her eyes at me in half-serious dismay.

'It's only Sophia. James is fine about it all. He enjoys the banter and he has a little following of young women who willingly read his poems and coo admiringly.'

'He's flirting with them?'

'Good heavens no,' I said. 'Well, only a little and not seriously.'

'I certainly hope not. I do feel rather *in loco parentis* with the young members. They can be very silly. It's the first time most of them have had a taste of unchaperoned freedom and it quite goes to their heads.' Dorothy looked serious. 'I shall have a word.'

'I wouldn't.'

She looked at me narrowly. 'What about you? There's no one listening. How's Michael? Aah! I can see from your blush what has happened. You are taking care, aren't you?'

I nodded, thoroughly embarrassed. I wasn't sure whether we were taking care or not. I knew so little about these things.

Luckily Millie came by, just as Dorothy opened her mouth to speak again, and the moment was gone.

Sophia went to stay with her mother, taking Freddie with her. She stayed there for a few weeks and Bradley moved in to keep James company – James who without Sophia was like a drifting boat. When Bradley was out working, or tapping on his typewriter in a corner of the house, James wandered around like the knight in the Belle Dame's thrall. Bradley, with the connivance of Doris, had hidden most of the drink, but that didn't stop James from going out and finding his own. Bradley's action had prevented excesses of the most sodden kind however. Paradise Street, without the organised influence of Sophia, began to resemble the house of Usher. Doris drooped around as if suddenly orphaned, giving desultory flicks of a duster to the furniture here and there, with little effect. Somehow the frays in the fabric, the patches of damp, the holes in the wainscoting, became more visible, and a kind of miasma of neglect settled on every corner of the house except the kitchen. Here, the warmth and comfort of the range and the ever-boiling kettle cheered the spirits. Every one of the workers found times in the day where they would settle there and replenish themselves.

At the beginning of November, an emergency meeting was called. We gathered in the drawing-room and listened as an excited Dorothy told us that Mrs Pankhurst herself was coming to talk to us on the fifteenth of that month.

'As most of you will know, Parliament broke up at the end of the summer without voting on the Conciliation Bill, so laboriously worked on by so many. We contained our disappointment then, as instructed by Mrs Fawcett and Mrs Pankhurst, since we understood the importance of the People's Bill which had taken precedence. However, Mrs Pankhurst fears the worst, that when Parliament re-opens on November the eighteenth, the Conciliation Bill will be sidelined. Should that happen, Mrs Pankhurst will undoubtedly wish to restart militancy. It is about that she will want to talk to us. So ...' Dorothy allowed her eyes to rove round the drawing-room with its chipped gilt paint and its patchy wall-paper, softened by the gas-light. She smiled. 'We want a full turn-out of as many women as possible at the Town Hall on the fifteenth of November, and we haven't long to organise it.'

Everyone was given a task to do to spread the news. Some chalked on the pavements, or on the sides of buildings. Posters were hurriedly printed and plastered all over the city. The high point however was a cluster of lanterns, powered by electricity, which threw up the words *Mrs Pankhurst, Town Hall, November 15th* on the side of the building, from where it could be seen by anyone in the city centre. A number of male supporters organised this display, which was certainly the crowning glory of our advertising campaign and entirely Dorothy's idea.

The ferment this planning caused in Paradise Street made me very relieved that Sophia and Freddie were still at her mother's. In addition to these preparations, and with a battle light in Dorothy's eye, she encouraged some of us to make a nuisance of ourselves at places like the Council House.

'Undoubtedly that is what our instructions will be,' she argued, 'when militancy starts again.'

'This is not an instruction from Headquarters then?' I asked.

'Well, not exactly...' She saw my expression. 'We're not going to do anything that could be classed as militant. Just – you know – be a nuisance, as I've said.' Her eyes danced. 'How you each define 'nuisance' of course, is up to you.'

So I found myself, with Millie, Clarice and a few others, chanting *Votes for Women* on the Council House steps as the Councillors left a meeting at the end of the day. No one could possibly say, in the November dusk, who threw the stone which broke the window of the chauffeur-driven car, come to collect one of the committee bigwigs. But somebody did and we were all arrested and taken to the police station.

The episode was reported in the local paper and we were brought before a judge but, though cautioned, we were not imprisoned, though my heart galloped like a horse in flight, from images of forcible feeding.

'We will not create martyrs of these silly women,' said the judge. 'Prison would only draw attention to them.'

So we were released.

The next day, Miss Nimmo called me in to her office. In front of her she had a copy of the newspaper in which my name and occupation was stated. Though I no longer wore my full suffragette regalia to school, I still sported the badge on my collar and, when I left school to go home, my scarf and hatband in the colours were proudly worn. The headmistress had never brought me to task for this. I felt that she still supported me, however silently.

Having asked me to be seated, Miss Nimmo looked me in the eye.

'This is not the first time I have had cause to speak to you. Last year there was a silly incident in the street, where you and a number of others were arrested for being disorderly and causing an obstruction. You had a journalist with you at that time, who gave a very different account of the incident and the reasons for it. I read both versions of the story, in two different newspapers, and felt that it was not worth causing a fuss about, though some of the older members of staff had a different opinion.

'You know all this. I only bring it up now so that you should understand that it is not plain-sailing running a school, when a member of my staff persists in drawing attention to herself and the school in an unwelcome manner. Parents I can put at ease. Colleagues I can manage. But the school board, to whom I am beholden for my post and for the finances with which I run the school, are another matter.' She looked at me gravely. 'You understand what I am trying to say?'

'Yes, Miss Nimmo.' I swallowed. 'Are you telling me that I must lose my post here?'

'No, and I hope that will never be necessary. You are an excellent teacher and your pupils love you. Even though your commitment to the W.S.P.U. has grown tremendously in the last year, you have managed to keep up with your work and I have no complaints on that score. But I cannot protect you should the school board ask for your head, though I shall try. They respect my word, up to a point. Should it seem that I am losing my good sense and protecting someone who does not deserve to be protected, who persists in flouting the school's good name, I should have to step back. I want you to be very clear about this.' She leaned forward and looked me firmly in the eye. 'In a choice between you and the good name and standing of the school, you would have to go.'

It was Thursday afternoon, the 17th of November, just a few days after the interview with Miss Nimmo and two days after Mrs Pankhurst's visit to Birmingham. This year, Thursday was a free afternoon with no teaching or pastoral commitments. Dorothy and I, along with Millie and Clarice, were on a train travelling to London. The two girls were full of excitement at the thought of visiting the capital. I was curious about seeing Headquarters, at Clement's Inn, and finding out why we had been asked to attend a briefing there. What more could there be to say, after the meeting only two days ago? Then Mrs Pankhurst had warned of the possibility of militancy and underlined how close the Conciliation Bill had come to success. And she'd asked organisers and one or two others to attend a further meeting at London Headquarters. It was time senior suffragettes knew how and where we work, she'd said.

Dorothy had thought there might be more to the invitation than met the eye. 'Perhaps she's afraid of reporters, who could spoil any surprise she may be planning.' Dorothy had sounded excited.

'Surprise?' I asked.

'Well, use your sense, Gladys – sometimes I think you haven't anything between those ears except Michael.' She smiled to take the sting out of her words. 'Don't you think she will have planned something to coincide with the reopening of Parliament?'

'That's on Friday! No, she wouldn't have asked for attendance without warning us how long we might have to stay. I will come up in the afternoon and return later that night – on the mail train if necessary.'

Following Dorothy here we realised how lucky we were to have her with us. She had worked at Headquarters and knew exactly how to get there for a teatime briefing. I should have plenty of time to attend and catch one of the late evening trains back to Birmingham.

The exterior of Headquarters was smart enough but inside was crammed. Every inch of space was used: desks, chairs, filing cabinets, piles of papers, trays of teacups, telephones ringing, the pattering and tapping of feet and of typewriters and the constant to-and-froing of women of all ages. The air was full of conflicting scents: ink and paper, dust and lavender, with a stuffy overlay of hot, tightly garbed bodies in close proximity. We thought Paradise Street was busy, but that was nothing compared with this.

A kindly young woman with a pencil wedged behind her ear gathered us in and invited us to follow.

'We're hoping to have new headquarters soon,' she said, apologising for the chaos. 'As you can see it's much needed. We've simply outgrown ourselves.' She waved an explanatory hand as we passed through office after office.

Finally she took us through to a larger room where there were already a number of people gathered, sitting on chairs wherever they could find a gap, or leaning against filing cabinets, or perching on the edges of desks. Millie and Clarice squeezed up next to another young woman on the edge of a table. I followed Dorothy, who appeared to know everyone and was calling out greetings within seconds. The cameraderie in the room, the shrieks and laughs and tattle of women's voices confused the ears, so that I felt disoriented and followed Dorothy's backview with a kind of desperation, as if she were a lifeline, until we came to a rest near the front of the room.

Soon the small but imposing figure of Christabel Pankhurst came in and everyone fell quiet. After welcoming us she made way for her mother, who I had not noticed sitting to one side of the room.

Mrs Pankhurst's face was tired and drawn, apart from those pansy-eyes that illuminated it. She came straight to the point.

'We are worried about the fate of our Conciliation Bill. It passed its second reading in Parliament last June but then the House broke up without a resolution on it. Tomorrow, Mr Asquith opens the doors of the House once more. We have asked that our Bill be brought to the forefront and will be told if that has happened. If not we will march into Parliament with the three hundred women we have gathered here for the purpose, to make a protest. We cannot allow the procrastinations of the Government to delay our rights any longer.'

We clapped and cheered her resolve but my stomach was sinking. I could not miss school. I leaned over to whisper my fears to Dorothy but she hushed me, as Mrs Pankhurst had not finished.

'Some of you have been in London for some time, for which I thank you. You endured appalling weather – I don't think it stopped raining for a moment the whole of last week – and travelled with me to every part of London to gather support. Meanwhile others were touring the provinces, and our visits to outlying regions were concluded this week. Our efforts paid off, however, for the Albert Hall, last Saturday, was full and the speeches, not just from myself but from the leaders of many other societies, were stimulating and hopeful.'

'Did we know about the Albert Hall?' I whispered to Dorothy as Mrs Pankhurst paused and took a sip of water. 'I'd like to have been there.'

A number of people turned to hush me.

Mrs Pankhurst cleared her throat and continued. 'I wish I could feel as optimistic as some of my colleagues. This

Government has proved shifty throughout, bribing us with promises and then reneging on them. Hence my hiring of Caxton Hall tomorrow, which is just a step or two from the Houses of Parliament themselves. Should anything happen to disappoint us again, we are well-placed to protest.

'I don't want to keep you long this afternoon. It is already dark, and still wet of course. Each one of you from the provinces has been allocated a bed with a London member and I shall see you all at Caxton Hall tomorrow.'

Mrs Pankhurst left the room but Christabel, with a friend, began to move around, matching up other recent arrivals like ourselves with their hosts for the night.

'That's Annie Kenney,' said Dorothy, waving at a narrow-faced young woman over the heads of the others.

I looked around for Millie and Clarice, but they had already been welcomed by other young people and were chattering merrily. I pulled at Dorothy's arm.

'I will need to catch an evening train back, Dorothy. If I miss a morning's teaching it'll be the end of my career. Miss Nimmo has already given me a warning and…'

Dorothy took my arm fiercely and marched me out into a corridor. 'You can't back out now. Why did you come? You must have known that you'd be roped into doing something here in London. And it's important, Gladys.'

'More important than my career?'

She threw her head back and sighed impatiently. 'It's your decision, Gladys. But this is it. This is the moment, the crux, where a choice has to be made. You've been sitting on a fence between two callings for long enough.'

I closed my eyes. I felt sick. 'How can I choose? What would I do without my salary? And what about the future?'

'Oh!' Dorothy growled in frustration. 'You know that if you lose your post because of your work for suffrage, Headquarters will instantly pay you a salary as an organiser for them. You're already doing that work. Money won't be a problem.'

'And when it's over? When we have the vote and I don't have a career?'

Dorothy shrugged. 'In my opinion the future always looks after itself. Some man will probably marry you. You're pretty and bright, though you always run yourself down. You'll find another career.'

I shook my head against the idea that marrying might sort my problems. If I could not marry Michael, then I wouldn't marry anyone. Did Dorothy, arch-suffragette with such a passion for the Cause, really think that marriage was a career choice? What about the freedom of women to forge their own path?

'Why were we not warned?' For the first time I realised that Dorothy was carrying a small bag. I'd thought nothing of it – I myself had my satchel, with a book for the train and some money in it, and an umbrella – but her bag was larger. It dawned on me. 'You knew, didn't you? Headquarters had told you of this by letter, and to keep it secret so that the authorities didn't get to hear. I'm right, aren't I? They probably told you about the Albert Hall too.'

She smiled and shrugged. 'If you'd gone to the Albert Hall meeting, you'd have known about the rest of the plans.'

Fury filled me. 'I'm not an outsider. I'm your friend. Your co-organiser. How could you keep everything from me?'

'I did give you some hints but … well, you needed a push, darling.' Her little smile was maddening. 'But you don't have to stay. As you've already said, you can return. Just go if you're going.'

I began to breathe hard, gathering the words that would wound deep enough to score the heart, but I hadn't even begun when Millie and Clarice came running out to find us.

'We're all goin' to stay in a posh house by the river,' Millie squeaked with excitement.

'Lots of rooms,' put in Clarice.

'She's an actual Lady Something-or-other, with a proper drawly kinda voice and servants an' all!'

'Your chance to find out how the other half live then,' said Dorothy caustically. She was still glaring at me. 'Gladys is going home. Gladys is deserting the Cause.'

'Gladys?' Millie's face had fallen.

'Did you know you were staying?' If Millie was also in on this, I'd never forgive Dorothy.

"Course not. But it's excitin', ent it? Clarice guessed there was summat more happenin."

I touched her cheek. 'It is exciting for you and Clarice but you know I must go back tonight. You can report what happens to me later. When you're back. I'll hold the fort in Paradise Street.'

'You cain't leave,' Millie looked lost, like the child that we often forgot she was. 'You were made for this. Lotsa people c'n teach, Gladys, but you – you inspire people. Like Dorothy. Both of yer are brilliant clever speakers and 'ow many people c'n do that?'

Clarice, whose arm was linked through Millie's, said, 'When you speak, Gladys, it's clear. It's easy to understand. It's a gift, I think. You're very lucky to have it.'

'Out of the mouths ...' put in Dorothy wryly, and something in me gave up.

At that moment, an imposing woman hoved into view, her pearl grey dress crackling around her and her umbrella stabbing the wooden floor with staccato taps. 'Ah, there you are! All ready? Got your bags? Good. Follow me.'

Firmly Millie took one of my arms and Clarice the other, while Dorothy fell into step with our hostess.

'Don't worry,' Millie said quietly as I protested. 'It'll be all right. Your headmistress stuck up for you before. 'Spect she will again, don't you? If you want 'er to. And it's only one day. Then it's the weekend.'

Later, when Dorothy and I were shown to our shared room she was still angry, while I was downcast. I felt as though I'd been steamrollered.

'I'm running out of patience,' she said. 'Now the decision's made, you need to snap out of it. Do things whole-heartedly or not at all. What did you think you were doing, coming to London but going back again before the real event?'

'I didn't know of the real event.'

'Of course you did. There were enough hints from Mrs P on Tuesday. You just hadn't used your brain. You have to commit. It's time. So stop sitting around looking whey-faced and peaky – if Millie and Clarice hadn't been charming our hostess with their enthusiasm, I don't know what would have happened. You're here now. The fact that you're in London at all tells me that you wanted a decision to be made for you. Well, it's made. Now live with it.' While she delivered this speech through gritted teeth, she was throwing off her clothes and pulling a night-dress out of her bag. I removed my stockings, skirt and blouse and, shivering, pulled the sheets up to my chin. There was a fire in the grate and the room was quite warm, but I felt cold with apprehension.

During the night, sensing that I was awake, I heard the rustle of sheets as Dorothy left her bed and pattered over to mine.

'I'm sorry, Gladys,' she whispered. 'I do understand how difficult it is to give up a career you enjoy. I can't go back to teaching either and sometimes I lie in bed and worry about that. But I do believe that the future takes care of itself. I know that I was meant to do this thing, to put my energy into the movement, and I believe you have the same calling. You're good at it, as the girls said. Without your job as a teacher you could travel around as a speaker. We could go together. Please don't be angry with me. I was just being selfish, I suppose. I want you beside me as a colleague but, most of all as a friend.'

She waited till I stopped snuffling, gave me a peck on the cheek and rustled back to her own bed. I rolled onto my back and lay still, my mind whirring.

How could I let Miss Nimmo know what had happened? At the very least she needed to know that I'd tried to contact her, that I was sorry. Perhaps I could telephone. Though Mama and Papa still had not got one of these devices, the school did and a rich house like this would surely have one. Or a telegram? No, I'd never find a Post Office to send one. But the school deserved to know…

I dozed and startled awake, jumbled thoughts still careering round my head like maddened horses. At some point, as I listened to the quiet breathing of Dorothy in the next bed, I began to face up to some of the things she had said. She was right. I could no longer juggle the two distinct halves of my life. Something would have to go. I had to make a decision.

With that realisation a measure of peace filled me. At last I slept until the grey dawn crept through the heavy curtains and the maid knocked at the door to bring us breakfast.

It was too early to ring the school when our hostess began to organise our departure. I caught hold of the housekeeper and left a scribbled note with her. Could she ring? But I wasn't hopeful. The woman looked doubtful and I had no number for the school. She would have to make enquiries. Looking at her polite closed face, I knew that nothing would be done. Before I could worry any further I was swept along with the others to Caxton Hall. As soon as we were there, waiting for news from Parliament, I forgot anything else.

When the news arrived it was exactly as the Pankhursts had feared. Far from voting on our Conciliation Bill or even mentioning it, Asquith had dissolved Parliament to force yet another General Election. The reason? Lloyd George's proposal to limit the power of the House of Lords, who had blocked the People's Budget for so long. The challenge to the Lords had thrown out of the window any hope of Women's Suffrage being on the agenda. This was explained to us, clearly and loudly, by a furious Christabel.

Angry at yet another sidestep, our band of three hundred women, from Ireland, Scotland and all over England, in whose number were Dorothy, Millie, Clarice and I, listened as Mrs Pankhurst instructed us as to how we should march, to deliver our Memorandum to the Government. Christabel read out its wording, copies of which were to be handed out peacefully by each region, in the order decided earlier that morning.

Dorothy, as Organiser, was given a copy of this, which read:

> *'This meeting of women, gathered together in the Caxton Hall, protests against the policy of shuffling and delay with which the agitation for women's enfranchisement has been met by the Government, and calls on the Government at once to withdraw the veto which they have placed upon the Conciliation Bill for Women's Suffrage, a measure which has been endorsed by the representatives of the people in the House of Commons.'*

'This is nothing but the truth,' Christabel told us all. 'The Conciliation Bill, which would have allowed some women to vote and which would have been the first stepping stone towards a general franchise for all women, has gone through two readings in Parliament and has been approved. All that was needed was ratification on its final presentation and we would have been there! And backed by the vast majority of the Liberal Members, who recognise and approve our Cause! But we are to be denied it. Again. Yet we will not break our word and allow our justifiable anger a free rein. Peacefully we will march into Parliament and present our Memorandums and peacefully we will withdraw, wrapping the cloak of our purity and dignity around us.

'Each contingent will present their Memorandums one at a time, with a short break before the next contingent ascends the steps to Parliament. At all times we will remain quiet and dignified. No one will be able to say that *we* reneged on *our* word.'

Every five minutes another contingent left Caxton Hall, starting with the representatives from London Headquarters, which included the Pankhursts themselves.

By the time it was our turn to march the short distance to Parliament, a quarter of an hour had passed and the scene on the steps and below in the square was hard to decipher.

Two lines of policemen stood in front of the doors to the House. They carried truncheons. The square itself was full of hecklers, men for the most part who shouted abuse at us. Behind them were more policemen. We were threatened from all sides and we drew closer together, shoulder to shoulder, under a barrage of oaths and threats. Dorothy held our copy of the Memorandum firmly in her hand.

Increasingly jostled by the crowds, our ears ringing with the din, we nevertheless made it to the steps and began to mount them. In front of us, the previous contingent had reached the top. Suddenly there was a roar of sound and a woman above us was picked up by two burly police constables and thrown down towards us. She rolled down the last step into the crowd and was immediately surrounded. Helplessly I watched as she was lifted above the heads of a group of men and passed over them. They pulled at her clothes and moved her around as if she were a plaything. The mad sound of laughter joined the cries and shouts that never let up. She was passed over the heads of the largely male crowd and disappeared from view.

Millie gave a kind of yelp as another woman was pushed down the steps and into her, so that she too lost her balance and fell. Clarice ran down to help her up, but from every side men pulled at them, pinching their upper arms and pulling their hair. I saw Clarice's hat being thrown like a ball in a children's game around the crowd.

I turned to rescue them but Dorothy grabbed my hand and pulled me upwards. Her hair was coming down and her blouse hung partly open.

'We must try to get to the top,' she said. 'Get through those doors. That is what is important.' She waved the Memorandum.

I looked up at the doors to Parliament, which were rendered almost invisible by a heaving, thrusting crowd of women and policemen who laid about them with their truncheons. One constable had taken off his helmet and was beating some poor woman over the head with it. The thread of her voice was lost in the tapestry of sound. Her mouth opened and shut like a distressed bird.

It was beyond belief. It was the closest thing to a picture of Hell I had ever encountered. And this was England.

Somehow Dorothy and I made it to the top and struggled towards a door.

'Not on your bloody Nelly,' said a rough voice, as a constable blocked my way. 'Have a feel of this,' he invited a fellow officer, as he grabbed hold of my breasts and twisted them. I gasped but did not cry out, though it was worse than the heckling in Birmingham, much worse. And there was no Michael to save me.

Through the shouts and screams I heard my skirt rip before I stumbled and fell and rolled down the steps, helped on my way by brutal hands, to the bottom where I was kicked, until I tucked my head under my arms and curled up like a hedgehog, while I prayed to be invisible.

After a while everything quietened down a little. Cautiously I pulled my head out from my arms and looked about. The sounds had died down, but for moans and weeping from the remnants of the proud, controlled women who had started the day. I lay still, listening to the police dispersing the rag, tag and bobtail of the crowds, who had seen the police attitude as a licence to let vent their own hatred and punish us – for what? Being women, I suppose.

The same constables who had beaten us into submission now pulled us to our feet and rounded us up into a terrified mute gaggle. I saw a group of police clustered around two still bodies lying in the square. They exchanged anxious looks before an ambulance appeared.

An elderly woman, clothes torn and hair adrift, her eyes dazed and roaming sightlessly over us all, was picked up and thrust into an ambulance. I stood in the group of women who had been rounded up, our numbers increasing as the police gathered up all the strays who had tried to find other ways in. I began to look about more purposefully for familiar faces, forgetting the police as I searched.

'Get back, you bloody bitch,' a constable yelled, pushing me back into the group, but I could almost ignore him, it didn't matter. Nothing mattered any more. I'd spotted Millie and Clarice. Dorothy, however, was nowhere to be seen.

The whole night was spent in the police station, in featureless brick cells, becoming colder and damper with the November night air as the hours passed. The cells were full of the cries of women trying to locate friends they had lost. I worried about Dorothy. It wasn't until the morning, when we were all taken into a courtroom that I saw her, her head high and proud, one large eye sparking with defiance, the other half-closed and weeping yellow matter. Dorothy had found her way round the side of the police cordon and actually got into the foyer of the House. But there she too met the police.

'I fought. I know we weren't supposed to, but how can you not, under such circumstances? It would take a saint, and I'm not that.'

'Look at us all,' I said. A night in the cells had not improved our attire; we were tattered and torn, bruised and exhausted. But our spirits were not beaten. A cluster of women stood defensively around Mrs Pankhurst, but she looked as though nothing would daunt her.

'I think she thrives on this kind of trouble,' I commented. Her head was up and, seeing this, I put my shoulders back and my chin up, as she did.

We listened as we were dismissed by a tight-lipped judge who told us, much as a much kindlier judge in Birmingham had, that he would not give us the satisfaction of having such a mass of women imprisoned, only to help their cause by creating a story for the newspapers to exaggerate. 'There will be no prison sentences for you,' he finished.

'I should think not,' whispered Dorothy. 'There are high-born women here, who can afford good lawyers. There'd be too many questions asked if we were imprisoned, after the treatment we received from the police. Who gave them licence to behave as they did, that's what I'd like to know?'

It turned out that there were many asking the same

question. Two women had died, hours after. I remembered the silent bodies I had seen as we were being rounded up. Died! Killed by police brutality or murdered by the crowd. My throat closed at the news and I could not swallow. It could have been Dorothy, or Millie. It could have been me.

Many others had been severely injured. Almost all had suffered manhandling of the crudest and vilest kind, clothes ripped, private parts handled and the crowd invited to treat us as if we were criminals or the lowest form of street life. Police and others had felt at liberty to behave as they wanted with us.

Dismissed from the court we wandered back to Headquarters, distressed and rudderless. Gone was my desire to go back to Birmingham to fight for my teaching post. I assumed that a day away would have completely ditched any possibility that I might remain. Instead I felt a companionship for all who had suffered what I had suffered. I wanted to be with them. If there were to be further demonstrations or fights, then I wanted to be a part of it all – anything to protest against the horror of what had happened.

Our hostess would put us up indefinitely, at her house overlooking the Thames. Christabel announced her intention to protest against the way we were treated, in rallies that needed to be as large as possible, to be held in front of the House on Tuesday the 22nd and Wednesday the 23rd. All of us committed to attending at least one of these and our numbers would be swollen by hundreds more, brought in from around the country. Once again we would be peaceful, armed only with banners asking for the vote and with copies of the Memorandum. We would show them that we would not sink to their level.

More women were foisted on our kind hostess. One young person, Ethel, from the East End of London, berthed with Millie and Clarice and was quickly absorbed into that friendship. In a separate room, next door to us, was an educated woman with intense eyes, who was introduced to us as Emily Wilding Davison.

She was tall and rather thin, with a feverish air about her that I put down to the agitation of the last few days. Her hair was red, like mine, though paler in hue and curlier and her eyes were an attractive green, though they looked golden-brown at times.

Dorothy had met her before and greeted her, rather coolly I thought. For my part I found her entertaining company as we exchanged background histories. Emily had a lot in common with me. From the far North originally, she had been brought up in London, had attended the Royal Holloway College and become a teacher, though she'd preferred the one-to-one of governessing, she said. My happiest years of education had been while studying the same English Literature degree as Emily. She remembered many of the tutors but she was two years younger than I. Though we had overlapped for a while, I couldn't remember her.

'I kept to myself largely,' she said. 'And I'd have been a humble first-year student when you were lording it in your third year.'

'Hardly lording it,' I laughed. 'I too had a tendency to bury myself in the library. Perhaps we were both being invisible moles. Who knows, you might have been in one dark corner of the library while I was in another.'

Her eyes shifted away. 'I didn't finish my degree there.'

'Why not?'

'My father became ill – in fact he died quite soon – and I went home to help nurse him.'

I took a breath, my thoughts immediately flying to Nina. 'Were you made to?'

Her expression was so shocked that I instantly felt guilty.

'I went to help Mother out of love. No one *makes* me do anything.'

'I'll second that,' said Dorothy, who had been unusually quiet so far.

Emily gave her a sharp look. 'You know I'd do anything for the Cause, Dorothy. Anything. It's the most important thing in my life. On it hangs the modern age, or so I believe. Until women can surge forward and fulfil themselves as equals with men we will remain in the dark ages.'

Later, over a hot supper provided by our hostess, Emily told me how she'd finally finished her degree in Oxford, another place we had in common.

'Though I couldn't claim it,' she said bitterly. 'I got a First, but only on paper, since women cannot have Oxford degrees. I cannot own it. Oxford is another province in which men rule.'

'It'll change,' I said. 'Along with everything else, when we have the vote.'

'And when do you think that'll be?' Emily's voice rose in pitch. 'Look at what's happened to us. Look at how Churchill, the Home Secretary, treats us. The police force is his domain. He must have given them the licence to treat us like animals. What hope is there if a prominent member of the Cabinet feels he can send out such a message to the country?'

'Churchill has never supported us,' Dorothy confirmed.

'Mrs Pankhurst and others are collecting stories of what happened to individuals,' put in our hostess. 'Then they will be put before Churchill, who will have to answer for them.'

'I've heard that he brought policemen in from the East End and Whitechapel, the roughest areas of London. Those men are brutes, trained to deal with robbers and murderers,' said Emily.

'But we're just women,' Clarice complained.

'Yes,' put in Millie, 'we're 'ardly criminals like some I could mention back in Birmingham. Me uncle fer instance, who's never done an honest day's work in his life, Ma says.'

Millie always brought a smile to everyone's lips, even though Emily's obvious anger rolled around the table like an unseen, barely leashed tornado. We talked instead of the plans for a further demonstration on Monday.

'We need to be more active, make it clear that we're not going to take things lying down,' said Emily. 'We have to make them notice us. We must find ways of being unforgettable.'

'What about two deaths?' I said. 'Isn't that unforgettable enough?'

'They won't be forgotten,' said Emily. 'Write their names with pride, and outline them with flame.'

There was something about Emily as she stood up and said this that made me a little uncomfortable. She sounded fanatical, unhinged.

'They have shown us the way,' Emily continued.

'They didn't plan to die,' I pointed out.

'We should stick to what Christabel has asked.' Dorothy caught Emily's eye and held it. 'A peaceful demonstration. The numbers in attendance will be what makes it unforgettable.'

Later, in our bedroom, Dorothy explained more about Emily Wilding Davison. 'She takes things on her self, doesn't ask Headquarters for permission but just acts. Mrs Pankhurst and the others are worried by her. There's no knowing what she could do. Christabel likes everything organised. Every member must know exactly what they're doing, and when, and where. You know Emily talks wildly about killing herself? She told Christabel that only a martyr for the Cause would make people take it seriously.'

'That's awful. Do you think she would?'

'I think she's unbalanced. And she's a loner.'

'Doesn't she have a close friend among the suffragettes?'

'She does. Mary Leigh – another woman who takes things into her own hands.'

'I know her! She was one of the women in Winson Green Gaol. Before you came, Dorothy. She began the hunger strike there. She was very ill afterwards.'

'You see what I mean? Another one who pushes things to extremes. You see how she and Emily are two of a kind.'

'Don't you admire them though? It was you who said that hunger striking was the most powerful weapon we had. That was the first time I met you.'

'I know. And it is. But now the Home Office…'

'Churchill again.'

'… has ordered forcible-feeding, I fear that more women will die of the brutal treatment. Then Emily Davison and Mary Leigh will have their martyrs.'

'Along with the two on Friday. Do you think such deaths will make a difference?'

'Oh, Gladys. I don't know. Black Friday they're calling it already. It does feel like a turning point. Would you be prepared to die for what you believe? A couple of days ago you didn't even want to sacrifice your teaching work.'

'I'm still here, aren't I? I too have reached a turning-point. I've made my choice.'

'But would you give your life?'

'I don't think so. Not out of choice. But what choice did those two women on Friday have? They hadn't chosen to die. The police, or the mob, killed them. It seems to me that death for the Cause isn't something we choose; it can just happen. If it happens to me, I can think of worse reasons than dying for women's freedom.'

'Me too.' Dorothy hugged me. 'Watch out for Emily though.'

'I liked her.'

'I know you did. Just be careful.'

This from Dorothy who was often called a firebrand herself.

'We could get into the Houses of Parliament themselves,' said Emily at the Monday rally, 'I know a way.'

'Look at the police,' warned Dorothy. 'You wouldn't get far.'

Emily passed a scathing eye over the numbers of women singing and chanting and waving banners. 'They're carrying on as they always do,' she said. 'It doesn't work. Anyone want to follow?'

Millie and Clarice immediately jumped to attention. There was a bit of hero-worship there. The previous night Emily had regaled them with stories of her wilder deeds and mentioned some plans for even more. Most of her tales had involved breaking in to some large house, church or public building. Millie, despite the abandonment of her roots, was still in awe of someone who could break the law and get away with it.

I watched with some anxiety as the two young girls disappeared round the corner in the wake of their heroine, whose curly hair was clamped under her flat deep straw. She had a determined set to her jaw and the pockets of her long coat bulged suspiciously.

After some thought I told Dorothy I was going to find them, but it was too late. Though I traced the outside of the Houses of Parliament, so far as I was able under the watchful eyes of the police, there was no sign of any of them. Perhaps they had indeed found a secret way in.

Later at Headquarters, where Christabel took the reports of those at the rally who had been, once again, molested by the police, I finally saw Millie and Clarice, sitting close to Emily. Their cheeks were pink and their eyes sparkled. Emily's face gave nothing away.

'Where were you?' I asked as I squeezed my way over to them.

'Wait and listen,' said Clarice proudly.

Millie bubbled with excitement. 'It were wonderful, Gladys, we...' Clarice nudged her as the room fell silent.

Emily Davison had stood up. 'A small group of us, armed with stones, went around the back and attacked the Government Offices there. We threw stones which I provided in order to break the windows of those offices. I take full responsibility for this action.' She sat down again.

Millie and Clarice tapped the tips of their fingers together in quiet approval.

The way Emily had presented herself struck me. It was confrontational. Perhaps Dorothy was right in her judgement.

Christabel looked at Emily for a short while before congratulating her in an even voice on her stand and the fact that she had not been caught and arrested. The window-breakers had vanished by the time the staff in those offices reported the damage. There could be no doubt who had been behind the action, however. A few of the stones had been wrapped round with copies of the Memorandum.

After this rally, we four made our way back to Birmingham, having decided to abandon London, though there were still more meetings and rallies later in the week. The hems of our skirts were muddy, torn garments held together with safety pins, boots covered in the dust of London but excitement just about prevailed over the horror of Black Friday. Millie, still pink-faced, relived the wonder of her Monday militancy. 'There were screams from in the office, Gladys, and faces pokin' out of it...'

'Lifting above the sill, so cautious, in case we threw a stone at them. Poor sillies,' added Clarice.

'Your first taste of the power of militancy,' commented Dorothy.

'But should people be afraid of us?' I asked. 'Isn't that rather against the point?'

'Oh, Gladys!' they all chimed together, laughing.

'Sorry. But isn't it? Against the point, that is? What if people become so afraid of us that they turn against what we stand for?'

No one answered for a while before Dorothy said, 'There's plenty of sympathy for what happened to us on Black Friday. The newspapers have reported it with shock. Most of them have been firmly on our side. When we get home, we'll brief Michael and Bradley with details from our experiences. We're lucky to have two tame journalists on our side. That will keep sympathy with us.'

It was as close to an admission that I may be right as Dorothy would make.

29

The staff room on the following day fell quiet and then buzzed with excitement as I entered. The two other English staff, Miss Hadley and Miss Sheldon, glanced at me and then made a great show of talking earnestly to each other, opening the pages of the exercise book that lay between them and studying it with attention. Only Amy approached me. She grabbed me by the arm and took me over to the window-seat, where we would be apart from the others.

She spoke in a tense whisper. 'Where have you been? You're for it, I expect, this time. They've brought in a temporary mistress to cover your classes. Look, she's over there.'

I glanced quickly at a middle-aged woman seated on her own at the far side of the staff-room and then back at Amy. Briefly I thought of my class, the way they responded to teaching. For many it would make no difference who taught them, but for one or two it would. I regretted those few and my desertion of them. I hoped that the seeds I'd planted in them would flourish despite my betrayal.

My temporary replacement had become aware of who I was and was looking over at me. She got up from her seat and wavered. In the end we met halfway across the room. 'My name is Meryl Drew and you must be the famous Miss Hazel.' She stuck out her hand and I took it.

'Gladys, please. And probably infamous.'

'This is awkward, isn't it?' she said.

'It is. I'm sorry you've been put in such a position and have had no time to prepare. I'll go to see Miss Nimmo now. And I'll give you a full rundown of what I've been doing with the girls and something of their strengths and weaknesses.'

'You're assuming that Miss Nimmo will dismiss you. I didn't get the impression she would. But if I am to be used again, thank you. Any notes you can provide would be useful.'

The rest of the staff were no longer pretending to be disinterested. It was in front of a firing squad of eyes that I returned to the window-seat to pick up my bag, smiled ruefully at Amy and made my way to Miss Nimmo's office.

Despite what my successor had said, I fully expected to receive my marching orders immediately, so I was surprised when Miss Nimmo told me that she had prevailed with the Board, against their advice.

'I can keep you here, as I dearly want, but because I have had to pay for a temporary teacher to cover your lessons, I am obliged to reduce your salary by half.'

This was so unexpected that for a while I was speechless. Eventually I found my voice. 'You are most kind and generous, Miss Nimmo. I shall never forget you and what you have been to me, a wonderful support. But I think I must decline your offer. What happened in London has made me realise that my priorities now lie with the W.S.P.U. I must give up my post. Keeping on with both responsibilities is no longer an option and, if I tried, both would be the losers. My time and energy can only go one way now.' I fought the welling tears as I spoke. I must not weaken.

Miss Nimmo gazed at me for a moment. 'You realise that you will never be able to return to teaching. The Board would not give you a good reference and it would be they to whom any other school would apply for knowledge about you. Your place is here, or nowhere. The school is facing exciting times of its own, Gladys. Do you remember? In the New Year we will move premises from Aston to Handsworth, bigger and better classrooms, no more drilling and gym in the narrow corridors.'

Her attempt at levity made me smile. 'It would have been fun to be a part of that move. I hope all goes well with it. But no. I am clear on this direction now.' I thought of Emily Davison. 'I could always become a governess if a teaching post is impossible. When it's all over and we have the vote, that is.' I got up and made ready to leave. 'I will leave full notes for Miss Drew. I liked her, by the way. Will you keep her on?'

'It's possible. She's a local woman, recently widowed, and could do with the work. We'll have to see how she shapes up. Your exuberant teaching methods will be a hard act for anyone to follow.' She reached forward and took my hand, keeping it in hers. 'Good luck, Gladys, whatever you do. Go out the back way, will you? I think it is unwise to allow your pupils to see you now. It will only upset them.'

I agreed and turned my back on that lovely gracious building and the work I had so enjoyed: on all those like Jane Evans, as well as all the bright-eyed pupils who were willing to learn, on Nina, on Amy and on five years of my life.

—⁂—

The new year in Paradise Street had its ups and downs. Sophia had at first welcomed my increased presence there but, as Dorothy had promised, I began to be away a great deal, as a speaker in other cities all over the country. I became a lover of trains. The views from the grimy windows allowed me to prepare myself mentally for different venues, while the time spent in them allowed me to relax, adjust my notes or just be with Michael.

Often he would travel with me. While Bradley spent more and more time in London, reporting on the doings of the Government, Michael became the chief reporter for the W.S.P.U. This made us both happy.

The wrapping-up of Parliament in the previous November had led to another General Election, the second in one year. Once again the Liberals were elected, but with no significant increase in their majority. Reluctantly, the Pankhursts had agreed with Millicent Fawcett to stem militancy once more while a second Conciliation Bill was drawn up and presented.

The only thing that loomed in this year of 1911 was the Census. Militancy of a more aggressive type may have been withheld, but the Pankhursts had urged us all to come up with schemes to spoil the Census forms. It was agreed that 'No Vote, no Census' would be written across the form and that no suffragette would spend the night of April 3rd at their own residence, to scramble official records further.

In March, the month before this event, Sophia met me in the hallway as I came in, weary from a journey from Liverpool.

'Can I have a word?' she said, before I'd even removed my hat and coat.

I could see trouble was brewing but couldn't face it right then, and said so.

'This won't wait,' she said. 'I've had a word with Dorothy already and she's agreed.'

'To what?'

'To moving your headquarters, as soon as you can.'

I put my bag down with heavy deliberation while I gathered my wits.

Sophia didn't wait. 'It's the whole chaos of having the offices and all the workers and in-and-outers in our home. The door is opening and closing a hundred times a day. It's not safe for Freddie, who's crawling now. And only today he had his hand stepped on, in his own kitchen, by a thoughtless girl who wasn't looking where she was going.'

'Can we sit down for this conversation?'

'No. I've said all I want to say.' She glared at me and pounded up the stairs. At the top she turned and shouted down. 'There is just one more thing. I want you to leave too. As soon as possible.' Whirling on her heel she flounced off towards their rooms at the end of the corridor.

I sighed and followed her up the stairs to my own room. With a heavy heart, I put my belongings carefully on the bed and looked around me. Paradise Street. My lovely room with its heavy dark furniture, its maroon flocked wallpaper. My desk at the window with its view down the street to Christ Church. To lose this place, which had been a haven for four years. To lose the friendship of Sophia and James. I lay on the bed and closed my eyes. To be truthful, since the offices had moved here, since Sophia's child had been born, there hadn't been many cosy chats. And there'd been very few long dinners with Bradley, where we talked about everything and nothing: ourselves, literature and politics – drinking and laughing and putting the world to rights.

Bradley was an infrequent visitor now, with more commissions and a small house in London. All around me there was change. Losing my work, cut off from my family. All of it was my fault. My decisions had slewed my whole world into unrecognisable patterns.

I turned my head into the pillow and closed my eyes.

There was a tap on the door. Dorothy's head poked round. 'Mind if I come in?'

'Of course not.'

'Oh look at you,' she scolded. 'You haven't even taken your boots off.'

She helped me remove my outer clothing and plumped up the pillows for me to lean against. 'There! That's better. I gather you've had an encounter with Sophia.'

'I should think everyone heard it.'

'They did. Most of them hid. Sophia in a rage is a snow-queen, all flashing blue eyes and sharp edges. I'm sorry you caught the brunt. I was out negotiating with a couple of people who might be able to house our next offices. John Bright Street looks suitable. A month, and we'll be able to move in.'

'She wants me out too,' I managed.

'I guessed as much. That must be hard for you. I know you love this place.' She stroked my hair as I wept.

'How about we find a place together? It could be fun.'

'I don't know.' I felt like a pile of useless blubber, floppy, wet and incapable of thought.

'If we found somewhere where we had our own apartment, perhaps, without a nosy landlord constantly watching our every move, then you'd have the freedom to see more of Michael.' She raised her eyebrows meaningfully.

I pulled myself upright. 'Really?' I'd only lived in a shared room where no visitors were allowed and then here, where I'd been very much a part of the household. Until now. 'Do such places exist?'

'Well, of course they do, silly girl. We could afford a little house of our own even, on our combined salaries.'

'That would be expensive. Mrs Pethick-Lawrence might classify such luxury as unnecessary expenditure.'

'No harm in looking to see what we find, though. Talk to Michael. He can put out feelers too.'

When she'd left I felt better. Dorothy and I had become

much closer since I'd committed to the Cause and given up teaching. It could work. And Michael and I might have somewhere to meet. At last. This thought lulled me into sleep.

Startled, I woke to the characteristic squeak of the door opening.

'Sorry,' said Sophia's voice. 'I've been up with Freddy and I couldn't go back to bed without talking to you.'

I tried to pierce the darkness to read Sophia's mood. She sounded all right. I fumbled for the matchbox kept by the bed and lit the candle.

Sophia picked her way through the belongings that Dorothy and I had left all over the floor and sat on the edge of my bed.

'I'm sorry,' she said. 'I was vile to you and you don't deserve that.'

'I think probably I do. I haven't given you much thought since Freddie was born. Too caught up in the Cause, I suppose.'

'I had no idea, when I decided that the offices could be here, what it would really be like. It's impossible.'

'I know. I can see that.'

'But you. How could I be so cruel after the friendship we've shared? But you've changed, Gladys. I don't recognise you any more.'

'What do you mean?'

'You've grown in confidence – well, I expect that's a good thing – and you've become very forthright and – I don't know – definite. You know what you're after and how to get it. You're harder somehow. Not the soft young woman I first welcomed into my home. I miss that person, Gladys. I'm not sure I like the new Gladys quite so much.'

That hurt. 'Does James feel the same?' I said softly.

'He agrees with me. I think we'll go back to our original

idea and advertise for a gentleman lodger, who we'll keep strictly outside the family. Oh, it's not that James dislikes you. Of course not. But both of us are missing a home for our child to grow up in.'

'Dorothy's going to look for somewhere we can share.'

'Well.' Sophia stood up. 'That's all right then. You'll suit each other. You're both fiery and determined. You can plan your speeches together.'

I heard the tone of her voice. It had reverted to a controlled anger. Perhaps admitting that I'd already talked through things with someone else and made a decision had hurt her somehow. I wished I understood people better. Everything seemed unnecessarily hard and I was tired, so very tired.

I was aware of Sophia standing by the door in her white nightdress, straight as the angel of banishment standing at the gates of Eden, but I turned my back on her and blew the candle out, expelling the image.

The next speech I was booked to make was in Leicester, at an *At Home*, a few days after Sophia had asked me to leave. I liked *At Homes*, they tended to be less formal than other meetings. Michael came with me. After he'd attended a few meetings around the country and had difficulty finding lodgings, he found that his presence became more acceptable as the 'official' reporter for the W.S.P.U. In this capacity the organisers of the meetings, rallies, or whatever we were attending, found him somewhere to stay, just as they did me. Sadly this was rarely under the same roof.

Neither of us knew Leicester. Both of us were given an address in Regent Road and my heart soared. We'd be together.

Number 120, Regent Road was a big house, three storeys,

with a garden at one side, adjoining the garden of the house next door. We were met by the owner, a doctor called Gertrude Austin. She had a narrow face, sharp blue eyes behind wire-rimmed spectacles and thin brown hair tied back into a wispy knot. We were kept standing on the doorstep as she looked us both up and down. I had the impression that we were being weighed up. Finally, whether we'd passed the test I could not tell, she opened the door further and stood aside to allow us entry.

'I did not realise that one of you would be a man,' she said. 'You can have the couch in my consultation room.' She beckoned Michael to follow. 'It's a Sunday tomorrow, so there'll be no patients.'

We followed her down a corridor. The room had a desk, two chairs and a battered looking couch heaped with cushions against one wall.

'Sometimes my patients need to lie down to be examined,' she explained. 'It's perfectly clean. I dare say you'll manage.'

She watched as Michael dutifully put down his bag and looked about.

'I'd rather you didn't go through that door,' she indicated a door at the back of the room, behind the doctor's desk. 'That's where I prepare the medicines. There's a sink and the necessaries just off the corridor. There.' She pointed, and then beckoned me to follow her.

Michael made to come too but Dr Austin flapped her hand at him. 'Wait here. There'll be tea soon, and cake.'

I rolled my eyes at him behind her back and followed her upstairs. There were four doors leading off the top corridor, all closed. I was shown to a spacious room and introduced to the bathroom with its large claw-footed bath. The room was cold, warmed slightly by the dark wood of the furniture and a rose-pink bedspread.

'I hope you'll be comfortable,' said the doctor, looking around with a kind of surprise, as if she'd never seen it before. 'I'll have the fire lit. And for the gentleman downstairs. When you're ready, come down for some tea. We'll be in the drawing-room, next to the front door.'

Michael and Dr Austin were sitting in silence when I descended, having removed my hat and tidied my hair. There was no sign of tea, but a fire crackled in the generous grate and reflected in the window-panes, where a purplish cloud had turned the sky to an unseasonal darkness.

'Brr!' I said cheerfully, intent on warming the atmosphere. 'You wouldn't think it's almost spring.'

'Oh, you would,' she said, 'if you saw the shrubs in my garden. All the fruit bushes are in bud. I'm very partial to fruit. I do hope this cold snap won't mean a bad year.'

I could hear the shuffle-shuffle of feet coming down the corridor and the minutes stretched out as we all looked at the door.

'That'll be the tea coming,' said the doctor. She looked at Michael. 'I wonder…?'

With noticeable relief, Michael leapt up and went out to meet the occupant of those hesitant feet. He returned, pushing a wooden trolley loaded with fruit cake and pretty china of navy blue and burnt orange in an oriental pattern. Following behind was an ancient person, so bent as to have a good view of her own knees and not much else. Her hair strayed out of a white lace cap and her eyes, when she lifted her head to look around the room, were milky and placid.

'Oh, good, Truda,' she said, clapping her hands together. 'Company! I thought I heard voices, and a gentleman too! Well I never.'

There were red darts of colour on the doctor's cheekbones and her eyes were very bright. She blinked rapidly behind the heavy glass of her spectacles. 'This is Maudie, my housekeeper,' she said. 'She's … been with me a long time.' There was an air of mild defiance about her last statement, which I found endearing. It seemed unlikely that much housekeeping could be done by this ancient person. And yet the cake was good and freshly made and someone had laid and lit the large fire.

I complimented Maudie on her cake.

'Oh, bless me,' she cried, her body shaking like a leaf straining to leave its branch. 'I don't cook now. Mrs Reynolds from the bakery comes in on three days a week and does what she can. And she has a daughter who pops in every other morning.'

'We manage, don't we?' said Dr Austin. 'We are a company of women and we help each other.' She looked at me with a small tight smile. 'Maudie is particularly good at dusting.'

Maudie nodded and shook. Her body, which had briefly achieved a sloping horizontal to view the room, now reformed into a hoop. She made sweeping movements with her right hand, as if banishing phantoms of dust.

'Why don't you sit down, dear Maudie? The cake is particularly good.'

'I am most partial to cake,' agreed that lady, collapsing into a chair near the fire and resting her head back against its green velvet upholstery. She took a mouthful of cake offered by the doctor and fell asleep.

When we returned after the *At Home* that evening, Doctor Austin met us at the door. She offered cocoa in the kitchen and listened with avid attention as I described the evening's doings and, at her insistence, a synopsis of my speech.

'I can't attend myself,' she said. 'There aren't many of us lady doctors in the country, you see, and my friend Bessie and I are the only ones at present in Leicester. Already, what we do to help our women patients attracts criticism so I cannot be seen to be a part of the suffrage movement or I'd lose the patients I have. But if you prevail, the world will change, and women like me will have no more need to hide away. So I do what I can. Offering the spare rooms in my home is something I can do to support your cause.'

Later, on our way back to Birmingham on the train, we laughed a little about Maudie, but then I sobered up. 'I rather admire Dr Austin. Maudie has no real use as a housekeeper, and yet she keeps her on in that capacity. She must be a loyal and compassionate woman, don't you think?'

'Not compassionate enough to take pity on us,' whispered Michael reaching for my hand, in a carriage empty apart from one business-man buried behind his newspaper.

'Well I never,' says Truda as she puts down the last page. 'How strange to see oneself through another's eyes.' Then she turns over the last few sheets and starts to read them again.

I can't bear to watch and leave the room to busy myself in the kitchen, feeling embarrassed at the thoughtless cruelty of my younger self, though it is true that I liked and respected the good doctor from the first.

Truda wasn't an easy person to get to know. It was some time before I was invited to call her by the shortened version of her full name – Gertrude – which only the closest of her companions used. I stayed with her numerous times when visiting Leicester's suffragettes and later lived more permanently with her when they made me District Organiser for that city. In all those years she kept her own council, never talked about her family or her background. It was as if nothing prior to her medical self existed. Nor was there ever talk of any relationships other than those she had with colleagues and women friends. Not from her or from anyone else who knew her. At that time Bessie Symington was her closest friend, but even their relationship was largely based on shared concern for the plight of women at the hands of men. I wouldn't say that Truda hated men in those days, but she certainly hated their unthinking sexual urges which left their wives to bear countless children, their girlfriends to suffer dangerous terminations and women to die from venereal diseases through no fault of their own. I like to think that having a boy child in the house after the War softened her towards men in general.

Further embarrassment heats my face as I remember the last sentence on that sheet. Compared to Truda's cool control, I have always been so messy in my passions, and I'm not just talking about sex here. Truda is a folded pair of hands in a still lap, feet tucked quietly under her, whereas I am a sprawler, noisily yelling, agreeing or disagreeing, never able to leave an argument alone but having to be right in the thick of it, sleeves rolled up to the armpits, fists flailing – I mean metaphorically of course. Not for me the watching and the slow acquiring of facts before making judgements that is Truda's way; mine is the hurried way, the scrambling, tasting and discarding way, the way of the blunderer, which might, just might, through trial and error, eventually get there – whichever *there* that is.

Michael and I were deep in the thrall of a sexual passion that consumed us both. Now, from the vantage point of watching others in love – Peter, for instance, when he first married Rosemary – I know how mutual passion proclaims itself through every look and every cell of the body. It's like fireworks, all fizz and sparkle, with underneath that slow burning simmer which suddenly spurts into flame at a look, a fleeting touch, the mere brush of a hand on an arm, the touch-paper of skin against skin. No one in the presence of such mutual desire can not smell it, feel it, taste it themselves.

Nowadays, with the raging of my body well and truly banked, I find the din of others' love abhorrent. Perhaps because I don't want to remember how it was for me.

Who knows how Truda views it all. Clinically, I suppose, as if under a microscope. This is how the species propagates ... how interesting ... but rather distasteful too and certainly nothing to do with me. But I could be wrong. Even after all these years there are areas of Truda's life and opinions which are firmly shut and locked away. I still do not know how to find the key.

30

With the move of the offices to John Bright Street in the second week of March, James, Sophia and I quickly fell back into our old companionable ways. Bradley, on a longer visit from London than usual, smiled round at us after an evening meal where we had talked about art, literature, poetry with all our old enjoyment.

'I'm having a break from politics and going down to Devon to see the site for a new building. It's to be called Castle Drogo, apparently, and it's the artistic brainchild of Edwin Lutyens. Should be a nice non-political relaxing commission for a change. Then there'll be the new king's Coronation to cover.'

'Sounds very tame compared with your usual hard-biting stuff,' commented James. 'That's because there are no howling banshees in suffragette costumes to shock the nation. It's all gone remarkably quiet,' Bradley teased.

Into this familiar atmosphere came Doris, with Dorothy close behind her. 'Sorry to interrupt,' she said, pre-empting Doris's announcement of her arrival.

'Enter one banshee, stage left,' laughed Bradley.

But Sophia's face had fallen. Since the offices had moved away it was as if she had developed a sudden allergy to anything to do with suffrage. 'If you want to talk to Gladys, I suggest you both go up to her room,' she said, stony-faced.

'I've found the perfect place for us to live,' announced Dorothy before we were halfway up the stairs. She was flushed and her eyes glittered.

My heart sank. I'd been enjoying the evening, had deluded myself that everything could go back to how it was.

Dorothy pulled me into my bedroom and shut the door. 'It's in Edgbaston, 34 Harold Street, the self-contained wing of a larger house. Two bedrooms, a shared bathroom and kitchen, and the further use of a small sitting-room with a dining table in it. It's not large but it's perfectly adequate. You could have the bedroom at the back. It's not overlooked by anything except a few overgrown shrubs, masking our part from the main house. There's a dear little path leading round to the back where there's a separate door. I thought of you straightaway. What could be more private and discreet?'

'Edgbaston? It sounds expensive.' I could hear my voice deflating her enthusiasm, but I couldn't help myself. On the wings of this evening, with Bradley, James and I in extravagant hyperbole seeking to outdo each other and Sophia our willing acolyte, I was back in love with Paradise Street and all it had to offer.

Dorothy appeared not to notice. 'The landlady has lost her husband. All she wants is a little income to help her get by, so she's divided up her house into two self-contained dwellings. And she's flirting with the idea of joining the Cause. Can't you see, Glad? It's perfect.'

'Edgbaston is quite a way away from everything.'

'Oh, what rubbish! There are trams. It's not so far. And lovely parks to walk in. A real feeling of countryside. It'll be wonderful to be able to throw off the cobwebs, go out on our bicycles, enjoy the fresh air as a contrast to our hothouse politics.' She gave me a sly look. 'A bedroom of your own. A separate entrance, with no landlady fussing about visitors…'

She was right. To be able to see Michael, to be with him whenever we liked. How we'd longed for that.

'All right,' I said, reluctant to admit Dorothy had won. 'I'll just have a look at it. I'm not making any promises.'

We moved in the last week of March, barely enough time to arrange our few belongings before the census was due on the 3rd of April. There wasn't time to enjoy the freedom of being our own selves. We were plunged into ideas and suggestions, to ensure that no suffragette would be in their own home on the night of the census.

There were parties organised, so that as many as possible could spend the night dancing and enjoying themselves in halls and rooms hired for the purpose. Some meant to picnic in the parks, though the weather was far from warm. A group of young women were going to spend the night in a restaurant with a couple of suffragette musicians playing dance music into the dawn. Dorothy proposed to stay in the office at John Bright Street, where she could collate feed-back from all the adventures of other Birmingham members into a grand document to be sent to Headquarters.

Having written in bold black ink, *Votes for Women* and, below that, in large letters: *No Vote, No Census*, across the official form, I gave it to our landlady, who was supportive and had already been primed by Dorothy. All I had to do now was to absent myself for the next hours, from late afternoon until the following morning. I thought of being at the office with Dorothy, but she had enough people who had volunteered to help her and was in fine fettle, full of annoyingly bossy plans. I wanted a break away from her. I toyed with the idea of going back to Paradise Street as invited by Sophia, who had returned to her friendly self once she had her home back, but I felt that this would be too comfortable and might miss the point, since I had left it so recently. An adventure would be more fun.

'Emily's hiding in the Houses of Parliament!' Millie had been in awe of Emily Davison ever since Black Friday.

I doubted the probability of such a plan.

'She's gonna creep in with one of them tours around Parliament and hide dahn in the crypt.' Millie shivered dramatically. 'She'll be with all them spooks and ghoulies, stayin' all night alone in the dark. She's ever so brave.'

It did not seem possible but it did have the ring of a typical Davison idea, full of drama. 'How's anyone going to know about it?'

'She said she'd pop aht like a jack-in-a-box and announce to all them M.P.s she'd been there all the time...'

'She'll be there this minute,' said Clarice, equally awed. 'She's taken food for two days, and drink, and she'll find a corner, under a tomb or something, to sleep – or maybe she'll shut herself in a cupboard.'

'There must be cupboards, she said.' Millie took up the tale. 'Even the Houses of Parliament need to be cleaned.' Millie grinned with delight at the thought of a broom cupboard in such a place of grandeur.

'Where have you got all this from?' I was caught up in the wonderful craziness of the idea, despite myself. 'Why two days?'

'She said the Government would be expectin' the suffragettes to do summat, so she was gonna go in earlier and stay two or three days, to catch 'em out. Ent it marv'lous?'

I laughed aloud. There was something about the daringness of an Emily Davison plan that made one rejoice. No one else would have thought of such a bold gesture.

The two girls laughed with me.

'So what shall *we* do?' asked Clarice. They both looked expectant.

My mind was blank. With their eyes still fixed on mine, an image of Millie with her damaged hands outside her place of work surfaced. 'What about the factory? When's it close for the night, Millie?'

'We'd never get in. We'd be seen.'

'What if you flirted with that horrible janitor you told me about? The one who was sweet on you?' Clarice was taken with the idea.

'Ugh!' said Millie, but her mind was working. 'You'd 'ave ter wait till the men 'ad all left. You and me, Clarice, could cause a diversion which would get rid of the janitor while Gladys went in. Then we could both scarper in while 'e was still safely aht the way.'

The details of this plan were sketchy and owed a lot to chance, but there was no time to refine them. It was already late afternoon. We made for the factory.

There was a little whimper from Millie as we reached those iron gates. She hung back.

Clarice put an arm around her and they whispered together as they waited for the bell on top of the turret to ring for the end of the working day. After a while Clarice broke away and approached me.

'Millie's finding this hard. What that janitor fellow did to her... well, it wasn't much – Millie swore at him – but he threatened her. He wouldn't leave her alone.' She gulped, looked back over her shoulder to where Millie stood, her head low. 'It's since Black Friday. Millie's not been the same – now she's afraid of men.'

Instantly I ran to her and said that of course she didn't have to do this. It didn't matter. We could go and sit in one of the tea-rooms that were staying open late to accommodate us, or sit in the Head Office with Dorothy.

But Clarice was determined. 'You won't be on your own, Millie. I shall be with you all the way, and just let that man try anything. He won't lay a finger on you or I'll give him what for.'

My goodness, she sounded more like a lover than a friend.

'I didn't intend that either of you should cause a diversion that would put you at any kind of risk,' I hastened to assure them. 'Look – how about stones.'

'Stones?' they echoed in tandem.

'Yes, like you did with Emily. Throw some stones at that big pile of metal on the far side of the yard. It'll make an almighty din. And he'll have to go and investigate. Then we can all sneak into the building and hide in that slop-room you mentioned, Millie.'

So Millie gave Clarice a leg-up from the back of the building onto the top of it. From my position out in the street I could see her white face as she wriggled on her stomach over the slightly shelved rooftop. Then came Millie. I saw them embrace before I melted into the shadow of a gateway a few yards from the factory gates and waited.

That embrace, could it be? Did women …? Like Michael and me? Surely not! … And yet – was it even possible? Feeling that another curtain had been ripped aside on my innocence, I brought my attention back to the matter in hand with difficulty.

The bell rang and I collected my thoughts as the janitor appeared and opened the large double doors to the factory. The male workers appeared in clots and clumps, some leaving singly and hurrying away, some milling outside the doors, noisily gathering others to them with much clapping on the back and shoulders. Then, as if obeying a signal, a knot of men would move as one towards the gates and disappear, laughing and talking, towards one of the public houses on their route.

After the men had disappeared, the women emerged, shyer, quieter, heads down and feet shuffling as they hastened away towards their homes. The janitor accosted one of these and pulled her out of the group. His voice, whose words I could not catch, was low and insinuating. I saw the white mask of Millie's face rear up like a snake from the rooftop and then the rattle and clang of a stone rolling into the metal waste at the back of the yard. The janitor's head moved sharply in the direction of the sound and the young woman he'd been talking to scurried rapidly away. The janitor stood still and, hearing no further sound, went into the building to turn out the lights and shut the doors. Another clunk from a thrown stone. Then a volley of sharp raps like pistol shots. With a curse the janitor approached the pile of metal with his truncheon at the ready. One of the girls threw a couple of stones further around the corner. The janitor followed and I acted. Through the open door I ran and into a huge echoing room full of heavy machinery. I hid behind one of these. Soon after, both girls reached my side and silently, Millie pulling at our sleeves, we were led into the slop room, a place where equipment was rinsed and cleaned.

It was dark and smelled of soap and old standing water around the long sluices and drains.

'No one comes in 'ere,' whispered Millie. 'Wait till it's quiet and dark in t'machine room. Then we can cum out. It'll be warm in theer and safe till morning.'

'How will we get out?' Clarice asked.

For answer Millie handed us three long robes that covered us to our ankles. 'We'll wear these. Everyone'll think we're slop wenches, the lowest of the low, poor ducks. No one'll look at us twice.'

We may not have had as much fun as some of the other rebels, but we were certainly some of the most unusual census dodgers. Dorothy congratulated us as we arrived cold and damp from our adventure. Donning those sluice-house robes had entailed getting wet; it appeared those clothes never dried out and I thought sympathetically of the poor creatures who would normally have worn them. In the hubbub of morning arrivals and clocking on, no one had noticed us leaving through the barred gate at the back of the sluice room.

The excitement of the census over, we were back to non-militancy and our usual busy but humdrum work. This allowed more time to see Michael. He had collated Dorothy's report and written his own version about census dodgers for the local newspaper.

At last he was free to see my new lodgings. Once there, after politely following my guided tour, he pulled me back up the stairs to my bedroom.

'It's the middle of the day,' I objected, conscious of Dorothy's imminent return. I felt strangely nervous. Michael looked so large in the little room: his big hands, the thickness of his neck and chest. I felt crowded.

But those large hands were tender, as was his expression, and soon he had soothed me, until we lay together on the bed and kissed until my head spun and I no longer cared what happened, or whether Dorothy came back home and knew what was taking place upstairs.

Though over the previous months we had kept up a kind of love affair in the countryside, hugging each other for warmth in the crackling frost and touching numb finger-tips to each others' stiff cheeks, since the heady shy days of our previous summer courtship there had been little chance for anything more adventurous. There had been journeys together to other cities where we had had a chance to talk and get to know each other, but even touching had been rare. In any case, I was always frightened before making a speech and Michael's main task was to talk sense to me and calm my anxiety.

It was strange that I didn't believe in myself or in the favourable reports made of my speeches. I convinced myself that people were just being kind. This infuriated Michael and Dorothy. When she asked how something had gone in Liverpool, or Newcastle, or Penzance, I always gave the impression that I'd made it through only by the skin of my teeth.

Then Michael's laughing eyes would meet hers and they'd both grin and tease me. 'I was always taught not to be boastful,' I said.

'Maybe boasting would stick in the throat a little, but honesty is not boasting. If something goes well, it's all right to say so. I certainly do. Both of us have won many converts to the Cause and we should be proud of that.'

I ducked my head and stared at my lap. Soon Michael's hand edged over and took hold of my hand, stroking it with his thumb.

'I like your blushes,' he said. 'In fact, I can't think of much that I don't like about you.'

'Oh, go on with you,' said Dorothy, looking away, her expression impatient. And I never felt comfortable 'going on' when she was around. Always there was at the back of my memory her words of warning. Even at the moments of greatest sweetness, when our bodies moved together in harmony and every part of me sang its own separate song, even then I heard her voice: 'Eventually you'll have to end it.'

I had thought that with a new place to live and the growing familiarity of my duties as co-organiser, I would quickly settle into some sort of routine, but there were always other demands. Requests for my talks and for Dorothy's were frequent. Dorothy had gone to Ireland most recently, which I envied her. To me Ireland was always as I remembered it, a quiet country place – empty lanes, patchy fields of potatoes, beautiful long beaches and the restless sea, a background litany to everything – so it was with astonishment that I heard of Dorothy's adventures in Dublin, shouting crowds, city noise, open abuse. She had been feted by the women there but heckled more than usual by the menfolk.

'You thought it was bad here. And it is, of course, sometimes,' she added. 'But there, the authorities will hardly let a woman open her mouth without throwing her into prison. I was shuffled from house to house, in at the front and out of the back before I could be discovered. The women are marvellous. Strong and vociferous…'

'And used to smuggling people from one place to another,' put in Michael grimly. 'Do you know nothing of Irish history, Dorothy?'

'Enough to know that it is a place of ferment on a number of counts. Yes, Michael, I know about the Home Rule issue, but that is not my immediate concern. Whatever happens to Ireland, whether it throws off the shackles of England or not, women are as voiceless as they are here.'

Michael laughed suddenly. 'I wish you could hear my mother after my father and brothers come back from a night's drinking. She can ring their ears with her opinion for an hour at least, without drawing breath!'

Dorothy glared at him.

'I know, I know, that's not the point.' Michael's voice became solemn and his eyes looked through our kitchen walls. 'Irish women do have a hard time, harder if anything than those in this country, except maybe for those in the slums. Those pretty little cottages, those scattered farmsteads, harbour large families, many of whose youngsters will not see adulthood. I have seen mothers kept alive only by their love for their children, since they have given every last scrap of food to them. Every time the potato harvest fails, the women come into their own: walking skeletons of sheer will, they keep the family together until their last breath.'

I had rarely seen Michael so passionate and vocal. Even Dorothy was silenced for a while. I laid my hand on his and remembered again the hot-eyed boy I'd first met.

'Will you come with me to Ireland one day?' Dorothy asked him.

Michael looked at me. He had seen my sudden shift in the chair and knew the cause. 'Gladys and I would be happy to accompany you, when the time is right.'

'Gladys and you!' she said scathingly. 'And you with a wife in Ireland, and offspring. I don't think that will ever happen, do you?'

'Dorothy?' I was so taken back by her tone I didn't know how to respond. 'Why so cruel?'

'And what difference would it make if I took Gladys or you?' put in Michael, holding tight to my hand. 'In the unlikely event that someone from Donegal would be around to recognise me ...'

'It's all right,' I hushed him. 'Dorothy didn't mean anything, did you?' though I thought she did. I felt she had heard Michael speak and had looked at him, really looked at him for the first time, not as the gorgeous creature she had so often referred to, but as a person with a mind and opinions which had value. I knew with sudden certainty that in that moment she had envied me and wanted Michael for herself.

So I wasn't surprised when she hissed, 'What you two are doing is shameful to the cause of women. You are betraying your wife and Gladys is colluding. That makes her a traitor to her sex. You must know that all I wanted was Michael as a guide to Ireland, someone who would make it easier for me the next time I visit as a speaker.' I recognised that she was covering her tracks.

Michael was pale with fury. I pushed him towards the stairs up to our room, fearing what might be said and broken by words spoken in anger.

Dorothy watched Michael stamp up the stairs and then turned away. Roughly I turned her back to face me. 'You realise that what you said will be hard to forgive, don't you?'

'You know me,' she answered with studied insouciance, her eyes belying her words. 'Always quick to retort. Words just spill out. You know I don't mean them.'

I looked at her, stretching out the moment until her eyes dropped. 'Are you trying to say you're sorry?'

A lift of her chin, her eyes meeting mine with an effort. 'Of course, darling. Aren't we the greatest of friends? Nothing can change that.'

When I joined Michael in our bed, he stripped the clothes off me without his usual care and took me roughly, one large hand on my forehead to keep me looking at him. His eyes were dark and stormy, his mouth a thin line. Nothing was said between us; there was nothing to say, for both of us knew that there was truth in what Dorothy had said.

Twice more, that afternoon and evening, Michael's body assaulted mine as if he was trying to lose himself in me, or obliterate me entirely. When he finally turned from me and slept without his usual closeness, without his warm arm over me, I lay on my back, sore and aching, and stared sightlessly at the ceiling. Was he punishing me or himself? He had never hurt me like that before. I felt a page turning in our affair and our future together looked suddenly less certain. Why was I letting this man treat me as a receptacle for his own anger, a vent for whatever feelings mastered him at that moment? I was supposed to be a strong woman and yet I wasn't. I was weak, weak, weak to let him back into my life when I knew there was no future in it, that Dorothy was right. Would I be able to follow her original advice and finish it all? I felt so dry and drained I could not even cry.

31

For a while after Dorothy's outburst Michael kept away; he had retained his rooms in Snow Hill, aware that moving in with me would have distressed our landlady. But it was not long before he drifted back, knocking with uncustomary reserve on the door before taking me in his arms and telling me that he was sorry, that without me his life was a desert.

Despite the hurt he had done me that night, my body had forgiven him sooner than my mind, and craved his attention long before this return. I found myself dwelling on the intimacies we'd shared in the past, heard my breath shortening as I played over scenes of abandon that quite shocked me in retrospect. Had that really been me? Was this passion a disease to so lay hold of me, body and soul? How could I cure myself and did I even want to be cured? The answer was no; Michael was my addiction and I couldn't let go.

After I had faced up with all honesty to my hunger for him, I was once again lost to common decency and the clamours of conscience. Ignoring those voices, all those who would agree with Dorothy, all the unheard horror of my family – unheard only because they remained in ignorance – stifling all dissent, even my own which rose in the grey light of dawn after passion was spent, I opened my arms and my weak craving body and answered the demands of his desire with equal demands of my own, till our sheets lay damp and twisted around us and we fell exhausted into slumber. The evenings of small talk with Dorothy which had been such a delight when we first moved to Harold Street – Michael enjoying my friend's sharp mind and acidic tongue, which he liked to waken with needling comments – gave way to longer and longer sessions upstairs in which we plumbed the depths of invention, till every tingling nerve end was glutted, numbed into silence.

At first our marathons upstairs were because Michael wanted to avoid Dorothy, but in truth we needed no excuse. I began to feel like a sleepwalker as I fulfilled my duties at the office, my thoughts already pulling me towards the evening when I would feed my desire again.

Dorothy remained strangely quiet during this time. Often, at our headquarters at John Bright Street, I saw her eyes roam over me and once, in front of Millie, she upbraided me for falling behind on some posters I had to produce for a suffragette Bring and Buy. When she had gone, Millie asked me what was wrong. Was I ill? She said I'd been acting strangely and not been my usual self. Playing for time, I said I had been feeling a little sick and then made good that fabrication by running to the lavatory and spitting out the acid contents of my stomach. How strange the body is, I thought as I spat and spat, to obey the slightest suggestion of the mind. Millie suggested I go home, that she'd tell Dorothy and organise the poster distribution herself.

At home, I stared at myself in the mirror and pulled my hair out of its fastenings. It had grown longer. Like a pre-Raphaelite damsel's, it corkscrewed down my back. After lovemaking, it was a torture to comb, so matted did it become. My face looked white and eyes larger than usual while my body was fuller, creamy and sated, breasts larger, nipples more prominent. Who was this stranger? I did feel not ill precisely, but a little giddy. I would lie in bed and wait for Michael to arrive.

I thought of Byron and Shelley whose lives, when I'd studied their poetry at the College, had appeared shocking, like something out of a storybook. Yet here I was, almost as bohemian as they and, despite the general lot of women, I understood I was living with a kind of freedom that most women could barely imagine. I had travelled far from the prim young woman who had first arrived to teach six years ago. Nina had been the first to break through my innocence and show what seethed under the coverlet of the world, but once I'd been woken there was no turning back. And now, on top of everything else, I was a woman living in sin. The phrase held no meaning for me, felt almost laughable; I understood that it was what society would see, but hadn't I broken through those chains? Yet by so doing, I had cut myself off from my roots. Knowledge and fear of the family's distress if they were confronted with my present life had cut me off. They did not even know I had given up my teaching. I was like a boat being whirled so fast away from the familiar shores of my upbringing that I felt alternately enthralled at the journey and terrified at my anchorless state.

I realised I'd stopped even thinking of Michael's wife. It was as if, after Dorothy's barb, I'd banished both her and guilt from my mind. Was that true of Michael too? Did he ever think of her, or his children? He never talked of them, but I recognised that that could be because he knew it would upset me. Surely, when he lay alone in bed at his lodgings, his mind must fill up with her, and with guilt. Both of us were burying our consciences the deeper we delved into each other's bodies.

Now, alone on my bed, I thought of his family in Ireland,

tried to imagine what his wife might look like, his children – how old were they? I tried to feel guilt, I really did, but it's hard to feel anything real about people you can't visualise. As with my own family, his life over there was a pin-prick which scarcely scratched my consciousness, or my conscience, because usually I kept it locked behind closed doors. That way the clamour was reduced to a background buzz, no more than a minor irritant.

As the afternoon progressed, the dizziness that had prompted me to tell Millie that I felt sick, increased. Once or twice I rose from my bed and tottered down to the lavatory, clinging to the banister. It seemed I was indeed ill. I looked in at the kitchen, realised that the thought of food made me feel worse, and crawled back upstairs to bed. There I tossed, alternately throwing off the blankets as I streamed with sweat and then pulling them up back around me as my skin cooled.

I was seldom ill and saw it as a weakness which must be fought against. Here was pain of a different kind and I was neglecting my duties. By the time Michael came I had struggled out of bed and, having drunk two glasses of water, had begun to feel better. I would be back at John Bright Street tomorrow.

When Dorothy arrived home, Michael had left again. He had been commissioned for a story in London and would be away for a few days. I felt too peculiar to care as much as I normally would.

Dorothy cast an appraising eye over my dishevelled state. 'What's wrong?'

'Some germ I've picked up no doubt. One or two girls in the office have been off sick. I must have caught it. They were back quite quickly and I shall be back tomorrow.'

'You sure? Take another day if you need to.'

But I didn't want to spend another day alone with my conscience. Work would divert me. I felt sure that my day at home had brought on a sickness that was more of the mind than the body.

———⊗———

July 6th 1911

Dear Gladys,

Lina and I are very worried about Mama. You will remember how last year she was still coughing at Rita's wedding. She has become very thin. I have written to Rita too. Nora is wonderful. Both she and her daughter come daily now and the house is cleaned and the food prepared. Lina and I take Mama and Papa for little outings, which they both enjoy. But a visit from you would be even better. Failing that, at least a letter. You promised ...

Kay's letter was kindly delivered to John Bright Street by Sophia with Freddie sitting up sturdily in his pram. Both had enjoyed the attentions of an admiring crowd of young women. Sophia was happier now that she had her home back but was still stiff with me.

'Have you not told your family of your change of address? This is the fifth or sixth I've had to bring here, and though Freddie needs to be taken out into the fresh air, it's not something I'm prepared to continue doing for you.'

I admitted I still hadn't got around to it and fell silent, turning away to avoid further questions. Each new piece of correspondence from home always spurred me to answer, yet I never did. From the others I'd received I knew that Jim was away more often than not, but that he kept up a limping courtship of Ida. Duncan had finished his examinations at the East India Company and had left to join Edgar at the tea plantation. Most treasured were Lina's brief scripts, always mispelt and laboured for, despite her studies, words scrambled themselves when she tried to write them, as if the twist in her body was echoed in her brain, eyes or her writing hand – who knows which? Usually she reported on some book she had read or some animal she had adopted, but she also informed me that Kay was still seeing the unsuitable Harry.

Reading the letters did not make me feel closer to my family. So far-removed, as if gazed at through the wrong end of a telescope, the family, tiny figures, walked and gestured as in a mime show. They held no present reality for me. Briefly my conscience would stir and I'd plan at least a visit. But then I would be swept up into another task.

Sophia's eyes narrowed as she saw me handling this latest letter, dipping into the news like a bird with a crumb and then looking round as if threatened by an unseen danger. 'Bad news?'

'No, no,' I assured, where once I would have unburdened to her willingly. What had happened to me? Instead of wanting to rush to my mother's side, thoughts of Nina surfaced. I knew if I went home I would be trapped there, unable to carry on working for the Cause, unable to be with Michael. I couldn't bear it. I knew that this letter would be buried like the others, for if I went home, under the eyes of those who knew me so well that nothing could remain hidden, the whole unsavoury truth would come out: that I had given up a promising career and was entangled in a relationship with a married man. Once my mother had told me my face always gave me away, that I was unable to hide my thoughts. I feared her sharp and knowing look. Now I was adept at lies and secrets and my face had become the mask of a deceiver. But it was easier to deceive people who knew me less intimately than my family. I did not want to put my new-found skill to the test.

The sickness did not entirely leave me. Perhaps I had returned to work too early but I wasn't prepared to admit it. I needed the diversion. In any case it came and went, leaving me feeling as well as ever between each bout. It was nothing.

It seemed I was popular with the Leicester suffragettes. In the next couple of months I travelled there twice to give talks and fire new members into enthusiasm for the latest head office plans. Both times I stayed with Doctor Austin. After the second of these trips, for the first time without Michael, she asked me to call her Truda. I understood that this was a compliment.

Maudie was still there, but now hardly moved from her room. Truda explained that she could not manage the stairs any more and wondered whether I could come up with a suggestion to help her get down. I looked at the stairs, steep though quite wide, but could think of nothing.

'Michael is more practical than I. Perhaps he could come up with something. I'll talk to him.'

'I hope you don't mind me asking, but what are you to each other?' She looked at me over the top of her spectacles. 'Not that it's any of my business.'

'We are friends,' I said hastily. 'Good friends. From childhood.' The easy lie slid out, oiled by frequent use since its first outing with the cycle scouts. She said nothing, but something about the quality of her silence told me she was not deceived.

I took Maudie's food up to her – she was half-asleep, but nodded and smiled at me vaguely – and then the doctor and I chatted in her pleasant drawing-room, with a small fire alight though there was no need, it being a mild October. Conversation was easier than on the previous occasions I'd stayed with her. I knew this was because Michael was not there. As he had said after our last visit, 'That is a woman who doesn't like men.' And we'd laughed together.

Now such laughter felt demeaning. If Truda had an ounce of nastiness in her it would be she and I laughing at him now, and then bemoaning that I was so weak as still to be hankering after him.

As the evening progressed, I found this strange quiet woman surprisingly easy to talk to. It was like conversing with myself, so little came back to me, though I was aware of approval and disapproval at some of the things I said. She listened to my talk of family, asked when I'd last seen them, and said quietly and firmly that she thought I ought to keep up visits to them.

'No time,' I prevaricated.

'Then make time,' she said. 'Families, even when they're difficult, are important.'

'Do you see much of yours?'

Truda had told me that she had only brothers, three of them, and that her mother was dead and her father almost dead. The last she'd said with a strange vehemence. She'd looked down at her lap, as if she didn't want to show her face.

When I pressed her for further information she told me that she would not speak of them again. 'I will see my brothers, but my father – never while he lives.'

I thought but did not say that her attitude to her father contradicted her assertion that families should be valued. Upstairs in the bed with the rose-coloured counterpane, I shuffled possible reasons for her attitude to her father and came up with the most likely: her desire to become a doctor in a medical world which did not welcome women. It was not long since nursing had become acceptable, thanks to Florence Nightingale, but doctoring required a good scientific mind as well as an understanding of anatomy and bodily functions that most men might consider unseemly for a woman.

I thought how lucky I was to have a father who had

encouraged me to study for a degree. But a propensity for English Literature was one thing – an airy enough subject for a woman's mind, along with music and painting perhaps – but what if I had shown a scientific bent? I thought of Caroline Herschel, Bill Waterfield's ancestor, her extraordinary ability and the lack of honour she received for it. By the time I fell asleep I had established firmly for myself that Truda and I were similar souls: both rebels, both gladiators in the arena of male dominance, both courageous in our different ways.

Not once during that night had I thought of Michael and I woke in the morning refreshed and rinsed clean, as if my whole self had undergone a holiday from addiction. Happily, and full of a bonhomie towards my new friend Truda, I tripped down the stairs and companionably we made breakfast together. What a lovely way of living, I thought to myself, far from the ups and downs of life with Michael, far from the needling of my own conscience.

There was a book on the dining table and Truda apologised for its presence. 'I like to read while I eat,' she explained, 'since usually I eat alone.'

When I professed interest in what she enjoyed reading I discovered a like mind, a polymath who was as happy to devour poetry or scientific journals as novels or Rudyard Kipling's tales of India. We talked so avidly and with such enthusiasm that Truda had not prepared herself for her first onslaught of patients. She was dressed, but still in bedroom slippers and her wispy hair left a lot to be desired.

I ran upstairs for her shoes while she twisted her hair into a knot, tamed it with a fence of pins and composed herself. Adopting a practical guise, I answered the door and let the first patient into the waiting room.

At lunch there was a short break before her afternoon patients. I had enjoyed acting as a receptionist and said so. On my previous visits, Michael and I had explored Leicester but with him in London researching a story I found I enjoyed even more the oasis offered by these simple tasks in the quiet peace of this house. Even my sickness had left me. Clearly my new friend was good for me, body and mind.

By teatime, when Truda was still working through the last of her patients, I had an ache in my lower belly that pulled at me so hard I doubled over. Investigation in the bathroom revealed spots of blood on my underwear. A nuisance, but not the end of the world. I always travelled prepared, and donned the clean cloths I kept for the purpose. Only the pain was unusual. I resolved to ask Truda for a pill to help me through my evening talk.

Dulled by aspirin, I managed the talk but sought Truda's eye, sitting at the back of the hall. She had come to hear me for the first time and as I trotted out some of the well-worn phrases I'd used at other venues since the census, barring outright militancy but warning that soon it may be used again and to be prepared, a stabbing pain caught me unawares and, with a gasp, I stopped mid-sentence, staggered and grasped the back of the nearest chair. In that strange dissociation I always experienced when my body was in the grip of pain, I saw my knuckles, white and pointed, as if belonging to someone else. People hovered around me, whispering, asking questions but one woman made straight for me and took me by the shoulders. Truda.

'Sit down,' she said, 'There now.' Those thin hands on my shoulders were surprisingly strong and reassuring. She asked if anyone had a carriage or automobile outside and in a matter of a quarter of an hour, we were back at Truda's house in Regent Road.

Later that night, after a good deal of cleaning up and firm but gentle questioning she explained that I'd had a miscarriage. About three months, she said as I gaped at her in shock.

'I did wonder,' she said. 'Your body shape had changed quite profoundly since last you were here. Sleep now, if you can. You must stay in bed for a couple of days. I'll keep an eye on things.' She smiled reassuringly at me. 'Don't be embarrassed. It's not as if I haven't seen it all before.'

When she'd left it wasn't embarrassment that caught me by the throat but just the fact that we'd made a baby, Michael and I, and that I'd lost it. Sleep was impossible. Instead other possibilities unfurled. Once again I spun dreams of escape with Michael, somewhere far away, when the Cause was won and it was all over. There we would have a child and I would love him – I felt sure that it'd be a boy – with a whole heart, for he'd be mine and Michael's, the fruit of love. Never mind that I'd never liked babies, never mind reality in any shape, the future Gladys was as different from the Gladys of the present as it was possible to be.

32

Suddenly it was November, and on the 7th, Asquith announced that in the coming Parliamentary session a Manhood Suffrage Bill would be introduced instead of our Conciliation Bill. The Manhood Bill would extend the vote for men but Government spokesmen said that women could negotiate, through yet another proposal, to be included. Both Dorothy and I saw immediately that this was a slap in the face.

We took a train to Headquarters to find out more and found it buzzing with news and very busy. It had been harder to find, because Dorothy had only known the old Headquarters at Clement's Inn. This new place, at Lincoln's Inn, was vastly different and surprisingly grand after the previous cramped quarters.

We stood in a large tiled hall where we were met by a pleasant young woman with an efficient manner. She took us up a smart tiled staircase, but I noticed there was an electric lift as an alternative and all the lighting was bright and electric too. There were even clocks driven by electricity on the walls.

We were met by a formidable lady, tall, stern-looking and considerably older than we were, called Harriet Kerr. She introduced herself as the office manager and asked us our business. When she heard that we wanted to talk to Christabel or to her mother, she took us straight through a large oak-panelled room with high vaulted ceilings, which was full of desks and the tapping of typewriters.

A gaggle of young women were giggling in one corner and Miss Kerr rounded them up and sent them back to their work.

'Young people!' she exclaimed, 'Doing this for the excitement rather than the vote.' Then her eyes rested on a sweet young thing, busily typing addresses onto envelopes, and her eyes softened. 'Of course, some of them have all the right motivation and are open to learning the proper way of going about things.' Miss Kerr might be a stickler for office rules, but she clearly had a soft interior under that stern front.

She ushered us into Mrs Pethick-Lawrence's office, since apparently Christabel and her mother were temporarily unavailable.

'It seemed quicker to come down by train than to wait for instructions,' said Dorothy, once we had all lamented over the latest insult from the government. 'What can we do?'

'On the twenty-first of November, I shall be leading a large group of suffragettes from Caxton Hall to the Houses of Parliament to protest. But such peaceful means are clearly no longer of any use, if indeed they ever were.' Her mouth made a grim line in her comfortable matronly face. 'On the same day, a large number of volunteers – we are in the process of choosing them now – will smash windows in a way that will bring attention to all those who we see as opposing our cause.'

'What do you mean exactly?' I asked.

'We are compiling lists of places who are openly against our suffrage: men's clubs, Government offices …'

'As Miss Wilding Davison and a few of our members from Birmingham did last year,' I said excitedly.

Dorothy nudged me to silence. Emmeline Pethick-Lawrence's face had folded into disapproving lines at Emily Davison's name.

'That's as maybe, but then it was not approved by us. Now it is.' Her hands made sweeping motions, as if to consign Miss Davison to oblivion. 'Add to the list the offices of newspapers hostile to us and anyone else who has openly stood out and spoken against women and their rights.'

'So, we should make a list of such places in Birmingham...' said Dorothy.

'I can think of a few already...' I added.

'Exactly. As you travel back to your own Headquarters start to compile your own local list. Now is the time for war, ladies, I think you will agree.'

Already she was getting up, pushing her chair back to show us we were dismissed but, seeing our willingness, she smiled and took one of each of our hands. 'You have done well with Birmingham, both of you. I have noticed the efficiency of your reports. That city is not the easiest of places to make a success of, but you have done it.' She squeezed our hands. 'Birmingham has always been a tough nut to crack. Yet you have made excellent inroads and built up a formidable membership. Well done.'

As we reached the door to her office, she called us back. 'Don't do anything on your own account,' she said. 'Miss Davison's example is not one to follow. Though we all recognise her enthusiasm for the Cause, her methods are not always welcome. They can result in embarrassment. Instructions will come from Christabel herself, who likes the idea of the suffragettes as an army, with the discipline to follow orders according to a plan. I suspect that she will want everything to happen at particular times and on particular days, to make as strong a statement, country-wide, as possible. Compile a list of willing volunteers for militant action. They must be prepared for imprisonment. Then wait for word from Christabel.'

On the journey back I wondered how Emily Davison would take to such an attitude from Headquarters. Hadn't it been she who first broke windows in Government Offices? Or so she had claimed. Now the Pankhursts were laying claim to the idea as their own. Millie and Clarice would have been incensed at Mrs Pethick-Lawrence's words. Dorothy, however, advised caution, at least as far as Emily Davison was concerned.

'For whatever reason, the woman is persona non grata with the Pankhursts. Best to keep a distance,' she advised, 'and wait to see what she does next. Meanwhile we have plenty to do finding Birmingham volunteers.'

The events of November swept away all other concerns, including Kay's letter about Mama's health. We were caught up instead in planning a military campaign to show the Liberal Party what we felt about being once again side-lined. Soon after we returned to Birmingham, news came of a further insult from the Government. Lloyd George had made a speech to party members in Bristol, where he boasted that with the proposed Manhood Bill *we have torpedoed the Conciliation Bill.* So that's what the Liberal Government, who had been stringing us along for so long, really felt: delight that we had, in one of my father's old naval terms, been 'scuppered.' They had lied to us and never intended to take the Conciliation Bill seriously.

The message from Headquarters came, using for fuel these incendiary words from Mrs Pankhurst: *the argument of the broken pane of glass is the most valuable argument in modern politics.* So the breaking of windows was to be our principal weapon.

It was not hard to draw up a list of prominent buildings as likely targets. To this we added the homes of all Council members who had spoken against the Cause. Millie, who threw herself into the whole campaign, took it on herself to find out which factory owners were particularly hard on women, allowed them no voice, or paid them absurdly little compared to men.

'Them owners spend most of their time with other bigwigs and 'ardly visit their factories at all,' she said indignantly. 'That's 'ow little they care.'

'They play golf, or drive off with their families in their new motor-cars to have picnics,' added Clarice.

'We could ruin them posh golf-courses for them!' Millie said with glee.

'Add them to the list,' I said.

'And museums, art galleries, libraries,' went on Millie, in a passionate rush. 'They're all big ol' buildings and it'd cause a stink if we damaged 'em.'

'Mmm,' I said doubtfully. This kind of action would be a little too near my own particular sacred cows. Beautiful buildings, art works, places where books reposed in sacrosanct peace.

Millie caught my expression. 'We're only talkin' of winders, Gladys.'

I nodded ruefully and added them to the list.

'Fire stations too, railway stations. All big buildings. Damaging them would cause a rumpus,' said Clarice.

In between planning meetings, Dorothy and I, with a few others, plodded around Birmingham and surrounding areas, house to house, trying to find women who would be willing to put themselves at risk by damaging property. We suffered abuse, doors slammed in our faces, wore out the soles of our boots, and often spent whole days harvesting just one volunteer. In the evenings, members would invite whole groups of women from their area to a meeting in their home and one of us would speak there, already exhausted after a day tramping the streets.

'It's dangerous,' I said to a group who had gathered at a member's house in Aston. 'I cannot conceal that from you. The likelihood is that you will be caught, arrested and imprisoned.'

'That's the point, isn't it? And the stumbling block,' said one woman. 'I have a family. How would they manage if I was imprisoned or, worse, my health was damaged? I have a baby to consider.'

'And I work in an office,' said another, 'as a secretary. Who's going to employ me again if I have been branded as a criminal?'

I sighed. Reasons like this were why we were finding it very hard to find volunteers. And I sympathised, of course I did. I knew, after all, that I would never be able to teach again. A woman who volunteered for certain imprisonment must be very sure that she can survive when she was released. Or be so passionate for the Cause that she did not care and trusted to Fate or God or Time to take care of the future.

But find volunteers we did, slowly. Some even had families but had husbands who believed as fervently as they did in the rightness of the Cause.

'I've a plan,' said one of these. 'Before breakin' winders I'll mek a large pie to last t' family a week. I'm already hoardin' coal 'n' taters. They'll manage.'

It didn't feel right to have Michael with us as we tried to persuade women to put their lives at risk. Instead, once or twice a week, I fed him a digest of what had occurred over a few days, for him to write up. The exhaustion of the work, the need for a release from it when possible, made me see Michael in a different light. I had reclaimed my priorities, or so I felt: the Cause first, Michael second. He was at one remove and this accorded with the thoughts I had had about him at

Truda's house. By not telling him either of the miscarriage, I was reclaiming something of myself even in our relationship. I could do without him, I felt, so long as I kept busy, and in time I would find the strength to make that break.

At the end of every day through the remainder of that year and into the first weeks of 1912, Dorothy and I staggered home and into our beds with no thought of anything but rest. After a few weeks of this, Dorothy insisted that we should each have at least half a day off a week, for sanity's sake. Those afternoons became moments of snatched happiness, where nothing else intruded between Michael and me. Yes, happiness: because I felt more in control, because his hands were tender, his body more respectful of the weariness of mine and this thoughtfulness on his part made me see him once again anew. I began to trust him, knew that he loved and, better, respected me while I needed the relaxation of his company, the release that our bodies in union gave me. Without that switch-off I felt I would not be able to continue the disheartening work we had been asked by the W.S.P.U. to do.

Soon, those afternoons became beacons that I needed as much as food and drink and, encouraged, Michael began again to arrive at night, creeping in late and slotting himself next to my sleeping body. I would half-wake and fall asleep against him, comforted, and dream of a quiet place far removed from the world I knew, where we lived together with a child which, once I'd woken, I recognised as the embodiment of the one I'd lost: a boy with Michael's eyes and the hay-coloured hair of his father's boyhood.

And then one afternoon Michael did not turn up.

I wrote up our digest for the week – another depressing review of failed enlistments – made a pot of tea, stood for dragging minutes at the front door, drifted upstairs again and peered from my bedroom window before I went down to the kitchen yet again. It was a cold day with wind blowing sleety drizzle against the windows, making visibility poor and damping the spirits.

When Dorothy returned, late in the evening, I was pacing up and down like a rat in a trap. She took one look at my face, hewed off a hank of bread and spread it with butter and jam. Then she pushed me into a chair, broke the bread in two and slapped one half down in front of me.

'Bet you haven't even eaten,' she said.

'No.' I swallowed. 'But he's never late. He would have sent word somehow if there was a problem.'

'What problem could there be?'

Wild stories of Irish arsonists and gun-runners ran through my mind. Perhaps they had always lurked there, ever since Bradley had told me of his brother being arrested at Liverpool docks.

'Something to do with his family perhaps?' I said lamely.

'You mean his wife,' said Dorothy, deliberately cruel. She fixed me with her look. 'I've watched you both these last months. I can see it's all growing cosy again. Your feelings are as clear as a rinsed window-pane, Gladys.'

'It's not like it was, not as – consuming.'

'Well, good.' She didn't look convinced. 'But it's settling into something else. You're like a long-married couple now. He's become a habit and habits are hard to break. Do you remember what I said?'

'I do remember,' I interrupted quickly, not wanting to hear those words yet again. Tears began to flow and, angrily, I wiped them away.

She took hold of my hand. 'It's a tragedy, Gladys. I mean it. Your love for him is real, I can see that, but it came too late. He was already taken – and I wonder, I can't help it, about a man who can change his affections so completely. Is that man to be trusted? I think not. The more I get to know him, the more I think of his wife and children back in Ireland. A man who can desert his family, leaving that poor woman to cope alone, that man is a rat, a traitor to the idea of love. How many children, Gladys?'

'Two. A boy and a girl. I try not to imagine them.'

'They must be quite old now. Old enough to hate their father for his absence and to feel protective towards their mother.'

I put my hands over my ears. Resolutely, I'd tried not to imagine those children, yet sometimes they surfaced anyway, always young, looking like the children in front of the Allen house the last time I was there, when I too was just a child.

'Gladys.' Dorothy's voice was gently insistent. She prised the hands away from my ears and held them tightly in her own. 'Here we are working to better the lot of women, when all the while you and Michael are perpetrating the worst hurt that you could on one poor member of our sex. And you are adding insult to injury by pretending she doesn't even exist. I blame myself too. I said make hay, because I believed it would burn out. But it hasn't.'

'It's changed … it's more … settled.' I gulped. 'He's not a … rat. He loves me truly, I know it.'

'More than you love him? Really?'

I gathered myself. 'I don't feel as I did towards him. I know he's weak, lost perhaps. He's just human. No better or worse than anyone. People make mistakes, Dorothy. His marriage was a mistake.'

'A mistake that lasted years. That kind of mistake must be honoured and lived with.'

'I know that deep in my heart. I do, Dorothy.' I felt like I used to when Mama or Papa upbraided me for bad behaviour. I knew that this relationship was the principal reason I had cut myself off from them.

Dorothy forced me to look at her. 'Look at you. One afternoon without him and you're a wreck. Where's Gladys the fighter?'

I looked up at her face. That sounded more like the Dorothy I knew.

She grinned that sideways smile. 'Use your knowledge of what's right as a lever. Break it off. Reclaim yourself.'

'It's not interfering with my work for the Cause. I've been careful to put that first.'

'First in your actions, yes. But not in your thoughts. And if your mind is otherwise engaged, you cannot be free to give the Cause your all.'

'So that is why you want me to break off with him?' I seized on the anger that rose in me, fed the flames and used them to quell those moments of guilt, of weakness. I would fight for my love as he had fought for me. 'No, Dorothy. There are hundreds of married women, which is how I think of myself too, thousands probably, who support the Cause without having to clear away the rest of their lives. Michael gives me the strength to keep going. He helps my work.'

I pushed the chair away and left her.

'One day you'll thank me for my advice. It's as hard to give as it is for you to accept.' She shouted the last up the stairs after my retreating back.

I slammed the door, threw myself on my eiderdown and piled pillows over my head.

Michael came to John Bright Street the next day. I was out with Dorothy, still looking for volunteers for the window-breaking campaign. Millie reported that he looked awful, unshaven 'like a bear', and that he had a young man with him. Instantly I assumed it was one of his brothers and forgave him. Hadn't I known it all along?

Dorothy and I had traversed parts of Aston, hardly

speaking to each other. She punctured the mood every few minutes with an airy comment about a building, a tree, a shop-front, all as neutral as possible. I responded with little more than grunts. I nursed my anger, kept it warm. Finally we wandered into familiar territory, frighteningly near to the school. I kept expecting to bump into Amy, or one of the English staff. But then I remembered that the school was no longer there, at least not the girls. The boys had remained in the building and presumably expanded to fill the rooms on the girls' side.

Dorothy was disappointed. 'I'd thought to wait for the staff to come out at the end of the day to canvass them. If prissy old you could be tempted away to join us there may have been others.'

I laughed aloud at the thought of terrifying Miss Bragge, or wispy Miss Hadley hurling stones at windows and for the first time felt free of the previous night's anger. 'Come on, let's go to my old lodgings. We'll try the Cartwright and the poor little downtrodden maid who looks after her lodgers. I can't even remember her name.'

'Is there any point?'

'Only for a bit of fun, Dorothy. We haven't had much luck today anyway.'

'A few more have promised support though. But it's true, no one is prepared to risk life and limb.'

We trotted down the alleyway I used to cycle through with Nina and arrived at the door of the lodgings in Walsall Terrace. I ran up the steps and banged at the door. A complete stranger answered.

'Oh,' I said, taken aback. 'You're not Mrs Cartwright.' The person who answered the door was tall and rather beautiful, with blonde waving hair. She wore a turquoise tea gown with yellow ruffles, though it was still morning.

'Indeed I'm not. How very perspicacious of you!' she cried. 'My name is Stella Swinburne.'

Dorothy raised her eyebrows as I hurriedly explained why we were there but the lady did not wait to hear me out. Instead she asked us in, 'because of your suffragette colours', and then indulged me further by allowing me to visit the room I used to share with Nina.

By the end of an hour, we had another volunteer.

'I'm recently widowed with no dependents. Francis was rather against suffrage, but he's not here now and I have little to do except keep this rather large house, which Francis wanted to fill with children.'

Dorothy dared to ask how he died. It was clear that Stella Swinburne was not grieving. She was dressed in the brightest of colours instead of sombre black, as if in celebration.

'It was an accident. A motor-car. Francis was a passenger. With his best friend. They met a tram. Both were killed.'

I listened carefully. Did her staccato delivery, said with humorous lightness, cover up some other emotion?

Dorothy said later she thought it was relief, that our newest conscript was enjoying her freedom. 'She's certainly one of us in spirit already. A non-conformist who dares to be different. Perfect! She's the most likely volunteer for militancy we've found yet.'

We had left with promises to meet at the next weekly *At Home*, which was to be a planning meeting for members, at John Bright Street. The rest of the day bore little fruit and at teatime we fell exhausted into a tram. Dorothy had some work to do at the office, but I went home to cook us both a meal for when she returned.

Michael sat on the step of the back door, next to a tall lad, all arms and legs and no 'filling', as Papa used to say about my brothers when they were fifteen or so.

'Hello,' I said cautiously, not wanting to fling my arms around Michael until I knew what was what.

'Gladys,' said Michael, his eyes speaking volumes of love and pleading. 'This is my son, Seamus. He's come over from Ireland on the boat all by himself, to find me.'

'My goodness,' I said. 'Then you'd better come in and have some tea. Would you like to stay for supper? I'm cooking for Dorothy and me.'

Already Michael looked more relaxed. 'I've told Seamus that I work for you and Dorothy and the Birmingham W.S.P.U. as a reporter. Like me, he has come to England to seek his fortune.'

Seamus looked far from the picture I had imagined after Dorothy's speech of the previous night. He was stick-thin, but so were many boys of his age. He had grown upwards before his body had time to gain muscle. He was bright of eye – Michael's intense blue, I noticed – and his hair was jet-black and glossy. More than that, he clearly worshipped his father.

'Seamus would like to do what I do, but he hasn't had the benefit of the education I had with Father Cullen. And besides he's still only fourteen.'

'Father Cullen's dead and gone, it's Father McNamara now, Da, and he's more the one for bible-bashing and drinking the dregs of the altar wine, says Ma, than the Latin and the Greek or the English itself.' When Seamus grinned there was a shadow of his father. He would be handsome one day.

'But your English is good,' I complimented.

'Ma taught us. She says that speaking English is important now.'

When Dorothy came back, she took the situation in her stride and the evening passed pleasantly enough. Michael explained, asking for support from us, how difficult it would be for a fourteen-year-old to find work.

'And how's your mother doing without you? Hasn't she another child?' Dorothy asked.

Seamus' face darkened. 'She doesn't know I'm here. She has my sister to keep her company. Maureen helps Ma all the day and wants nothin' more.' He looked at his father. 'But I do want more, Da. More than working in the fields for some English landlord, or fishing like Grand-da, who can't fish any more with his bad arm, nor pull an oar neither – so what good is he, but for moaning and drinking of the ale? Or there's learning a trade like boat-building or putting stones together to make a field, or cutting peat for the fire. That's all my uncles do, Da, save fer Uncle Patrick, and we're not allowed to talk about him or know where he is. England is where to be and where I want to stay.'

By the end of this speech Seamus' lower lip was mutinous and his eyes were stormy.

I faced him. 'Seamus, you did a very brave thing coming all this way on your own. But your mother must be worried sick and what your father tells you is the truth: you'll find no work here until you're older. If you don't want to be a labourer working on the fields, or on the new roads, or the railways, you'll need to have more education.' I looked to Michael for help. 'Surely, if the priest won't teach him, there must be schools where he can learn?'

'Da could teach me. I could live with you,' he told his father, 'and you'd teach me all you know and I'd be all right and away from Ma and the girls.'

'The girls?' asked Dorothy.

'Maureen and baby Una,' said Seamus impatiently. 'But the bairn doesn't count yet and she's no trouble.'

My ears rang and I could not hear any more. I stared at the stove, made a pot of tea, spooned out some more stew, clattered the plates in the sink. Baby! When had the baby been born? But I knew. Michael had gone home and resumed his relationship with his wife and made a baby with her. While he was seeing me. After he'd told me that I was his love.

Michael knew what I was feeling. I could feel his eyes on my back, as I crashed pots together in soapy water.

Dorothy talked for a little about schools and how to find one in a nearby town. If Killybeggs was insufficient, then Seamus could find a compromise – be away from home at school in the week-days and come home to help his mother at weekends. All the time, she was trying to negotiate man and boy away, so that she could catch me before the breakers crashed over my head and swept me off.

And at last they were gone, and she held me and clucked and cooed, and took off my clothes and put on my night-gown, while the copper warming-pan took the chill off the stiff sheets, before she tucked me in my bed and left me to the pounding surf in my ears, which insisted, beat by beat – echoing my heart – that it should have been me who had his baby, not the woman who he'd told me he didn't love, but that now and for ever it was too late. I clasped my arms over my empty womb and did not cry. Weeping did not dig deep enough but spilled over the surface and ran away. Weeping presaged healing and I knew I would never heal. That now I would never have a child, a son like that beautiful boy Seamus who had looked at me with Michael's eyes, or any child at all.

33

Dorothy helped me through it all. She didn't say I told you so. She didn't speak about it at all, but she watched me carefully and made sure I had plenty to fill my time. There had been one wave of window-breaking already, organised by Christabel, and more than two hundred women had been arrested and imprisoned and then forcibly fed. We knew another wave was planned, even bigger and more spectacular than the last, involving all the department stores and grand shops in London's West End. Dorothy and I would go, with others from Birmingham, like Stella Swinburne, and Millie and Clarice, of course. We waited to hear the dates and times.

There was no time for Michael. No time for thought.

Meanwhile, Emily Wilding Davison had caused another furore. Millie told me about it. Nowadays I had to be told everything, for I had stopped reading newspapers and eagerly gathering news. I was an automaton, a clockwork toy whose mechanism was always one cog away from halting.

'She's done it again,' Millie announced excitedly. 'This time she's gone beyond stones. She set fire to a letter-box.'

'Not before she'd rung the press and the police to make

sure that it was reported and that then she'd be arrested,' added Clarice.

'Maximum publicity,' said Dorothy wryly. 'That one likes to be in the limelight.'

Millie rounded on her. 'That's the point, ent it? We want people to know wot we're doin'. What'd be the point of settin' fire to a letter-box at dead of night?'

'There are other ways of letting the press know – and the police. You don't have to make a song and dance about it,' said Dorothy.

'How did she do it?' asked our newest volunteer, Stella. 'It can't be as easy as it sounds.'

'It says here she had a piece of cloth soaked in paraffin. She lit it and dropped it through t' slot,' said Millie reading out from the press report. 'Oh, blimey! She'd already set fire to quite a number befower that one.' She giggled. 'Imagine how awful 'er clothes must of stunk. Paraffin's 'orrible stuff.'

'What's the point of it?' asked Stella.

'To make a nuisance of herself,' said Dorothy. 'If people's letters are not reaching their destination, they get upset. It causes a rumpus. It makes a statement.'

'A statement that we're prepared to go even further than before,' I spoke for the first time that morning. 'First stones and now fire.'

'What will she think of next?' Clarice wondered.

'Bombs, I 'spect,' said Millie, wide-eyed. 'Like those troublemakers in Ireland.' I flinched. Even the mention of Ireland was a body-blow.

'Says here she will be sentenced at the Old Bailey!' said Stella. 'And that her bail has been set at £1,000. That's quite some statement.'

'Don't get any ideas, Stella,' said Dorothy. 'This is another example of Miss Wilding Davison going her own sweet way. I doubt whether her actions have been approved by Headquarters.'

Dorothy had made sure there was no time to think of Michael. His face was not seen at John Bright Street and Millie and Clarice must have been primed, because his name was never mentioned in front of me. I heard him call outside my window at Harold Road, once, early on, and hid my head under the pillows. But it did not stop me wondering: what was he doing – was he finding enough work? Where was Seamus – had he gone back to Ireland? The questions ate at me until I asked Dorothy directly.

'He's gone back to Ireland, Gladys. With his son. It's the right thing for him to have done and I think better of him for it.'

'Did he look all right?'

She hesitated. 'He looked broken, truth be told. But it was still the right thing to do.'

Then she comforted me, though I did not weep. Right thing or no, it's not such an easy thing to give up love. I felt scoured out by emotion and knew he would be feeling the same. I wondered if I would ever see him again.

———

Word came from Headquarters. Volunteers should arrive before the end of February to be prepared and briefed. They should bring a bag with them, containing a nightdress and a change of clothes. All should wear clothes suitable for action and make as little fuss on public transport as possible, to avoid detection. It would be helpful if we could arrive not all together, hence the leeway of 'before the end of February', since many of the more prominent suffragettes were known to the police. We were given different addresses around London to head for.

Millie and Clarice travelled to somewhere in the East End of London, Stella to Kensington – 'nice and convenient,' she sparkled – while Dorothy and I went to an address in Muswell Hill. Our host and hostess, a Mr and Mrs Winfrey, both in their sixties, toasted and fed us on arrival before giving us a black canvas bag each which would hang over our shoulders, concealed by our coats. On our first day there a fresh blue sky greeted us, with scurrying clouds harried by a bitter wind. We turned our coat collars up and wrapped scarves around the lower halves of our faces. Mrs Winfrey lent me a scarf of her own, of a pretty pink, since all I had was my suffragette one.

'Best not draw attention to who we are,' she had whispered hoarsely – as if policemen lay behind the wainscotting with stretched ears and handcuffs – before we were packed into a smart Vauxhall for a jaunt. Their chauffeur, a man called Sharp, would take us all, with a loaded picnic hamper, out into the country North of London.

'Hampstead Heath would have been nearer,' said our hostess, still whispering, 'but too many people walk there.'

So we drove towards Boreham Wood and turned into a lane across the common there. Our task was to find stones and fill our bags with them. I was glad that I'd brought my black gloves, not my white ones, for finding stones after recent rain was a muddy business. I tested each one in my hand, making sure that the weight and shape fitted nicely into the palm. While Sharp laid out the picnic on a folding table he'd brought for the purpose, Dorothy and I practised throwing at a nearby tree. She, the former teacher of Physical Education, was far more accurate than I and soon both of us were giggling helplessly, as we watched my stones hurtle to this side or to the other of that patient tree.

'Focus, Gladys,' ordered Dorothy. 'Aim for that branch over there.' This was a deliberate ploy to glean more mirth from the situation as the branch was narrow and high up, but focus I did, and the branch shook off a couple of dead leaves that had sheltered there since Autumn.

Laughing even harder, we felt like a couple of children when our hosts called us over for lunch.

'Now I see why games with stones are the mainstay of entertainment for the lads of Birmingham,' I puffed, as we lowered ourselves to sit on the running-board of the car. Mrs Winfrey assured us that Sharp had cleaned it, to protect our coats from dirt.

'Luckily,' commented Mr Winfrey from the car seat where he was ensconced, 'a shop window will be a far easier target.'

'Make sure you have replenished your stock of stones,' added his wife, before Sharp brought us plates of cold meats and bread, dotted with butter that was too cold to spread, but which melted in the mouth in little delicious explosions.

The following morning, Mrs Winfrey gave us a small hammer each to conceal in a coat pocket.

'You've done this before,' I joked to hide my nerves.

'Once only. Before Christmas.' She looked solemn. This more than anything made me realise the danger we were going into. I felt the weight of the stones pulling at my left shoulder and hoped that I would not have to carry them for too long. Both of us were told to make for Bond Street in the West End. I was given the large department store of Asprey's as my starting point, while Dorothy was instructed to head for another store further down the same road. Our hosts drove us to the Underground Station at Camden Town and waved us goodbye.

Asprey's was impossible to miss. Its huge arched windows, which stretched from pavement level to the division between the first and second storeys, flashed and winked at me in the fleeting sunlight. Purple flags hung at intervals above those windows, proclaiming the name of the store in curly gold lettering. I approached with awe. It was like a glasshouse, a vast conservatory, only a band of gold-coloured metal separating each enormous pane. These were what I was sent to demolish. I had had no idea of the nature of the task and how daunting it was. I began to feel sick.

I approached cautiously, dodging vehicles – far more vans and smart cars than were yet evident in Birmingham. The vehicles screened me from view, so that I was able to lurk behind a chauffeur-driven Rolls Royce and assess the situation. It was half past ten o'clock. Half an hour to go. Now my stomach tightened and I began to taste bile.

How could I do it? I couldn't, morally or ethically, but I must for that is what I had agreed to do.

The pavement was colourful with women chattering and commenting on the displays in the windows, those very windows I'd been sent to break. I felt that everyone must see me for who I was, that I stood out like a signpost advertising my intentions. I could see my reflection in the windows. Nothing about me looked or felt normal. Compared with those wealthy women planning their wardrobe or searching for fine fabrics to decorate their homes, I looked dowdy, plain, clearly a misfit. Any minute now one of those women would expose me as a charlatan. There would be a tap on my shoulder. Any minute.

I made myself focus on a particular group of women and moved closer to them, trying to look as if I were one of their party. A laugh rang out from one and I smiled too, as if I shared the joke. Though I hovered on the edge, clearly invisible to them since no one gave me a second glance, I felt more visible than I'd ever felt in my life. Surely the bag of stones under my coat swelled and grew to giant proportions and the dangerous shape of the hammer deformed my pocket. And I could not make them more obvious, for again and again my fingers searched and found them – stones, hammer – stones, hammer – as if to reassure myself.

I checked my watch, as I'd been doing countless times since I arrived. At ten to eleven a smart woman, accompanied by a number of store lackeys carrying vast bags of goods, was ushered out of the main door by the commissionaire, a bull-like figure dressed in the Asprey's uniform of lilac and gold. His wide legs, above small feet encased in shining black leather, turned this way and that as their owner scanned the street in both directions. I wanted to duck but made myself stand still. Together we watched the lady being absorbed into the vehicle and tucked in under a white rug, surrounded by her purchases. Another five minutes as the chauffeur started the car and returned to his place behind the wheel. Majestically, the car purred away. It was five minutes to eleven.

The commissionaire eyed me haughtily. Perhaps I did not match the standards he had come to expect of Asprey's customers. Defiantly I moved close to another of those great windows, a little further off. It was very clean, so that standing there I could see myself reflected, while admiring the display of shoes and clothes – for sporting weekends in the countryside – that was displayed there. Covertly I pulled my watch half out of its pocket, felt again for my arsenal.

We had strict instructions not to begin until eleven in the morning. Then Christabel, whose organisation this was, would have the satisfaction of knowing that everywhere in the capital, there would be destruction happening at the same time. As soon as the police received a report of damage from one source there would be other reports from elsewhere, from all over the West End. The idea was to overwhelm the police so that they would not know how to cope.

The pocketwatch felt slippery in my hand. Even my palms were damp and the sweat trickled cold down my back and under my arms, swathed in the bulky coat. No one else was wearing such a thick coat. It stood out in the light March sunshine. Was that man looking at me? He could be a police detective. Maybe word of our plans had leaked out after all.

I tried to look insouciant, as though I was just admiring the display and had all the time in the world. I concentrated on particular items, to focus my mind. There was a special hat which was tied under the chin by a scarf, for use in open automobiles. Dorothy and I could have done with that yesterday, on our trip to Boreham Wood. There were skirts, narrow at the bottom and leaving the ankles exposed, to make it easier to step up into a motorcar without dirtying the hem.

When I glanced up again the man had gone, but the shop commissionaire in his smart braided uniform eyed me suspiciously. His shoes were polished like a soldier's. I made a greater play of pretending to admire a particular pair of narrow boots, with fur lining and fox fur rim. My acting, despite having to fight the inclination to check the whereabouts of the hammer and to ease the weight of the bag dragging on my shoulder, must have been convincing, because he flexed his feet a couple of times, so that the leather creaked, and strode purposefully off towards the next doorway along, several yards away. There a bunch of people, a man and two young women, carried their purchases out of the door and stepped out into the street to locate a hackney carriage.

At the same moment I heard a clock whirring, ready to strike, from a nearby church tower and took a quick glance at my own pocket watch. It was eleven o'clock. Now! It had to be now!

The commissionaire still had his back to me. He stepped out into the road to flag down a cab for the customers. He was tall and very broad with a neck like a tree-trunk. His braided hat sat on top of his head like an acorn. My heart pounded. He opened the cab door to help the two lady customers in and I acted.

Taking up a position at the edge of the pavement, a good distance from the shop-window, I released the hammer from its confinement, turned the waistband over so as not to trip over my skirt, and ran towards the window where I raised the hammer in my right hand, shielding my eyes with my left hand as we'd been told to do, and smashed it into the glass. A ripple shook the vast sheet and it shivered for an instant before it splintered into thousands of pieces. My hair and coat glistened with hard drops like diamonds, and the pavements crunched and glittered.

Having begun to run I kept going, hitting windows as I passed. Everywhere was shouting and screaming. Through the broken windows I could see people crawling about on the floor. Were they hurt? There wasn't time to think.

All around I could hear vehicles grinding to a halt, the blaring of horns... men's voices shouting... more screaming. I kept running. My face felt stiff, so shocked by what I was doing that the muscles had frozen. But the movement, the hitting of the glass, the feel of tiny splinters settling on my hands and face, built up inside me in a kind of whoop, half terror, half wonder. I bellowed aloud, drowning out all that was happening around me, all that noise that sought to halt the power of what I was about.

Close behind now were grunting breaths – the commissionaire – and suddenly his broad arms caught around my waist and his vast belly jostled my back. But my hand was still free and the momentum of my speed kept us both moving, so that I managed another window until he trapped that arm, but I was still moving in a kind of joyous desperation and succeeded in transferring the hammer to my left hand, with which I took out yet another window before, sliding on broken glass, the commissionaire, his breath bellowing out of his lungs, brought me to a stop.

'That's enough, you little bitch,' he wheezed. 'The police are on their way.'

Eyeing me warily he stepped back, taking the hammer and making sure that he held me still by the left arm. A grey-suited man with pursed feminine lips and a high collar emerged from the nearest door. Behind him were four or five others, holding in front of them absurd items as shields: a half-dressed mannequin, a chair, a picnic hamper. These surrounded me, holding their items in front of them as if to ward off the devil himself.

I felt a crazy desire to laugh.

'Thank you, Streatham, you can let go now,' said the grey suit. 'You will have to bear witness against this young woman in court.' He turned to me, his lips pursing into a point like the beak of a bird. His eyebrows had risen into his pomaded hairline. 'What possesses you, Madam, to wreak such damage on our premises? Have you any idea of the cost of all this damage? You'll answer for it I promise you. You will have the whole weight of the Law against you. Look how many witnesses there are.'

I did look, and saw heads raised from behind furniture in the devastated shop, mouths in round 'O's of shock. I saw that everywhere glass shone, as if the whole display had been scattered with glittering jewels. The shop floor was a lavish Aladdin's cave, hit by a hurricane. Diamonds of glass sprinkled the hats of customers and the hair of shop-girls with frost. And I had caused it.

The laughter bubbling in my belly began to rise and surfaced as an astonished surge of joy, the kind of joy which arises from a task well completed against all odds and in the face of danger.

'Votes for Women' I shouted and heard, further down the street, the cry picked up by others and the far-off tinkling of glass.

The shop-manager, or whatever official of Asprey's he was, took a step back and said with alarm, 'You're one of those mad suffragettes, aren't you?'

'Yes,' I cried and reached into the bag under my coat. Both hands cradling a stone, I began to run again, letting fly with stones as I went. Too late the manager and his supporters started after me for I had wings today, the wings of rebellion and freedom which allowed the breaking, not just of windows, but of all the taboos of my upbringing. Yelling, I ran and threw and skidded round the corner into a quiet side-street where the store windows were as yet untouched. There I threw again and barely registered the satisfaction of that noise, that destruction, as I ran and threw until three policemen caught me and pinioned my arms.

I was still fizzing with excitement when I was taken to a police-station where I was bound over to appear at court the following week.

The night before the court hearing, spent back with the Winfreys in Muswell Hill, did little to calm either of us down. Dorothy and I each had a bag ready, with books and clothes, assuming we would be imprisoned for some time. Neither of us had slept a wink, but spent the entire night whispering to each other, reliving those few moments of dangerous glory.

The courthouse was an austere stone building, weighted down by Latin promises and quotations honouring Justice and Mercy, though we knew that these grand sentiments would not apply to us. Not only had we broken the rules, but we were women.

I looked around to see how many of us there were. A big excited crowd of suffragettes of all ages, with flaming eyes and reddened cheeks, squashed together in the foyer, while on the other side stood those who were bearing witness to our deeds. The fat commissionaire caught my eye and shook his head in disbelief.

When it came to my turn and the judge saw the disparity in size between the Asprey's doorman and myself he was briefly speechless. 'You say that she broke more windows *after* you had hold of her?' he said as we stood in front of him, close together. I came up to my accuser's waist. A single one of his arms was wider than my head.

'She's a firebrand, sir,' said the commissionaire, mopping his sweaty forehead, 'and stronger than she looks.'

The judge raised his eyebrows and the curled tips of his moustaches twitched.

'No privileges,' he said wearily, cutting short my plea to be treated as a political prisoner, the plea we all made, for political prisoners are treated with more respect and allowed more privileges than common criminals.

Having listened to all the damage we had caused in a few short minutes, the judge sent most of us to Holloway Prison, though there were too many for that prison to accommodate us all, so some were sent elsewhere, even to Winson Green in Birmingham.

I wished I could have gone there, where I'd have been among friends and supporters, who would have visited and cheered us up, as we had done for Mary Leigh, Alice and the other first-time hunger-strikers. But that was not to be.

We too would be hunger-striking. It was the next thing on our agenda, but we had to wait for the word from Headquarters. The strikes must start together, and word must be passed to the other prisons, so that all of us acted as one.

I entered the portals of Holloway Prison with a feeling of unreality. It was a vast red-brick place, four storeys high. Set back from the street, it had the look of a castle, with a driveway and grass lawns separating the building from the busy street outside. We walked up the drive to the brooding crenellated mass of the gatehouse and we were in. Noises from the street, all the teeming outside world, were suddenly cut off, as if we had walked into a different universe.

This was a place of metal and stone, a hard place. Huge metal doors clanged behind us and I heard the finality of outsize bolts being driven into their sockets. As soon as they fastened behind us, the natural light of outside, with its yellows and greens and rainbow prisms, was replaced by an unnatural electric whiteness that bleached our skins to the colour of bone. Metal staircases and corridors divided the floors, and the cells too had metal divisions driven into exterior walls of sooty brick.

A harrassed wardress, who was trying to take down the details of us all, complained to another that there had never in her memory been such a large influx of prisoners at one time. The noise was incredible. Something about this place enhanced sound, extended it into gong-like echoes. Some of us were shouting about our rights as political prisoners. All of us were hanging onto our sanity, our feelings of self. I clung to my bag of belongings as if it were a life-raft.

At last we were separated and sorted. In smaller groups we were taken to a cloak-room, where we were divested of our outer clothes and handed black sack-like dresses, with big loose sleeves, tight at the wrists. Arrows were loosely sewn all over the dress, pointing accusingly upwards, and a round disc, embroidered with the letter H, was sewn to the upper left side. This prison-wear was finished by a large white half-apron, tied around the waist, which I was glad to see covered most of the ugly arrows. A small white cap, rather like that of a nurse or a lady's maid, sat on our heads.

The group I was in laughed and joked about the clothes. One young East-End woman said she'd never had anything so smart in her life and that caused much jollity. A couple pretended to be in a fashion-show, pointing out the practicality and unusual features of today's garments for the modern woman. Being so small, I was swamped in mine. A wardress gave me a thick black belt, so that I could hitch up the length. The shoes I was given were also too large and I hoped I would not have to walk far in them, though the thickness of the darned stockings might save my feet from blisters.

Of course I knew that the mirth around me covered up as real a fear as I felt. It took courage to laugh. Perhaps I would find that ability in time. This group were lucky. They were all from London branches of the W.S.P.U. and appeared to know each other quite well. Since our arrival at the courtroom I had lost sight of Dorothy. There was no one I knew, no Millie or Clarice for comfort.

Once dressed and still clutching my bag, I followed a wardress up to the first floor, fearing to look down through the gaps in the metal links of the stairs and the corridor, because it made me feel dizzy and disoriented.

'Here you are,' said the woman, standing outside a stout wooden door. Her uniform was better cut than that of the prisoners: a long navy skirt and blouse, covered in a full length calico apron from neck to floor, but with a similar white cap to mine, only wider, with white wings like a nun's.

She opened the cell door and noticed my bag. 'You can't keep that,' she said, but before she could take it from me, she was called downstairs to fetch another prisoner. With relief, I hid the bag with its precious books under the narrow flat bed, relieved that my cell door had not been closed.

The cell smelled dirty, with a background reek of carbolic and urine. The floorboards creaked under my feet and were slippery, as if with a layer of grease or old dirt. It was the bed which took up most of the narrow space of my cell. My bag would not be really hidden, of course, not if they cared enough to remove it. The bed, which I sat straight down on to test it, was hard, just wooden slats, with a thin crackly mattress that I imagined was filled with horsehair. On it were two blankets, a worn sheet, much darned and a thin pillow. A plain wooden chair sat under the tiny window – too high to see out of, except by standing on the chair. Which of course I did, immediately, peering through the little segments of glass to see what lay outside. No trees, but a big square of grass, about the size of a hockey pitch, with a gravel path around the whole perimeter. All of this was surrounded by a high red-brick wall. I supposed this was the closest there was to a garden and wondered if we would be allowed to walk in it. At least there would be fresh air.

Investigating my cell further, I noted a couple of hooks on which, I supposed, clothes could be hung. I unpacked my own night-dress and hoped it would be allowed. In the corner by the window there was a low commode and a jug and basin for washing. A cracked sliver of soap lay at the bottom of the basin and made me shudder. This detail brought home to me, more than anything else, that here I would be for the duration of my three months' sentence.

I was about to take a book out, to fill the time, when a cheery voice at the door asked me if she could come in. It was Clarice.

'I said we'd find you. Here you are!' She gave me a huge hug. 'It's not so bad, is it?'

Dear Clarice. She and Millie were always so positive about everything. I reflected that living for the moment, as they did, was probably the best solution to the present predicament.

———

At first things were, as Clarice said, not too bad. We were allowed a surprising amount of freedom, being locked up only at night. In this wing there were no other prisoners than suffragettes and I guessed that they were keeping us all together and separate from the other inmates. We were waiting for news of what was happening to our leaders, especially Mrs Pankhurst. They were being tried separately at the Old Bailey. When they were sentenced, word had it that we would start to hunger-strike.

Meanwhile, it was a bit like being back at the Royal Holloway College – a large group of women, many of them well-educated, with whom to talk and exchange views and laugh. The age-range was wider. We had one or two who were grandmothers down to a couple younger even than Millie, who was now nineteen. Our belongings had not been taken from most of us, dependent on the wardress to whom we had been allotted at the start, so there were books to share and poetry to sustain us, as well as the interest garnered from tales of people's lives from every echelon of society and numerous different occupations: writers, actresses, teachers, shop owners, milliners, secretaries, lady's maids, factory workers. Most of them, like myself, had had to let go of their professions to serve the Cause but none of them regretted the choices they had made.

In the evenings we sang, especially Dr Ethel Smyth's recently composed *March of the Women*, or Clarice and Millie, with their sweet voices, entertained us with some of the folk-songs with which they had been brought up. The pair were quite aware of the bawdiness of one or two of these, and enjoyed leading us up the garden path with a pretty tune and a suddenly suggestive line which surprised us into laughter.

This happy state of affairs – discounting the poor quality of the food, which favoured potatoes for their bulk, and gobbets of greasy fatty meat floating in tasteless juice – could not last. But it passed a couple of weeks.

Every day we were allowed into the exercise yard, that very same green patch with the gravel path around its perimeter that I'd seen from my window. There we were not allowed to linger, but had to walk two by two around the edge. It was on one of these walks that I spotted a tall familiar red-haired figure: Emily Wilding Davison.

She had not been part of the window-smashing because she was already in prison on an arson charge. As such, she had been kept away from the rest of us, until someone in charge deemed it better to keep all those troublesome suffragettes in one place. So she had been moved to our wing, where, as it turned out, she was in a cell almost opposite mine.

I was pleased to be re-acquainted with her, despite Dorothy's warnings, and of course Millie and Clarice were over the moon. I spent time with new acquaintances when the younger girls were with Emily, since I did not like to see her influence over them, but there were many times when we talked congenially, about our college days, about teaching, and of course about the Cause, to which she was more passionately devoted than anyone I'd met. For most people the Cause was, of course, the most important thing in their lives, but they did have other claims on their attention: husbands or children for the main part. Until recently I could have claimed Michael as filling a significant part of my life and keeping me in balance. Now there was a void where he should have been. But Emily had placed the Cause at the very centre of her being. There was no room for anything or anyone else. She lived and breathed it and never ceased to plan ways of accomplishing the end result: women's franchise. On this hung everything else. The lives of women would change. They would be empowered. There would be a new modern age in which women could do anything equally with men.

Of course I believed this too, though I would have put higher than the empowerment of women for its own sake, which I saw as potentially selfish, the ability to alter the lot of the poor. This Emily scarcely mentioned. She was also very critical of the Pankhursts, who she saw as power-crazy, especially Christabel. I did not feel I knew enough about them, so held my peace. Emily had worked for some time as a researcher in Headquarters and had seen the family and their friends at close quarters.

Somehow, Emily always seemed to know news from the outside before the rest of us did. I don't know where she obtained it. So it was from her that I learned first of the arrest of the Pethick-Lawrences and others on the charge of incitement to cause criminal damage. Christabel, it seemed, had got wind of imminent arrest and had escaped to Paris. So there were a number of people arraigned with Mrs Pankhurst at the Old Bailey. Perhaps the number on trial extended the time we had before being told to hunger-strike. Whatever the reason, those days were a surprisingly pleasant lull before the storm.

Change came suddenly and brutally. We were given the new instruction, each one of us in the morning when, contrary to previous days where we had eaten together at long tables in a downstairs room, we had a bowl of watery porridge thrust at us through a hatch to the side of the door. Then we were told, again through the hatch, that we were to be kept separated from each other and would remain locked in our cells except for exercise periods. My bag of books and clothes was confiscated.

Needless to say there was vehement objection. We beat on our doors and shouted till we were hoarse, the strange echoing quality of the building creating a weird effect of overlapping and disharmony, like a piece of modernist music.

When we were let out into the exercise yard we refused to come back in, whereupon we were seized one by one, and carried in as supine as logs brought to a furnace. One by one – it must have taken them at least an hour to fetch in everyone – we were locked in our cells. There, as we had agreed outside, shivering in the damp morning air, we broke our windows with our chairs, in strict order, so that as each heard the window of the next cell shatter, we would follow by breaking our own.

The result of this was immediate. As soon as the window had broken, two wardresses barrelled into my cell and dragged me out of it, fighting as hard as I could. I was taken down the stairs, where I arrived bruised with a ringing head, from being dropped so many times on the way, and thrown into another cell on the ground floor. The previous occupant had not made her bed nor emptied her slops. The smell of urine and worse, seeping into the stagnant air, made me happy to break the window of this cell too. But then I waited, sitting on a chair in the middle of the cell, from where I could hear the shouts and screams, the banging doors and breaking glass all around me. At one point the Governor came in to our wing and walked up between the cells talking sternly to us through the closed doors. All the answer he got was 'Votes for Women', which was begun by one voice and then picked up as a defiant chorus from all.

After this I was returned to my original cell and soon after the hunger strike began. They left us for five days, perhaps to test our nerve, perhaps to ready themselves for the massive task of subjecting so many to forcible feeding. I remembered what Mary had read out, of her sister Alice's experience in

Winson Green Gaol and shivered. The practical account had contained many details that did not help my already nervous state.

Then I remembered what Jim had made us do when we were children. We were to be brave, utter no sound of pain or complaint, whatever happened. Our training, or so he said, would make us the most courageous children alive.

We had all watched each other's faces when we were put to the test, for signs of fear or of cowardice. I would remember that, whatever happened. I would not make a sound and, whatever I felt inside, no one would be able to read fear in my expression.

I wish I could say that I found starving myself easy. I did not. I'm sure I was not alone in that, though keeping us apart had that effect – of making me feel that I was the only one who suffered such pangs. *A trouble shared is a trouble halved*, Mama used to say, when extolling the benefits of a large family. Our suffragette family were kept apart to allow fears to prey on us and to make us feel that there was no one who cared. Perhaps they thought that loneliness would drive us to seek favour, as naughty school children will fawn on a stern master, hoping to deflect punishment.

When the time came for forcible feeding to begin, I am ashamed to say that I welcomed it – in my thoughts at least – as the lesser of two evils. To have food thrust into me against the idea of starving to death. I did not want to die. I thought of the sweetness I had enjoyed when lying with Michael and I did not want to die. I thought of the familiarity of my family and their love; particularly I thought of Rita, of running to Canada to find a new life with her, however unlikely that was, and I did not want to die. I thought of Spring, just around the corner, and the rising sap of the flowers, the greed for life of Nature, and I knew I shared that same greed.

Thoughts like this weakened my resolve, all the long ticking minutes that I waited for it to be my turn in the queue for forcible feeding. Later I heard that it had taken two hours, as so many managed to delay the event by barricading their doors or by escaping from the wardresses. I was almost the last. Plenty of time to hear the screams, the banging of doors, the scraping of chairs and the crash of their overturning on the concrete floors, along with the shouts and sobs of those who came before me. That trick of picking up sound and magnifying it, which I had noticed from the start in our wing of the building, meant that I had plenty of time to wonder what each groan, howl and shout meant. By the time they came to me, I was like a trapped animal, waiting in line for the knife, smelling her fate coming closer, hearing her friends and family suffering and knowing that in five minutes – in two – in one – it would be my turn. No avoidance was possible but to bow the neck to the inevitable.

But when it came to it I didn't bow my neck. I suspect none of us did. By the time they arrived I was in such a state of panic that I fought like a maniac. In the end, they wrestled me to the floor and I was dragged by one foot over to my chair, then hauled up into it. There I was stretched backwards, with a large heavy wardress sitting across my thighs, her meaty hands on my shoulders, and a wardress holding each arm and leg, and another with a cloth across my forehead holding my head back. One of the wardresses was crying as she held me still.

I became aware that the doctor had come in. He had been doing this to women for two hours already and his hand was shaking so much that he could not direct the tube up my nose as he was supposed to do. Instead it dabbed feebly around my mouth and lower face, until a more senior doctor came in and took the tube and pushed it, with a slow but strong impatience, through my nasal passages and down into my throat. I could feel it scraping and pushing, meeting obstacles and pushing again, until finally it stopped, when apart from a horrible awareness of the presence of the tube, all I felt was the slop they were pouring into me down all its burning length. Throughout this process, I hung onto the memory of the courage game, and did not emit a sound.

Twice a day all of us, old and young, were subjected to the same treatment. There was nothing to do but to submit. For my own part, each hour became just a dull waiting for the next forced meal. Day by day the pain grew worse. It was harder to force the tube down my swollen nose and throat. And once, I am ashamed to admit it, the pain was so bad that I screamed. Yes – to my shame, I did. Just once. I heard Jim's voice in my head, so disappointed in me, but I could not help myself.

After some days, a kind of langour filled me, which was compounded of hopelessness and despair. There was nothing to distract me, no comfort, since they had taken the books. In between feeding times, I just lay on my hard bed with my eyes closed and floated in dreams of the past.

One day I was disturbed from this pleasant activity by the unbolting of my door. A wardress came in, her body tense.

'Please come,' she said. 'It's Miss Davison. She's threatening to kill herself. We noticed that in those first weeks you two talked to each other. You seemed to be friends. So perhaps she'll listen to you.'

Dazed, I followed the woman. We went along the corridor to the part of the wing where the metal stairs linked the four floors one to the other with galleries of wire fencing. Between each floor, from side to side of each gallery, wire netting stretched as a safety device. We climbed up until we were on the top level.

Emily stood, swaying slightly, near the top of the fence, thirty feet or so above floor level. I saw her wild white face, the tangled knot of her hair, and the intentness of her expression. She meant to do it. She was too far caught up in the white light of her own decision to know I was there.

I was filled with a kind of envy and in a rage I shouted, 'Let her go. What's the point of everything after all? Perhaps she is right and only a death will make them listen.' And I turned away, brushed past the shocked face and rigid body of the wardress, and made my way back to my cell.

I heard the sound as she jumped. Soon after I heard the lock turn on my door, but no one came to tell me whether she'd succeeded. I passed the time as I waited for news, sure that she would be dead, contemplating ways to manage my own suicide. Nina had had the courage to do it. And Emily. How much more fitting it would be that I should follow suit, I who had betrayed everything and descended to the level of an animal. Like a rabbit in the jaws of the fox, as the teeth bit deep I had screamed.

The next day the same wardress came into me and told me that Emily had jumped but been caught in the wire netting and had not died. Then, though already hurt, she had pulled herself up to the top of the staircase and thrown herself down a second time. And again she had failed, though she was badly damaged and had been taken to hospital. Having delivered her news, the woman looked at me as if to say, *Show something. It is your fault, for you could have prevented it.* But I showed nothing. I felt nothing. If Emily Davison wanted to die then that was her choice and her right. Who was I to persuade her to embrace a life that had betrayed us all?

'I suppose you'll try too,' said the wardress angrily. 'The trouble you lot have caused us. You should think of that sometimes, you who talk all the time about making women's lives easier.'

I was stung out of my sombre mood. 'And you held us down and forced food that we didn't want down our throats. Look at the women we are now compared with the women you saw first, when we were fit and healthy. For we still trailed around the exercise yard once a day, a sorry sight. 'Some are so weak they look close to death,' I went on. 'None of us are well. Have you thought of that? Have you thought of yourselves as murderers? There will be women here who will die because of what has been done to them.'

'And isn't that what you want? It's what *she* wanted. She talked of making a statement. Seems to me you're all busy making useless statements. And just look where it lands you.'

As rage held me in its grip, so that I shook with it, suddenly I knew that I wasn't like Emily. I didn't want to die, but to embrace glorious life. I felt washed in sudden light as this realisation bathed me. I closed my eyes the better to appreciate the rush of warmth that filled me up. And my breathing slowed. I calmed down.

The woman was still talking. For a moment I had not heard what she said. She appeared to be telling me that none of them felt good about what they were doing. They went home and cried. Then she caught my eye. I was listening again. 'Most of us have families, see, and this is paid work, isn't it? I can't afford to lose it; none of us can. If we don't do what we're told we'll lose our posts and work isn't easy to find.'

Her words were another realisation. What choice had these wardresses? How could I hate them? Though I did reserve feelings about the large woman who regularly sat across my lower body to hold me down. Her face looking down at my helplessness, as she weighed down my thighs and confined my wrists with hands like steel bands, that face had showed only a bovine relish for her task. But yes, occasionally

I had seen a wardress look distressed. And on that first day, one had cried. This was food for thought.

I must have been standing with my mouth open, looking like some kind of fool, for she spoke to me again, the wardress who had opened my eyes to seeing things from another perspective, and made me take all my belongings downstairs to a cell on the bottom floor, from where I could not run and try to kill myself as Emily had. They need not have bothered. I was past thinking of means to kill myself and doubted now whether I would ever have had the will to carry it through, though shame still bothered me when I was alone. Nonetheless, I hung onto the pride I was building up, that I had never screamed again. Despite the torture, the agony that ripped my nose and throat right down to my stomach every time, I had never again made a sound.

I do not know how long it was afterwards – I had heard Emily was out of the hospital and in an observation cell – when a wardress came and said that she had asked to see me.

She looked ill and exhausted. She told me she had been interviewed by a number of doctors and officials, who were trying to prove that she was insane. There was a strange glitter in her eyes, that looked to me like triumph. Despite her pain and weakness, she was enjoying herself.

'They cannot prove me insane,' she declared. 'I'm certainly not, and they know it. You see, Gladys, not one of these men – doctors, the Government – understand outrage, the outrage of so much that is done to us women. The outrage of what we were all being put through, with their tubes and clamps to make us stay alive at any cost. But what those men do understand is death. I thought, if I killed myself they would stop forcible feeding. That's all.'

In the face of such blind dedication, such certainty, I could add nothing. I kissed her forehead, where the bruises from her collision with the stairs on her second attempt were only just fading, and left her to go back to my cell.

～✦～

Not long afterwards, it was over. The hunger strike was finished, since the Home Office had given in to our demands to be treated with privileges, as political prisoners not convicts. Suddenly we were allowed books again. My bag was returned. And soon after that we heard we were to be released, via doctors who would assess whether we were fit to return to our lives or would need a spell to recover, in a clinic or a hospital.

For my part, all I could think of was home, not with Dorothy where the absence of Michael would hurt me further, but Rowstock and Mama and Papa. I was sure I would be allowed respite; Headquarters and our office in Birmingham would manage without me and Dorothy, whichever prison she was in. I went into the room where the doctor would assess me. It was the junior doctor, the one I had seen at a weak moment that first day of forcible feeding. He held out his hand to feel my pulse and I mistook his gesture for a handshake, took it and clasped it in mine. Quickly he pulled away and we both laughed awkwardly, realising my mistake. He stopped abruptly and slid his eyes from my face.

'You would have shaken my hand?' he asked in disbelief.

'Of course,' I said, full of the bonhomie of impending release and the new perspective in which I now regarded those who had tortured us.

'Then I thank you,' he said humbly.

When he asked me how I was, whether I experienced pain in my throat, my lungs, anywhere else, I lied. I wanted to go home.

We were released in a group and met at the gates of the prison by a committee from Headquarters, dressed in white, with flowers in their hair, as if, like Persephone, we had come back from Hades to bring Spring to the upper world. Some of us, like Eurydice, would return to those depths, for the campaign was not over and many of us would be tested again. For my part, I hoped it would never again be me.

Briefly I saw Millie, thin as a straw, with the corkscrew lustre of her hair flattened and dimmed. She leaned on Clarice's arm. I met the bleak look in Clarice's eyes. She looked older. I expect we all did. She gave me a wave of her fingertips and bent back, her face softened with love, to her charge.

34

Headquarters contacted Birmingham on my behalf. I had their blessing and could go home for as long as I needed to gather my strength. Once there, I lied again, afraid of shocking everyone with the events that had worn me down.

By some miracle they did not know that I had been a part of the window-smashing, nor imprisoned. They were too caught up by Mama's illness, which had hollowed her till she was mere skin and bone. So I was able to achieve two things for the price of one. I could give Mama some time, reassurance and love, while enjoying the spring and the heat of the early summer at Rowstock. The excuse – the lie – that I gave them was that I had been working too hard at school and had been given time off to recover.

'What a thoughtful person that Miss Nimmo is,' said Papa approvingly, while Kay and Lina fussed about, describing the organisation of Mama's sick room.

'I can take my turn in helping with Mama,' I insisted, and did so. After the last months of hard work and then imprisonment, anything else was a rest. I had five weeks, which was not enough to heal either my body or my mind.

Sophia had sent one or two letters that had arrived at Paradise Street on to Harold Street. From there, our landlady had sent them to the office at John Bright Street. Finally they'd found me here. One was from Ireland; I turned it over in my hand, fought those fingers which wanted to fondle the paper, despite everything, because he had touched it, then I tore it into a myriad of shreds. The thickest letter called me to read it immediately. It was from Rita and had been crossing the waves towards me all those many weeks I had been in prison.

March 18ᵗʰ 1912

Dearest sister,

This comes all the way from Canada, where at last the snow is lessening, after months and months of it. Yesterday we had a heavy rainfall, which washed some slopes clear, and the sky is laden with more. I long for it to go at last. We are quite snug, of course, in our little cabin, with a fire blazing. I have forgiven Bill for allowing me to think that the cabin was some kind of palace! A palace would be difficult to keep warm in the long winters. But I do worry about room for children, when we can afford to begin the family we so want to have.

Bill is quite an important personage here in Nakusp, which is no bigger than Harwell but has pretensions. He dazzles all with his telescope, which has been set up in a house in the main village, whose roof was removed and rebuilt to accommodate it! Bill, ever the showman as you know, delights in inviting people to look through it on the clear starry nights we have here. I confess to being a little jealous of his popularity but am beginning to make my own mark by teaching English cooking to some of the women here, who come from all over: Holland, Sweden and even Russia, as well as some from England and, especially, Scotland. They are encouraging me to write that cookery book I always threatened the family with, and perhaps I shall.

These things – music, neighbourliness, cookery classes – can take place comfortably in the wintertime. Summertime, however, is when we continue to dig and plant. Sometimes we need to remove boulders as big as houses and trees as tall as Nelson's Column. How? By enlisting the help of the whole neighbourhood, who will always lend a hand when a task is too great. But the rest we do ourselves and it's hard work, the hardest I have ever done. I have muscles you would never believe, in places you would never guess! And Bill was right, I do like Elspeth tremendously – his cousin Horace too, who is kind but rather formidable. Elspeth took a little getting used to as she's very forthright. She has no patience with 'namby-pambies' – as I fear I was when I first arrived. She is small and wiry, with a wonderful smile. Despite her Hampstead upbringing, she can now shoot as well as a man – last year she killed a grizzly that had wandered onto our land and mauled one of Horace's dogs! I pity any marauding Indian or other troublemaker that happens onto her territory!

Elspeth tried to show me how to shoot, but I was useless and went around for days moaning about my bruised arm and shoulder. However, in the summer – my first summer here and not long enough in my opinion – I came into my own and helped Bill to teach all the youngsters to swim in the Upper Arrow Lake. Both of us are good swimmers, but the Lake – which isn't really a lake at all but a kind of swollen part of the Columbia River – is challenging because it is full of currents and undertows. Mama would definitely have forbidden us even to enter it!

I wish I could describe the beauty of this place in summer. The mountains, the lakes, the forests. All that space. The light on the water. Even in the winter the colour of the snow was a surprise – we think of it as just white, or dingy grey when the cartwheels have gone over it, but here it's blue, and sometimes greenish in the shadows, and even pink when the dawn or sunset hits it. And the wildlife: moose – such strange mournful-looking creatures, Gladys, with great sad eyes – and bear and wolves – yes, really – I've not seen any yet, but I am told when they're hungry, they'll come and take one of the domestic animals. Oh, and wonderful soaring eagles, which are as common as pigeons here! Probably more common, since I expect they've eaten all those poor birds!

You don't hear the cooing of pigeons or the sound of twittering, that very English sound, out here. The birds are loud, as if saying 'this is all ours, and you poor humans cannot lay claim to it' or they are completely silent – probably hiding from those eagles! The pine forests are so quiet when you walk in them, but you feel, all the time, as though you're being watched. I don't like them, but couldn't admit that to brave Elspeth, or even to my own husband, who looks on everything around him with a child-like delight. As you can see from the picture I've tried to paint for you, my new home is beautiful but terrifying too. Sometimes the terror wins and I wish I were back at Rowstock and safe.

The best times are the summer evenings, when Bill and I go out in our canoe – a kind of boat invented by the natives here – and watch the sun go down behind the mountains, and the flaring red of the sunset on the water. Those times I am happy and don't miss home at all. Other times, it is all so strange and wild and full of unknown dangers, that I feel terribly homesick. And then I'm ashamed because I have so much to be happy about.

More than anything I miss you, Glad. I miss having a sister who knows me so well that I don't have to pretend. I hope one day you'll visit. Or stay?

How are you doing? How is the Cause doing? When I told some of the women here what you were up to, most were amazed. This place demands so much from us in the way of simple survival that to worry about things like the vote is as extraordinary as growing plums in the mountains – something Bill aspires to but cousin Horace laughs at.

Mama writes me that you haven't visited or even written since the wedding! Really? That's unlike you – you did promise me. She says she's much better, but that's not what the others tell me when they write. PLEASE go to see her and REPORT BACK. I feel so cut off here and helpless to do anything about our parents. Would I even know in time if anything happened to them? Or to any of you precious people, my dearest sisters and brothers. WRITE, Gladys – that's an order!

Your sister Marguerite Waterfield [can't resist writing the whole name!] It looks good on paper, don't you think?!

P.S. Think of the journey this letter will have taken before it reaches you. There is a postal service here, thank goodness. So I hand my letters over the counter in the post office. But there are no roads as yet, or rail, just some old tracks made by the miners in the boom time, and now by the foresters who cut down trees and drag them to the sawmills. The first miles that letter travels then, are on the paddle steamer – here they call it a 'sternwheeler' because the wheels that drive the boat are at the back, not the front as at home. The sternwheeler will take it to Revelstoke, *where the train track begins. On a train it goes, chuff chuff chuff, till it reaches Vancouver. There it will be put on a large steamer, with all my wishes and kisses and hugs wrapped up in its frail packaging. I hope none of them escape and that the long journey treats this letter kindly. It will be weeks till it reaches you, probably we will be snow-bound again by then. Think of me! Xxx*

P.P.S. I've written this letter over days, a bit here and a bit there. Hence all the crossings out and arrows as I seek to improve its literacy, before my school-teacher sister sets eyes on it! I'm thinking of you. Your Rita. Xxx again.

Rita's voice, her whole personality, leaped out at me from the pages. She spoke of fresh things, of new life and hope and adventure. The shadow of the prison had no place there and this letter alone did much to lighten my darkness. I began seriously to consider joining her and Bill there. When we had finally won the vote, for I could not desert the Cause now, not after suffering so much. Surely after the torture of so many women, something would give. Popular opinion would sway the Government and it would all be over. Surely.

By August I was back in Birmingham and I knew it was too soon. My body was thin and weak and there was a fierce pain in my throat and lungs which would not leave. But I could not stay at home, not after Mama's sister Aunt Louise had arrived and blown my lies to kingdom come.

'How are you, Gladys?' she said as we greeted her. 'Found time out of your busy schedule to visit your ailing mother then?'

'It's school holidays now,' said Kay protectively.

Aunt Louise arched her eyebrows at me. 'Oh, really? How does that affect you?'

That's when my heart began to sink. She knew. Somehow, she knew. Then I remembered the many committees, the passing of gossip that went under the heading of news at those events. During my teacher training years I had sometimes sat in on those committees – the ones where my aunt presided – so she could show me how very respected she was in the society she had chosen. And Oxford too, of course, had its suffragettes. The network of news through them was efficient.

But why now, some weeks after our release? Names would have been bandied about but I had been only one of many. Perhaps it had taken her some time to realise that I was a part of it. There are not many Hazels but she was a Holland, a name she had reverted to after her husband's early death, like my mother had been before her marriage. Her friends in Oxford might not realise the connection, or remember any but the first names of those poor little waifs so kindly taken in by their aunt.

The sword did not fall just then; it shivered slightly on its hanging thread, however, and promised to fall directly on my head very soon. With a look compounded of humour and malice, Aunt Louise marched up the stairs, her other nieces in her wake. I watched as her fashionable backview in its red hobble skirt and over-tunic ascended the stairs, displaying narrow bony ankles in beige stockings. Once she looked down at me over her shoulder. Her narrow lips curved and with a flick of her lacy tunic she was gone. I heard the door to Mama's room open and waited.

When nothing had happened, no cries or hubbub of any kind. I slunk off to the kitchen where Nora, almost as old now as Gertrude Austin's Maudie, poured me a cup of tea the colour of an Irish peatbog. Regretfully, my mind drifted to Michael. Anything was better than to think of what might be happening upstairs.

'Are you feeling all right?' Nora asked as she scattered flour over the scrubbed oak tabletop and began to roll out pastry.

'I'm fine, thank you.' I got up and passed Nora's daughter, Eve, as she bustled in with a pile of laundry. Down the stone-flagged corridor, nursing my doom in the pit of my stomach and the cup in my hand, I emerged into the brightness of the sunshine and made my way towards the tennis court, hearing the soft thuds of the ball in my memory as, home from school, Duncan and Edgar thrashed it out crowing with delight at every point gained over the other. Next my memory served up the sharp rap of the croquet ball as we played one of our endless family games together. I saw Papa standing close behind Mama, his hands over hers wielding the mallet, his chin resting on the top of her head. Lina and Kay set out their lead farm animals on the close-mown grass of that same court. Oh those endless games in the endless summers of our youth.

My feet took me next to the sloping bank below the court where once Rita and Bill had lain and kissed, between Bill's Oxford friend Victor and myself. It had come after one of their many rows – Bill had to tease and push that teasing to the limits. He always got the reaction he wanted, ruffling Rita's mood till she was all prickle and spikes of fury. Then would come the making up, the caresses and the kissing. Perhaps that was all it was about. I never could understand it, used to worry for their marriage when I remembered how Bill always had to be in the ascendancy, how he loved to manipulate her so that she fled away and returned – a yoyo to his hand.

That day had been different. It was in the early days, when in my naivete I still thought it was me he and Victor visited. I had seen how he needled her and how she rose to the bait and stormed off. But then she'd returned and thrown herself down between Bill and me and Bill had turned towards her, risen up on his forearms and bent to kiss her. Even innocent I sensed the lightning charge between them and was shocked at the touching of those bodies, one of which had been so close to me always. It was a presage of our eventual separation but it was the raw desire in both of them that I felt and, I suppose, envied. It is that which etched the moment on my memory. Now, with more understanding of the workings of sexual desire, I sat on that same sloping bank and wished myself with Rita, or failing that wished her here with me. She might be equally shocked by Aunt Louise's revelations, but in the end she would forgive and support me. She always had.

The afternoon crawled slowly by. No shouts or demands from the house. No screams of shock or surprise. But after a while the doctor arrived in his pride and joy, the little Singer automobile he'd bought a few years before, and climbed out with a grunt, patted the bonnet of his car and, seeing me, gave a cheerful wave.

'How do you find your mother?' he said. 'Your father just gave me a call.'

'She's too thin,' I said cautiously, 'and she has little energy. Would it do her good to take her out?'

'Your father should buy an automobile.' He looked fondly over his shoulder at the black rather flimsy-looking vehicle parked behind him. 'I've never looked back. A cover for when it rains and for all those night visits when infants insist on being born.' He cleared his throat and looked me up and down. 'But you must know why your father has called me out, surely? Something new must have happened.'

'I've been sitting out here for ages,' I said vaguely and he gave me a puzzled look before making for the house.

Lina came to fetch me for supper. It was still warm outside, but a dew had started and my skirt was soaked.

'I said I'd fetch you,' she said. 'Better than Kay, who might be fierce. Perhaps you'd like to come to the barn to feed the animals with me first?'

The animals turned out to be a number of cats and a small dog on a long chain who greeted her ecstatically. She dropped down beside him and kissed his head. 'Isn't he a sweetie, Gladys? I'd love to have him in the house, but Papa won't allow it. He says the hair would make Mama cough.'

The cats curled around her ankles while Lina unloaded the contents of a couple of small bowls, tucked into the pockets of her favourite cardigan, which was stretched to the utmost by such treatment. 'The thing is,' she said as we sat on the sweet-smelling hay and watched the animals eat, 'Mama is very upset. She took a funny turn when Aunt Louise told her what you'd been up to and that has made Papa very cross too. You'd better be prepared for fireworks.'

I thought this was worse than facing prison, worse than waiting for forcible feeding. No, nothing could be worse than that. I took a deep breath. Courage, Gladys, courage, I told myself and straightened myself, chin up. The sooner I faced it, the better. What was the worst that could happen? We were family after all.

Banishment. That was the worst, and it had happened. Under Aunt Louise's sharp gaze at the dinner table, Papa had pronounced that he did not want me in the house. That he could not support a liar. That seeing me and knowing how I had betrayed everything I had been brought up to be, would be too much for Mama. Kay sat very upright at the table and raked me with her blue eyes. Mama's place at the end of the table opposite Papa was an emptiness that felt full of her presence. Only Lina looked at me softly, with the kind of regard she turned on any orphaned abandoned creature.

In my worst dreams I could not have imagined such an outcome. Now I had no family and no lover. I had nothing but the Cause.

I am up on the Downs, no horses today, but a sweep of blue full of scudding cloud that sends shadows racing over the ground. I remember that judgement from Papa, the looks from my sisters and it still makes me shiver to think of the harshness of it. Did Mama forgive me? I never saw her again, but the Mama I knew would not have held with such a punishment for long. I like to think that, despite Aunt Louise, she would have found it in her heart to bring me in from the cold to the warm comfort of her affection if she had had the strength to write.

Truda has a large pile of pages to work through. It is why I have left her to it, that and embarrassment. There is a lot in those pages that makes my skin flush and my armpits prickle. There is a lot, too, of my own weakness and shame. I suppose I worry there might be another banishment, a rejection, or at least a punishment for all those failings which I've never before confessed to. How can Truda still like me, or even respect me, when she knows what I really am?

Two hawks circle in the sky, their mewing cries filling the air. All the little birds in the bushes that line my pathway back home are silent under their searching gaze. They crouch low and keep still under the few tatters of leaves that remain, to avoid the plummetting fall, the stretched claw, the cruel beak.

I reach the shelter of the village and choose the road to the shop. I will go back home laden with food stuffs to make a stew. Truda loves soft foods with plenty of gravy or sauce which are kind on her brittle teeth.

Back home in the kitchen I try to judge, as I unpack my bag, where Truda is. Has she finished reading? I have been gone for long enough. Perhaps she cannot bring herself to talk to me, is wondering what to say or how to say it. My hand trembles and I cannot find the strength to cut through the turnip I've selected as first for the knife.

There is a sound behind me. Truda stands in the doorway, her head on one side, glasses off which makes her eyes look soft and watery, one hand supporting her against the doorframe.

'Dear Gladys,' she says. 'Thank you so much for trusting me with the details of those hardest times in your life. How very brave you were and are.'

And she comes over and puts an arm round my shoulder while I weep.

35

Once back in Birmingham I threw myself into my duties. What else was there? I worked as never before, made sure there was no time for thought. But at the end of 1912 I was transferred to Leicester as District Organiser. The women there had requested me, apparently, having found my talks inspiring. From the start I lodged with Truda, in her familiar house in Regent Road.

It had been weeks since I'd heard anything of Michael. But he tracked me down. He had known where to come, of course, and had knocked on Truda's door just before I was due to leave to give my first talk in my new role to the Leicester W.S.P.U. Tactfully, Truda ushered him into the drawing-room and absented herself. I was distracted and impatient, knowing that I would have to speak soon, and nervous as always.

'I'm sorry, Gladys. I had to come. I went to Birmingham first, to Harold Street, and there was no one I knew staying there. So then I went to Paradise Street, where Sophia told me that you had moved away. She also told me you were ill, that she thought you were still unwell, that you had not given yourself time to recover after that long spell in prison. Is that true? You look so thin.'

In my family, sickness came into the same category as pain, to be borne without complaint. So I brushed off his concern, knowing he wanted to put his arms around me and fearing I would shame myself, for my throat was still swollen and to speak, to project my voice to reach large numbers, was agony. But the pain had to be conquered, so I stepped away. And I told him coldly that I could not carry on a relationship with a married man.

'You knew I was married.'

'But then I met your son. And heard about your other – children. Your new baby.'

His voice dropped. 'I wish they had been *yours*. I wish we'd had a parcel of children.' In spite of how he'd hurt me, the vast betrayal of the baby, my reserve broke. I couldn't look at him, but I whispered, 'I wish that too. I wish I'd held our child in my arms. But that can never be, Michael. You know that. It's done.' And I ran out of the room.

A moment later Truda's driver, Brown, came to the door and said the car was ready. I could feel Michael behind the drawing-room door, not knowing what to do. Half-expecting him to catapult out and carry me off or some such nonsense, I scooted out myself, forgetting my notes, so that when I arrived at the Leicester headquarters, I made a speech that was entirely from memory, and received congratulations afterwards for the sincerity and freshness of my words.

When I returned, Michael had gone and Truda said nothing to me about him. It was as if he had never been there. But that night, I crept to the window over-looking the street, from the bedroom with the rose-coloured counterpane, and imagined I saw him, standing in the sudden shower that misted the window. Or perhaps I did not imagine it. Perhaps he was there, shivering in the rain and looking longingly up at the window, a wavery shape distorted by the water running down the pane, like some tramp that had been denied warmth and comfort.

My days in Leicester followed the usual pattern for an Organiser. By then I could do most of it, even the paperwork, with ease – though the time it all took was dreadful. The weekly reports and financial breakdowns were no longer sent to Mrs Pethick-Lawrence. She, with her husband, had been expelled from the party for reasons none of us really understood. They had always been so loyal, had financed many of the important enterprises, including the printing of *Votes For Women*, which we'd handed out on street corners and by bicycle for so many years. The new paper was called *The Suffragette*, but it was in most respects the same as its predecessor.

The days, as I've said were straightforward, but the nights … oh, those dream-filled nights.

I couldn't see a bicycle without thinking of Michael. Would it always be like that, or would there be a slow fading of memory until I could let him go at last?

I dare say Michael would have been expelled along with Mr Pethick-Lawrence had he still been a reporter for the W.S.P.U. Christabel appeared to have developed a dislike of men in a society formed for the enfranchisement of women. I could understand that. It was men who troubled my dreams.

One of my recurrent nightmares arose out of the brutal manhandling which I and many others suffered from the police. Those incidents had become combined somehow with that aggressor who'd knocked me off my box and handled me lewdly, and with the distorted face of a man, half real, half imagined, who rose up out of a heckling crowd. His lips were flecked with spittle and his eyes burned. He could have been anyone. I don't remember a particular person, a particular voice or class or facial type; he was a composite, I suppose, the combined hatred of all those men whose status was threatened by our challenge.

By this time I was beginning to see no end to it all and to dislike immensely what I was being asked to do. On the one hand I had committed to the Cause and there was nothing else but to obey; on the other I was losing respect for Headquarters. Not for Mrs Pankhurst, for whom I had and will always have the highest regard – but for Christabel, who I felt was using her mother as a figurehead for her own motives.

Like Emily Davison, Christabel had much to be angry about. She had trained in the law, achieving the highest grades, but was not allowed to practise it because she was a woman. She was always in the limelight, and that takes its toll. The authorities were gunning for her, determined to bring her down, so she spent two years trying to order everything from Paris, where she had fled. I think through those final years she became a little unhinged.

I don't blame her for that. Didn't I also become more than a little mad? It didn't show yet, in the last weeks of my Leicester appointment, but by the time I was in Bristol, my final posting, it did. There I didn't have Truda to look out for me and I knew no one. Everyone looked up to me, hung on my every word, expected so much, were awed by my experiences, those same experiences that haunt me still. There was not one person I could turn to.

Fear stalked me.

The start of the fear arose quite logically. While in Leicester the Government had passed a new law which became known as the Cat and Mouse Act. It was a devilishly clever plan which at first sight appeared humane.

The idea was that when a woman had been forcibly fed to the point where she was ill, she would be released and sent to a clinic, or some equivalent, where she could be nursed back to health. Here is the sting in the tail: once declared by a doctor to be fit, she would then go back to prison to complete her sentence.

A sentence of three months, for instance, under this new ruling could take a year or more to complete. The victim would be in and out of prison, force-fed to the point of near-death, brought back to life, re-arrested, and so ad infinitum. It made my head spin when I thought about it later.

In my stupidity, I had not seen the horror of the implications of this Act. Needless to say, every one of us worked hard against it, and this Act alone added a thousand-fold to the burden of being a District Organiser.

We all contributed to compiling a network of safe houses which could shelter a Mouse on the run. Truda could not participate, because my being there would make her house too obvious. But she did become a safe house when I moved away. The Mouse would move from safe house to safe house, always one step ahead of the police, to avoid being sent back to prison. In the majority of cases we were successful in keeping our brave Mice safe, but the tension, the constant fear of arrest was dreadful. Especially when our leaders in Headquarters were being arrested, often for as little as housing inflammatory material, or inciting acts of militancy. I began to lie in bed at night, stiff as a board, with every muscle tensed, waiting for a knock on the door from the police.

I could not speak of the real fear, which was that I would have to go back there, to Holloway, and suffer the same horrors as before. Or worse, sometimes I would lie awake thinking that surely the authorities would stop forcible feeding – what good had it ever been? – and instead would simply allow women to starve themselves to death. Why not? That is what we professed to want, after all.

In my mind as it pursued this idea, I saw acres of skeletal women – hollow eyes, clawed hands outstretched – left to die by their own choice, of starvation. And people walked on by – not just men, the police, the Government – but everybody. Women too. They walked chattering by, shopping, gossiping, all utterly impervious to our suffering. And not just impervious but ignorant of it. As my mind followed this through, I saw a world that forgot us all, that went blithely on, totally unaware, as if it were all nothing. For in these darkest moments I not only saw the uselessness of our striving, but that no one cared one whit.

Yet, with no alternative, still I went through the motions. I carried on my duties as an Organiser, but I no longer saw any of it as exciting, or enjoyable, or even meaningful. As time went by, our acts of militancy: the spoiling of golf-courses, the burning of houses, the bombs set at railway stations, the defiling of art work in galleries, all of these things and more which I helped to organise and often participated in, seemed like a roller-coaster to disaster which could only end one way: going back to the nightmare, going back THERE, where this time I and others would be left to die. And it *would* all be for nothing. For it seemed to me that we had gained nothing whatsoever in all the years of trying.

At these darkest times, when the thought of death surfaced and became at once a fear and an occasional temptation, Emily Davison inserted herself once more into my thoughts. Six months into my tenure with the Leicester W.S.P.U. I heard of her death at the Epsom Derby. Shocked to the core, a number of Leicester suffragettes including me travelled to London for her funeral, though her burial I understood was to be a family affair up in Northumbria from where she came.

Despite the doubts with which Emily was viewed by Headquarters they honoured her with the kind of show that the London W.S.P.U. excelled at. Her funeral procession was long, her coffin draped with suffragette banners and white flowers, while the horses and carriages were flanked by suffragettes in white, symbolising the purity of the Cause and, I suppose, of Emily's motives. So many suffragettes had turned up from all over the country that central London was brought to a standstill.

I took my place in the procession and, to my delight, saw Millie and Clarice following the second carriage. Both were wearing white, as I was – for that was our instruction from Headquarters. Millie's eyes were red with weeping. I wondered if she still thanked me for making her a suffragette.

After a tiring day following the funeral cortege and listening to the eulogies given for Emily by Mrs Pankhurst and by Emmeline Pethick-Lawrence and others, a sense of unreality grew in me, so that I was glad when Clarice found me and suggested we meet for tea at the Lyons Corner House in Piccadilly Circus when it was all over.

Over tea we all agreed that there was something hypocritical about the whole event. 'I can't help thinking that Headquarters are taking advantage of all the fuss that's built up in reaction to the event,' I said. 'It's marvellous publicity of course.'

'They never liked 'er,' agreed Millie. 'But she were bloomin' wunderful, that's wot I think and 'spect ah'll always think. D'you think she meant to kill 'erself?'

'Some are saying that she just wanted to drape a banner round the King's horse, as a statement,' said Clarice.

'I'm a bit confused about it: it's hard to make sense of

all the rumours that fly around in the newspapers. But only an idiot would think that in a horse-race anyone could spot which one of a knot of galloping horses belonged to the King. That's my first reaction. I think that it was just chance that it came from the royal stable – and of course that chance makes for better copy. One or two of the photos show that the horse – Anmer, wasn't it called? – was some way behind the others. More likely she saw a gap and simply walked out into it.'

'Cos she thought it wouldn't 'arm 'er?' Millie had leaned forward, eyes big as saucers. Her lips trembled. 'Like wot you said abaht 'orses, Gladys, that time wiv the mounted perlees – that they won't step on yer.'

'Millie told Emily about that, about how you stood in the path of the horses and they sidestepped around you. And about your sister – that story you told us afterwards – the horse on the beach.'

'You told Emily about that?' I looked at Millie. She nodded. 'When?'

'It were at a rally in Lundon, after you'd gone 'n' left fer Leicester. She were there and we were too. She were that pleased to see us.' Millie smiled at the memory and then burst into tears. 'Oh, I cain't seem to stop blarting.'

'I think it's the idea that she meant to kill herself that upsets Millie – isn't that right, sweet?' Clarice stroked her cheek and handed her a damp handkerchief.

Millie nodded. 'But then, if she thought she'd be safe? Would it be my fault for telling 'er?'

I took Millie's hand. 'What would be worse – if she meant to kill herself or if it was an accident because you'd told her horses would rather avoid hurting a human being if they could?'

Millie just shook her head.

'Either way you'll just have to come to terms with it, dear

Millie. But I think she probably wanted to die, to make a huge statement for the Cause. And what greater statement could she have made? In front of thousands of people? I'm sure she'd be delighted at the effect she's had.'

On the train back to Leicester, after tearful farewells with my two Birmingham friends, I thought further about Emily. I remembered what she'd said to me after her failed suicide attempt in prison. She'd wanted to be a martyr. She'd sincerely believed it would make a difference, a memorable statement that would swing public opinion in our favour. How sad she would have been at the attitude of certain members of Government who, instead of seeing it as the brave action I thought it was meant to be, dismissed her as a hysterical woman whose actions only proved further what certain men had always held, that women with their uncontrolled emotions did not deserve the vote.

———

After I was sent to Leicester, contact with Dorothy or my other Birmingham friends became rare. Dorothy left Birmingham too, and returned to work for a while at Headquarters. Both of us kept travelling and speaking, for we were both much in demand, and sometimes our paths crossed. The second to last time they did was when she came to Leicester to speak, in the autumn of 1913, at my request.

We embraced each other and Truda, whose house she stayed in, tactfully left us to it.

'How are you, old darling?' she cried, pushing me out at arms' length to scan my face. You don't look too good. Aren't you eating enough?'

Because we had been through the same regime of forcible

feeding, though Dorothy was one of those sent to Winson Green, I felt I could say to her without it being construed as fussing that I still found it difficult to eat, my throat and lungs were so sore all this time later. 'It's difficult to project my voice too.'

'Not what I've heard,' she said. 'Lots of people comment on your inspirational talks. Headquarters are always receiving requests for you to travel to Leeds, or Edinburgh, or Bristol – all over the place. I'm quite jealous. You appear to be going places I've never been. But now – guess what.' She looked around theatrically, pretending to search for eavesdroppers, and lowered her voice to a stage whisper. 'I'm being sent to Ireland again. A big campaign to get Irish womanhood with us – they're still quite scattered over there.'

'They have other things to think about,' I said.

'Well yes. The Home Rule issue and all, but still … So I thought I'd contact Michael – he's over there, isn't he? – to ask for his help. A strong Irishman like he is would be a useful chaperon amidst the wild Celts or Gaels, don't you think? Do you remember, I asked him once before? And he said he would, if you came too. But that's impossible now, isn't it?'

She looked at me with her lop-sided mischievous smile, that remembered expression which meant she was unsure but was going to dare anyway, to push the barriers whatever the consequences.

My face felt stiff with shock.

Her smile faltered a little. 'Or are you still seeing him, despite …?'

'Of course not.' I found I could force the words out after all.

'Well, then.'

I began to shiver. Was this really Dorothy speaking? Dorothy who knew, none better, how it had been between Michael and I? Then I remembered that Dorothy had always flirted with Michael. I knew she found him attractive.

'You're cold?' She started forward. 'You *are* ill, I can see you are.'

I jerked away as her hand reached out to me.

'What is it? I thought you'd left the man behind, as I told you so often. But you still care, don't you? I don't understand how you can when he betrayed you like that.'

I could not speak. Dorothy stepped back with a puzzled frown. 'I'm sorry if I hurt you. It was clumsy of me.' She sketched a smile and adopted a light air. 'But you know me – I like to tease. I didn't mean it.'

But I knew she had meant it. And even though I knew Michael would never come trotting to her heels, I could not forgive her.

So I was cool with her for the rest of the visit and I did not see her again for a long while. I heard of her, though. She was awaiting trial in Ireland when the war broke out the following August. With the Pankhursts declaring the end of militancy for the duration of the war, all imprisoned suffragettes were granted amnesty and allowed out. All but Dorothy, who languished in a Dublin gaol for a few more weeks, before she too was finally released.

After the last time I was at home I did not expect to hear from any members of my family. The parting was too bitter, my disgrace too great. But at the beginning of January 1914 I received a letter from Lina: kind, extraordinary Lina, who was so clever in her own way. She could remember everything she read; could quote huge chunks, with extraordinary accuracy, after only one scan of the page – and she didn't read just silliness. Her mind was voracious and she had gone right through that rectory library with all its dusty tomes. But spelling was a torment, which meant writing a letter was a burden for her and therefore a rarity. We often marvelled as a family, that she could photograph whole pages of words with her mind, so that they'd flow from her mouth without a single mistake, yet the formation of those words, the ordering of the letters, would scramble somehow, as if her brain had a kink in it.

Recognising her untidy hand sent alarm bells through me. I ripped the envelope open.

Deer Glad,

> *Mama dyid yesturday and she wil be berrid in 2 weeks. You must cum. Mama always had a speshal place for you, Glad. She talkt abowt you so much. I no she fergav you. She understood that you did wot you felt you had to. She told me that herself. Cum soon, Lina*

Those few weeks, before Aunt Louise's arrival had destroyed the closeness of our family, were all I had had with Mama. Nothing, however, could keep me away from her funeral. Lina knew that, knew what was right, and had made sure I would be there.

So I went and I was not well myself. It was a chill January day. Mama had died on the first day of the New Year. She never saw the war, never experienced the fear of having children in peril, never saw her first grandchild.

When the others saw how ill I was – I could hardly walk upright and my cough troubled me terribly – I was ashamed. It may have softened their feelings towards me, but that only added to my guilt. Jim, smart in black topper and tails, eyed me with concern. It was a shock to see him out of his Royal Marine uniform.

My eyes sought out Papa, who looked stern and straight in his own formal black. I knew he was trying desperately hard not to show emotion. He avoided everyone's glances, not just mine. Especially not mine, I suppose, since anger was not appropriate at a funeral.

Rita, Duncan and Edgar were not there and would not even know yet of Mama's death, but Kay and Lina had clearly had black dresses run up by a local seamstress, quite plain, but for some simple ruffles around the neck and sleeves. Funerals had not featured in our family so far, except for Aunt Mary's and before that Uncle William's. We had been too young when Papa's brother William had died, suddenly, when Rita and I were at school, and Aunt Mary's death had occurred when the younger ones had still been adolescents and I had been away teaching. Black drained the colour from my sisters' faces, but brought out in sharp relief the intense blue of Kay's eyes and the curvature of Lina's spine.

My own black had been lent by Truda. I was now as thin as she, but nowhere near as tall, so she had taken up the hem herself, with those neat precise stitches she used on wounds whose edges must be pulled together. She had not wanted me to go, so worried was she about my own health and the fact that I was still working, despite all her admonishments. But she knew my own mother's funeral was something I must attend, however much it cost my health and however much I feared the reception I might receive from the family.

Lina came forward and pulled me into the family grouping behind the hearse. We were to walk the journey to Harwell Church, as we had so many times on a Sunday. All but Papa, who was being taken by the doctor in the little Singer automobile.

The car followed the hearse and Jim walked behind the car, which groaned and sputtered its protest at the crawling pace. We were relieved when the doctor moved the car out from the line and overtook, to arrive at the church first, where

Papa could wait by the lych-gate and from there walk the rest of the way.

With the car gone, Jim walked behind Mama in the funeral carriage, which was pulled by two black horses plumed with black feathers. There were wreaths on Mama's coffin that looked more fit for Christmas, with holly berries nestling in winding ivy.

After Jim, we three girls followed. Kay thrust a posy of hellebores into my hand, that had just bloomed, white and purple, in the shade of the garden hedge. Mama had called them Christmas roses and would always watch for their appearance as a promise of spring to come.

Behind us were Mama's two sisters, Papa's only remaining sibling, dear Aunt Sarah, who had gone to live with a friend when Aunt Mary died, and our two cousins. I dreaded speaking to Aunt Louise, could feel her eyes boring into my back, laden with blame.

Sure enough, when the service was over she overtook me on the way to the graveside and said through gritted teeth, 'I hope you realise that you killed your mother. You and your suffragettes.'

When it came to it, the waiting for her spite was much worse than the reality. What a thoroughly nasty woman she was and how could she have come from the same parents as my loving Mama?

I looked her full in the face, noticing that time had not been kind to her. She was still smart, but her face was grooved with deep furrows and her hair, what I could see of it under a preposterous concoction of black lace and beads, was an unattractive mottled grey. The dress she wore, as expected, was fashionable, with a narrow skirt and quantities of beadwork and lace all down its front, unlike our unfashionably wide skirts and high tight necks.

'I believe,' I said in a clear voice, 'that if there is blame for my mother's death, then you should bear at least a part of it. Your eagerness to give her news that I had protected her from was a terrible shock to her already weakened system.'

Aunt Louise opened her mouth to speak again, revealing yellow teeth like a horse but her sister, Jane, stepped forward and drew her away, while at the same time, Nora, our cook from the village, dressed wonderfully in a black dress with a bustle and quantities of black netting like Queen Victoria used to wear, took my arm and led me to the graveside beside my sisters.

The walk back for the funeral supper almost finished my strength, but I kept my head up and, if I leaned rather too heavily on Lina's arm and had to stop twice and cough so hard that it was like daggers in my chest, it did not matter. No one commented on that walk home, with Mama left behind in the orange clay of the churchyard, but the walk was salutary. By the time we were back at Rowstock, everyone had softened a little out of concern for me.

'Well done. You deserve a badge for not making a fuss,' whispered Jim leaning over me.

Even Papa, who looked at me in a baffled way, as if he could not think of a way of approaching, finally came forward and said, quite kindly, 'You should have that nasty cough seen to.'

I explained that I lodged with a doctor and he nodded, relieved. I did not tell him that I had just received word that Headquarters were sending me to Bristol as District Organiser. I had been in Leicester for a year and that was long enough. The W.S.P.U. policy was never to leave an Organiser in the same position for too long. They felt the more entangled one became with friendships and loyalties, the less you gave to the Cause. I don't know whether that was true or not but it accorded with what Dorothy had told me when I was involved with Michael. So far as I knew I had not wavered in my duties to Leicester, but it would be no good arguing for staying there, despite my fear that without Truda my health might not hold up.

⁓

Once I was cast up in Bristol, still sick and a prey to the nightmares and fears that had dogged me since Holloway, I could no longer control what was happening to me. Waking and sleeping I lived with terror and then I was ashamed. Hadn't I been trained to conquer fear? What would Jim, or any of my siblings, say now, if they saw the wreck I had become? Shame drove me to extreme measures. I got into the habit of punishing myself. Every time I felt fear, or sickness, or shame, I denied myself food for twenty-four hours.

Then sometimes I would lie awake thinking of how all this had started: of Millie, and Sarah who prostituted herself at the age of twelve, of the misery of the slums and the appalling deprivations of the men and women there, who had no chance and no real choice. And this would follow by my feeling guilty again, that I was afraid for myself, that I felt ill and weak when I had so much more than them, that I was so intrinsically selfish and self-obsessed. And I would punish myself once more: another twenty-four, or thirty-six hours of starvation.

The final cycle of memory and punishment was the violation that I felt at the hands of men – the police, the man in the crowd who had fondled my breasts, the composite horror-man with his white-flecked lips, the tubes thrust down my throat by male doctors. I would lie in bed, shaking with revulsion at myself, reliving it all, seeing the faces of the violators as they leered and winked lewdly with wet lips, open mouths. Even Michael's face in memory, as he entered my body, distorted in some strange way and became unrecognisable, as if he were in some strange ecstasy all his own that had nothing whatsoever to do with me. What was it about being a woman that caused men to want to defile us so?

In a paroxysm of self-hatred I threw myself to the floor beside my bed and scraped with my nails at my breasts, my stomach, all my tender parts, until they bled. Then, because again I had forgotten why I was there, what role for the greater good of women, and ultimately the poor, I was supposed to be fulfilling, I denied myself food once more – because what I really wanted was to deny myself, to cross out that selfish part of me that thought always of ME, ME, ME.

So it went on for three or four months, till near the end of June 1914, when I was discovered lying on the floor beside the bed in my Bristol lodgings, by a co-worker who was concerned that I had not come into the office that morning. I was raving, apparently, certainly not lucid. It says much for those kind women in Bristol that I was not sent straight to some clinic where I might have remained for years, deranged and lost. Instead they contacted Leicester and put me on a train like an unwanted parcel with its packaging unravelling. I ended up back with Truda Austin who, as a doctor and a supporter of the Cause, must have seemed to them a very fitting answer to a problem too puzzling for them to handle.

36

The house in Regent Road was quiet, and I sank into its peace and slept. But after a couple of months my illness was too much even for Truda. She was a busy woman and I needed special treatment. Her spectacles glinting with determination, she used her new telephone and persuaded Papa, Kay and Lina that the orchard at Rowstock was the best place for me, now that war had closed the doors to sanitoriums in Europe.

Joe, now fully in charge of Higher Farm, took a bed out for me. I would sleep in the haybarn with the door open while a lighter camping bed, plumped up with pillows, was placed on fine days under the lime tree at the far end of the orchard – always one of my favourite places. There I slept, dreamed, slept and woke again while Lina brought me food and left it within reach but did not touch me.

Truda had explained to everyone that tuberculosis, which she diagnosed me with, might be catching. Fresh air was the answer, in the absence of mountains in some foreign clime, now inaccessible because of the war. Touching, particularly embracing, should be avoided. This was the excuse Kay and Papa needed, I supposed, for they rarely came to visit the family pariah in the orchard.

At last Rita came back from Canada with Bill and she took over my care from Lina, who had enough to do coping with a crotchety and ageing Papa. By now Kay was in London, training to be a nurse. This was her courageous response to the death of her Harry, early in the war. It was all change at Rowstock.

Bill joined the Royal Artillery and after training left for the war, his chin set with determined optimism in the face of Rita's fears.

'It's all right,' Rita said. 'He told me that as an Officer he'd be well out of reach of the enemy's firing power.' She was quiet for a bit. Then, 'I'm pregnant,' she whispered and, later, 'I hope he sees his baby.'

Speech was hard for me without a coughing fit, but listening to Rita talk about her life in Canada, her hopes and fears which, as her belly swelled, became focused on the inevitability of giving birth, was pleasant and strangely soothing. I dipped in and out of her conversational stream, pleasantly buoyed up by it, knowing that whatever else, she at least still loved me.

'The Red Indians just squat at the side of the path while the rest of the tribe moves on. Then they pick up their baby and catch up. It's that easy,' she informed me. And, later, 'Elspeth has had three children already without even a groan. It can't be too bad, can it?'

I smiled reassuringly and blew her a kiss, my mind full of that mess of blood I gave birth to at Truda's house.

Not long after, little Hugh was born, soon after we heard that our cook Nora's eldest grandson had been killed in the trenches. Living in the midst of Nature, so close as to be a part of it, I was struck by the rhythms of the seasons, the pushing up through the earth of the shoots, the falling of the leaves, in direct counterpoint to all that was happening over the Channel. Men died but babies still came into the world.

One day I saw a tall figure in uniform come through the trees. The sun was behind him, casting a long shadow. With his mother beside him baby Hugh lay on a rug under a tree, his hands and feet waving in response to the leaves above his head.

'Rita!' I called. 'Look!'

It could only be Bill. No one else in the family wore a soldier's uniform.

He greeted us sombrely. There was nothing of the pride and certainty of the last time we saw him, when he was first off to the Front. His face looked gaunt and shadowed. He would not talk about the war.

'I have a few days leave,' was all he said, before admiring the baby and looking at his glowing wife. What a contrast they made, she round and bursting with the juice of motherhood, he still walking in the shadow of death. I noticed he did not touch Rita, or his new son. Perhaps he could not. There must be a transition from the land of the dead to that of the living, and it must be taken slowly. We had that much in common, Bill and I.

The short time he was here was the blink of an eye and once more he was gone, leaving a Rita distraught with weeping. Only the noisy suckling of little Hugh dried her tears.

'I feel that I have been so lucky to see him again when so many have lost their men, that now that luck will change. It has run out, as luck does. I feel it, in my head and in my heart.'

Soon it became evident that another child was on the way.

As Rita became heavier we drew towards another Winter. This one was not as cold as the previous year but so wet that every step we took was mired in mud and stained the hems of our skirts. Soon we were turning them up so as not to face the eternal need to scrub them. We heard that France was suffering from the same conditions. It was the final month of 1916 and I was improving slowly, able to walk a yard or two.

Rita was wan and listless. She waited avidly for every scribbled note sent by Bill and, in between, scanned the Harwell noticeboard outside the church, which published the lists of local boys who had met their end. 'Thank goodness our little boys...' [in her mind Edgar and Duncan were always trapped in naughty little boyhood] ...'escaped the war. That's one good thing about their being in India.'

Kay had finished training now and after a spell with the severely wounded at a temporary hospital in Surrey, she too left for France. Another one to worry about. Lina looked after Papa who was perfectly fit in his seventy-second year, but always in need of entertainment. Lina fulfilled that job perfectly by reading endless stories of derring-do to him: Ryder Haggard, Jeffery Farnol. Though he called some of the episodes 'Piffle' and 'Claptrap' when they became too romantic, Lina said he smoked furiously on his pipe during those sections, with a far-away look in his eye. 'Thinking of Mama,' she thought aloud, and then looked hurriedly away from me.

It was clear to me that I was never really going to be forgiven. Yes, they had taken me in when approached by Truda, who had told them in her clear and uncompromising way, that if they didn't they'd have my death on their hands. But Aunt Louise's words – and I hadn't been in the room to hear what she said, so would never know how she had presented me – had bitten deep and Mama had passed on a good deal of what her sister had told her to the rest of the family. Yet though Aunt Louise had told me to my face at Mama's funeral that I was to blame, that it was the shame at my imprisonment and my militancy that killed her, I had my doubts.

Mama was more than that. She approved of the fight for suffrage. It was just the means I chose that upset her, and my disobedience as I had promised not to embrace militancy. I don't think the shame of her daughter being imprisoned was to blame either. Mama was more than that too. *Shame* was an Aunt Louise word. She would have hated one of her prissy Oxford acquaintances to point out that her niece was a criminal and one of those harridans, like the woman that took a whip to Winston Churchill.

Quiet little Harwell and its surroundings could not have cared less who or what I was. Most people – farmers and their wives for the main part – had probably never heard of suffragettes. So my *shame* would not have affected the family's standing with their neighbours, or so I thought. Maybe Papa thought differently. But Mama, if she'd been well enough, would have eased everything with the village, if she'd had a chance.

How I wished that I'd been braver and gone up to see Mama after Aunt Louise had spoken to her. Maybe she had taken a turn for the worse then, as I'd been told, but maybe if I had disobeyed my father and delayed my exit a few hours, I could have paid her a visit and shown her how much I loved her. Would that have changed things?

I asked Rita what she thought.

'Kay wrote me what Aunt Louise said. She was very angry and shocked. It sounded as though you had been violent and loud and all the kind of things that Mama would have hated. But I knew you weren't like that, Gladys. And I expect she did too. Anyway, by the time Bill and I came back because of the war, you were in such a dreadful state, no one could be cross with you any more.' She bent to look at me, still trapped for hours at a time on my daybed, though coughing less.

I hated her pity but brushed it off. 'I *did* say and do violent and loud things. But I had violent things done to me too – far more than anyone could deserve.'

She leaned over me gently and her face was soft. 'Don't you think it's time you told me all?'

Which, omitting all reference to Michael, at last I did. There was no one else who understood me so well, who could be a receiver of everything that had happened. I told it without feelings, without trimmings, just the facts of it which, God knows, were bad enough.

Afterwards I felt the first inklings of peace in my soul. Ignoring my warnings, Rita put an arm around me and sat squeezed next to me on my chair. Our heads touched. Neither of us spoke, but the connection between us continued, like a river flowing from one to the other. Little Hugh, sleeping humped up with his bottom in the air, on a rug at our feet, shifted and sighed and she turned towards him. The connection was broken, but not completely, never completely.

37

In 1918, the final year of my sojourn in the orchard when it was clear that I was at last almost completely better, Rita asked a question. She had pondered, she said, on all I had told her and discussed it a little with Lina. Lina had been inclined to think of what had happened to me as something equivalent to an animal beaten by its owner. She failed to see that it was my own decisions that had put me in the way of abuse. Clear-eyed Lina had taken the blame from me and put it firmly onto the leaders of the W.S.P.U. It was they, she argued, who had sent their followers into danger, just as the generals in this dreadful war ordered their men over the top of the trenches to die. In both cases Lina felt that those who followed the orders were exonerated from blame, for what choice had they? Dear generous Lina, but I knew different. Unlike a soldier ordered to the Front, there had been no compulsion on we suffragettes to join up, or to remain on the field of battle when the going became tough. At any point I could have raised my hands and said, *Enough*. And I would not have been shot as a deserter.

Rita listened to me as I embraced my own blame. Then she asked did I feel it was worth it? Did I feel that endangering my health and causing such a breach in the family – she didn't say and killing Mama, but mentally I added that to the list – was worth it now, when we had failed and not even got the vote?

This was a hard question to answer and to do so I had to remember what I felt when war was first declared and the Pankhursts pulled out of the fight for suffrage.

My first feeling had been relief. Now I could rest without guilt that I was no longer in the fight. Then Dorothy came to visit me, here in the orchard in October 1914. It was only a few weeks since she'd been released from prison in Dublin. She was incensed.

'We have been betrayed,' she cried. 'The Pankhursts have betrayed us.'

After a rant she noticed the state I was in. 'Gladys, what are you doing? It's a damp misty day and you're sitting outside. Are you mad?'

'I think I have been for quite a long while,' I croaked.

She looked at me hard. Then she sat down on the wooden chair kept for visitors, though it collapsed from the changes of weather before many weeks had passed and was used for firewood that Christmas.

'I think you and I are probably still on the same side,' she began.

'I am no longer on any side,' I said wearily.

'Oh dear, perhaps you have not heard. Well, the Pankhursts stopped making a nuisance of themselves to the Government because of the war...'

'I knew that much.'

'... and appear to have forgotten what we were fighting for altogether. Now it's all the men at the Front, the money needed for guns, for boots, for tanks and they've been using *our* money, the money we sweated and slaved to bring in for the coffers at Headquarters, to finance the war effort. It's absolutely not on, don't you agree?'

'Wars are expensive.'

'Oh, Gladys! I shall scream! It's not just the funds we raised… we're talking vast amounts … I happen to know that one rally in London brought in two thousand pounds. Two thousand! In one day! Now think of all the rallies, the American teas, the bring-and-buys, the selling of our goods…'

'All right, all right, I get the picture.'

'That's the spirit, Gladys, at last I'm needling you into some kind of reaction. Now listen…'

She tallied all the crimes she thought the Pankhursts had committed: laying off the Organisers without warning or pay – 'They owed me quite a lot of back-pay from the weeks I was in Ireland and in prison. It's outrageous!' – closing all the shops that sold goods for us – 'Millie, I gather, was reduced to selling off what she could just so that she could live. I saw her, she's just the same, living with Clarice now, who's gone back to work in the shop for her father, so they'll survive despite their loss of salary.'

'Oh, I'm so glad.' Hearing of Millie brought the happy times in Birmingham flooding back.

'I know you were fond of her. She'd come to see you if she could but without money…'

And she was off again, raging, raging. 'You know, when Christabel came back from Paris, last month, she made a speech encouraging men to sign up. An old friend of hers shouted 'Votes for Women' and you know what she said? *We can't discuss that now.* As if everything we had been through and believed in could just be brushed under the carpet.'

I was beginning to catch something of her fervour now. What I was being told undermined everything we had been doing for the last few years. I listened as Dorothy told tale after tale of listless organisers with nothing to do and no money – some of them even lacking the funds to travel back to their own homes, clearing shops that had been sold on, packing up all that paperwork in offices that were being reclaimed by their owners.

'Some of the W.S.P.U. ex-workers have been rung up and asked to advertise Mrs Pankhurst's efforts to persuade men to join the forces. She hasn't stopped her eternal travelling around the country. Only the subject has changed. And she expects us to support her in that as we supported her before.'

Exhausted by emotion, Dorothy fell quiet for a moment. 'All that we've worked for, all that we suffered for, all that some of us died for,' she said finally, her voice choked with tears. 'Look how ill you are. There are many who were force-fed, as you and I were, who are as sick as you. Some died from the feeding – it's all coming out now. I'm in touch with a lot of suffragettes. Apparently sometimes the tube went the wrong way and deposited that foul stuff they called food into women's lungs instead of their stomachs. Those ones died.

'Not in prison of course – that would have embarrassed the Home Office. No those 'mistakes' were smuggled out to hospitals.' Her voice became more bitter. 'Of course that was at the start. The doctors got better at it. They had plenty of practice, didn't they?'

The talk of forcible feeding had brought back the taste of nightmare. I could hear the sounds, smell the 'food', the sweat on the nervous doctor's shirt, the breath of the wardress sitting on my pelvis and leaning over, close, to trap my arms. *Welcome*, the nightmare whispered in my ear. *I will never leave you, Gladys, never. Get used to me.*

Dorothy noticed my distress and grabbed my hands, asking if there was anything she could do, for I was coughing and choking, and I could taste blood.

'I'm sorry,' she said. 'I'll leave you now. Just wanted to bring you up to scratch.' I nodded, unable to speak.

'I'm not going to let it go, you'll be pleased to hear. There are a large number of us, angry women all. I'm thinking of forming another suffragette society and, despite the war, we'll keep fighting. Because it's important, isn't it? What we've done must not be forgotten.'

I was glad that I had that glimpse of the true Dorothy, the fighter and rebel who had caught my attention so strongly when I first heard her speak in Birmingham. It undid the anger I'd felt when she visited me in Leicester.

That was the last time I saw her, though later I heard from friends that she did indeed fight on, heading not just one, but two breakaway suffrage groups. I heard too that after the war, after suffrage was achieved, in a limited way, she stayed true to her rebellious free spirit and had a child, a daughter, though she was not married to the father. I envied her. Was the father of her child married? I wished I could ask her.

She had advised me so differently, when it came to my relationship with Michael. I should have ignored her and done what she had now done herself. Perhaps then, I would have had a son to watch as he grew towards manhood, a boy with hay-coloured hair.

At the start of those long years in the orchard, nursing my health and with plenty of time to brood, I had one or two visitors, before the ties that bound me to my old friends had slackened and broken from lack of upkeep. Sophia was one, trailing a reluctant Freddie, a naughty five year old obsessed with war. Despite our worries about the friends and family we had at the Front, it was hard not to laugh at the little boy, pouncing out from behind trees with broken apple twigs for guns.

Bradley was a war correspondent, she told me, and James an officer in the army.

Later I learned that Bradley survived the war but James was mentioned in despatches and received a posthumous medal for leading his men through the German wire to capture a few yards of muddy slope. Such useless gestures made heroes in those futile battles.

At least James's son would have something to be proud of as he grew up. I hoped it would be more than for Nina, whose sole knowledge of her father had been a faded photograph of a man with a lavish moustache. Freddie would have a medal in a box to handle, but as he grew older his father's poetry would mean more and offer a key to his real self.

I wondered what had happened to Paradise Street. Sophia wrote me that she and Freddie had moved in with her parents.

<hr />

At the end of the war, when Bill returned, Rita and he travelled back to Canada. She asked me another question then. Would I consider coming out myself, to stay with them?

'There is nothing for you here,' she said.

The wrench at losing her again after our sojourn back at Rowstock where our sisterhood had been reaffirmed, would be hard, but I knew I was not ready, though I'd often dreamed of going to be near her. My health still fluctuated, so Truda had suggested I come to stay with her for a while in Leicester.

I thought of the quiet of her home, a quiet that I had once found strange because I saw it through Michael's eyes but was now appealing. In the rush of returns – Bill, Jim, Kay – much altered and still grieving for her Harry – the noise of welcomes, the crying of Rita's two children, upset by the sudden surge of change in their lives – I felt exhausted. But Truda's house, so silent with its large light rooms, the softness of her voice and the way she kept to herself, beckoned.

I wanted to write, had jotted a few things down about the suffrage years, especially the time in prison, but now I wanted to leave behind those years, all that stress and suffering. Poetry called me. The summer heat warmed my bones with its promise. I needed a change, but not to Canada, which I saw as a place of cold and hardship, despite Rita's assertions otherwise. For the moment, I needed ease and peace; a little time on, who knew? The call of adventure might once again appeal.

So back to Leicester I went. I was still there when the news that suffrage, limited to women who were householders and over thirty, was granted. When that news came through, Truda looked at me through those narrow spectacles of hers, with her sharp blue eyes and held me while I laughed, in a kind of hysteria because, though I was over thirty I was not a householder. I still could not vote.

I heard Rita's voice in my head. *Was it worth it?*

I did go to a celebration or two in the houses of some of my ex-suffragette friends in Leicester. There I was informed that women with degrees were also on the list of those who could vote. By the time I learned this it seemed almost inconsequential; there were so many of us who still couldn't, brave warriors for the Cause like Millie and Clarice, and many many others – the offices in Birmingham and Leicester had been fuelled by those keen young people.

Resolutions were made to keep pushing the Government for universal franchise, and I listened to their arguments.

'Look how the men have all been given it, now they're back from the war. They couldn't have the embarrassment of all those young heroes returning and unable even to vote, could they? All men can vote now, without having to be householders,' said one woman.

'That's because the armed forces don't own houses, isn't it?

How dreadful it would be for those men to come home and not have a say in their future,' said another caustically.

'But we did our bit too. Look how we turned our hands to factory work, to driving buses and ambulances.'

'Farm work, too,' reminded another.

'We kept the nation going!' exclaimed one eager young woman.

'But if we do keep on at the Government, let's have no militancy this time,' said the first speaker. 'I think in the end that ploy was turning people against the Cause.'

We were all silent after that, thinking of the things we had done. Soon after that I made an excuse and was taken home. I wanted none of it. Something in me had turned over onto a new page.

After a few months, I became anxious that I was not contributing in any way to Truda's household. Her tonics, that she made herself in her little back room, had built my strength, but there was still something not right – a residual ache in my lungs sometimes, a lack of energy. When I had been here as District Organiser, she had received a part of my salary as rent. But now I had no means of supporting myself and I was still too weak to seek work as a governess as I had planned. I could not expect to live off her good will.

She was kind enough to salve my pride by coming up with another solution.

'I haven't had a housekeeper since Maudie died, not a proper one. I've made do with Mrs Reynolds and her daughter popping in to see to me and bringing me pies and meals to warm up in the oven. I could do with a proper, live-in housekeeper.'

I explained that in my family Rita was the cook, I was no more than adequate, though I had helped my mother in childhood. And I wasn't very tidy either, but I supposed there was nothing much to dusting and polishing.

'You won't have to do all that, Gladys dear. I'm not badly off, you know, as a doctor. I have a car now and Brown, the gardener, doubles as my chauffeur when I make home visits. We'll get a girl in to do the heavy work, until you're fully better. We shall manage very well, you'll see.'

And I had become fully better, physically, though I never felt quite as I used to. Something had snapped inside me. Fourteen years after Holloway, I still had nightmares, when I'd wake covered in sweat with the sounds of that echoing building filling my ears and something heavy holding me down, so that unspeakable things could be done to me. Worse, in dream after dream, I could hear myself break that courageous silence to which I was sworn. I could hear myself scream.

Often, too, I dreamed of Michael. I saw him as he used to be, the boy with the hot eyes and hair the colour of dry grass left out in the rain. Now that he was gone I felt free to acknowledge that I had truly loved him, that I would have liked to spend the rest of my days with him, if only that could have been. And that I was so weak that had he walked in then and there I'd have thrown my arms around him and forgiven him every betrayal – all.

I reached into the drawer beside my bed and felt for his letter. It had come to me, worn and softened from being carried around in his pocket, the ink blurred by rain, or my tears, I could not remember now which. Every day that I could bear to, I read it:

My dear sweetheart, my little love,
If this is in your possession then I am dead. And if that is so, there is no longer a chance to say all those things I wanted to say, but could not because of the manner of

*our parting. I am so sorry. If I had known that in a grimy
Birmingham street I would have rescued a mermaid with
sunset hair from a sea of struggling bodies on the filthy
cobbles, if I had known that, I would have saved myself
for you, my darling. It would have been worth the wait.*

*I thank God that we had the years we had. I treasure
every memory of you, my dearest, and hope that you
will find peace and a new love one day, for you deserve
it. Take care of yourself now that I am not there to take
care of you.*

You are locked in my heart, Michael

When I'd received that letter, it had been brought to me
by Rita, struggling through the unkempt couch-grass of the
neglected orchard. She carried baby Hugh in one arm, the
letter in her left hand, and her belly was swollen with her
second child, Margaret. She was distracted and fractious
with the heat, and with the difficulty of negotiating a passage
through the orchard with her bulk and the heavy baby, who
wriggled to free himself so as to practise his crawling. She
passed it over without comment, as if I had letters every day.
Then she put Hugh down with a sigh and leaned herself in the
crook of a tree to watch him. She fanned herself with her hand
and blew upwards to cool the perspiration on her upper lip.

It was August, 1917.

I couldn't read it with her there, though my fingers itched
to open it. I knew who it was from; I'd know his handwriting
anywhere. For some reason I made no connection between the
war and Michael. I thought this letter must be from Ireland.
For a crazy moment I imagined he was writing to say he was
free – able to marry and be with me. I had not heard from
him, or seen him, since that dreadful time when he followed
me to my new posting in Leicester.

So many wishes. I wished that sight of him, shivering on the pavement and looking up at my bedroom window, was not the last one I had. I still wished I had his son. But I was forty-six now; it was unlikely I'd ever grow a baby in my womb. Holding Rita's babies, which as the war drew to a close the doctor pronounced me well enough to do, had been so sweet. The smell of their little bodies, the fat folds of them, their soft vulnerability. How different I was from those earlier days, when babies and anything to do with them made me cringe. Rita laughed at my enjoyment of Hugh and Margie, as little Margaret was called from the first, and teased me over those charity visits in Ireland.

What had brought about this change? It may have been just that they were Rita's babies, as near to flesh of my flesh as I was going to get. But I think it was more. I knew that Michael was gone and, with his death, I knew I would never have a child of my own. Those years of the war and just before, with Emily Davison's final tragic gesture at the Epsom Derby, and then Mama. I'd been surrounded by death – we all had – and had come close to it myself. But that little child in my arms was life. My conversion was as simple as that. I wanted to move out of the grey ash of death into the vibrant colour of life.

In Truda's quiet house where I had little to do but get better, cook light meals and organise my thoughts, the dreams were finally beginning to recede. Perhaps one day they'd leave me entirely. I hoped so. Even the dreams of Michael. Until I could separate him in my thoughts from all the horrors.

What had come to the surface of my memory, again and again, were those separate violations done to my body. It was all mixed up somehow with Sarah in the darkness of the alley, Millie, who had been raped by her uncle and the fear she had of the janitor where she worked, all those mothers and children who had to prostitute themselves for a loaf of bread.

Even my own family were part of the confused distress that I carried around with me, at least the older male members: Papa, who looked at me without any of the gentleness I remembered from childhood, Jim who put us all through the courage game and made life a competition, in which we would be judged by success or failure. It was that one time when I screamed that I could not forgive myself for, the only time that I failed the test of forcible feeding. I had endured so many in silence.

It is harsh of me perhaps, to place some blame at Jim's door. He had only been twelve years old, and I remembered how sweet he was with Lina and Kay when they were tiny, how we all looked up to him and trusted him to lead us – something he did so naturally. When I saw him at home after the war was over and he related how it was to be in the battle of Jutland, what he dwelt on was only the final part, when the German fleet had surrendered and the British fleet escorted them in a triumphal parade of three columns, the British ships flanking the German ones. He made light of everything else. The horrors of that naval battle I have learned of since, but never from Jim. Not a word.

And I thought – why did we button up so? Was that courage or stupidity? Did Jim suffer nightmares, as Mama told us Papa did after the Crimea? Old habits die hard. I found it as difficult as I suspected Jim did, to talk about what troubled me so.

Instead I wrote it. I produced many poems and had a volume published – a volume which I sent to Bradley with a further copy to Sophia, in memory of James. Poetry was a way of working things through, since talking about it all appeared to be denied me. And that was not the fault of Truda. Quite the contrary, she encouraged me to talk, convinced that I'd heal faster. But despite wanting to, recognising that I needed to, I could not break the habit of years. I could not look deeper into my own self without feeling that I was indulging in selfishness and should snap out of it. Maybe that was just the way I had always been.

38

Truda was a strange person to be living with. We shared a love of literature and often read aloud to each other. She was a good reader, surprisingly for one so reticent, and it was relaxing to close my eyes after our supper and listen to her voice. But she was as closed as me about her inner troubles. I knew that there was something unacknowledged about her father and I'd met her brothers, who were also difficult to know. Brothers and sister spent many hours together, just sitting in near silence.

Brought up by Mama to be a polite hostess, I found this difficult. I wanted to jolt them into laughter, to sharing memories, to the kind of noise such a meeting in our family would engender. All attempts at drawing any of them out – there were three brothers – failed. They visited – rarely, thank goodness – and all four siblings sat there, showing nothing and uttering only a few words here and there, before they departed.

Later I thought of these meetings, not frequent but quite regular, and recognised that something important did happen between them as they sat together. I would never know what their childhood had been like, but they all must have suffered the same, or at least knew of each other's suffering, and these meetings were the way they had of acknowledging that and of giving each other mutual support. Her family, our family, had different ways of showing it, that's all. But we were all participants in the courage game, and the Austin family had mastered it.

In our family it was fine, even expected, to show emotion. Weeping, anger, joy, all were noisily celebrated, though tears as a valve to alleviate suffering might be frowned upon. I wasn't sure. I was always a weeper, though latterly I'd learned to master that better. The boundaries between what was and was not allowed were never well defined in the game. In fact, the precise rules of many of Jim's games were rather wobbly, and might change according to circumstance. If only we had not embraced that game of our endurance and nerve so completely, so without question, it would not have caused me so much guilt, such terrible nightmares of failure. It was only a game, and a game is not reality. In fact, reality, life, love, the problems life throw at us defy any rules. The premise of a game does not fit the strife of living, is in fact defeated by it. For no child, even Jim who had adulthood forced on him by parents with little time to spare, can understand the challenges that life will bring. To help us, to give a structure to our chaotic childhood, he had constructed games, for games are all he understood.

It was something I realised about him in retrospect. When we did go to school it was games that again offered us rules and structure and from what I heard of military and naval training there was not much difference. Games train us to follow rules and we do not question them. Instead we follow without counting any cost; gladly we will offer up our lives. The Pankhursts, by treating the suffragettes as an army understood the lessons of the game well and profited from it.

Though I could not talk of the worst things and neither could Truda, there was a deep shared current of understanding between us. In her house I felt as though I had been washed up on a quiet shore, where the wind and the stormy waves were stilled and life could pass me by. So the years passed, evenly enough, and Truda and I fell into a comfortable routine.

On a September morning in 1926 I woke up to an achingly blue sky and there was a snap in the air, a whisper of approaching winter.

Throwing the window open, I took deep breaths, and realised that at last the pain in my throat had receded to little more than a memory. Running downstairs I made tea for Truda and took it up to her bedroom as I usually did. Then, still feeling energised, I pottered in the kitchen, cleaned the big range and enjoyed the feeling of growing strength in my arms.

I heard the letter fall on the mat and wiped my hands. Letters were rare. Picking it up I recognised the handwriting on the envelope – an old man's wobbly hand. Papa.

There was a dull stirring in my stomach, an anxiety. Papa never wrote. We had remained distant with each other. What could have happened?

For a while I just stared at the envelope, listening to the sounds from above of Truda getting ready for the day. I found a knife and sat, ready to slice through the seal. A footfall on the stairs. Quickly I got up and went into the dining-room where I knew I wouldn't be disturbed.

The words jumped out at me, the only ones that mattered.

Rita is dead, drowned. Please come home.

He could have rung, but Papa never believed in telephones.

Immediately I rang Rowstock and got Lina.

'It's true,' she said. 'She was drowned in a canoeing accident on that lake they live by.'

'When was this?' Had there been a world without Rita for weeks and I did not know it? Mail to and from Canada took ages.

'It was a few days ago. We were wired by someone called Elspeth. She sounded very upset.'

'Of course she would. She's a cousin by marriage. And they were close neighbours.' My stomach felt hollow. I could not take the news in.

'There's to be a trial, apparently. Someone called Willie has been accused of killing her.'

My knees gave way. I pulled out a chair and sat down in it, hard. Willie was Bill. Horace and Elspeth, from the start had called Bill and Rita the Willie Waterfields. Rita had laughed about it in one of her letters.

'Hello? Hello? Are you still there, Gladys?'

'Yes, dear. I'm here. Tell Papa I'll come immediately.'

On the train back home I felt light in the head, empty, as if I had been scoured out. I was filled with a kind of waiting, which I supposed was the way my mind was coping with the shock. It had not really taken it in, but half an hour into the journey the pain began, real physical pain, and I doubled over in my seat, so that others in the carriage looked over at me in fright.

Adopting a stiff unnatural smile, I moved out into the corridor, away from their prying eyes. I knew at last that it was true. My heart felt it. Rita, my truest friend, my companion and sister, had gone. With it went the idea of going to Canada to be near her. Would it have prevented anything if I'd gone at the end of the war, when she first suggested it? I remembered how Bill was then, as if a darkness travelled with him. Of course it was all that he had experienced in the trenches. No one had come back unchanged.

I thought over the letters that had passed between us in the last few years, a constant flow of them. Were there clues there as to what may have happened? The happiest ones had contained news of Hugh and Margie and then the latest child, Peter, who Rita said was pure Hazel in his looks, unlike the others who favoured Bill. Little Peter, only two years old. Would it be worse for him to be without his mother, or for Margie and Hugh at nine and ten? Terrible for all three, I thought, gazing sightlessly out at the passing scenery.

Rita had never complained in these letters – trapped like the rest of us in that same childhood code – but reading between the lines there had been ups and downs in their lives: two fires – two houses burnt down from Bill's smoking habit, and each time the children only just rescued in time. Once she'd said how Bill enjoyed teaching the young women of the town, to swim, to play the piano and was often out in the evenings, and I sensed something there, a loneliness in her. Was Bill neglecting her for other women?

I had asked in my next letter, but her answer made light of it and moved on instead to their shared canoe rides in the evenings and the colours of the lake. That same lake where she had now perished. I shuddered. All of us were good swimmers after our childhood by the sea. Why would Rita have drowned?

I hoped the answers would come when I reached home. I prayed they'd know more. They did, of course. Papa had telegraphed Elspeth in Nakusp, asking for more information. She had replied saying how shocked they all were, she and her children especially. She touched on how hard it was for Rita's three children to have only one parent.

I remembered that she was a single parent herself, since Horace Waterfield had been killed in the last weeks of the war.

Then she confirmed that Bill was to be tried in court but

hastened to reassure us. Of course it would all turn out to be a mistake.

After we had all read the telegram, which ended by sending us love and strength to cope with our loss, Papa turned to us, his face ravaged with grief.

'I don't believe a word of it,' he announced. 'Bill kill my Marguerite? Impossible.'

So that was that. The family verdict. But I remembered some of the past rivalry between Rita and her husband, how Bill had always to be in the ascendant, how he felt that he was always right. Then I added to those memories how Bill was when he returned from the trenches: alternately gloomy and moody, and then feverishly excitable and full of a kind of spurious enthusiasm. He spent the few days before they returned to Canada furiously striding around our grounds, examining the apple trees and hurling advice over his shoulder, or sitting outside in the dark, where we would just see the glow of his pipe, as he sat for long silent hours in the garden.

He had dazzled Papa with descriptions of the night sky in Canada – the showers of meteors which he charted – pacing, pacing all the while as he spoke, so that our heads were always swivelling to follow him. Then he would fling out of the door and be gone, no one knew where, for hours.

This Bill, I thought, just might have done something, not with intent but on the spur of the moment.

I stayed at Rowstock waiting for news with the others, joined intermittently by Jim and his wife Ida, and their two daughters, Nancy and Janet. Jim was on leave, which was a blessing, since we all needed his kind of quiet commonsense. The girls, who were close to Peter's age, just brought home how dreadful was the loss of Rita. Those girls, with their childish tender limbs. I remembered Hugh's plump thighs. No difference at that age between the sexes – their skin, the round limbs, the innocence of their eyes.

It seemed there was nothing else to learn. We heard that Bill had been exonerated at the trial.

'Didn't I tell you?' said Papa triumphantly. 'Why, that boy was a family friend. He was one of us.'

When it was clear that there was nothing more to be learned about the mystery of Rita's death and Bill had been exonerated, I returned to Leicester. I knew that if I stayed at Rowstock with my questions and doubts I would not be welcome. I could not afford any more upset in the fragile relationship I had with my family.

'Bill had an uncertain temper,' I said to Truda one day.

And later, 'She was a good swimmer. At the trial Bill said she couldn't swim. Why do you think he said that?'

Then on another day: ' They couldn't prove anything at the trial because there were no witnesses, but that doesn't mean…'

Till Truda, quiet even-tempered Truda, told me to leave it alone.

'You're like a dog with a dead rabbit, shaking it and shaking it to try to get some life back into it. Let it go. Probably you'll never know what really happened. You cannot bring her back and what do you hope to achieve? Those poor children need their father. Have you thought about that? And what about the youngest?'

Bill and the two elder children, along with the Herschel telescope, went to Harvard, who had once before put out feelers, trying to tempt away this descendant of such famous astronomers from the charms of Canada to an academic life. He didn't stay. Whether that restless energy I had seen in him when he returned from the war was still driving him, or whether he just could not settle in the United States, I do not know, but within a few months he went to South Africa, to settle near the observatory from where his grandfather, John Herschel, had charted the stars of the Southern Hemisphere.

Little Peter, the youngest child, had been sent to England, at the time when his remaining family made the move to Harvard. The idea was that Peter should be taken in by Bill's brother Percival, who already had a large family.

'He's alright,' I said, sulky at being reprimanded. 'He's with his uncle and his cousins.' I imagined a kind of replaying of our own childhood: masses of children happily mixing together, all taking care of each other.

'Why did they not ask if you would have him?'

I shrugged; I didn't want to think about it.

'Do you think it could be because you were a suffragette?'

That stung me. 'Why would that be relevant?'

'Just that you may not have been considered quite … suitable.' She saw my expression and gave me a look over the top of her spectacles. 'Well, if you don't think that's the reason, why don't you go to see him anyway?'

I didn't want to go. I don't know why. Perhaps it was that he would remind me of Rita too much. Maybe I was afraid that he would remind me more of Bill, who I still harboured uncomfortable feelings about. I only knew that my reluctance to go was deep-seated.

I invented excuses. Truda's eyes sharpened.

'I wouldn't want to tear him away from the wonderful fun he'll be having with all those cousins.' Then, obscurely, I added, 'Duncan and Edgar spent half their childhood wishing for cousins to play with.' As if that explained everything.

Truda sighed.

Some weeks passed before she tried again. 'He's just an infant, you know. Two years old. You should check that he is as alright as you keep telling me. Don't you think you owe your sister that?'

I ran upstairs and cried where she couldn't hear me. I cried for all the children who wept in the slum houses for lack of food or because they were cold or sick. I cried for the children I had failed to reach with my teaching, and for those I had deserted by leaving. I cried for Mama, that she thought I had abandoned her when she was ill. For Rita, who was still too young and vital to die and who had abandoned her own children without meaning to.

Lying on my bed, with the wash of the sun on the ceiling, I cried myself out. But not before my mind had moved on from the people and memories that were part of my life, to encompass the whole suffering world, with its millions of abandoned children, old and young.

When I had finished I must have fallen asleep, for I woke to find Truda sitting on the edge of the bed.

'I'll go with you,' she said. 'If it helps. You need to find Rita's boy. You need to find Peter.'

A very haughty lady met us. She was Bill's brother's wife, who I remembered slightly from the wedding. She looked both of us up and down, her expression saying that she found us very much wanting.

'It was too much,' she said at last. 'Peter was far too young and needy. He simply did not fit in.'

'So where is he now?' Now that we were here there was nothing more important than finding the child. Gone were any fears. Instead, I was filled with an energy I hadn't experienced for years. I had a Cause again.

'There was a couple in Guildford we were told about. A respectable pair.' She looked disparagingly at both of us again, her eyes settling on Truda. 'A doctor and his wife. I believe they had tried but could not have children. It seemed a good opportunity for all parties.'

'You gave Peter to an unknown couple in Guildford?'

'He will be much happier there.'

Truda looked sideways at me. She could see that I was about to burst with anger.

My body shook with it. I opened my mouth.

Quickly Truda stepped in front of me. 'Dear Mrs Waterfield,' she said. 'Gladys has travelled all the way from Leicester to see her sister's little boy. Just to check that he is all right.' She waited.

Mrs Waterfield appeared to be weighing up a great many contradictory reasons why she should or should not help us. At last she relented.

'You understand that we did what we thought was best. I will telephone the couple now, and warn them you are coming to visit the child.'

It was another whole day before we could see him. By that time I had built up an imaginary picture of the doctor and his wife as ogres and grasping manipulative kidnappers. I saw Rita's child locked in a cupboard and fed on scraps from the floor.

But it was a charming woman who met us and invited us into her front room. She introduced herself as Mrs Blighe, said that the doctor was busy in town where his surgery was, and described what a dear little boy Peter was.

'But sad,' she said. 'He misses his mother. He's very quiet. I don't think it helped that his cousins were so boisterous and confident, too young to understand his feelings I imagine and what he has gone through: ripped away from everything and everyone he knows. Losing his whole family at a stroke – bad enough a mother, but to lose brother, sister and father too!

And his home! I can't imagine how the poor little darling must feel. And of course, he has stopped talking.'

After warning us not to do anything too noisy or sudden, she said she'd take us to him now.

It was a warm spring day. Rita had been dead for six months and Peter was now three years old. The doctor had made the child a swing and Peter was sitting on it, listlessly rocking, almost imperceptibly, to and fro. Though the swing had been set low, the boy's toes only just touched the ground.

'He's been sitting like that all morning,' whispered Mrs Blighe. 'Ever since I lifted him on to it. When I try to encourage him down he just grips tighter to the ropes. To be honest I don't really know what to do. He needs a lot of love and understanding. But I think it'll take a long time.' There were tears in her eyes. 'Peter,' she said. 'Peter dear. Your aunt has come to see you. Look!'

I stepped forward and looked at him. Rita was right, he was pure Hazel: Jim and Mama's full lips. Rita's straight look and the fine curve of her eyebrows.

'Peter?'

This time the boy looked at me, a sudden quick darting look like a bird's. Then he was down, jumping off the swing, so that it swung sharply forward and would have caught him on the back of his legs, except that he was running towards me and his face was alight.

'Mumma!' he called, 'My mumma,' and hurtled into me. His arms went round my knees and his head burrowed into my skirt. He sighed.

We waited for Dr Blighe to return whereupon for the umpteenth time Mrs Blighe related what had happened, as she had to her cook, the postboy and the next-door-neighbours. 'It was incredible… the boy spoke for the first time … called her mummy… quite had us all in tears.'

Peter had not let go of me. Now he sat on my lap and I felt the warmth of him there and thought of Rita. My hair had faded from its brightness and darkened as I got older. To a small boy, I may have looked very like the memory of his mother.

The Blighes did nothing to retrieve the boy they thought they had adopted, kind people that they were. 'He's never really been ours,' said Mrs Blighe. 'It's as if he was waiting. Don't you think, dear?' she said to her husband.

'What beats me is that no one thought of this – of *you* – before. Why did his father send him to his brother's family?' Dr Blighe said.

'I don't suppose he was thinking much,' I said. Truda gave me a warning look. My tone had been condemnatory. There was no reason why this nice couple should learn any of the circumstances that had brought Peter to them. 'He had two other children and perhaps didn't think he could manage a little one as well. And I'm not married. I expect he thought a family would be the best solution and *they* thought a couple who wanted a child…'

I didn't mention the shocking fact that I had been a suffragette, though I was sure Bill's brother would have known. I was also sure now that Truda had been right. It was my unsavoury past that had ruled me out, even in Bill's mind.

'Exactly. And now what?' Dr Blighe continued.

'I must have him,' I blurted. I looked at Truda. 'For Rita's sake.' I could have said for my sake, for I was suddenly full of joy.

Doctor Blighe said, 'But what about the Waterfields, Mabel? We made a promise to them.'

'I'll deal with them,' said Mabel Blighe stoutly. 'Look at him. He's made his own choice. You can see he isn't ours to keep.' There were tears in her eyes, but she blinked them back and smiled through them.

I looked up at Truda, aware suddenly that it was not my choice to make. I lived in her home.

She held my gaze and nodded.

39

Peter ran back from school and told me about his day, as he always did over his tea.

'We learned about bad people and prisons today,' he said. 'Do you know anyone who's been to prison, Aunt?'

He always called me Aunt, as soon as I was able to tell him about his mother and to give him a photograph of her to keep for himself.

I laughed. 'I've been to prison many times.'

'*You* have, Aunt? Crikey!' His wide blue eyes regarded me with awe. Then a little crease of anxiety appeared above his nose. 'But you're not a bad person, are you?'

'No, dear. I was trying to make the world a better place and I wasn't alone. Thousands of other women were trying too.'

'Did they all go to prison too?'

'Quite a number did. We went to prison on purpose, to try to tell the important people who rule this country that things needed to change.'

'How many times were you there?'

'Lots of times just for one night. Once I was there for many weeks. But there were friends with me, so it was alright. Look, I've got something to show you.' I got up and went to the dresser drawer where my medals were kept. I got them all out and arranged them on the dining-table in front of Peter.

'They're a bit like the ones Ronnie Clyde's father has. He said he got them in the war. For courage, he said, in the face of battle.'

'Well, ours was a different war...' I watched as he fingered them, running his hands over the silver bars of the prison gate, on the one I got from the W.S.P.U. after leaving Holloway, and then carefully lifting the other from its leather casing, where it hung from its strap of purple, green and white between his hands.

'It's got your name on it,' he said. 'None of Mr Clyde's medals have his name on them.'

'No.' I was speaking mostly to myself now. 'The W.S.P.U. were good in that way at least.'

Peter turned it over in his hands, picking out the difficult words about forcible feeding.

'Can you see that first one you looked at? It's in the shape of prison gates. Because of the time I spent there.' I could say it, finally, after years of nightmare, of hiding from the memories. I could say the words without my stomach knotting. It was over at last.

Peter thought for a long while. 'You won't go again, will you?'

'No. We got what we wanted and things did change. Not as fast as we would have liked. But after the war, came the first change. Some women were allowed to vote after that. We had to wait another ten years before the rest could.' Peter's eyes were beginning to lose focus. I cheered my tone to keep his attention. 'I don't suppose you remember a party we had here. It was 1928 and you were only four, so I expect not. Lots of my friends came, lots of those women who'd tried to change things. We had a party because finally it had happened. We were allowed to vote at last. All women over the age of twenty-one.'

'I know what voting is. We voted Dickie Attenborough as blackboard monitor this week. Next week I hope it'll be me.'

'Good, so you understand that it's when everyone has a say about who gets to be in charge. That's why so many of us went to prison. Because we weren't allowed a say about who should govern this country. We couldn't vote.'

'But now you can?'

'Now we can.'

'That's all right then.' He gave me a quick hug and ran off to play. I heard his feet thundering up the stairs to the attic, where he had his playroom.

I closed my eyes. I could speak of it. The shadow had lifted its hem. Slowly I packed those medals away, infinitely more hard-earned than those little red badges awarded by Jim when we were children. I understood more about courage now. It cannot be sought, or trained into you. Everyone has it in them, to a greater or lesser extent and everyone is tested at some time in their lives. For most there are no badges.

I was fifty-two, unmarried, with love of a man and the hope of it, far behind me. But I had my child, my boy – as near to mine as could be. And I had the truest friend I could wish for. It was enough.

———

Truda puts the last page down on the table and removes her spectacles. Her eyes are wet. 'Well done. Did it help? Has that shadow left you now?'

'As much as it ever will.' The parade of faces from the past, sensing an opportunity, surface and clamour for attention but I blink them away. I smile at her but cannot resist a naughty 'Your turn now.'

'One day perhaps.' She gets up dismissively. 'We need to lay the table. Peter's coming, with his family. Had you forgotten?'

The Hazel Family 1888

The Hazel Family 1887

The badge received by everyone who signed up as a suffragette. Notice it is handwritten.

Received for multiple imprisonments

HUNGER STRIKE

PRESENTED TO

GLADYS MARY HAZEL
**BY THE WOMEN'S SOCIAL AND POLITICAL UNION
IN RECOGNITION OF A GALLANT ACTION
WHEREBY THROUGH ENDURANCE
TO THE LAST EXTREMITY
OF HUNGER AND HARDSHIP
A GREAT PRINCIPLE OF POLITICAL JUSTICE
WAS VINDICATED**

AFTERWORD

Most of the characters in this novel were real people, whom I have listed below. However, the book is a novel, not a biography, partly because I used the 'I' persona, so as to wriggle myself thoroughly into Gladys's skin and partly because, even though she was a writer herself, she chose to write very little about her childhood and family life and left out tantalising details which I had to imagine. She did outline Jim's game, however, which gave me a title for the book. It took a particular kind of courage to be an active suffragette.

All the suffragette incidents that feature in the book are real and Gladys Hazel took part in every one of them.

The main characters who were actual people are:

Suffragettes: Emily Wilding Davison, Dorothy Evans, Christabel and her mother Emmeline Pankhurst, and Gladice Keevil. Reference is also made to Catherine Osler, Millicent Fawcett, and Emmeline Pethick-Lawrence in particular, plus numerous others who worked at the W.S.P.U. London Headquarters.

King Edward VI School, Birmingham, then in Aston where
the present boys' school is:
Miss Nimmo, the headmistress, Miss Bragge – the Second
Mistress, and the English staff, Miss Sheldon and Miss
Hadley.

Doctor Gertrude [Truda] Austin was one of the first women
doctors whose pioneering work was about contraception for
the working classes. After the War Gladys and my father lived
with her, first in Leicester and then in Blewbury, Berkshire,
until Gladys died.

All other characters are inventions of my own. Gladys's
tantalisingly brief jottings about all the period covered by this
book, talks of a colleague she lodged with, who introduced
her to the slums and the women's club. This I made into Nina.

33 Paradise Street and 34 Harold Street were both real
places [the latter known about because of the census form].
33 Paradise Street did indeed become one of the offices for the
W.S.P.U., but the whole street has now disappeared. Dorothy
Evans and Gladys did really share lodgings at Harold Street.
I have a poem written by Gladys which is dedicated to D.E.
– could that be Dorothy? Other poems indicate a forbidden
love and her desire for a child of her own. Out of this I was
able to spin the story of Michael.

ACKNOWLEDGMENTS

A huge thank you to the patient readers of the first draft: Nick Waterfield, Susan Elkin, Mary-Rose Farley and Judy Phillpotts, with a special thank you to Judy, who also proof read the last version and who spotted all my grammatical weaknesses. I couldn't have done it without you, or without Anne Kennedy and her ongoing support with all the drafts in between.

A sad thank you to my father, Peter Waterfield, who happily heard and loved the first draft, but died before the project was finished. From him I received so many important details about Dr Austin and the house at Leicester and about Blewbury. And yes, he was best chums with Richard 'Dickie' Attenborough at this first school, while younger brother David was allowed to tag along with them at times!

Thank you too to Alison Wheatley, Foundation Archivist for the schools of King Edward VI, Birmingham, who sent me invaluable material and photographs of the school in Aston as it had been when Gladys taught there.

The books I found most useful as research were:

Suffragettes – The Fight for Votes for Women edited by Joyce Marlow

Women of the Right Spirit by Krista Cowman – about the work of the organisers

The Girl from Hockley and The People of Lavender Court by Kathleen Dayus, who was brought up in the back to backs at the same period as Gladys was there. Invaluable for the Birmingham accent.

Unshackled by Dame Christabel Pankhurst

My Own Story by Emmeline Pankhurst

+ maps of old Birmingham, a visit to the back to backs museum in Birmingham and many hours of trawling through back copies of Votes for Women, available on line.